THE JAPANESE ASSASSIN

A KIRA NOMURA THRILLER - BOOK ONE

JACK ARBOR

WRITE MORE STUDIO

For Yukinobu, Shoko, Yayoi, Minamo, Neo, and Sota

Kazoku wa taisetsu na mono nanka ja nai. Kazoku koso subete da.

家族は大切なものなんかじゃない。家族こそすべてだ。

Family is not an important thing.
It's everything.

ONE

A faraway bird sang a long melody.

Farther away, a frog croaked.

A creaking branch and the scraping of wood on wood sounded overhead.

Silence descended, and she drifted into a dreamless state.

Sometime later, the song of the colorful bird returned. At least that's how she pictured the bird in her mind. A bright red thrush with a dominant plume of purples and yellows.

I've arrived, all ye female birds. Behold me in my glory.

The bird sang again and again until its song died away, but the damage was done and her eyes creaked open to slits.

Lightning bolts of searing fire lit up her nervous system until she squeezed her lids tight. Instinct prevented her from crying out, and she clamped her mouth shut.

More noises crept into her awareness: chirping, croaking, and buzzing. Something cackled far in the distance, and the image of a monkey formed beneath her closed lids.

Underneath her, an animal scurried through grass stalks and palm fronds.

Underneath?

Where am I?

Panic surged through her mind and into her amygdala, the ancient part of her brain regulating flight or fight, and her eyes flew open. It was self-preservation. She endured the sharp tacks poking her eyeballs and the stars of white light crossing her eyes. She blinked back tears until her vision cleared. Brown rafters and beige thatch were above her, and an unlit oil lamp hung from a chain.

What is this place?

Her brain suggested moving her head to see more of her surroundings, so she made the attempt. Nothing happened. An anxious sensation flooded her nerves.

Am I paralyzed?

She willed her eyeballs to look down her chest and stomach. A moth-eaten army-green blanket covered her body. Her toes formed a small tent near the end of where she lay. She flexed her toes. Nothing happened.

This is ridiculous. I'm not paralyzed. Flex, damn it.

Still no movement.

Wait. How do I know I'm not paralyzed?

I just know.

With a force of will conjured from somewhere deep, she concentrated all her energy along her arm and through her hand and into her pinky.

Move, damn it.

The finger twitched.

I knew it.

A breeze picked up, and a sprinkle of something rained onto the thatch. Water? Leaves? Dirt?

After resting her pinky while she examined every inch

of the thatch above her head, she compelled one hand to move before she concentrated on the other. That's when she noticed the deep ache enveloping her entire body, from her temples to her toes, the kind of ache resulting from a beating. Or many beatings.

The thought was intuitive. It appeared in her mind unbidden.

She switched her attention back to her feet and toes. The big toe on her left foot tensed, followed by the big toe on her right foot. She focused her attention on her calves and worked her way up her legs to flex each muscle and relax it. She performed the exercises again and again until elasticity returned and her feet rotated in circles. As she worked her arms and shoulders, the wool blanket fell away and a breeze washed over her.

Under the blanket she wore briefs and a T-shirt. While her skin was covered with scars, scabs, and dried blood, the T-shirt was ripped and stained with something rust-colored. The cuts and scrapes stung and throbbed.

She bicycled first one leg and then the other while ignoring the deep soreness from working her muscles. She hugged both legs against her chest to stretch her back. With energy summoned from the deepest well of her soul, she sat up.

A wave of nausea overtook her, and she almost heaved, but she fought it off and remained upright with her arms bracing her. The rest of the room swam into focus. Spacious by hut standards, the room was square with waist-high railings of cypress wood which were the only thing between her and the forest. Thatched overhangs blotted out the view, but a bird with green and blue feathers fluttered through the opening, sailed to the roof, and perched on a rafter.

The military cot she rested on was in a corner. A folding table sat on the edge of the room, and a counter with a wash basin was to the right. A metal mirror hung on a rusty nail over the basin, and two plastic bins sat next to the counter. Otherwise, the room was empty.

She swung her legs so her feet hit the floor and rested a moment before she stood.

Big mistake.

Vertigo swam through her head until she sat back hard onto the cot.

The bird chattered.

I know, bird. Shut up.

Instinct screamed at her to get up and become mobile.

Make my body functional.

Her safety depended on it.

My safety? Where did that come from?

Their prey was close. The two men with the machetes and sweat-stained shirts almost smelled her. It was a test. An initiation into the crew. Hunt her down and execute her. The bloodier the better. Take pictures. Enjoy themselves and report back when done.

With a curse directed at the heavy jungle heat, the lead man swung his machete at a vine to clear a spot in the trail. He squeezed his girth through the opening and left a button snagged on a branch. The ripped shirt brought a laugh. He would buy a new one with the spoils from the hunt. One with rhinestones like they wear in America.

Behind the lead man trudged a skinnier and younger version of him. This one wore a dirty trucker cap and a stained T-shirt and a snarl on his face. "How much farther?"

"How do I know?" The heavy man swiped the machete at a vine. The oppressive jungle took a toll on the adrenaline-laced glow of the hunt. "You heard the same thing I heard. Follow the trail. Can't miss her."

"Hold up." The skinny man leaned on a tree and sucked from a plastic bottle of water with the words *Pure Life* on the label. When the bottle was empty, he crushed it against his hip and tossed the trash into the forest. "How do we know this isn't a trap? What if she's actually hunting us?"

The larger man slapped him on the head, and the younger man's cap flew to the ground. "Scared of one little woman, huh?"

The smaller one snatched his hat from the ground and glared at his companion. "Fuck off, I ain't scared." He touched the pistol handle at his waist. "Do that again and I shoot ya."

The bigger man's smile disappeared as he brandished his machete. "Go ahead. Draw it before I slice your hand off."

The youngster's hand twitched as it rested on the gun butt, but he let it fall away.

With a wave of the big knife, the plump man laughed. "That's what I thought. Let's go see what treats she has to offer."

He pointed along the trail with the business end of the machete. "Lead the way, young 'un."

Ten more minutes of hiking led them to a clearing in the trees where they found the cold remains of a campfire and a thatch-roofed hut built on stilts. The lead man put his hand on his young companion's shoulder. "Let's watch for a bit."

The skinny man slapped his hand away, jogged into the middle of the clearing, and headed for the hut.

The big man cursed and followed.

When she stood, she held on to the cypress wood railing next to her cot until the dizziness faded.

She took a step.

Hold on to the railing.

Another step.

Let go of the railing.

The room wobbled, but it passed, and she took another step.

One hand hovered over the railing as she made her way to the wash basin, where she caught a glimpse of herself in the mirror. Scrapes on her cheeks, bruising around almond-shaped eyes. A small flat nose was humped like it was broken once. Shoulder-length black hair in a tangle. Petite chin with a tiny cleft.

She didn't recognize the reflection.

As terror welled inside her, she grasped both edges of the washbasin and bent to avoid peering at the image in the mirror. Brackish water sat in the bowl and she splashed some on her face and stood to face the mirror again.

The water intermingled with blood to form mud on her cheeks, and she wiped her face with a dirty cloth hanging on a nail.

It didn't help. There was no recognition.

Who am I?

Images flashed in her mind. A vacant and clean city, hazy visions of men and women in olive green uniforms, knives dripping in blood, and violence—lots of violence. She shuddered.

How did I get here?

She took hold of the edges of the bowl again and held on as she heaved and retched. Nothing came up.

A search of her mind brought up no memories of how she got here. Or who she was. Or where she lived. There was nothing except instinct, and her instinct screamed at her.

Get out. Run.

A pair of army-green cargo pants hung on a nail. She yanked them on. They hung loose and were as soiled and frayed as her T-shirt. The cuts and abrasions were alarming. There were a lot of them, and most were scabbed over or in the process of healing. A deep cut in her shoulder was held together with a dozen stiches. She poked at the wound, and a drop of blood oozed from a corner. The laceration was new.

A search of the plastic bins yielded supplies. A crusty enamel mug. Some jute rope. A folding pocketknife with a red handle. Cooking utensils and a crusted pan. And lots of dirt. The second bin contained a gallon of water and a stack of beige-colored packets labeled Meal, Ready-to-Eat. No weapons, other than the pocketknife.

Why did that come to mind?

With the pocketknife, she cut a length of the rope to use as a belt. She ripped off the bottle lid and guzzled from the gallon jug before using the blade to slice open a beige packet labeled "vegetarian bean and rice burrito." The bland food tasted like heaven. Her balance returned, and her mind cleared.

A sound came from outside the hut.

The noise was foreign to the cacophony of animals and plant life filling the jungle. Footsteps. Heavy, lumbering.

A man?

Cocking her head, she focused on the sounds.

Two men.

Two men approaching the hut at a run.

TWO

The thudding footsteps turned into the squeaking of wood against wood, and the hut swayed.

A ladder.

Two men. One heavy, one smaller. The thoughts appeared from nowhere. Unbidden. Automatic.

Nowhere to go. Except over the edge. Face what's coming.

She snapped open the pocketknife to reveal a rusty blade as she cast about the hut for other weapons. The mirror over the washbasin was a square piece of metal. A makeshift knife, perhaps. The cot could be disassembled into a stack of thin metal poles. No help against an immediate threat. She padded on bare feet to the middle of the room. All she had was the knife.

And my hands.

It's enough.

Her racing pulse slowed, and calm flooded over her. She squatted on her haunches and waited.

A head appeared, followed by a torso. A skinny man

with glistening brown skin stepped into the hut, and a larger man followed.

The thin man wore a tattered T-shirt, jeans, and a dirty trucker cap. While he leered and licked his lips, his hand rested on the butt of a pistol stuck in his waistband. The second man was older and wore a soiled cowboy shirt stretched over a big gut. One button was gone and brown skin showed through. This one carried a rusty machete. Both men had scraggly facial hair, and sweat glistened on their faces.

"Well, well. What do we have here?" The skinny man with the trucker cap spoke in Mandarin.

She understood the language.

A clue.

Am I Chinese?

"Looks to me like we found our toy." The one wearing the cowboy shirt sneered. "And she's even tastier than they described."

Who are they?

As she rose to her feet, a gentle pulsing energy formed in the middle of her chest and calmed her.

Child's play, these two.

Cowboy Shirt grinned as he stepped into the middle of the room and waved his machete. Trucker Cap shifted from foot to foot as his eyes roamed her body.

While balanced on the balls of her feet, she sidestepped left away from the larger one and closer to the skinny one, the one with the gun. She shifted the knife in her hands so her fingers grasped the blade. The balance was off, but it would do.

She was calm with a quiet confidence, and the colors in the room swelled in vibrant technicolor. Her attacker's motions bloomed in prominence, and the smells of the jungle popped in her nose. She saw, noticed, sensed, and took in everything. All stimuli were aroused and worked in unison to optimize what she was about to do.

These two men are about to die.

The thought neither pleased her nor upset her. It was a fact, just as the sun sets in the west. There were no emotions about it.

"Little girl, why don't you get on your knees." Trucker Cap's fingers tapped on the gun handle. "I'd hate for—"

Her feet moved into an attack position with her weight on her back foot. With a flick of her arm and the shifting weight of her body, the knife was airborne. She rushed after the flying knife. End over end, it sailed through the air until its blade sank into the neck of Trucker Cap.

As Trucker Cap's face switched from the lascivious leer to a surprised gape, his hand fell away from the gun and went to his neck.

Cowboy Shirt was frozen in place with his mouth open.

She launched a flying kick at the skinny man, and her foot landed on his chest and propelled him back until he crashed against the cypress wood railing. The wood cracked at the impact but held. His hands clawed at the blade handle sticking in his throat as blood dribbled from his neck.

"ARRRGGGHHHH!!!" The big man charged.

After landing on her feet in a crouch, she whirled to see the heavy man lumber at her, his machete held over his head. The attack was slow and clumsy, and she ducked to evade the blade as it arced through the air. She danced to the center of the room and turned to face the attacker.

Again the big man lunged at her, intent on lodging the rusty blade into the side of her neck. She leaned away as the blade swished through the air, and she whipped around to see him take another short swing.

Cowboy Shirt's attack was off-balance and lacked power, but the tip of the blade caught her abdomen and sliced a thin cut across her oblique. A line of blood seeped into her shirt. The wound was superficial, but it stung.

I'm rusty. Get it together.

When the next attack came, she dodged to her left before she leaned into the attack and caught Cowboy Shirt's arm as the blade swung down. With his arm caught in the crook of her elbow, she let the heavy man's momentum carry him. As he fell, she used a slight weight shift to take him hard to the ground before she wrenched the arm and a *snap* cracked in the tiny hut. The heavy man screamed.

She rolled, let go of his arm, and bounded to her feet. He writhed on the ground as the long blade lay forgotten on the wood floor. She pounced on his back, put the crook of her arm against his windpipe, and pulled so his back was bent at an angle and he faced the roof.

I need intel.

"Stop struggling or I'll break your neck." The Mandarin came to her innately, which struck her as a clue, which she stowed away for later.

Focus.

The man in the cowboy shirt gasped for breath and pounded a hand on the hut's floor.

Across the room, the skinny man yanked the knife from his neck as he collapsed to his knees. He dropped the knife and pawed at his waist and grabbed the gun. The pistol wavered, but it was pointed in her direction.

She rolled off Cowboy Shirt as the gun roared and a bullet spit past. She rolled again as another bullet thunked into the wood floor, and she leaped to her feet and scampered at the skinny man as the gun fired a third time. A slug cut a furrow along her thigh muscle, but her momentum carried her to the attacker.

Trucker Cap swung the gun around, but she was already on him. The palm of her left hand struck out and batted at the pistol as she pummeled the skinny man's jaw with the heal of her right hand. The attacker's head snapped back and rapped against the cypress wood railing before he slumped. Blood from the knife wound spattered. She snatched the pistol from him, shifted the weapon to her left hand, aimed, and fired. Point blank. The bullet penetrated Trucker Cap's forehead and he slumped.

I'm left-handed.

She pivoted and held the gun in a two-handed grip pointed at Cowboy Shirt, who rose to a sitting position. He sobbed as he cradled his broken arm. "Please don't. I have a daughter. Please..."

The pleading elicited no emotion from her. The man intended to end her life, that's all that mattered.

The gun was comfortable. By feel, it was a Glock 19. The numbers scrolled unbidden through her head: 9 mm, 102 mm barrel, 855 grams loaded, standard magazine capacity of fifteen. Unknown number of cartridges remaining—can't assume Trucker Cap started with a full magazine. The pistol was grimy to the touch, with gritty action. Poorly cared for.

"Any more of you out there?"

"No! I mean, I don't think so. I don't—"

She stepped closer. "How many?"

"I don't know! I swear. It was just the two of us."

"Where are we, damn it?"

He furrowed his eyebrows. "You don't know?"

"Answer the question."

"On an island."

"What island?" She jabbed the pistol at Cowboy Shirt's forehead. "Come on. Answer the question."

"Uh, it's called Xisha."

She searched her memory. Nothing. "What ocean?"

"In the South China Sea."

She edged to the plastic bins near the washbasin while she trained the pistol on the big man. "How did you get here?"

"By boat."

"Where's the boat? You two came alone?"

Cowboy Hat's eyes shifted. "Yes. Two of us." He looked at his fallen companion, who now lay slumped against the latticework in the railing, his blood in a pool.

She rummaged in the bin and emerged with the jute rope. After the gun went into her waistband, she wrenched the heavy man's hands behind his back, which elicited a scream, and she wound the rope around his wrists. "Who sent you?"

Silence.

The stench of onions and body odor assaulted her as she grasped his sweaty hair and banged the pistol barrel against his temple. "Who sent you?"

"I die if I tell you that."

"You die if you don't tell me."

Cowboy Shirt clamped his mouth shut.

She whipped the pistol butt across his forehead, and he grunted before he toppled to his side. She jerked him upright. "Who?"

His mouth stayed closed while his eyes went wide.

He's more scared of them than he is of me.

The wound on her leg throbbed, and blood seeped into her pants.

With more of the rope, she secured his legs and dragged

him to the far edge of the hut, where she tied his neck to the wooden railing. A search of both men's pockets revealed a wad of red-and-green Chinese yuan, which she pocketed, and nothing else. "Where's the boat?"

Blood dripped from an open cut on his temple. "West of here. About two klicks."

She used two rags tied together to blindfold her captive, and checked the skinny man's pulse to ensure he was dead before retrieving the knife from where it fell from the dead man's hand. At the washbasin, she dropped her pants and examined the thigh wound. A furrow about three inches long.

Lucky.

Blood oozed, but not much. She rinsed the knife clean and cut a length of the blanket, tied it tight around her quadricep as a bandage, and pulled the pants back up.

A piece of the blanket served as a satchel, which she filled with the MREs and the water jug. The skinny man's boots fit loosely, and she yanked on the laces to cinch them tight. The satchel went over a shoulder and the machete hung from her rope belt. The pistol stayed in her hand. The polymer grip was reassuring. She dropped the magazine, confirmed there were eleven bullets, slammed the magazine back home, and checked to ensure a round was in the chamber by pulling the slide back just enough to see the bullet's copper jacket. Twelve rounds total. Trucker Hat was smart enough to carry his weapon with a full magazine and a chambered round.

How do I know these things?

After she wiped clean everything she touched, she went to the ladder.

A man hid in the lush tangle of vines and overgrowth surrounding the hut's tiny clearing. He was small in stature and Korean in features, with leathered skin and deep crow's feet from years in the field.

The man, who went by several monikers, including Tracker, Watcher, and Outpost, slowly, carefully shifted his legs to relieve pressure as the two thugs appeared in the clearing. He checked a chunky watch on his wrist.

Right on time.

Careful not to disturb the vegetation, he sipped from a canteen before he returned his eye to the scope. The scope was attached to a Remington 700 hunting rifle, which rested on a bipod so the muzzle pointed at the hut's front door. The Remington was the base model for the M40A1 sniper rifle used by the US Marine Corps. The man knew this, although he wasn't fortunate enough to enjoy the same modifications, so he made do with the Remington. The rifle was old but well cared for and reliable.

For Outpost, a shot from this distance was effortless, even with the old Remington, and he centered the scope's crosshairs on the larger man as the duo blundered across the clearing.

One of his canteens was empty, and he had peed several times while in the blind, letting the urine run along his leg and soak into the mud under his torso. Not only did Outpost not want to violate his cover by rising to pee, but the urine also served to cover his human odor. Minutes after he relieved his bladder, the two thugs disappeared up the ladder and into the hut.

A minute of silence was followed by a scream and three gunshots. The scream was male. A second later there was a fourth gunshot and another scream. Lower octave, also male. Guttural, panicked.

A compact satellite phone with a stubby antenna rested on the ground next to the rifle. It was expected at Control that the woman would make short work of these two, but Outpost hesitated to provide an update until he had confirmation. After he placed his eye to the scope, a tiny raven-haired shadow dropped from the rear of the hut to the ground. The shadow made no sound.

The figure crouched in the darkness beneath the hut for what felt like a long time while Outpost, who was used to remaining motionless for hours at a time, grew antsy. If she found his hiding place, he was dead. Momentary panic washed over him, but he fought it. She was good, but Outpost had decades of operational experience under his belt, and he reminded himself to trust his skills.

He scanned the shadows under the hut with the rifle scope and cursed his lack of night-vision or thermal optics. He was aware such things existed, but his handlers didn't have that technology. As the watcher resisted the urge to scratch his cheek, a frond wavered in the shadows under the hut. The movement turned into the small figure of the woman as she entered the dense foliage to the rear of the structure.

Outpost exhaled, surprised to find he was holding his breath, and typed a short text message into the satellite phone and hit send.

THREE

Before she descended the ladder, she crouched and listened. If there were two men, there might be more. The gunshots were not quiet.

The metallic scent of blood mixed with charcoal and sulfur from the gunfire permeated the hut's interior. The trussed attacker moaned softly from his spot at the rear of the hut. Outside were only the sounds of the jungle and the smells of loam, vegetation, and sweet flowers, the screech of a faraway monkey, the titter of some unknown animal, the cry of a bird. She didn't hear anything foreign to the jungle. There were no human sounds.

Rather than descend the wooden ladder, where she may be a sitting duck, she peeked over the rear railing to judge the distance to the ground. She tossed the machete out and stuffed the gun in a pocket before she vaulted over the railing, hung briefly, and dropped silently to the ground, where she crouched in the shadows.

A clearing opened in front of the wooden stilted structure. Beyond the clearing, the jungle extended in all directions. Where the open space ended and the jungle started was a dark and forbidding barrier of vegetation, tree canopy, and thickets of vines. A trail led away from the building across the clearing and into the jungle. An old fire pit was a dozen paces from the hut in the center of the clearing. Nothing moved except for the gentle sway of foliage.

Behind her, the undergrowth disappeared into inky darkness. She used the machete to cut away a dozen vines and stepped into the jungle behind the hut. Soil, moisture, and decaying plants assaulted her nostrils, and more vegetation blocked her path. An animal in the trees scampered through the branches, disturbing the canopy. Cutting through the jungle to avoid the trail would take too much time.

I need to get off this island.

She returned to the clearing, skirted the open field by following the tree line until a trail came into view, and crouched to examine the trail's soft earth. Dense with vegetation, the narrow track had only two recent sets of boot prints. One was from a lighter and smaller person. The other was heavier with larger feet. The boot prints pointed in the direction of the cabin.

How did I get to the hut, and how long was I there? Maybe the rain washed away my track or the tracks of the people who brought me?

No memories surfaced. So many questions, no answers.

Where am I going?

No clue. Figure it out when I get there. Off this island, that's for damn sure.

She set off along the trail, machete in her right hand, pistol in her left.

The blind was carefully crafted in the week prior to the mission, but Outpost fought to stay confident that he was hidden from sight.

The woman materialized in his scope, and he stared at her injuries, which appeared in crisp focus through the high-definition reticle. He made mental notes about her condition. Damaged eye socket, cuts and scrapes, and bruising. Blood seeping through her pant leg. She skirted the clearing with a slight limp. Her eyes, though, were clear and alive. Outpost froze. For a moment, he feared he was the helpless prey in the predator's sights.

She drew closer as his hand crept to the pistol in the holster at his belt. Using deadly force was forbidden unless absolutely necessary. He would not return home in disgrace. There would be horrible consequences for his family. Sweat rolled along his back and pooled in his palm while he grasped the pistol handle. Better to die than fail in his mission, and it took all his willpower to let go of the gun.

The woman halted five meters from his position and cocked her head. The rapid shifting of her eyes was visible to Outpost's naked eye. Caked in dust and mud and vegetation, he froze and relied on his training to calm his racing heart. There was no offending odor from him or his gear after the week spent living in the jungle. He smelled more like the jungle than the jungle itself. Still, her darting and wild eyes were unsettling. A cornered animal was the most dangerous kind. He let his breath out slowly, pulled in oxygen, and held it again.

It was endless agonizing minutes before the woman crouch-walked to the trailhead, where she knelt to examine the ground. When she slid into the undergrowth, he waited thirty minutes before sending a long message to Control through the satellite phone.

The trail was several kilometers in length without any forks or spurs. All her senses were alive, and she relied on her ears to tell her if someone approached on the trail. As she hiked, the earthy aroma of the jungle mixed with the smell of salt and something else. Something man-made. As the trail opened up, she picked out the new smell. Engine oil and diesel fuel. The dirt turned into sand as the trail widened and the vegetation changed from thick jungle to widely spaced ferns and palms. Azure blue peeked through in pockets, and light surf ebbed and flowed.

She stopped and crouched behind a flowering tree and examined the sandy area. A rickety dock extended into a calm expanse of sea. Old tires, driftwood, and rotted netting littered the beach. A small, blue fishing vessel bobbed at the dock, its bow pointed out to sea. At ten meters in length, the boat had a small cabin in the aft, three antennas on the cabin, and not much else visible. No humans were in sight.

It's too good to be true.

She watched the beach and ocean for sixty beats and nothing happened, so she pushed aside the vegetation and tracked through the underbrush in an arc around the beachhead. There was no evidence anyone was present. With the pistol in her left hand and the machete in her right, she stepped onto the beach, trudged through the sand to the water's edge, and approached the boat.

The boat's decrepit condition became apparent. It was badly in need of a paint job, chunks of wood were missing from the railings, and bullet holes littered the gunwales. In faded white paint, the words *Tai Zhang Fu No. 0713* were stenciled along the dulled blue hull and the name *Maria* was painted on the stern.

Taiwanese markings.

How do I know that?

She crept onto the dock, leaped over the gunwale, and came face-to-face with an old man.

He stared at her through rheumy pupils. His cheeks were lined with deep wrinkles. A wool cap was perched on his head despite the heat, and tattered cloth pants hung on a gaunt frame. The old sailor had emerged from the cockpit's narrow door and stood leaning on a boat hook. His laughter crackled, and he grinned. "Took ya long time."

After he hitched up his heavy pack, Outpost gripped the rifle and hustled across the clearing to the hut. The text came in from Control indicating the woman had reached the boat, so it was safe to emerge from the blind. He scaled the ladder and went into the hut.

One of the hired thugs, the young one, was face down in a pool of blood. The other man, the larger one, rested against the rear railing, his face covered with a cloth and his neck secured to the wooden railing with a rope. His chest rose and fell.

"Who's there?" The man's breathing increased.

The woman was supposed to kill both men. If the men somehow managed to overcome her, Outpost's directive was to kill them as they exited the hut. This unlikely outcome was not considered in their mission planning, but there was only one thing to be done.

After Outpost checked the pulse of the young man who lay in the pool of blood to confirm he was dead, he drew his pistol.

"Hey. Anyone there?" The man's barrel chest heaved.

The pistol shot was loud in the tiny hut. The heavy man's head bounced off the wooden railing as the bullet entered his forehead before his head slumped, his chin on his chest.

There wasn't much time. Outpost pushed both bodies over the hut's edge and they landed on the ground with a thump. Perspiration flew as he used a folding shovel to dig a shallow grave.

"Who are you?" She held the machete low. The old man wasn't much of a threat.

The fishing boat captain was unarmed, except for the boat hook, and he smiled to reveal pink gums and no teeth. "Does not matter. Where would you like to go?"

"Where are we?"

"Ah, yes. Indeed. Where are we?" The old man hung on to the boat hook with both hands so it supported his slight weight.

He may be senile.

She surveyed the deck of the boat. Despite the decrepit state of the decking, gunwales, and cabin structure, the craft was clean and shipshape. Rope was coiled neatly, bumpers were stowed, and the fishing nets were neatly folded.

"Enough nonsense, old man. I can drive this boat alone if I need to."

The faint crack of a gunshot echoed from deep in the jungle.

The shot brought a brief smirk to the old man's face before it disappeared. "We go. Talk later. Stow lines." After he secured the boat hook to the exterior wall of the cabin, the old fisherman hobbled into the tiny cabin. The engines coughed before they rumbled to life.

With a glance to the jungle behind her, she secured the pistol in her waistband, jumped to the dock, unwound the bow and stern lines from their cleats, and stepped onto the boat as it motored away from dock. Moving to the aft, she stayed partially hidden behind a fifty-five- gallon drum as she scanned the coastline for any evidence of someone with a gun. No movement on the beach, even the palm trees were still.

She went into the cabin, where the captain stood at the helm on bowed legs with one hand on the throttle and the other on the massive rudder wheel. A short crate helped him see over the rudder wheel and through the window. The cabin was outfitted with a modern array of electronics, including sonar, radar, a new radio, a small laptop, a tablet, and a large screen with electronic nautical charting. With one eye on the old man, she searched the meticulously organized but tiny room. A few cans of pork. Instant coffee. Boxes of cigarettes and two bottles of a Chinese alcohol called *baijiu*. First aid kit and a flare gun. Everything had Chinese labels and markings. No sign of any weapons, mobile phones, satellite phones, or any other communication gear save for the ship to shore radio.

As the old man watched, she pored over the electronic nautical chart. It was all in Chinese, which she easily read. The cryptic codes of the chart's elements came easily to her. Reefs, rocks, and soundings. The boat was a blue triangle headed north. Elevation contours surrounded a sprinkle of islands named the Paracel Islands. She worked the controls to zoom out on the screen. Nothing but ocean, so she zoomed out more. A land mass to the west appeared that she recognized as Vietnam. As she kept zooming, an island to the north came into view labeled *Hainan Island.*

China.

"South China Sea." The fat man had spoken the truth. The maps and geography were familiar to her.

The old man nodded and cackled.

She glanced out the rear, and the island was a speck on the blue-green horizon. "Stop the boat."

The engine throttled back, and the boat settled into a drift on placid seas.

She put her hand on the captain's arm. "What's your name."

A shrug. "Li."

"You're Chinese?"

Another shrug. "Yes."

"What are your orders? Who do you work for?"

The fisherman smiled wide and his eyes sparkled.

A Chinese name, Chinese products on the boat, but Taiwanese boat markings. A story jumped to her mind. Something she read once, or maybe she knew through discussions with someone. It was about a Chinese fishing boat using Taiwanese markings to illegally enter Taiwanese waters. Somehow she knew the Paracel Islands were disputed territory with claims by the Chinese, Vietnamese, and Taiwanese.

What are my options?

North to China. West to Vietnam. East to the Philippines.

Fatigue hit her, and her muscles screamed with aches as the adrenaline wore away. The gunshot wound throbbed, and even the cuts and scrapes prickled her skin. She banged her hand on the dash.

Why can't I remember anything?

Where should I go?

She peered at the map and willed an answer to appear.

"Āi yā!" The old man rapped his knuckles on the massive steering wheel and pointed.

Through the window, making good time across the flat seas, cruised a large-hulled yacht.

And it was headed directly at them.

FOUR

South China Sea

Spray shot from the bow as the yacht sailed along the smooth gray ocean. With the old fisherman's binoculars, she examined the craft. The bow was steeply vertical in an inverted bell shape that cleaved the waves rather than planed above them. The blue gray hull was tall, with three large windows and two portals, and topped with a steel railing. The cabin took up most of the aft, and a flybridge was atop the cabin, where a man stood at the helm. Next to him was a second man who toted an automatic rifle. At the bow were two more men, also armed with assault rifles.

The old captain's wry grin disappeared.

She checked the Glock. It was worn and dirty but functional, with twelve bullets in the magazine. The gun and a machete were her only weapons. And the folding pocketknife with the red handle.

The men at the bow of the approaching craft raised their rifles. Bullets plunked into the side of their hull and spit into the tiny cabin. A volley tinkled through the glass and it spidered before more bullets shattered it and the glass fell in shards.

As she dove to the floor, the heels of her hands landed in the glass, drawing blood. She grabbed the old man by the trousers and pulled him to the floor. Too late. A blossom of blood spread on his dirty white shirt. More rounds plinked through the thin wood slats and whizzed past her head. She dragged the now-dead fishing boat captain over her torso and let his body absorb stray bullets.

The rattle of gunfire grew louder as two more rifles joined the volley. Soon the tiny wooden cabin was filled with holes, and splintered wood and glass shards littered the floor. She kept her head down.

The gunfire ended. The fishing boat dipped as the larger boat bumped it and there was a *thunk* as if a landing hook was deployed. Pistol in hand, she pushed the bullet-riddled body of the old fisherman aside, wormed along the floor to the narrow cabin door, and glanced around the jamb.

The yacht's gray hull towered over the fishing boat's port side. Two dark-clad men stood on the attacking ship's deck with rifles trained on the cabin while two men climbed down a rope ladder to her boat. Turtled on her back and with the pistol out in two hands, she leaned through the cabin door and squeezed off two shots.

A man on the ladder spasmed as two bullets hit him and he landed on the deck with a thud. A second attacker was already on her boat, creeping along the gunwale. She fired twice, hitting him in the leg and torso before automatic fire erupted from the yacht.

Glass and splinters of wood rained on her as bullets chewed through the cabin. She pulled herself into the tiny structure, put her back to the instrument panel, and let the thick wood of the dash and the electronics absorb the gunfire.

Eight bullets left in the Glock. An unknown number of men.

A voice in Mandarin bellowed through a bullhorn. "Throw your weapon out the door and come out with your hands up."

Shit.

"You're outgunned and outmanned. Toss the gun."

Under her feet was a crawl hatch leading to the bilge and engine compartment. From somewhere in her murky mind, she remembered the story of the Spanish conquistador Hernán Cortés who, upon attacking Veracruz, Mexico, ordered his own boats scuttled to motivate his smaller army to fight and discourage retreat.

"I'll kill anyone who steps on this boat!" She shoved the pistol into her waistband, snatched the flare gun and the two bottles of Chinese alcohol, heaved the trap door open, and dropped to her stomach. She wrenched open the bottles and emptied the booze into the bilge water, where the alcohol blended with a shimmering slick of oil. After she tossed the empty bottles into the sloshing liquid, she rose to her haunches and fired the flare gun into the bilge and slammed the trap door.

The bullhorn blared. "This is your last warning. Toss the pistol out the door and show your hands!"

She peeked over the helm's dash. Two men stood at the yacht's rail with automatic weapons. Two more soldiers made their way forward along the yacht's deck.

Smoke seeped from the edges of the trap door. No retreat now, the boats were burned. Hidden from view and on her knees, she aimed the pistol out the shattered window and fired twice. Both shots missed, but the men dove for cover.

The wooden structure of the cabin facing the attackers was torn to shreds from the gunfire, but the opposite wall was intact. She went to work on the wall farthest from the yacht and tore at the old, sea salt-encrusted wood. As she kicked and ripped planks away, the air was filled with more automatic fire. Bullets ripped into the cabin and sang past her head. With a final yank, she opened enough of a hole to wiggle through. She took only the Glock and the pocketknife and abandoned the homemade backpack of rations.

After she squirmed through the opening, she slipped over the gunwale into the sea, careful not to make a splash. With a deep breath, she ducked under the *Maria* and swam underwater to the far side of the yacht, whose dual propellers churned in the water.

This far from land, the ocean water was hazy. She avoided the spinning propellers and surfaced at the starboard aft corner, where she snaked up onto a fiberglass swim platform. The boat's name, *Jin Teng*, was painted in white letters on the steel-blue hull. The gunfire ended, and the bullhorn blasted again.

"This is your last warning."

She glanced over the transom. Four men in dark uniforms stood at the railing and scanned the fishing trawler. Another man stood atop the flybridge with a bullhorn to his mouth. All five were short in stature with Asian features. They wore old-fashioned uniforms that made her think of Chairman Mao's old army. The pocketknife went between her teeth, and she kicked off her boots and set them gently on the swim platform.

One hundred nautical miles to the east of the *Jin Teng's* position, a fish factory vessel named the *Damanzaihao* bobbed in calm seas under hazy gray-blue skies. Gunmetal water extended in all directions and blended into the sky at the darkening horizon. An occasional white cap alluded to approaching weather. With a 150-meter beam, the former oil tanker was large enough to handle any swells the South China Sea might throw at her, and with twenty years floating these waters under his belt, the captain didn't blink twice at the dark bank of clouds to the west.

The ship's markings and flag were Chinese, but her crew was North Korean. The boat was a working fish factory, with the ability to transfer, process, freeze, and store huge quantities of fish while at sea. The crew of one hundred souls continued its fish processing operations as trawler after trawler bumped alongside to transfer their day's catch.

The fishing and processing operations were a cover. Hidden behind locked doors in the boat's aft-cabin were enough electronics to operate a massive surveillance operation, which was in fact the boat's primary purpose. Antennas and radar arrays bristled on the roof of the three-story cabin, which also housed barracks, a mess, and a common room to service the North Korean Reconnaissance General Bureau (RGB) staff.

Three well-trained young men wearing naval uniforms sat shoulder to shoulder while a lean man with a weathered face paced a narrow aisle behind them. The older man wore an army uniform with two thin red bars and a single silver star on the epaulets. If he were in a military parade, his breast would be covered with medals. Out in the field, however, the epaulets were the only indication the man's rank was *sojwa*, roughly the equivalent of lieutenant commander in Western naval rankings. He preferred his men refer to him as simply *Commander*. His name was Pak Yong-ju, and his unit was code-named Control.

None of the *Damanzaihao*'s crew realized this team of four were from the RGB, a secretive department of operators trained to execute the most dangerous missions outside North Korea's borders. The ship's crew only knew these were special men, and they knew enough not to ask questions or look them in the eye.

A bank of monitors in the cramped room displayed satellite and drone feeds borrowed from the Chinese, and several radar banks showed the South China Sea. Another row of monitors displayed maps with GPS locations of all shipping and pleasure craft in the South China Sea. The largest monitor showed a small fishing boat in black, white, and shades of gray, and the small wake behind her indicated the boat was under way.

"Sir, the *Jin Teng* is three minutes out from the *Maria*." The report was made by the young man on the end of the row.

The commander put his fingers to his cheek and briefly traced the scar there before he addressed the communications officer. "Have we heard from Outpost?"

"Negative, sir. Not since he reported that the target left the island on the *Maria*."

All talking ceased, which left the clacking keyboards and the commander's measured footsteps clicking on the metal deck like a metronome.

"The *Jin Teng* is approaching the *Maria* now, sir."

On the black-and-white image, a larger craft appeared off the *Maria*'s bow. The RGB commander marveled at the quality of the images from the Chinese Wing Loong 1 UAV. While no people were visible on the *Maria*'s decks, he assumed both the target and the old captain were in the cabin. Seven men were visible on the deck of the *Jin Teng*.

"Get me audio." The commander crossed his arms.

A switch was toggled, and the tiny room was filled with the sound of gunfire. After a pause, the *Jin Teng* captain's amplified voice sounded in the room. The team in the *Damanzaihao* watched the gun battle unfold through the crisp audio feed and black-and-white drone imagery.

When the lithe form of the woman snaked out of the water and onto the *Jin Teng*'s swim platform, an analyst spoke in an alarmed voice. "Should we warn the boat's captain?"

The commander paced with arms crossed over his chest and his lip curled into a grin. "Negative."

Silently she crept over the gunwale and slid onto the rear deck, where she was hidden from the attackers by the cabin. Her bare feet were light on the fiberglass deck as she took the steep stairs leading to the top of the flybridge and stopped so her head peeked over the edge. The knife was clenched in her hand.

The man with the bullhorn stood on padded seating next to the steering wheel to see over the bow and into the smaller fishing vessel. As he lowered the loudspeaker he issued an order, and two men dropped over the yacht's side, clambering down the rope ladder and onto the fishing boat.

She darted up the remaining steps and across the flybridge. In one motion, she clamped her hand on the man's mouth and dragged the rusty blade across his throat. She helped him sink to the cushions, out of sight from the men at the bow. She wiped the blade on the dying man's tunic and stowed it in her pocket before she plucked his pistol from its holster.

With a pistol in each hand, she took a flying leap and slid along the angled cabin windows. As her feet hit the foredeck, both pistols bucked as she fired and ran at the two men who stood at the bow.

Warriors run to the fight.

The two enemies spasmed as bullets hit their torsos. The Glock emptied, and the slide locked open. One man spun and tumbled over the railing while the second sagged to the deck.

Shouts erupted from the fishing boat, and bullets sang overhead. She darted along the side of the cabin so the structure was between her and the gunfire, shoved the empty Glock into her waistband, and took the steps to the flybridge two at a time.

The yacht's engine was purring at idle. She jammed the throttle forward and cranked the wheel. The dual 500 HP diesels roared, and the boat leaned into a turn. With her head low, she kept the boat on an arc so the men on the trawler had no angle of fire. The fishing boat's aft sat low in the water as smoke poured from below deck. The soldiers who remained on the fishing trawler were fish food.

When she was a safe distance away, she slowed the yacht, idled the engines, and drifted. An examination of each dead body revealed little. Some yuan notes were wadded in their pockets next to waterlogged cigarettes. She took the cash but ignored the smokes. The assault rifles were AK-47s and the pistols were Type-92s made in China.

Who are these guys?

Everything was in Chinese, but they were not law enforcement.

Hired guns? Mercenaries?

While she searched the cabin, she levered open an access panel with the pocketknife to uncover a bank of electronics. After a brief hunt, she pried off a tangle of computer circuits and cords comprising the GPS transponder, which she pitched into the ocean. The lower cabin contained nothing of interest except a small backpack, which she carried to the flybridge.

Back at the helm, she consulted the navigational screen and pointed the boat in the direction of the island of Hainan, the nearest land mass off the Chinese mainland, and after setting the headings, she activated the autopilot. She acted on instinct—there was no rational thought behind the choice of Hainan other than she wanted to get away from the scene of the attack and her last recorded GPS position.

When she was a safe distance away from the last known GPS transponder location, she cut the engines and let the boat drift while she cleaned up the mess. After a more thorough search of each body, she heaved each one over the side. She opened the stern wash closet and used the freshwater hose to spray the blood from the decking, and she tossed all but one of the AKs into the ocean. After gathering the three Type-92 pistols, she emptied the magazines. She refilled the Glock's mag with three of the 9 mm Parabellum cartridges and test-fired into the ocean. The Parabellums were standard, and the Glock could be reliably shot with almost any quality of ammunition, but better to be safe than sorry.

How do I know these things?

After she satisfied herself the Chinese bullets fired in the Glock, she refilled the magazine and racked the slide to chamber a round, dropped the mag to add another bullet, and slammed it home. Fifteen in the mag and one in the chamber.

The backpack sat on the captain's chair, and she opened it. The first item was a satellite phone with the battery level at the halfway mark. The second was a pack of cigarettes in a red box with Korean hangul instead of Chinese. She recognized it as a North Korean brand called *Paeksan*. As she stared at the pack, an image flashed of an outdoor dirt yard with three cages made of bamboo large enough for a human. As fast as it appeared, the memory was gone, but a cold vein of fear ran along her spine.

The last item in the backpack almost sent her to her knees. It was a rumpled and dirty picture taken with a Polaroid camera showing a young black-haired woman in an army-green uniform and cap perched on her head with a red star was emblazoned on the front of the hat. The uniform was buttoned to the woman's neck with gold buttons. A leather belt and strap ran across her chest, and a red pin the shape of a flag was on her left breast. The flag had two blue stripes, two white stripes, and a red stripe, along with a red star on a white circle—the uniform of the North Korean army.

The young woman in the photo was her.

FIVE

South China Sea

As a shiver ran through her core, she wrapped her arms around herself. The sun was inches from the horizon, and a damp breeze fluttered her wet clothes and forced her into the lower deck's cabin. Her movements were robotic, her mind elsewhere.

I'm in the North Korean army?

A nauseating sensation filled her gut. She let it pass and contemplated the idea dispassionately as she searched her memory for any indication it was true. Through the haze of memory loss appeared pictures and video reels. Images of a civil war, the heavily mined demilitarization zone, and soldiers standing guard among low-slung blue huts. North Korea's string of dictators, its isolation, and its ties to China and Iran. Visions of a famine appeared, and a slow-motion video of thousands of villagers, bent over and gaunt from malnourishment, staggering along a roadside. Vague memories of radio addresses and state-run television programs touting the nuclear might of the People's Republic of Korea ran through her mind.

Are these memories of real experiences dredged out of the fog of my own living history, or were they known to her through books and the internet?

Did I ever live any of these memories?

If she was once in the North Korean army, it appeared that was no longer true.

What happened to me since the photo was taken?

Maybe her lack of memory was a blessing in disguise. Perhaps this was an opportunity for a fresh start. She pushed the thoughts away as she searched the lower deck's cabin more thoroughly.

The boat was once a luxury yacht with teak wood trim, leather in the main cabins, and a full galley and commode, but the teak was dry and cracked, the leather was stained, and trash littered the interior cabins. As she sifted through the detritus, she found a pile of clothing, some of which loosely fit. She shed the wet pants and T-shirt and tugged on a pair of stiff canvas trousers, which she secured with a webbed military belt, and a tunic two sizes too large. She stuck the Glock in the belt.

The galley contained cans of meat and vegetables, tea, and cartons of cigarettes. After setting a kettle on the gas stove, she used the rusted folding knife to open two cans of food, which she ate cold while sitting on the flybridge as the sun sank lower in the sky.

A new thought occurred to her as she spooned cold meat into her mouth, the kind of mind-bender that probably meant nothing.

If I was once, or ever had been, in the North Korean army, isn't it likely I wouldn't hate the idea as much as I do?

If she only experienced the North Korean army in her

life, it would be the only context she would know, and she would not experience such a visceral negative reaction. As the spoon scraped on the bottom of the can of meat, she decided the past didn't matter. Alone, in the middle of the South China Sea, with nothing but her wits and her skills, the world was hers to do with as she pleased. The newfound feeling of confidence and freedom made her smile.

The yacht floated under darkening skies as the wind ruffled her hair. Someone, somewhere, wanted her dead. But the world was a big place. A warm self-assurance crept over her.

I can disappear where no one will find me.

From somewhere in her murky mind, the image of a brown palm tree-lined beach appeared. The memory was patinaed, like it was an antique postcard from the 1950s, yellowed, and worn along the edges. An image of a place she saw somewhere, maybe a magazine or a guidebook, but where she never visited. Surfers bobbed in the waves, the sand was smooth underfoot. When the memory returned to her so strongly, the scent of coconut oil wafted across her nose. Or did it?

Did I just imagine that smell?

Something told her she had never been to this beach, but it was a dream, something she held on to that gave her hope.

She dug into a can of green beans.

I'm free. I can find this sandy brown beach.

The beans were cold, but it didn't bother her. It was nutrition, and she required sustenance.

If I run, will I ever find out who I am?

Something didn't sit right. Running went against her instinct. She was trained to attack, not run. After she scraped the remaining morsels of cold green beans from the can, she tossed the empties into a trash bin and gulped from a bottle of water.

So now what? Run or fight?

While the boat idled, the fuel tank read three quarters full. Wherever the boat came from, the sailors only used at most a quarter of the tank. The navigation equipment was modern, and she studied her current location. Three hundred nautical miles from Da Nang, Vietnam. One hundred and ninety nautical miles from Sanya, Hainan, China. Calculations appeared in her head, as if by magic. This size of craft, a quarter tank of fuel used. Enough gas to get to China, so China was her destination.

What will I do when I get there?

The self-confidence bubbled just beneath the surface.

I'll figure it out.

After she turned the rudder to the northwest, she set the autopilot on a course for the Chinese island of Hainan, sat back in the cracked leather captain's chair, and finished the water bottle while the breeze ruffled her hair.

The three North Korean analysts' faces registered shock as the single woman decimated the trained soldiers on the yacht.

The commander, however, was stoic. Indeed, he would have been surprised if the *Jin Teng*'s attack on the *Maria* was successful, and he would have been shocked if the woman had ended up dead. So far, their little experiment was paying off in spades. Eventually the woman would die. But not yet. It was too early.

The senior analyst who sat on the end found his voice. "Sir, shall we track the *Jin Teng*?"

"Affirmative." The commander fished a packet of French cigarettes from his pocket and lit one with a gold lighter. The operations team had access to only one UAV feed from China, so they followed the *Jin Teng* as it sped away on a northerly course until it slowed in the middle of the ocean. The *Maria* would sink, and the men stuck on it would die, which mattered little to the commander. According to their radar, the nearest boat was a hundred nautical miles from the *Jin Teng*'s position. On the monitor, the tiny figure of the woman tossed bodies overboard and cleaned the decks before she disappeared below.

After a period where nothing happened aboard the *Jin Teng*, the woman reappeared from below decks and tossed something small overboard.

An analyst spoke up. "Sir, the *Jin Teng* disappeared from the GPS map."

"She disabled the GPS transponder." The commander stroked his chin.

The room grew silent as nothing happened until the woman climbed to the flybridge.

The youngest and most junior analyst spoke up. "Sir, the *Maria* has also disappeared from the GPS map."

"It sank." The commander scowled, ashamed the fact wasn't obvious to his team. "She scuttled it before she swam to the *Jin Teng*."

The commander remained in the cramped operations room long enough to watch as the *Jin Teng* resumed her northwesterly course. Once he was satisfied the woman was headed to China, as predicted, the commander exited the operations center and the sailors of the *Damanzaihao* made a hole for him until he pushed open a door and exited into the humid and now blustery sea air high above the ship's main decks.

There he lit another cigarette with the gold lighter, one of the many luxuries his position afforded him, and smoked while the ship's fish-packing operations went on below. When the cigarette was done, he flicked the smoldering butt into a bin of wiggling fish five decks below and removed a chunky satphone from his rear pocket, unfolded the antenna, thumbed it on, and dialed a long string of digits.

A man on the other end grunted by way of an answer.

"So far the operation is as expected, sir." The commander's voice was measured and respectful. "She easily dispatched the two men on the island and took out the seven soldiers aboard the *Jin Teng*."

"Excellent. And now?"

"Headed to China, sir."

"As we predicted."

"Agreed, sir. From our vantage point and reports from Outpost, she had no trouble. The only anomaly is she left one attacker alive on the island."

Momentary static filled the receiver before the gravelly voice spoke. "That's unusual. Note the details in your report." The voice on the other end was Colonel Ryo Ungsok, Commander Pak's direct supervisor, and the director of the RGB. After his predecessor defected to South Korea, Ryo ascended to the top spot in the RGB.

"Yes, sir. We'll shift to phase three. I've already activated the welcome party in Hainan."

SIX

Hainan, China

Three groups of hidden eyes followed the fifty-five-foot, slate blue-hulled Azimut Magellano yacht named the *Jin Teng* as she approached the shoreline. The pitch-black sea was lit by a quarter moon, sending slivers of shimmering light across the rippling water. Nothing stirred on the remote beach running along the western side of Lingshui Wan bay. China's voracious developers had not yet set their sights on this strip of beach. Far to the west, around a series of jagged peninsulas, was the sleepy town of Sanya, while to the east was a pearl cultivation farm and a tiny resort, both of which were dark.

Ten thousand feet above the Azimut and unseen to its sole occupant was a Chinese-made Wing Loong 1 unmanned arial vehicle (UAV). The drone was operated by a Hong-Kong based Chinese-controlled company on behalf of the China's Ministry of State Security. That spy agency in turn lent the usage of the drone to North Korea's Reconnaissance General Bureau, which is how the RGB commander and his staff on the *Damanzaihao* were able to observe, via black-and-white thermal imagery, the *Jin Teng* as it approached the desolate shoreline.

Also watching the yacht were four soldiers, who were dressed as civilians, but they wore tactical vests and carried Type 88-2 assault rifles that were North Korean-made copies of the Soviet AK-74. The four soldiers lay on their stomachs at the top of a dune and tracked the yacht's progress through night-vision goggles.

As the boat appeared on the horizon and purred into the bay, the team leader toggled his comms. "Control, we have a visual on the boat."

On the opposite side of the bay, a third set of eyes tracked the yacht's progress. Near the pearl cultivation farm, a woman lay prone on top of a van. The van was positioned so it was partially hidden from the bay by a dune, but the woman's vantage point atop the van offered a clear view over the dune. Like always, the woman craved a cigarette, but she dared not smoke in the middle of her operation. Instead she chewed on a wad of nicotine gum.

Next to the woman lay a sniper rifle fit with night vision optics. A spotting scope sat on a tripod. Two members of Japan's Special Forces Group (SFG), that country's version of the American Green Berets, were in a protective formation around the van, armed with assault rifles but hidden from sight.

Inside the vehicle, a communication technician was illicitly patched into the thermal imagery beamed from the Wing Loong drone. The young comms technician, who called himself Neo after the character from *The Matrix* movie, spoke into her ear. "The yacht is three klicks out."

"I have visual." The woman spoke in a whisper as she

eyed the yacht through the spotting scope. "Any movement over on that dune?"

"Negative, ma'am," said Neo. "I count four men."

"Damn it. How many times do I have to tell you. Stop calling me ma'am."

"Yes, ma'am."

The woman's name was Wu and her title was colonel, although she hated the title's formality and went by only by Wu. While her past was a complicated cocktail of conflicting loyalties, at present, she served as the number two in charge of a Japanese spy agency so secret only the prime minister and his immediate staff were aware of its existence. Neo, who served in the same agency, was an accomplished computer analyst.

Wu leaned over to her rifle optics to recheck her calculations. A light breeze carrying moisture had picked up in the past thirty minutes. Distance was 600 meters, and one of the North Korean soldiers' foreheads appeared grainy and green in her rifle scope. Colonel Wu and her team had limited knowledge of the North Koreans' operation. They knew a drone beamed imagery of the beach and the bay to a North Korean fishing factory ship out in the South China Sea. They knew the North Korean tactical team lay in wait for the woman on the yacht gliding gently into the bay. That was about it. "Neo, are you recording the drone feed?"

"Aye, ma'am."

"Confound it, stop—"

"The *Jin Teng* is slowing, ma'am."

"Copy that." Wu rolled her head to crack her neck, toggled her mic, and spoke to the SFG team leader. "Reminder. We are observers only. We are not to engage unless fired upon, copy?"

"Copy that."

"Or if I give you orders otherwise."

"Also a good copy."

While the rifle remained trained on the group of men on the dune, Wu used the spotting scope to track the tall-hulled yacht as it glided slowly into the bay and slid to a halt a hundred meters from the beach. No one was visible on the flybridge. The entire vessel was dark. Her running lights were cut, and the dark fiberglass blended in with the black water.

Where are you, girl? Wu panned the spotting scope from bow to stern. Nothing.

That's when a *whoosh* sounded from the dune where the four North Korean special forces troops lay in wait.

Colonel Wu ripped her eye from the scope as the rocket-propelled grenade swished through the heavy air, slammed into the yacht's cabin, and exploded in flashes of yellow and red. Another rocket-propelled grenade whooshed from the dune, followed by a third. Two more explosions sounded as plexiglass and wood sprinkled on the water around the boat.

"Holy crap," said Neo.

No shit. Wu's heart sank as the *Jin Teng*'s fuel tank exploded, which sent the boat's aft flying into the air. By the time the explosions subsided, what was left of the yacht crackled with fire.

No one could survive that. Sorrow washed over her.

"Ma'am? Now what?"

Wu stayed silent as she searched the water through the spotting scope for any sign of survivors. Nothing stirred save for the flames licking at what remained of the cabin structure. Bits of flotsam, some ablaze, littered the water surrounding the boat, and a slick of fuel meandered out to sea. The gas slick caught, and flames spread out around the boat. Colonel Wu bent back to her rifle scope to see the dune where the four North Korean special operatives lay in wait.

She stopped chewing her gum as elation washed over her. "Activity on the beach," she reported into her comms.

The dune where the four men were positioned and from where the rocket-propelled grenades launched was a frenzy of combat. Two of the North Korean soldiers lay motionless on the ground. The other two were in a melee with a small, dark figure who fought with a quiet fury.

There was something tiny and metallic in the fighter's hand. The attacking figure spun and planted a kick on one man's neck, fell to the sand, rolled, and rose to a crouch to meet the second man's attack. She parried one strike, blocked another, and moved so fast Wu didn't track the counterattack until the North Korean soldier lay on his back bleeding from the neck.

The last soldier yanked out his pistol as something sailed through the air. The North Korean soldier jerked and dropped the gun, and his hands went to his throat. The small attacker darted at the struggling man, snatched the soldier's pistol, and fired it twice. The soldier slumped to the sand as the reports reverberated over the water. She stopped and plucked something small and silver from his throat.

That's that, then. Wu smiled.

The woman on the sand dune stood over each of the fallen soldiers and fired two shots into each man's head. The cracks of the pistols echoed over the water. After a brief search of each body, the small shadow vanished into the sea grass.

Sirens sounded in the distance. The wrecked yacht

crackled and popped as the fire burned. Otherwise, the bay was still.

"Wrap it up." Colonel Wu spoke into her comms as she broke down her rifle. "We need to go." After she stowed her gear in the van, the team of four sped north along route G98 on the way to the town of Haikou on the northern side of the island where they would catch a ferry to the Chinese mainland.

On the ferry, the two Japanese soldiers plus Neo remained with the van in the car hold while Colonel Wu paced the empty top deck with an encrypted satphone to her ear. Her free hand pressed a cigarette to her lips. So far, the quarterly medical checkup mandated by her agency showed only clear lungs. Healthy as an ox, the Japanese doctor explained, as if she should be happy with the prognosis. She didn't bother to tell him that an ox is a castrated bull, which didn't seem all that healthy.

The male voice on the other end of the satphone was deep and measured. "Where is she now?"

Wu let out a stream of smoke through pursed lips. "In the wind."

Joe, the man on the other end of the phone, matched his voice in physical appearance: tall, muscular, and long-limbed. "The North Koreans aren't going to let her get away that easily."

"They'll have to send better men." Wu inhaled on the cigarette, and smoke escaped her mouth as she spoke. "We're monitoring. When they find her, we'll know."

"Any guesses on her intended destination?" Joe asked.

Wu paced and considered the question. *How much does my boss need to know?*

"I have some ideas."

"Maybe she'll take the out. When will you present it?"

The out. It was Joe's biggest hope, but Wu had reservations. A part of the recruitment process designed to force the candidate to make her own choice. A conscious choice bred commitment and was the cornerstone of her recruiting strategy. A strategy her boss disagreed with. "Soon."

"Why don't you bring her in? Tell her everything. Let the chips fall where they do."

"We talked about this." Wu flicked the butt of her cigarette over the ferry's rail, and a trail of sparks arced before it fizzled out when it hit the water.

A deep sigh came from the other end of the line. "I remember, but the clock is ticking."

"We're only two days into the kinetic portion of the operation," Wu said. "You can't recruit an asset in a day, or a week, or even months. She's a ready-made operative that won't take years and years to train and condition. The North Koreans made a terrible mistake, and now they're cleaning up their mess. But she needs to trust us. We need to earn her trust. She's a wounded animal right now. Emotional. Unpredictable. This is how operations go. We take large risks to gain large rewards."

"I'm aware of how operations work. I'm also aware of the risk-reward tradeoffs." The man on the other side of the call went silent. Joe Nomura, the head of Japan's new, top secret agency called Department 82. Her new boss. A man under tremendous stress after only weeks on the job.

She pictured Joe standing near the broad windows of his office in Tokyo with the phone to his ear while he peered out over the grounds of the Imperial Palace. He probably wore his trademark dark blue suit, white shirt, blue tie. While Joe wasn't an emotional man by temperament, he was close to this operation. Too close, in Wu's estimation. Closer than she was, if that was possible, and it was the true basis for his concern. "Trust me, sir. This will bear fruit in the long run."

"It's not the long run I'm concerned about," Joe said.

Wu knew when to push and when to release the pressure valve, so she said nothing.

"I'll trust your judgement," Joe said. "For now."

The line went dead.

SEVEN

Guangdong Province, China

The combat-induced adrenaline faded as she sped north along the G75 motorway, away from the island of Hainan and in the direction of Zhanjiang, a large city on the Chinese mainland. The ebb and flow of the chemical was a familiar sensation. It coursed through her bloodstream and heightened her awareness and sensitivity before it receded into dullness. Her body and mind were conditioned to handle the adrenaline highs and lows and to use them to her advantage. The fresh air and the mindfulness required to pilot the motorcycle at a high rate of speed renewed her mind and kept her alert.

The bike was a Chinese-made Bullit Hunt S with a 125cc engine. The cafe-style racer resembled a superior-quality bike made in Britain by Triumph. How she knew these facts niggled at her while she kept the throttle wide open and wove among traffic. She seemed to possess many innate skills, like how to ride the motorcycle and defeat the kill squad on the beach. Yet she didn't know her own name or where she came from or who her parents were. Anguish threatened to wash over her and she pushed it away to focus on piloting the motorbike.

Stay focused.

She had found the bike in an alley and waited for the owner to get off work while she ate a cold dinner from the nearby dumpster. She grabbed the bike's owner from behind, and he never saw her face. After she bound him with a length of thin cord from the dumpster, she stuffed a rag in his mouth. The bike keys were in his pocket. There was also a wad of cash, which she left. For now, the yuan she lifted off the dead soldiers was enough.

One benefit of the motorcycle, besides the fact that there were thousands of similar bikes on the road, was the anonymity of the helmet, which she had jammed onto her head before she pulled into traffic.

As she sped east, the theft of the motorcycle gnawed at her. What if the young man wouldn't be able to get to work to earn a living to feed his family? The guilt after the fact was surprising; it hadn't occurred to her before she took the bike. Instead, she acted on instinct. She needed the bike and so she took it. Confusingly, the deaths of her attackers in the hut, on the yacht, and on the beach generated no emotion at all, as if that part of her brain were dead. If someone strapped her into an EEG machine, would the device register any activity in that part of the brain? It was a simple equation. They meant her harm, so she eliminated the threat. Simple.

The fights went through her mind time and time again. She replayed the combat sequences, and they streamed in vivid color and minute detail. While she didn't remember anything about herself, the attacks in the hut and on the yacht and on the beach were crystal clear. Her memory functioned, so why didn't she remember anything from before she woke in the jungle?

There was the attack by the larger yacht with the soldiers that she dispatched with ease. Seven fewer bad people on the planet. Her arrival in the bay near Sanya, where an impulse told her to slip into the water at the mouth of the bay and swim to the beach. She knew to expect the unexpected, and to act before acted upon. Every move was done out of instinct. Don't think, act. It was when she let herself think that she would end up in trouble.

Who am I?

I don't even know my own name.

Do I want to know who I really am? Will I like the answer?

She didn't know, and so she drove east.

After killing the four men at the beach, she had made a cursory search of their pockets. Other than some cash, which she kept, and cigarettes, which she tossed, there was a scrap of paper tucked between the cellophane and the cardboard of a box of cigarettes. On it was an address written in Chinese. 383 *Lockhart Rd, Causeway Bay, Hong Kong.*

When she read the address, something clicked in her mind.

Hong Kong.

It was familiar and filled her with hope. And a little dread. It was a place she had been, a place she was familiar with. She was sure of it. The combination of the tiny clue and the familiarity of those two words added to a calm sense of purpose.

Hong Kong.

Am I from there? Do I live there?

Without another plan, Hong Kong beckoned. And so when she reached the sprawling city of Zhanjiang, she found the G15 highway heading east and followed it.

A kilometer behind the speeding motorcycle drove an ordinary delivery van. Outpost piloted the van with one hand on the steering wheel and the other arm stuck out the window. Rust dotted the panels and the windshield was cracked. The logo of a chicken toting a messenger bag was emblazoned on the side. Inside, empty coffee cups and Styrofoam ramen bowls rolled on the floor as the van took the gentle curves of the motorway. A small tablet was attached to the dash, which showed a red dot moving on a map. He drained the cold coffee dregs from a cardboard cup and tossed it into the back, where the cup rolled among its brethren.

So far, the mission was right on schedule.

A sign flashed past Wu's window indicating they were sixty kilometers outside Macao. Half of Wu's blood was Chinese and she read the sign easily, which was a result of her childhood in Hong Kong. One of the Japanese SFG soldiers drove the van, while Wu rode in the front passenger chair. The other Japanese SFG soldier rode on a bench seat and stared ahead blankly. Both Japanese soldiers were dressed in civilian clothing, which included gray ball caps and T-shirts over bulging muscles. Neo sat in the rear with a laptop and monitored the illicit feed from the Chinese drone. Wu cracked a window and lit a cigarette with her lighter.

"I wonder how they're tracking her?" Neo chewed on the tip of a pencil. "This drone feed is broadcasting her geo-coordinates every five minutes." The analyst connected the signal to Wu's mobile phone, which showed a green dot moving along a map of the G15 highway approaching Yangjiang.

"Where do you suppose she's heading?" Neo tapped on the keyboard.

Wu gazed out the window as lights flashed by. This late at night, the highway was mostly empty of cars, but lorries roared and groaned their way to and from the massive population centers of Shenzhen, Guangzhou, and Dongguan. "She's going to Hong Kong."

"How do you know, ma'am?" Neo asked.

"She'll go somewhere she's comfortable." Wu flicked the butt through the window crack, blew smoke from her nostrils, and closed the window. "Unfortunately, comfortable doesn't mean safe."

When the green dot exited the G15 and turned onto the S32, also known as the Xuanda Expressway, Wu nodded to herself. The S32 would take her to Macau and over the bridge that spans the Zhujiang River Estuary to Hong Kong. As the van hummed along the pristine motorway, Wu's thoughts turned to a meeting she attended six months ago in Seoul. A meeting that launched her on this path. A meeting that gave her renewed hope, an emotion she had grown unfamiliar with.

None of the neighbors in the wealthy neighborhood of Seocho were aware the house was owned by the National Intelligence Service of South Korea. It was the kind of neighborhood where residents kept to themselves and asked no questions. The sight of government-looking SUVs at the curb and armed guards on the roof generated no double takes, as they were common accoutrements of the wealthy and powerful. Indeed, only two blocks east from the NIS safe house was the compound of Samsung's CEO, and next to the safe house was a mansion owned by the pop singer Jaejoong. Both residences deployed armed guards, and a helicopter was often seen ferrying the Samsung CEO to and from his office on the Samsung campus.

Colonel Wu marveled at the size of the estates while the smoke-windowed SUV motored her from the Seoul Gimpo airport where she had arrived via private jet. It reminded her of where she was raised in Hong Kong's Peak neighborhood, and to distract herself from the memory, she lit a cigarette. When she pushed the button to roll the window down, the window didn't budge.

"No smoking in here, ma'am." The driver, a young Korean in a black suit and dark sunglasses, gripped the wheel at ten and two. "The windows don't roll down for security reasons."

Wu blew smoke into the front seat and glared at the young man in the rearview mirror until they drove through a wrought iron gate, motored along a drive lined by flowers, and parked in a four-car garage, where they waited for the heavy door to descend before exiting the SUV. Wu ground the cigarette out under her boot and followed the young man into the house, where she was greeted by four Koreans in blue suits, all of whom scowled at her before the one with the grayest hair stepped forward to issue the rules.

"You are to remain at least ten feet from him at all times. Under no circumstances are you to touch him. No smoking. Any electronics you brought with you are to remain outside the room, as are any weapons. You're to take no notes. Any pens, pencils, or other writing implements will remain outside the room. Your conversation will be recorded, and you will be monitored the entire time. You have fifteen minutes, not a second longer."

Wu nodded.

"And Colonel Wu, a reminder that you are here because the defector demanded it and our government assented. Any violation of the rules will result in your immediate ejection from the interview room and you will forfeit any future access. Are we clear?"

"Got it," Wu said.

After depositing her phone, a Zippo lighter, and a sterling cigarette case into a box, she was ushered along a hallway and into a bedroom, or what once was the master bedroom. The only furniture were two chairs standing ten feet from each other. A video camera was on a tripod, and the red light winked on as she walked inside. One wall was outfitted with a mirror the size of a projection television that she presumed was one-way glass.

A man turned from the window. His teeth shone in the overhead fluorescents when he smiled, which was a sign of privilege where he came from. The man extended a hand. "My name is Choe Su-gil." The Korean was small and gaunt, with hollow cheeks, and he wore modern rimless glasses with violet-colored lenses. His suit hung on narrow shoulders, but his eyes flickered with energy. Choe's grip was strong, and he took Wu's shoulder in his other hand.

They already violated a rule. Not her fault. Can't expect her to be rude, after all.

Wu squeezed the man's hand. "Don't you mean Colonel Choe Su-gil?"

Choe shook his head and pointed at a chair. "That remains to be seen. I forgot your past, Colonel Wu. Your accomplishments at the Chinese Ministry are well known to us. Sitting where I sit now, I may claim some empathy with your own choice to, how do the Americans say it? Switch teams over to the Japanese? Please, sit."

"My time at the Ministry was never a choice." While Wu took her seat, Choe pulled his chair closer, and they sat knee to knee. Second rule violation.

"I'm told we only have fifteen minutes," Wu said. "Why did you demand to see me? I'm told you refused to provide any intelligence to the South Koreans until after you spoke to me."

Choe put his hands up. "My only leverage is information. The South Koreans, rightly so, take their intelligence-gathering seriously. While I trust them implicitly, what I have to say to you they will deem as inconsequential, while you will recognize the value of the information. No sense risking ambiguity along the communication route when you and I can speak directly, no?"

Wu nodded. "You are the most senior official to defect from North Korea since, what, Hwang in 1997? And you're the only member of the Reconnaissance General Bureau to ever come across the border, correct?"

Choe nodded. "Your information is correct."

Wu crossed a leg. "So the South Koreans' attitude is natural. The last thing they want to do is share intelligence with the Japanese. At least until they can parse your knowledge and distill it and decide what to share and what to keep secret."

The North Korean defector waved his hand. "And they

will have their information. Yes, I chose to defect to the South instead of the West. After all, it is my homeland. But for now, the information is mine to do with what I please."

Wu's mind spun. Since receiving word through the South Korean embassy in Tokyo twenty-four hours ago that a high-level North Korean defector wanted to speak with her, she had been unable to focus on anything else. She had many questions for this man, but none could be asked in front of the South Koreans. "I am deeply appreciative of whatever information you wish to share, Colonel Choe."

The North Korean bowed his head and steepled his fingers before he raised his eyes once more. "I believe you are searching for a young woman, yes? Someone you have been looking for since a long time ago?"

Wu's skin tingled, but her face stayed stoic.

Choe's eyes darkened. "I have information about this young woman I believe you'll find helpful. She is in deep trouble, but you, unlike me, may be in a position to help her."

EIGHT

Mong Kok neighborhood of Hong Kong

The cash she had plundered from the four soldiers was almost gone. A chunk of the yuan went toward prepayment for a room in a rundown hotel in the Mong Kok district of Hong Kong called the Nga Shing Hourly Hotel. Good marketing in the name, which is how she made her lodging selection. A bit of the cash went to fill the motorcycle's petrol tank. Some of it paid for a bowl of noodles and two mangosteens, the sugary fruit popular in Southeast Asia. She spent more of the cash on a fresh change of clothes, including a pair of olive-drab cargo pants, a black ball cap, and a gray zip-up hoodie. The rest went toward a leather shoulder bag for the Glock.

Calling the Nga Shing a hotel was generous. It was little more than a flophouse where the proprietor, a wizened Chinese man with white hair sprouting from a large mole on his chin, sat behind thick plexiglass and stared at a tiny black-and-white television. A mottled orange tabby lay on a sunny windowsill and hissed at her when she put her hand out. Her hotel room contained little more than a double-sized bed, a credenza decorated with cigarette burns on the laminate top, and a set-top television that only played snow. But the room was clean, and she wedged a chair under the door handle and fell fast asleep with her hand wrapped around the handle of the pistol.

The city was both foreign and at times familiar. She navigated the streets without the use of a map, and innately knew where to find a hotel that took cash and didn't ask questions. The mangosteens triggered far-off memories of time spent here, as did the crowded living conditions, the towering skyscrapers, and the missing fourth floor in the hotel. She knew the word *four* sounds like the word *death* in Chinese, so builders omitted the fourth floor to avoid bad luck. Despite the instances of déjà vu and familiar discoveries, she was unable to dredge up specific memories of time spent in this city. Was her time here fleeting? Did she know people here? Was her family here?

Despite her frustration, she was energized by sleep and alert from a cup of black coffee from the pot in the hotel's lobby. She stepped onto a sidewalk slick from an early morning rain. The cacophony of street noises and shoulder-to-shoulder pedestrians was comforting, and she tugged the brim of her cap and walked south. She had memorized the address written on the slip of paper: *383 Lockhart Rd, Causeway Bay, Hong Kong*. The address was across Victoria Harbour from the hotel and so she decided to do a short surveillance detection route, known as an SDR, before finding an entrance to the MTR, Hong Kong's expansive subway system.

As she crossed Argyle Street, her eyes roamed the crowded street and recorded faces. A man in a trench coat leaning against a building reading a paper. A homeless person wearing soiled military garb lying on a cardboard box. A woman with gray hair and sunglasses and smoking a cigarette had been window-shopping ten minutes ago but now was paying for a coffee at a bodega. There was an earbud in one of the woman's ears. *Threat, or my imagination?* By the time she hastened along Fa Yuen Street and jaywalked through traffic to get to the opposite sidewalk, the gray-haired woman had disappeared.

A scooter honked as Colonel Wu crossed the road. She dodged an old Chinese woman pulling a wire basket of groceries and shouldered through the crowd. Although Hong Kong is one big Chinatown, the narrow alleyways and market stalls of Mong Kok serve as a Chinatown within a Chinatown. It was Wu's home turf.

The only child of a Chinese banker father and a Japanese mother, Wu was raised across the bay in "The Peak," Hong Kong's wealthiest neighborhood, where she was subjected to private boarding schools and au pair-supervised play dates. Each time she ran away as a teenager, she ended up in Mong Kok among the blue-collar Chinese of her father's extended family. They were a salt-of-the-earth people she easily connected with, but who were ultimately compelled to return her to the chauffeured cars and a two-nanny-per-child ratio. But not until after her relatives fed her traditional noodles or hot pot and filled her head with stories from *real* China, as they called it.

Now, she stopped at a noodle cart belonging to her aunt's nephew's son, paid cash for a bowl, and sat at a rickety table to eat. The youngster, who wore a soiled white tank top and a dangly earring with a gold clipper ship, didn't know her. As she slurped the salty broth and sucked in the noodles, she avoided thinking about her father. Aloof, unavailable, and immensely successful during her childhood, he now lay in Tokyo's poshest nursing home, cared for by an attentive staff, but unable to recognize anyone because of the Alzheimer's ravaging his mind. *You reap what you sow, you prick.*

The mobile phone buzzed in her pocket and she answered it to hear Neo's voice. The analyst sat in the rear of the van, which was parked along Nathan Road. "Asset left her hotel, ma'am. Proceeding south on Canton Road."

"Copy that." Wu handed her bowl to the cart's proprietor, who tossed it onto a pile of soiled dishes. She shoved a tiny Bluetooth earbud in one ear that connected to her phone.

The next part of the operation would be delicate, but her team had pored over the logistics endlessly and practiced it dozens of times. The target had to be made aware of something without knowing the source of that something. Under ordinary circumstances, they may send an anonymous text or email. But the asset didn't have a mobile phone or an email account. How do you pass anonymous information to someone in an analog fashion without them knowing? The information had to stick—in other words, the target needed to take it seriously. Drop a handwritten note into her handbag? Pay a stranger to hand her a message?

In this case, Wu thought it important that the woman later recognize her, Wu, as the source of the information. Alone and isolated, the target would naturally connect with the source of the information, a lifeline so to speak, and later this connection would be critical. The individual approaching her needed to be non-threatening, and so they rejected the idea of using any of the young male operators in the Special Forces Group or a stranger who would mean nothing to the asset later. Wu, in her late forties, with gray hair and deep crow's feet at the corners of her eyes, selected herself as the messenger. A matronly figure conveyed more trust than a young hotshot operator. That was the theory, anyway.

Recruiting an asset was a seduction. It was an apt metaphor, but they didn't want her as an agent as much as they wanted to recruit her to become a member of the team. An employee rather than a contractable resource. Bring her into the family. Therefore, to instigate the initial contact, Wu needed to be intriguing and mysterious, yet helpful and, most of all, non-threatening. Questions needed to be asked and some answers needed to be given. Give the target a taste so later she will want more. Whet her appetite. Position Wu as someone with answers to her many questions. Uninterested in, and frankly poor at, real-life seductions, Wu was an expert in the art of asset recruiting. Everything relied on a foundation of trust.

Wu pushed aside the ruminations on asset recruiting theory as she walked along Tung Choi Street. The narrow avenue ran parallel to the much busier Canton Road. Her phone buzzed, and Neo was back. "You're roughly opposite her."

"Copy." Wu stepped into the street and wove through honking traffic and dodged motorbikes until she came to a side road, which she turned onto. At this pace, she would emerge onto Canton Road behind the target. "Any idea where she's going?"

"Negative."

Wu turned onto Canton Road and dodged around pedestrians.

"You're twenty meters behind her."

As Wu quickened her pace, her quarry came into view. Dressed in olive pants, a dark T-shirt, a gray zip-up hoodie, and a black ball cap, the asset carried a leather satchel on one shoulder. Wu estimated the woman was armed with at least one pistol and the knife. It was possible she had picked up another weapon along the way. One wrong move and she might blow six months of operational planning, and the North Korean defector's intelligence would go to waste, or worse, she might get shot in the process. Wu's pulse quickened.

If Wu stayed in this position, the asset would soon make her. She only needed a glimpse of the woman, so Wu hung a left into an alleyway and broke into a sprint. While she ran, she turned her jacket inside out. Five minutes later, she slowed to a walk as she emerged back onto Canton Road, now ahead of the asset, and spoke to Neo through the comms. "Tell me if she stops or turns."

"Yes, ma'am," Neo said into her ear.

"I'm going to initiate contact." The faintest sensation of a pit in Wu's stomach formed, which was a surprise. As a veteran of two-score years of field operations, nerves were rare. But it had been a long time since the stakes were this high.

What happened next played out behind her, so Wu heard it but only saw the aftermath. Tires squealed, the door of a van clanked open, and men shouted. "Stop. You there." Gunfire erupted in two short bursts. Civilians screamed.

Wu whirled. The tiny dark-haired woman stood in a two-handed shooting stance, pistol out. The gun cracked twice again and a black-clad man emerged from the van into the volley of fire and fell to the street. Two men in similar dark uniforms lay in a pool of blood on the sidewalk. The shooter whirled and disappeared into an ally as sirens sounded.

"Shit." Wu scanned the scene from a position near a store window.

Neo's voice sounded in her ear. "What happened?"

"Someone just tried to snatch her. Black van. Three dead. She'll go to ground now. We might not have another chance."

"Watch your step, she'll be trigger-happy."

No shit. Wu shoved the earpiece into her pocket as she slipped through the gathering pedestrians and darted into the alleyway nearest to the asset's last location. At the far end of the ally, she glimpsed a form carrying a brown satchel before it disappeared into the shadows.

I only have one chance. A unique opportunity to help a wounded animal, but approach with caution.

Wu used her scarf to cover her hair and face and grabbed the lapels of a man who was about to mount a small motorcycle. Her foot took his legs out from under him, and she helped the man to the ground and threw her leg over the motorbike's seat. With a wrench of her wrist on the throttle, she took off through the alley, made a right turn, whizzed past a yelling shopkeeper, made two lefts, and almost plowed into a tiny form in olive-green army pants and a dark t-shirt. The woman's left hand was buried in the shoulder bag.

A puddle splashed as Wu pulled to a stop. "Get on."

The dark-haired woman froze with her hand stuffed in her bag.

Wu lowered the scarf to reveal her face. "If I wanted to kill you, you'd already be dead. Now get on."

After a brief hesitation, the small woman threw a leg

over the seat and grabbed Wu's waist as they took off. Wu dodged a pull cart of parsnips, weaved around a man carrying a dozen shopping bags, and turned into another alley. After three more turns, Wu emerged onto the Kowloon Highway, where she opened the throttle.

NINE

Hong Kong

The lights winked out as they entered the Western Harbour Crossing tunnel and the motorcycle's running light illuminated a yellow path through the murk. They emerged into the sunlight on the Hong Kong Island side, screamed around a curve to enter Connaught Road West, and exited onto a side street two blocks from Western Market. After she wove through narrowing side streets, they turned into a tight courtyard between two abandoned warehouses. Graffiti covered the crumbling brick walls and no one was in sight.

The young woman leaped off the rear of the motorcycle, whipped out a pistol, and trained it on Wu. "Who are you?" Her finger was tight on the trigger.

Wu froze with her hands on the motorcycle's grips. The young woman was haggard, her stringy hair was in need of a wash, and there were cuts and bruises on her exposed skin. Her eyes were hooded but alive. Alive with fear, adrenaline, and something else. A mission, maybe. Her clothes were new, but there was a feral quality about her. She was surviving, but also dangerous. *Tread lightly.*

The young woman waved the gun and stepped back. "Who are you, damn it?"

Wu put her right hand in the air, palm out. "I'm going to reach into my pocket. I have something I want to show you. Okay?"

The raven-haired young woman hesitated before she nodded her head. "Do it slow."

Wu slid her hand into her jacket pocket, withdrew a mobile phone, and held it out to the young woman. It was an older flip-style phone that had seen better days.

Guarded hope appeared in the woman's eyes, but she remained still. "What is that? Why are you giving that to me?"

"It's from a friend."

"Who? Who's the friend?" She was jittery and her eyes darted everywhere.

"Do you want it or not?" Wu waved the device in the air.

The young woman snatched it from Wu's hand and stepped back. The gun never wavered.

The attack on the asset's life was just the thing Wu needed to start the trust-building process. The stark contrast of the rescue worked in her favor. "Keep it safe," Wu said. "Turn it on only when you need it so you're not tracked."

"Please. Tell me who you are."

The pleading expression of hope and fear tugged at Wu's heartstrings. "I can't right now. We can't be seen together. I'm... I'm sorry. There is a file on the phone that will help you."

The raven-haired woman grabbed Wu's arm in a death grip and waved the gun. "Wait. Please..."

I need to go. Put as much distance between her and the woman as possible. Just as a little trust would start things off on the right foot, too much may ruin it. If Wu gave her too much information, the woman might be distracted. And distracted could get her killed.

"You're all I've got..." The asset's eyes were wide.

Damn it. Wu relented. "Your name is Kira." Wu pried Kira's hand from her arm, held it a moment and squeezed. Their eyes caught, and there was a flicker of gratitude in Kira's smile. "Remember this word: *Jiāting*. Got it?"

"Yes, *jiāting*." Kira's eyes were wide, hopeful. "*Family*. Why do I need that word?"

Wu pushed the motorcycle's starter button and revved the engine. "Just remember it."

"Wait—" The gun sagged in Kira's hand.

The whine of the motorcycle's engine drowned out Kira's voice as Wu pulled away from the curb. When she glanced back, Kira was gone.

Four blocks away, Wu left the motorbike parked between two cars and doubled back to Western Market, where she blended into the crowd. It was a venue she knew from her childhood. She darted among stalls and found a door to the back rooms, where she dodged fishmongers and vegetable farmers carting their wares from lorries into the market. On a loading dock, Wu reversed her jacket and tied the scarf over her hair. When she was sure there was no possibility the woman had tailed her, she inserted her earbud and dialed Neo. "Handoff complete, can you establish tracking?" The mobile flip phone was specially modified to emit a signal even when the user thought the device was powered off. It was a signal trackable only by Department 82's technical team.

"Hold please, ma'am." Neo's rapid typing came through the headset. "Got her. She's walking along Morrison Street. Opposite direction from you."

"Good. I'm going to run an SDR. Send me periodic updates on her location."

"Copy."

The transmission ended and Wu put her earpiece away. As she hastened along Jaffe Road, she chastised herself. *Damn it, why did I do that?* Wu almost told her more. It was Kira's eyes, alone and afraid, that caused her to relent. Wu turned into the Wan Chai MTR station and hopped a train while observing those around her.

One wrong move, revealing too much, might tank the entire mission. *Keep your head on right, damn it.* Millions of yen and her own burgeoning reputation in Department 82 were at stake, of course. But there was more, wasn't there?

Kira is at stake, and that means more than anything.

I have a name.

Kira.

She let the word roll around in her head to see if it was familiar.

Kira. Kira. Kira.

It wasn't.

Kira what? What's my surname?

At an internet cafe, she googled the name *Kira* and found the usual internet junk. The name was derived from either an Irish word meaning black or a Hindi word meaning beam of light. Go figure. She searched for records of missing females with that name and found nothing. The name Kira was multi-national and popular in America, but plenty of Russians, Canadians, and Germans also used it. No clues there. Kira was a common name in Japanese manga graphic novels. Add an A to the beginning and you get a popular pornographic entertainer. A sinking sensation washed over her as she realized the search was fruitless. *Is this really my name, or was the gray-haired woman lying?* After she erased the search history and wiped off the keyboard, Kira left the cafe.

Right back to where I was before.
Still, it's nice to have a name.
I'm Kira.

Her thoughts switched to the gray-haired woman on the motorbike. A guardian angel who appeared out of nowhere. Well, not out of nowhere. She was walking behind her on Canton Road prior to the attempted kidnapping but was ahead of her when the attempted snatch occurred. The woman's appearance on the motorcycle was not a coincidence, but it wasn't this fact that led Kira to jump on the back of the bike. Under ordinary circumstances, the appearance of someone on the street during an attack like that would have prompted her to shove a knife in the intruder's throat.

But something held her back. When the woman pulled aside her scarf to show her face, there was a glimmer of recognition. Something in her gut, something she trusted. Maybe it was the woman's action to uncover her face. By revealing her face, the woman signaled familiarity and trust. But it was more. It was the woman's eyes, nose, chin. Something about her. Kira knew the woman but couldn't place her. She trusted the thin lifeline.

As she walked, Kira remained vigilant of the people

around her, cataloging them, watching for repetition, staying aware of faces that looked familiar or anyone taking an interest in her. The attack in broad daylight on Nathan Road was a sign it was time to leave Hong Kong. Whoever wanted her dead was closing in on her and tightening the noose. After she killed three men in broad daylight, the police may be after her as well.

A billboard caught her eye. It was attached to a building high overhead and displayed a prominent bottle of beer against a blue sky, a green ocean, and a sandy beach. The billboard made her think of the brown sandy beach, the one in her dreams. The fantasy.

Golden-brown sand fine enough to be soft on my feet. The shallow water so hot, it burns my toes. A dark-skinned local hands me a fresh coconut with a straw. A surfer rides gentle waves as a breeze rustles my hair.

A taxi honked, and the city brought her back to the present. The swirling mass of bleeping scooters, cycling commuters, and groaning lorries was oddly comforting. It was home. There are answers here. Clues to her past, to who she is. And the gray-haired woman is here.

The phone was heavy in her front pocket, and she yearned to get to a safe place to examine it. People all around her walked the streets with their phone out, balanced in one hand, oblivious to those around them. The device in her pocket was precious, and she didn't want to chance dropping it or that someone may attack her or try to take it. So it remained stowed away.

She was unsure whether to be grateful for her survival skills or horrified by them. *Survival skills.* Yeah, that's a good one. What world did she come from where survival was a matter of killing before being killed? And how was she able to catalog and remember hundreds of people on the street naturally, without trying? Instinct saved her from the black van, and her reaction time and skill with the handgun allowed her to drop her attackers on a crowded street. How did she acquire these skills? Maybe the gray-haired woman knew.

After an hour of meandering the streets, Kira was satisfied she was alone. At one point during her walk, she ducked into a department store and bought a black hoodie and stopped to give her gray sweatshirt to a homeless woman. Returning to the Mong Kok neighborhood was risky, but she had paid in advance for three nights. She tugged at her hat brim and turned onto Nathan Road, where she expected to see a police presence. It was only an hour after the attack by the three men in the black van, so there should be hordes of police, and the area should have been cordoned off to enable them to investigate the attack and shooting.

There was none of that. The street where the attack took place was busy with throngs of pedestrians, but there were no police. The black van was gone, and there were no bodies on the ground. Even the blood was gone.

I didn't dream this attack, so what happened?

Someone cleaned it up and quickly, that's what.

Kira made a right turn onto Shantung Street and hastened away from the scene. She passed the Hollywood Shopping Center and entered the Ladies' Market, where she bought another change of clothes and traded the black ball cap for a navy blue one with a NY Yankees insignia.

After a street meal of fried wontons and noodles, she returned to the Nga Shing, where the same old hotel manager snoozed with his head propped on his hand. The mottled orange tabby lay in a fabric chair and struck out at Kira with razor-sharp talons when she stroked its fur. A gaunt old man sat on the teal-colored vinyl couch and stared blankly at a television that showed a black-and-white kung fu movie. A cigarette with an inch-long ash dangled from his fingers.

After a quick shower, where she put the phone next to the sink and left the curtain open so the device was visible, she dressed and used her fingers to comb out her wet hair. Seated cross-legged on the bed, she picked up the mobile phone. It was a scratched and dented Samsung. Once she thumbed the on button and it booted up, she immediately turned off the Wi-Fi and the cellular connections. Once again, she was surprised to learn she innately knew how to navigate the phone despite having no recollection of ever having used a device like it before. As she dug through the phone's contents, there was nothing other than the standard functions like contacts, text messaging, and a calculator.

Her heart sank and she rose to watch out the window at the street below when she remembered a trick. In the settings menu, she toggled something called *system and hidden files* and accessed the file system. There, among a litany of items with esoteric names, was a file folder titled *Read Me*. Hope surged.

She opened it.

A password prompt appeared.

"What the—"

The woman didn't say anything about a password. Was she accessing the right file? Another search revealed nothing but applications and files required to operate the phone. She tossed the phone onto the bed and lay back on the thin pillows as car horns, sirens, and other street noises filtered in through the window. A scream from somewhere above was followed by laughter.

I must have missed something. She forgot to give me the password. Maybe she's waiting to give me the password.

After closing her eyes, Kira forced the street noises to fade away as she visualized the entire interaction.

The attack by the three men in the van.

She shot the three men and ran.

The motorcycle appeared. "Get on," the woman said. When Kira hesitated, she said, "If I wanted to kill you, you'd already be dead. Get on."

Bold statement, but maybe true. Who knows what skills the gray-haired woman possessed.

When they reached Hong Kong Island, Kira asked questions. More like she begged. Silently, she chastised herself. *I'm not that desperate. In the future, do not make yourself vulnerable to strangers.*

"Who are you?" Kira said. "Who are you, damn it?"

The woman gave her the phone, and Kira begged until the woman revealed her name. It was as if she did it reluctantly.

She knows more about me.

Otherwise, all the nameless, gray-haired woman said was, "We can't be seen together. There is a file on the phone that will help you."

As she played the interaction back in her mind, two things struck her. One was the gray-haired woman hadn't shown a flicker of fear when Kira pointed the gun at her. The second was that she was able to remember this interaction clear as day but had no recollection of her past life.

Kira grabbed the phone and tried various combinations of the words spoken by the woman, including her name. Nothing worked. Frustrated, Kira pounded the bed with a fist. As she lay there, rhythmic thumping and moaning came from the other side of the wall.

Great.

Fatigue eventually overtook her and with her hand on the pistol, Kira fell asleep.

The crash of glass woke her, and Kira jolted up, pistol out, head on a swivel as she searched the dark room.

Stillness. Laughter trickled in from across the hall and music blared. Another tinkle of glass outside the window was followed by hooting and hollering. At least the amorous couple next door was now quiet. The clock indicated she had slept for three hours, and it was midnight.

The interaction with the gray-haired woman played through her mind again as she lay on the scratchy sheets. She went through it all again. Maybe it was the much-needed rest, but she remembered something she hadn't thought of last night. The woman made her repeat a word.

Jiāting.

The Chinese word for family.

At the time, it didn't mean anything to Kira, so she promptly forgot about it. Now she grabbed the flip phone, accessed the *Read Me* file, and typed the word in the password field.

The file opened.

Relief made her slump as emotion surged.

The file contained a short phrase in English. *Stall 42, temple street night market.*

Disappointment flooded her, and she tossed the phone on the bed.

What? That's it? All that for this simple message?

She rose from the bed and went in the bathroom, where she splashed water on her face.

The brown sandy beach appeared in her mind, and she leaned both hands on the sink and peered into the mirror. The beach beckoned. Safety, a fresh start. An escape.

Kira banged her fists on the sink. The beach was an illusion, something she anchored in her mind to try to forget her circumstances. She cupped her hands under the faucet and rubbed the freezing water into her cheeks and eyes. Through the mirror, she gazed at coal-black eyes and stringy, raven-black hair.

Run to the fight.

The answers are out there.

Stall 42, temple street night market.

A vision of the gray-haired woman's face appeared. Ashen skin heavy with wrinkles and yellow teeth. But the voice was commanding, strong and confident. No fear while staring directly at the barrel of a gun. The woman's eyes were hard, iron-like. She knew things, and she definitely knew Kira. There was more there to discover.

All thoughts of the sandy beach left her as she packed her shoulder bag with the pistol wrapped in her scarf. She shrugged on the hoodie and pulled the ball cap on tight before she exited the hotel to find the Temple Street Night Market.

TEN

Hong Kong

Outpost was equally adept at blending into urban environments as he was operating in the jungle. Gone were the sniper rifle and scope and 9 mm handgun, and in their place was a small set of powerful binoculars and a compact .22 caliber pistol of Chinese make. He had not showered in days, and instead relied on the filth to augment his disguise as a homeless person.

He lay sprawled on a filthy stoop in a doorway across from the Nga Shing Hourly Hotel on Argyle Street in the bustling Mong Kok area of downtown Hong Kong. He wore a military-style bucket hat, camouflaged shirt, and cargo pants like the ones he wore in the jungle, except these were tattered, frayed, and smelled as rank as the dumpster five feet away. While he passed the time, Outpost marveled at the irony that the same outfit served him equally in the jungle and in the city.

The small tablet with the blinking red dot was in his

pants pocket if he needed it. He preferred to rely on old-fashioned, tried-and-true methods of tracking, including his own skills and a citywide network of sympathetic Koreans who were organized into a surveillance network and reported back on her movements.

So far his quarry had come and gone from the hotel several times, changed her outfit, and slurped some noodles. He was happy to see she had upgraded her wardrobe, but the savage glint in her eyes remained. Feral, unpredictable.

An odd sensation filled his stomach when he learned she survived the attack by the three men in the black van: relief and some other warm emotion he didn't want to think about, so he pushed away all the feelings.

Too dangerous.

It was after midnight when the target exited the Nga Shing and turned south. He toggled his radio to notify a watcher who sat several blocks south on Nathan Road, then burrowed into his sleeping bag, thumbed on his satphone, and made a quiet report to Control.

It was midnight, and party-seekers filled the streets in Mong Kok. The air was now cool, but humidity clung to her skin as she searched for a scooter to steal.

She avoided the crowd by ducking into a narrow alleyway running behind a row of nightclubs. The asphalt was torn up, and the cramped thoroughfare was filled with overflowing dumpsters, chairs strewn haphazardly, boxes of rotting vegetables, and a dozen two-wheel transports probably belonging to kitchen workers. A man in a soiled kitchen smock sat in a chair smoking a cigarette, and his eyes tracked her as she walked near a Honda motorcycle.

She feigned disinterest as she strolled by. When she turned, the cook was gone, so she darted to the motorcycle. It was a 400cc that lacked a fairing, and its pipes were rusted. She straddled the bike, found the key switch, popped open the plastic housing, and used the pocketknife to cut a two- inch wire, which she used to complete the circuit. A click sounded as the bike switched on. She held in the clutch and tried the starter. The bike coughed, sputtered, and caught, and she darted into traffic and puttered south on Shanghai Street.

The Temple Street Night Market was a multicultural melting pot located in the Jordan neighborhood of downtown Hong Kong. Kira parked the motorcycle and killed the engine before she plunged into the milling throng of trinket-seekers, street-food purveyors, and tourists, many of whom carried open beers. To the left was a booth where an old man hawked grilled seafood on a stick, while tables laden with cheap bracelets and earrings were to the right. Some stalls were simple tents erected on the street, others were storefronts packed with knock-off bags, T-shirts, souvenir chopsticks, pendants, and rings. Even at this hour, hundreds of locals and tourists with a mix of skin colors filled the narrow alleyways. Odors of curry fish balls and fried pig intestines wafted through the dense crowd.

She scanned the market as she hunted for the right stall. When she found it, disappointment overtook her. Number 42 was a narrow temporary lean-to of tattered blue plastic sheeting over bamboo poles in a row of similar shelters, all in disrepair, each with a sign in Chinese advertising fortune readings. A mixture of locals and tourists waited outside several of the stalls, but no one stood outside Stall 42.

Kira made a quick pass by the booth. Inside the leaning shelter was a woman with deep wrinkles throughout her face and a lavender shroud over her hair sitting in front of a small table covered by a purple cloth. The woman's head was bowed, and on the table was a small rectangular package wrapped in blue fabric. It was clear why Stall 42 had no customers despite the crowd. While the other stalls charged 200 HKD for a face and palm reading, the advertised prices in Stall 42 were ten times that. A glance each way along the street revealed no one who seemed to have a particular interest in her or the stall. She stood and kept a wary eye on the fortune teller for thirty minutes. No one went into the stall, and no one paid any attention. The old woman was frozen in place.

Kira sidled into the shelter and stood next to the wall of plastic sheeting, unwilling to sit on the tiny stool with her back to the street.

While her eyes were cast downward, the old woman murmured, making it difficult for Kira to hear.

"Hello, my child."

"Uh, hello."

"You're here for a reading?" The old woman spoke in code-switching, a mixture of Cantonese and English. The Cantonese, Kira knew, meant the woman was likely a Hong Kong native.

Kira stole a glance behind her. "I, uh... I don't have any money."

"I know, darling." The woman pulled back the shroud and swept her arm over the table. Arranged on the table near the blue cloth package were a single candle, a stone worn smooth in the shape of an elongated heart, and a single feather. Three crystals sat near the feather.

"Please, Kira. Sit."

The use of her name jolted her, but she remained standing. "How do you know me?"

The old mystic touched the bundle wrapped in the blue cloth with a crooked finger and smiled. The blue cloth contained a pattern of tiny white stars.

Kira snorted. "Do I know you?"

The smile waned on the hag's face. "I am unknowable, my dear." She unfolded the cloth parcel corner by corner to reveal a deck of cards. Stacked neatly and face down, they were old and worn.

"I'm all riddled out, lady. Let's get on with it." A stick of burning incense filled the tiny stall with the pungent aroma of sandalwood, and her head swam as vulnerability washed over her. "Can you help me? I was told to come here."

The old woman waved a misshapen hand and pointed at the stool. Her knuckles were swollen with arthritis, and her nails were cracked and yellowed. "Sit, my young friend. You are safe here."

After a glance at the street, where she saw no one, Kira sat but kept her knees pointed to the side. She didn't like the exposure of her back to the open street. Behind the old woman, the plastic sheeting overlapped in what appeared to be a way out. One swipe of her pocketknife along the lean-to's sidewall would make another exit.

Why do I think of these things?

The old woman's skin was covered with deep wrinkles and large warts. Black hairs stuck out randomly from her crooked face. When she raised her head, her eyes were overly large with black irises and no visible pupils, which was unsettling, as if perhaps the old woman was blind.

The old seer placed her gnarled hand on Kira's bare arm. The warmth of the touch was electric, and Kira's despair washed away and was replaced by a feeling of calm and safety.

What on earth?

The old fortune teller withdrew her hand and shuffled the tarot deck with dexterity belying her crippled knuckles. While she manipulated the cards, the tip of her tongue stuck out of the corner of her mouth and her big eyes sparkled. "You're fighting a battle within, aren't you, my dear?"

Kira started. "How do you—" She rolled her eyes.

Everyone is fighting a battle within. She's just spewing generic babble that applies to everyone.

The old lady smiled and held the deck out. "Please, shuffle."

Without thinking, Kira took the deck, cut it in two, pushed the two halves together, and repeated the process another time.

The seer received the cards. "You're trying to decide whether to follow your gut or perhaps run away from your problems."

Ugh. More blather.

Kira stole a glance behind her.

"You have a decision in front of you." The mystic shuffled the deck. "Perhaps a decision between safety and risk. A choice any normal person would make. But not you. You're tempted by the dangerous path, and you seek answers. What path do you follow? Where do you go from here?"

Kira's mouth hung open.

This is BS. Except it's true.

The truth of the old hag's words stuck.

"Someone gave you a gift," the old seer said.

Kira snapped her mouth shut. "You can't know that." Unless the gray-haired woman had spoken to the fortune teller.

Kira's eyes narrowed as the game became clear. The

gray-haired woman had enlisted the help of the old woman to manipulate her. Still, she was intrigued. Maybe this lady possessed some kind of insight, some new information or angle. Anything to help the path ahead become clearer.

The old seer gave the deck a final shuffle and offered the stack to Kira. "Make a cut."

Kira hesitated before she selected part of the stack and set it on to the table next to the remainder of the cards.

The mystic assembled the deck again and flipped over the top card to reveal a drawing of a moon in the night sky. Despite the card's disheveled state, its hues were vibrant and lush. A dog and a wolf sat in a field, both howling at the moon, while a crayfish crawled from a pool of water in the foreground. A pair of towers faced each other. The card was upside down to Kira, the moon end of the card toward her. With a cluck of her tongue, the old woman placed a hand on Kira's hand, and the hair on Kira's arm stood up.

"The Moon card, reversed." The soothsayer sucked air in through her teeth. "The dog and the wolf represent two sides of your animalistic nature, one civilized, one wild and feral. One tower is good, the other is evil. The crawfish is your ego. The creature's hard shell represents your protective nature, but the soft underbelly is your vulnerability."

A cold sensation crept along Kira's spine.

"The Moon card in reverse means you battle confusion, anxiety, and self-deception. You sit at a crossroads between your two selves, your two paths. Ahead of you are your fears, which must be faced. Your choice has deep consequences, and you cannot run from it."

"What the—" Kira pursed her lips.

What is my intuition telling me? Am I to be feral like the wolf?

The choice had a certain allure to it.

"Please. Make a second cut."

Kira swiped a lock of hair behind her ear as she cut the deck.

The old hag flipped over a second card. It showed eight golden cups, three stacked on top of five with a gap where one was missing. A red-cloaked man with a walking stick appeared to be hiking away from the stack of cups. A golden moon illuminated the path ahead, and he walked near a river with mountains looming in the distance.

"Eight of Cups." The old woman's long fingers stroked her craggy chin. "Reversed, again."

"What does it mean?" Kira leaned her elbows on the table.

The old woman peered at her through iris-less pupils. "It's a moment of transition. You are leaving your old life behind, that's the eight cups, because you're dissatisfied with the path, even if you didn't fulfill your ambitions. That's the missing cup. The path ahead will be dangerous, that's the mountains. The river is your ever-changing emotions. The card's reversal indicates you're confused about what path you should take."

"But I don't know my old life. How can I transition from something I don't even know?" Kira put her hand to her mouth.

"Your confusion is manifest. Let go of the feelings that don't serve you so you can progress. Is your past relevant to your future?"

Kira sat back and crossed her arms. *This lady is bonkers.*

"Please. Another cut."

After she made the cut, Kira put her elbows on the table and held her breath.

The old mystic turned over a third card and put her fingers to her mouth. "Ten of Swords, upright."

Kira gasped. The card showed a man lying on the ground, his face in the dirt, his torso covered by a red cloth. A mountain range loomed in the distance, past a body of water, and the sky was dark. Ten swords were stuck in the man's back.

The old hag's eyes clouded. "A major disaster is imminent. Watch your back, young lady. Betrayal is likely. The end is unavoidable, but there is a bright spot in this card. Although the skies are dark, the waters are placid, and the sun still rises to show the mountains in the distance. Perhaps by letting go you can see how bright your future may be."

"Why are you putting a positive spin on this one?" Kira was unsettled by the image of the swords in the man's back. Did it mean if she sought the truth of her past and of herself it would end in treachery and betrayal? And what was she supposed to let go of? The idea of learning about her past?

That's not happening.

The fortune teller tapped the Moon card, tapped the Eight of Cups card, and touched the Ten of Swords. "You must sit with your uncertainty, my dear. Do not fight the grayness in your mind. When you think you are clear on something, you are not. Be open to messages, but ease into their meaning. Sit in your patience and trust your instincts. The truth will become known in time."

Kira glanced behind her. A trio of raucous beer-drinking sailors passed by the tent. When she turned back, her eyes lingered on the Moon card.

A crayfish is my ego?

Because we all form a hard shell around ourselves?

The old mystic smiled to show a single crooked yellow tooth. "Don't ignore your intuition, Kira. Trust your gut. Let go of your negativity and dwell in what you know is right. Eventually you will rectify the mistakes of the past."

The old woman's eyes dimmed as she wiped the cards from the table and made the tarot deck disappear.

That's it?

Kira put her hand to her chin.

Trust my intuition, beware of betrayal.

The old woman swept her hand across the table a second time, and two small velour bags appeared on the table. Each was identical to the other except for the color. They were each two inches by two inches and were held closed with a gold braided silk drawstring. One bag was a deep burgundy red while the other was a royal blue.

"You face a choice, my dear." The fortune teller clasped her hands on the table. "Seek the truth of your past or start fresh. Face your demons, whether they be good or bad, or build something new."

She touched the blue bag with a crooked finger. "In the blue bag, you will find a key. That key will open a safe deposit box with a new identity. A full set of British papers, enough cash to get you started on a new life. Bank accounts, credit cards. There is a modern flat with your name on the deed in London. Leave all this behind and make a new life."

The woman's finger shifted to the red bag. "Or choose the red bag and discover your true self. Explore your authentic self and find your past. Face who you really are, for better or worse."

The old woman put a finger on each bag. "Know this. There are no guaranteed outcomes with either bag, only opportunities." She smiled, and the yellow tooth appeared. "And you may take only one bag."

Kira furrowed her brow and put her palm on the table. "What if I take both? Who will stop me?"

The old hag cackled. "You will not be successful."

Something about the old woman's confidence made Kira withdraw her hand. A video reel of the past forty-eight hours played in her head. Waking up in the jungle, hurt and alone, the fight in the hut, and the skills she discovered. The attack on the yacht, and the ease with which she killed the attackers. No remorse for their deaths. The discovery of the picture of her in a North Korean soldier's uniform.

Do I really want to discover who I am?

The brown sandy beach flickered in her mind, and the mirage was replaced by the gray-haired woman's face. There was something there. Compassion? Empathy? Real human emotion behind the hard steel eyes. There was a connection there. The gray-haired woman offered hope, and she had sent Kira here to be offered this choice.

Her thoughts returned to the tarot reading. What began as a farce turned into something tangible. A lesson she needed to hear.

Face your fears.

Move away from the savage and in the direction of civility. Leave the past behind, but only after knowing it and coming to terms with it. Let her old self die so a new self may rise in its place.

Face the truth so I may overcome it.

Trust my intuition.

Run to the fight.

She snatched the red bag.

The old woman bowed her head, pulled the lavender shroud over her head, and disappeared through a flap in the rear of the stall. The blue bag was gone.

ELEVEN

Hong Kong

Kira found a dark stoop away from the hectic Temple Street Night Market and crouched with her back to the door. It smelled of urine and rancid meat, but she didn't care. Her stomach rumbled. A woman laughed, and a motorbike whined. A man in a dark coat ambled by with a lit cigarette dangling from his lips but paid her no attention. When he was gone, Kira examined the bag she was given by the old mystic.

The bag was the color of wine with a braided gold silk drawstring, finely made with tight stitching and thick material, but it was worn with an aged patina and the drawstrings were tied in a tight knot. The bag itself was about two inches square and through the silky velour, the contents felt small and lightweight but hard and tubular. She pried at the knot, undid the drawstring, and dumped the contents into her hand.

It was an ornate antique key made of bronze. About two

inches long, its business end was comprised of squared-off bits, while the handle was an ornate carving of a seahorse.

Great, what am I supposed to do with this? More damn riddles.

Kira shoved the key back into the tiny sack, stuffed the sack into her pocket, and left the confines of the doorway. As she threaded through the crowds in the night market, her thoughts went back to the fortune teller. Somehow the old woman had orchestrated the choice, used some kind of sleight of hand to make those three cards appear, and filled her head with the tarot nonsense to influence her to pick the red bag. Now she had rejected the safe option.

But why?

Her stomach rumbled again, and she used some of her precious cash on a meal of roasted sweet potatoes, steamed rice with chili sauce, and a bowlful of curry fish balls. She ate while standing and observed the faces around her. No one was interested in her, so her thoughts drifted back to the tarot card reading.

The Moon card symbolized making a choice between good and evil and facing her fears. The Eight of Cups represented transition from one life to the other, while the Ten of Swords portrayed danger and betrayal, yet also hope. Any of the tarot cards could be interpreted to fit her situation, but maybe the cards were meant to speak to her. As she licked curry from her finger, the idea of running was a distant memory. The brown sandy beach was a figment of her imagination conjured to offer an escape. Escaping was weakness. The answers were in front of her, meant to be chased headfirst. But would she become civilized like the dog or feral and wild like the wolf? Or perhaps both?

What if I don't like what I find?

Better to know and deal with it, for better or for worse.

Run to the fight.

She tossed the napkins and paper bowl into a trash bin and exited the night market. After an hour of meandering through the city on various MTR trains and buses, she was satisfied she was alone. It was 3 a.m. when she entered the Nga Shing to find the lobby empty, the television off, and the skinny man fast asleep behind the protective glass of the proprietor's booth. The angry cat was gone. Kira glided past silently and went to her room, where she levered a chair under the door handle, crawled into bed, and fell asleep.

TWELVE

Hong Kong

"I need you back here in Tokyo." Joe Nomura was on the other end of the line.

Wu took the phone and her cigarette to the hotel's open window and flicked ash into the outside air. The tiny black flecks of carbon disintegrated into thick humidity. Outside the hotel's window, hundreds of wires crisscrossed overhead and dozens of neon signs advertised drinking establishments and massage parlors.

"Did you hear what I said?" Joe's voice was always slow, never hurried.

Wu sucked on the cigarette and spoke through a cloud of smoke. "Why?"

"In case you forgot, we have a department to run. Namely, budget meetings."

"Denki can handle it. He's prepped and knows the numbers better than I do." Denki Ito was her lieutenant, officially her deputy director of the black ops section of Department 82.

"Protocol says the department head is to be in attendance."

Wu sucked air in deep through her nose as carbon monoxide and rotting fish wafted from the open window. The cigarette was trapped between two of her fingers and burned forgotten. "When I agreed to join Department 82, you and I discussed that we wouldn't let bureaucracy get in the way of operations. The idea was to build an agency that cuts through the red tape and prioritizes outcomes over protocol."

Joe remained silent.

Wu sighed. "If it will make you feel better, I'll send Neo and the SFG team home. The operation has entered a phase where I can run things alone." This wasn't a budget meeting issue. Joe wanted the operation to end. He had his reasons, which Wu respected, but he was wrong.

"We also need to get to a place where our department heads aren't in the field all the time," Joe said. "You have a department to run and a dozen open positions to fill."

"Denki can handle—"

"Denki doesn't have your touch when it comes to recruiting. We brought *you* on to build the department, not Denki Ito."

Wu bowed her head and took another puff on the cigarette before blowing the smoke through the open window. In the ally below, a car horn honked and a bicyclist threaded through pedestrians. "Not true, Joe. We hired Denki specifically for his management skills. We agreed I'd spend my time in the field."

She flicked the cigarette butt with her fingernail, and ash

sailed into the breeze. "Besides, if you want me to focus on recruitment, I'm right where I need to be. I can hire a half dozen soldiers from the ranks of the Special Operators Group and not get anyone near to her abilities." Neither Joe nor Wu was about to mention the real reason Joe wanted the operation to end. He was professional enough not to let his emotions influence his decisions, which is why Wu pushed back.

More silence from the other end of the phone. Someone yelled out in the street below, and somewhere a baby cried. Wu exhaled and sucked air in through her nose deep into her solar plexus in an effort to calm herself. Years of meditation and breath work helped her to observe the moment between stimulus and response so she might choose an appropriate answer. If they abandoned the operation now, years of work would be forfeited, not to mention their asset may disappear forever, or worse, get killed. She had said what needed to be said.

"Send the team back tonight," Joe said. "I need Neo back here in Tokyo. You have forty-eight hours to work your plan. If it doesn't yield fruit, you're to extract her and bring her in. We'll just have to take our chances."

The line went dead.

South China Sea

Fifty nautical miles from the 200 islands comprising Hong Kong, the Kowloon Peninsula, and the New Territories, the North Korean fish factory ship *Damanzaihao* chugged on a northeasterly course. The factory ship rendezvoused with a North Korean fishing vessel and commenced operations to shift the haul of yellowfin tuna to the factory ship, where it would be filleted and frozen for transport to North Korea. While the factory ship filled her belly with lucrative and illegal catch, Commander Pak and his team of RGB operators tracked their fugitive.

Using the Chinese drone, CCTV footage, his expert tracker on the ground in Hong Kong, and the large contingent of local human ground informants, Commander Pak's team followed her trail. It wasn't enough merely to use the tracking device implanted in her shoulder. Accurate on-the-ground intel was required. An informant glimpsed her on the street in Yangjiang. A police report of a breaking and entering where security camera footage revealed a small, dark-haired woman who picked a lock and made off with food provisions in a suburb of Macao. A stolen car in the city of Shanwei was found outside Quanzhou, wiped clean of all prints. Pak's team plotted the appearances on a map showing a jagged route northeast and overlayed it with the GPS tracking to confirm she was headed in the direction of Hong Kong, just as they had predicted.

On day three of the operation, as they tracked their target into the warrens of Hong Kong, and as the *Damanzaihao* floated off the coast of Kowloon Peninsula, Commander Pak received a call, a special kind of call, one requiring he clear the room of all his staff. It was the kind of call that made perspiration break out on his forehead even though the air in the room was frigid from the chugging air conditioner.

A secretary's voice droned through the earpiece. "Please hold for Army General Yun Sun-nam."

Commander Pak stood with a satellite phone to his ear, his back rigid as he stood at attention. His skin prickled despite the frigid temperatures in the room, and his fingers endlessly traced the long scar on his cheek.

"Annyonghasimnikka, Commander Pak." The voice on the other end was high-pitched with a singsong quality. General Yun served as the Chief of the General Staff of the Korean People's Army and had direct authority over the Reconnaissance General Bureau. This was Pak's boss's boss.

"Annyonghasimnikka, sir." Commander Pak bowed to the empty room. The call, which skipped Pak's chain of command, was irregular.

"Dear Leader wants an update on the progress of Operation Gumiho."

In North Korean mythology, a *gumiho* is a nine-tailed fox with the ability to shape-shift into a seductive woman. No one said the RGB didn't have a sense of humor, although Pak disagreed with the moniker. It was disrespectful.

"Of course, sir."

There were good odds that North Korea's supreme leader was listening in on their conversation. Despite Army General Yun's insinuation that he would provide the country's mercurial leader with an update, it was common knowledge Dear Leader liked to listen in on his subordinate's phone calls.

"Everything is on track," Pak said. "The target is in Hong Kong, as we anticipated."

"The body count is more than we thought."

"We knew it would be a difficult task. She is well trained, by our own excellent training programs, sir, and it is quite a test for our men." The offhanded compliment would not go unnoticed.

"We're at fourteen dead, correct?"

"Fourteen of our weakest performers, sir, and two Filipino contractors. I projected twenty dead, all of them laggards in our training programs or expendable third parties. The tests will motivate our trainees and soldiers to be better. As we progress, our more capable operatives will test themselves. By the end, we'll have identified our strongest agents and eliminated those who are the weakest links—"

"And we will have killed the problem asset in the process."

"Correct, sir." Commander Pak bowed again.

"And the fail-safe?"

"In place and ready for activation." A drop of sweat rolled down Pak's temple.

Don't let it come to that.

"And the trigger for the fail-safe?"

We've been over this a hundred times. But you must insist on parading for Dear Leader.

"There are several. One trigger is when we exceed twenty dead. Another is the moment she tries to run or disappear."

"Very well, Commander Pak. You may proceed."

The commander waited for the call to end before he turned off the satphone, exited the communications center, and stepped out to the balcony to light a cigarette.

God help us all if I have to deploy the fail-safe.

THIRTEEN

Hong Kong

383 Lockhart Rd, Causeway Bay, Hong Kong.
   It was the address written on the scrap of paper she had found tucked between the cellophane and cardboard in the cigarette pack on one of the soldiers who attacked her on the beach.
   She stood on Lockhart Road and gazed up at the building at that address. The soldiers who attacked her on the beach were well trained and well equipped. They used night vision goggles and modern assault rifles, and wore commando-style clothing. Not to mention the rocket-propelled grenades. The scrap of paper was a rookie mistake, or perhaps a lapse in training. The commando team was equipped to be effective but lacked preparedness and professionalism. Unless, of course, the scrap of paper meant nothing. Maybe it was the address of the soldier's mother or girlfriend. Still, it was her only lead to discover who might want her dead.

Lockhart Road was an upscale city street with one lane in each direction separated by a narrow concrete divider with greenery planted along the middle. Expensive cars were parked along the street, and the buildings were between twelve and twenty stories tall. A fancy kitchen goods store was next to an upscale men's clothier on the ground floor of the building at the address. The pedestrians were a mixture of locals and tourists.

Through the building's glass door was a set of stairs which she guessed went up a floor to an elevator lobby. The facade of the building was beige and speckled with air conditioning units. Scaffolding covered with plastic sheeting lined floors one through four, although no workers were present. The city block was an ordinary street of bustling citizens going about their daily business. Except for the steady stream of men filing in and out of the glass doorway at 383 Lockhart Road.

She posted up in a coffeehouse across the road with an easy sightline to the building's door. On the table in front of her was a Yuanyang tea, a concoction of coffee, black tea, and milk.

While she watched the front of 383 Lockhart Drive, she periodically glanced at the television. She was too far away to hear the sound, but the headline at the bottom read *North Korea Tests Missile over Japan*. The closed caption text at the bottom of the screen indicated the missile was launched from near Pyongyang and flew over mainland Japan about 1,000 kilometers before it splashed into the North Pacific.

When the newscast switched to the war in Ukraine, Kira tuned out and resumed her surveillance of 383 Lockhart Drive. At least two dozen men went into the building, and the same men exited between thirty minutes and an hour later. The men—and they were all men—were all shapes and sizes. Old and young. Fat and thin. Well dressed and disheveled. Office workers and construction workers. One man was dropped off by a long black sedan and was picked up seventy-five minutes later by the same sedan. A student with a backpack arrived on a bicycle, locked his transport to a metal ring near a tree, and entered the building. Fifteen minutes later the student exited, jumped on his bicycle, and disappeared. It didn't take a trained surveillance specialist to figure out what went on in 383 Lockhart Road.

Kira trapped some yuan under her empty cup, grabbed her bag, and tugged the ball cap tight on her head as she exited and crossed at the corner. A narrow alley ran behind the row of buildings on Lockhart Road, and she ducked into it, where she found most of the stuff one expected to find in an alleyway. Dumpsters, delivery scooters, and men in soiled cooks' outfits smoking. The beige metal door to the building of interest was labeled with three stick-on metallic numbers. Three eight three. She ignored the stares of the cigarette smokers and yanked open the door.

Inside a corridor was lit with yellow light. Surveillance cameras were missing, which, given the business that went on here, wasn't surprising. She followed the hallway to a door. Next to the door was a sliding window, and behind the window were two young men in a small room. Both were short and both had a sheen of sweat that came from working in a poorly air-conditioned office. One young man wore a white tank top while the other sported fuzz on his chin, a poor excuse for facial hair. As she tapped on the window, both men appraised her from head to toe.

White Tank slid the door open. "You must be new here. We don't get many outside girls."

She let her tongue brush her lip as she leaned close. "This was a special request from my agency. They didn't tell you I was coming?"

"Aw, yeah, they probably did. We're a little busy though."

Kira winked. "I can tell. I have a special client, if you know what I mean."

White Tank creased his brow. "You got his name?"

Kira cocked her head and raised her eyebrow. "Come on, you know they won't tell me that. I was told he was here in the last couple of days."

"Do you know what he looks like?"

Kira searched her memory of the fight on the beach, which was clouded by the narrow vision that accompanied battle. Four men in olive uniforms, but only one held a pack of cigarettes with a scrap of paper hidden between the cellophane and cardboard box. His face appeared in her mind and triggered a memory. "All I know is he's a soldier, and he has a large birthmark on his neck."

White Tank's eyes went wide, and he glanced over at Peach Fuzz. "We weren't told he was coming back."

The young man with the wispy chin beard shook his head.

Kira shrugged. "I was told I'd get your best room for him. VIP, you know?"

It was a shot in the dark, but from the young man's reaction to her description, the soldier was clearly an important guest of the facility. Her plan was to check the room where the soldier had stayed for any clues before she returned to have a more spirited discussion with the two youngsters about the soldier's identity and where he came from.

White Tank scrutinized his phone. "I got nothin'."

"Oh no." Kira frowned. "Is that bad? He's supposed to

be here in fifteen minutes. I need to get ready, if you know what I mean." She winked.

White Tank grinned. "It's all good. Someone must have forgot to tell us he was coming, that's all." With a glance that went up and down Kira's frame, he produced a key. "Penthouse. Top floor. Been empty since he was here last week."

As she grabbed the key, White Tank held on. "Make sure he's happy."

She yanked the key away and smirked over her shoulder as he buzzed her through the door. "I always do."

The elevator contained buttons for fourteen floors and a penthouse, and she punched the P as the overpowering smell of urine permeated the small elevator.

The lift dinged when it stopped at the sixth floor, and as the doors opened, fluorescent pinks and blues blinked from holiday lights strung along the hallway. Trash littered the linoleum, and music blared from an open door. A young woman who looked no older than fifteen, dressed in short shorts and a halter top, stepped on, her eyes downcast. The girl leaned against the elevator wall and rubbed her temples.

Kira's heart sank.

Where was this girl from?

How did she end up here?

Was she here by choice, or was she forced to be here?

Kira almost opened her mouth to say something, but the girl got out on the tenth floor without looking back. The doors sighed shut.

Stay focused.

At the penthouse level, Kira stepped into a dingy entryway with peeling paint on the walls. The key opened the double doors, and she entered the suite. There were two rooms, one for sitting and one for sleeping. The sitting room contained a small kitchenette, two dingy cloth couches, and a rickety table holding a soot-encrusted ashtray. Soiled curtains covered the windows and as she yanked them open, dust danced in the sunlight.

A half-full bottle of vodka was in a cupboard along with some mismatched glasses. In the sleeping room was a queen bed, sloppily made, and a bathroom. The previous occupant had left a gift behind in the toilet bowl, and the sink was full of hair and dried white stuff that might have once been shaving cream.

Am I wasting my time?

In the bathroom was a woven reed receptacle full of trash. She dumped it out on the bed and poked through it with her pocketknife. Tissues, a Kotex wrapper, cotton balls with makeup and smelling of makeup remover, two condom wrappers, and yes, two used condoms. Nothing else.

A ding came from outside the tiny apartment, faint but unmistakable. The elevator. With a glance to ensure she had swept all the trash back into the receptacle, she pulled the Glock from her bag and stepped next to the wall dividing the sleeping and sitting rooms. When the door to the penthouse suite opened, a voice yelled, "Hey."

It was White Tank.

"Where is she?" Peach Fuzz's voice was lower.

"How should I know? Probably in the damn bathroom. Hey, lady!"

The two punks appeared in the transom between the two rooms, unaware Kira was standing with her back to the wall. White Tank's hand rested on the butt of a pistol in his waistband, and Peach Fuzz held a mobile phone in one hand. She pushed the Glock's barrel against White Tank's neck as the two men took another step into the bedroom.

"Oh, shit." White Tank's face drained of blood.

Peach Fuzz dropped his phone.

"Who did you call?" Kira asked.

"What... what are you—"

"You called someone to check on my client's arrival. When they told you he wasn't due to be here, you decided to come and investigate. Big mistake. But if you tell me who you called, I'll let you two walk out of here alive."

"I don't... I can't..."

"Toss both your phones on the bed," Kira instructed. For emphasis, she pushed the Glock into White Tank's neck.

The thug complied, and Peach Fuzz bent to pick up his phone and threw it onto the soiled bedcover.

"Lie on the ground. Do it. Now."

Peach Fuzz dropped to his front, but White Tank hesitated. "The building is on lockdown." His voice strengthened. "No one gets in or out if we're not in the control room."

"I won't have a problem getting out of the building." Kira pressed the Glock into his neck. "Get on the ground."

The thug hesitated, and Kira weighed her options: Threaten them and leave them alive, or kill them. An image of the young girl in the elevator flashed in her mind as White Tank made a move.

With a swing of his arm, something he might have seen in a kung fu movie, White Tank attempted to swat the gun away. Unfortunately for the thug, he was slow and projected his attack by widening his eyes.

She stepped back to evade the clumsy strike and fired twice. Both bullets plunked into his chest at close range. The white tank top instantly turned crimson, and the room was filled with the smell of gunpowder.

As White Tank spun from the impact and collapsed,

Peach Fuzz stayed rooted in place, on his hands and knees, wide-eyed and slack-jawed. Again, the image of the young girl in the elevator entered Kira's mind, and she aimed and fired twice more. Both bullets punctured Peach Fuzz's forehead and he collapsed to the floor.

Blood pooled on the linoleum as she wiped down everything she touched. She checked the men's pockets. There was a few hundred Hong Kong dollars, which she took, and nothing else. With the Glock in her hand, but hidden in her bag, she left the suite, banged open a door to the stairwell, and descended the concrete steps.

FOURTEEN

Hong Kong

When she reached the eighth floor, Kira got an idea. It was risky, especially given the two dead bodies in the penthouse. The safest thing would be to exit the building and never return. But the image of the young woman in the elevator weighed on her, and she opened a door and found herself in a dingy hallway lit with yellow overhead fluorescents. The hallway was clean of trash, but the linoleum floor was cracked and dirty. If her plan worked, she would be able to solve her cash problem and maybe help the young women trapped in this building.

Her hand clutching the pistol remained hidden in her shoulder bag as she made her way along the hall. Many of the doors were closed, and Kira guessed some of the floors were used to house the young girls while other floors were used to service paying customers. She paused at one door to listen. Silence. She repeated this at several doors, and at the fifth door, there were the telltale sounds of a female at work with a male customer.

After she returned to the stairs, she ran down to the sixth floor, where the young woman had entered the elevator. This floor was a different story. Food wrappers littered the hallway and music thumped behind a closed door. After another twenty paces, Kira encountered an open doorway, and she peaked inside. The room was illuminated by purple light. Four twin beds were arranged in what would ordinarily be the living room. Women's clothing, including lingerie, leggings, bras, and miniskirts, were draped on the furniture. The bedding rustled, and a leggy girl with bottle-blonde hair crawled from the bed and padded into the rear of the apartment, her eyes downcast.

Kira returned to the stairwell, and by the time she reached the main floor, she was committed to her plan.

Kira knew enough about human trafficking operations such as this one to know it was most likely operated by one of the Triad gangs in Hong Kong. While that didn't scare her, it made her more cautious. A quick check of the Glock revealed eleven bullets left in the magazine and one in the chamber. With the gun held out in one hand, she pushed open the door and exited the stairwell into the lobby.

The operation appeared simple. Customers entered through the glass front doors and ascended the stairs to the main lobby, where they checked in at a desk that was once a security desk but now served as customer service. The service desk was manned by two young men who made an attempt by dressing in Oxford shirts, but who sported neck and face tattoos. Kira guessed these young men took payment in cash and assigned the customer a room number. They phoned back to the dispatch room, operated by White

Tank and Peach Fuzz, who assigned the girls to the customers.

When Kira appeared in the lobby, the two young men behind the service desk looked over, startled. One of them froze at the sight of her gun while the second stooped and rose with a short-barrel shotgun. Kira fired a single shot, and a red blotch appeared on the white shirt of the man with the shotgun. He staggered back and the gun faltered. Kira shot the second thug before he reacted.

She ran to the reception desk and checked to make sure the two men were dead before she ransacked the drawers. A handful of banknotes were in a box, which she scooped into her leather shoulder bag. This was not the mother lode—most of the cash would be stored in the back where security was better. The Glock went into her bag and she grabbed the modified single-barrel shotgun of Chinese make, a knockoff of a popular German model. Somewhere in her memory was the fact this model took four cartridges in the magazine and one in the chamber. A quick check revealed the chamber was loaded.

A button under the counter activated the door to the back with a metallic click, and she hastened across the lobby and through the door with the shotgun up.

The room where White Tank and Peach Fuzz worked was behind plexiglass and a secure door. When she came through from the lobby, she fired a round of buckshot at the doorknob, which burst into bits. She pushed the door open with the shotgun level.

When she peeked around the transom, a gargantuan Chinese man was standing with his hands in the air. He wore jeans, and a white button-down shirt strained against his belly. Tattoos crawled up his neck, and his eyes were wide open. "Don't shoot."

The small room smelled of body odor and onions. A desk was pushed against a wall and two metal chairs were strewn haphazardly. A bank of screens showed black-and-white images of the lobby.

Kira eyed the huge man over the shotgun barrel. "What's your name?"

"Kong."

"Appropriate," she said. "Whose operation is this?"

The man gulped. "14K."

"Triad, yes? They're going to be pissed?"

His jowls shook as he nodded.

"You have a mobile phone?"

"Yes." More vigorous nodding.

"Take it out."

"What?"

Kira waved the shotgun. "Take out your phone. Slowly."

Kong complied and held up his iPhone.

"Dial 999."

"What?"

"Dial 999. Put it on speaker."

The man did as he was told, and a dispatcher's voice sounded through the speaker phone. "What is your emergency?"

"I'm calling to report a human trafficking operation at 383 Lockhart Road," Kira said.

"I'm sorry, ma'am. Please repeat yourself."

"You heard me. 383 Lockhart Road. Dozens of women are locked in here and forced into prostitution. It's apparently run by the 14K triad. I've eliminated the men running the place. You need to send someone to rescue the women."

"What is your name, please?"

"Doesn't matter. Get over here immediately. 383 Lockhart Road." Kira shook her head. "Hang it up."

Kong tapped at the phone to end the call.

"Put it back in your pocket."

The large man complied. "Are you going to kill me?"

Kira shook her head. "I want you to take a message to your boss."

Kong groaned. "Don't make me do that."

"Well, I guess you can disappear. They'll think you ran off with the cash."

"They're going to think that anyway."

"You must have security footage from the lobby that will tell a different story."

Kong nodded. "What do you want me to tell them?"

"Any members of 14K who come after me are dead. Got it?"

Kong squinted. "You know who these guys are, right?"

"Don't worry about that. Repeat the message."

"They send anyone after you, you'll kill them. Who should I say sent it?"

"Doesn't matter. Where do you keep the cash?"

Sweat beaded on the large man's cheeks as he nodded at the desk. "Top drawer."

"Turn around." As Kong complied, she shifted the gun to one hand and yanked open the top drawer, where an aluminum lockbox sat among pens, stained take-out menus, and paper clips. "Where's the key?"

"On the hook by the door."

Kira found the key hanging on a leather lanyard. "Very secure, Kong."

She used the key to open the lockbox. Inside were dozens of rolls of cash, each held together with a rubber band. She dumped the lockbox contents into her leather satchel. Before she exited the room, she found the security video system's storage box, opened it, and fired two rounds of buckshot.

Kong jumped and turned around. "I thought—"

"You didn't think I was going to leave footage of myself around for everyone to see, did you? Goodbye, Kong. I hope for your sake we don't cross paths again."

She ducked into the hallway and sprinted to the rear door. After glancing both ways, she saw no one. As she hastened through the alleyway and turned south on Marsh Road, sirens rang out in the distance.

FIFTEEN

Hong Kong

The surveillance detection route did its job. Someone was tailing her, and they were amateurs.

After leaving 383 Lockhart, Kira tossed the shotgun into a dumpster after wiping her prints from the stock using the tail of her T-shirt. She hustled along Lockhart and jogged to Hennessy Road. She wanted to get to a train station and put some distance between her and the building before it turned into a hornet's nest of police activity. On Hennessy Road, a bustling thoroughfare with tall buildings and hundreds of neon signs, she jumped onto a white tram. The narrow streetcar was jammed with tourists and locals, and she remained by the front door but kept an eye behind her.

That's when she first noticed the tail. A young Chinese man wearing a gray T-shirt stepped through the rear door as the streetcar started up. Ordinarily he would not have triggered her interest, except the same young man had been in the coffee shop earlier when she was watching 383 Lockhart.

Coincidence?

From the corner of her eye, she watched him. He wore dark trousers rolled at the bottom and well-worn Converse high-top shoes, and his T-shirt was frayed around the collar. He removed a phone from his pocket and scrolled, but his eyes darted from the street to the car interior and back to the street. She got the impression he only pretended to scroll on his phone.

She rode the tram until Hennessy Road intersected with Johnston Road, which is where she dropped to the street from the tram as it started away from the stop. As luck would have it, one of the yellow double-decker buses was stopped at the Anton Street bus stop. She darted through traffic, jumped on the bus, and glanced behind her in time to see the young man in the gray T-shirt standing on the street. As the bus trundled along Johnston Road, Kira peered through the window while the young man eyed the bus, his phone plastered to his ear.

———

"Ni hao." Outpost had a tiny Bluetooth earbud stuck in his left ear which was connected to a phone hidden in his pocket. The idea was to be seen mumbling to himself. No homeless man in his purported condition was likely to own a modern mobile phone. Mumbling to oneself, however, was perfectly acceptable.

The voice on the other end belonged to one of his street watchers, a troop of locals he employed to track the target's movements and report back. "She made me."

Outpost almost chuckled. The young man must have heard that phrase in a Western movie.

"She's on the 5B bus going east on Johnston," the youngster reported.

"I'll have someone pick her up." Outpost ended the call and immediately connected with another member of his loosely knit team. This man was stationed on Lockhart Road and sat astride a scooter awaiting instruction. A minute later, the new watcher was puttering along Johnston Road behind the 5B bus.

Kira stepped off the bus and tugged her cap low while she hurried along O'Brien Road. Thunder rumbled, and umbrellas appeared in the hands of pedestrians. If her unreliable memory served her correctly, O'Brien would butt against an alleyway that would return her to Hennessy Road, where there was a train station. She needed to get off Hong Kong Island and over to the Kowloon mainland, where she might hide among the city's grittier neighborhoods. While Gray T-shirt appeared harmless, he might be part of a larger surveillance team.

Sure enough, O'Brien Road turned into an alleyway. She stepped over potholes filled with stagnant water and ducked into the Hennessy Road MTR station, where she used cash to add fare to her MTR card before hurrying along the brown and tan speckled tile hallway as if she were late for a train. An escalator took her down to the platform, where she waited for the next train. She strolled to the end of the platform, watching those around her, and tapped her foot while she waited.

No sign of Gray T-shirt.

"I've got her."

Outpost nodded to himself as the report came through his earpiece.

"Subway platform at Hennessy Road."

"Copy that," Outpost mumbled. "Stay with her and tell me where she exits."

The transmission ended, and Outpost permitted himself a tiny sigh of despair. An hour ago he had received an urgent call from Control. Apparently the target had gone off script—way off script—and now there was hell to pay, which is why he and his team were drawing the noose tighter. Despite his orders, he permitted an illicit feeling to creep in.

Good for you.

Ordinarily he would never allow such a thought to rise to the surface. It was simply too dangerous to permit himself such empathy, but *good for you.*

The thought made him grin as he thumbed on the satphone and prepared to give an update to Control.

Wave after wave slammed into the *Damanzaihao* as the massive ship rolled gently in the roiling surf. Overhead the skies turned a bruised black and blue, and the clouds were thick with moisture but had not yet opened. On the horizon, lightning cracked as Commander Pak stood on the metal grated balcony, one hand gripping the railing. Beige paint peeled from the metal.

The fishing operations below had ceased due to the lightning, and the sailors were all safe below decks. Pak violated one of the captain's rules by remaining above deck, but Pak had a job to do, and the captain would keep his mouth shut. Outside was the best satphone reception, and Pak was also away from the prying eyes and ears of his staff.

Reports were streaming into the control center below deck about the shitstorm at 383 Lockhart, and now RGB leadership wanted heads to roll. Pak's primary objective now was to make sure his head remained squarely on his shoulders. There was only one way Pak could think of to protect himself.

The satphone buzzed.

"Shì de." It was Outpost.

Commander Pak received the update from Outpost with clenched teeth, and Pak gave him an order before he ended the call and dialed another number by heart.

As the phone rang, a large raindrop hit Pak's shoulder.

Kira took the train north, under Kowloon Bay, into Hong Kong proper, and exited at Jordan station into a warm, blustery wind carrying moisture and a few raindrops. The pedestrians had thinned out, and those remaining all hurried along the sidewalk with their heads bowed against the wind. After she walked west along Bowring Street to Canton Road, she turned north and into the Kowloon King George V Memorial Park.

Which is when she realized she still had a problem. An old man with fluffy white hair she recognized from earlier in the train station was behind her. The enormity of her problem was made clear to her when Gray T-shirt showed up again. The young man followed as she went under the Chinese gate and into the park.

This meant the tail was an organized effort. There were multiple members of a team, all coordinated by a central dispatch. There may be a dozen people tailing her, but she needed to shake this group somehow. An icy trickle of sweat rolled along her spine, and she hugged the satchel full of cash as she exited the park.

"Our friends in Hong Kong are not happy, and that's putting it mildly." Colonel Ryo's voice was gritty.

Commander Pak pinched the bridge of his nose with his free hand. The rain pattered consistently now. A drop hit the railing and spattered. Another drop hit his glossy black boot. His hand went to his face where the scar running from his temple along his cheek to his chin burned. Was it his imagination, or did the scar always pulse and smolder when he was under stress? Probably his imagination. "An unfortunate and unpredictable occurrence, sir. It was a onetime event."

"Is that how you want me to explain it to our friends? An unfortunate occurrence? One of our men, through his ignorance and poor training, led the target to our friend's operation, and she destroyed the entire thing. Lucky for you, that… er… facility was not a partnership between us and them."

"Operations like this are unpredictable. You know this, sir." Pak stood ramrod straight with the phone shoved against his ear.

"Maybe so, but our side is worried. If this continues, she may negatively impact our… how should I say this… our more direct business with our friends."

The two men were purposefully opaque. Their target's

recent actions disrupted a 14K triad trafficking and prostitution ring, which angered the 14K leadership. The prostitution outfit was not a joint 14K-North Korean endeavor. The 14K triad, however, operated the Chinese side of a massive smuggling operation moving Western luxury goods into North Korea and trafficking counterfeit American currency out of North Korea. Commander Pak oversaw the Chinese side of the enterprise from his home base in Shenzhen, about thirty kilometers to the north of Hong Kong. It was this business relationship that concerned the two men.

"That is a very unlikely scenario, sir."

"There have been calls to bring in the fail-safe."

"No." Pak immediately regretted his outburst. "I have another idea. If our friends are so upset, why don't we feed her to them? Add our friends to the hunt. They can throw all their foot soldiers at her and extract their vengeance."

The silence on the other end lasted for a long stretch as the rain increased in intensity. In fact, Pak had already taken steps to enact this plan. He had instructed Outpost to tighten the noose on the target and teased the idea with his counterpart on the 14K side. Wind blew at Pak's shirt and ruffled his hair. Steady rain hit his shoulders. A lightning bolt cracked into the sea not far off the starboard bow.

"Do it," Colonel Ryo said.

The transmission ended.

The order Outpost received from Control caused a knot to form in his insides. Tighten the noose, spook her, force her to make a mistake. It meant Control was about to commence some kind of attack. As the knot blossomed, an idea formed in his mind.

Why not warn her?

He rejected the idea as quickly as it occurred to him. That type of action was grounds for termination. He would be executed, and his mother and father would be put in a labor camp for the rest of their lives.

Instead, Outpost let himself hope for the best. She was the best Pyongyang had ever seen; she was prepared for the attack. She would persevere and survive. A thick elation replaced the knot, and he was overtaken by momentary euphoria.

The strange emotion surprised him. After decades of distinguished service to his government, Outpost found himself older and with no wife, children, or family other than his aging parents. Is it possible these were paternal feelings for a daughter he never had?

He took a moment to observe the sensation before deciding it wasn't too much. What was the harm in enjoying the warmth of the emotion, as long as he never expressed it to anyone? It was his own private feeling. No one could take that from him.

Hope surged in his veins as he dialed Control and provided the target's location to the man on the other end.

SIXTEEN

Hong Kong

Despair crept into the edges of Kira's mind.

She saw faces in the crowd that weren't there.

Her ability to memorize faces and people, a skill that ordinarily served her, turned into a liability.

A young man who appeared to be Gray T-shirt, the same one who was on the bike in the park, now materialized in front of her. Except it wasn't him. It was another young man on a skateboard in a slate-blue T-shirt who sailed past her on the sidewalk.

A young woman in a raincoat, who Kira recognized from the train, hugged a young man before jumping onto the rear of his scooter and motoring away.

The rain helped. It was steady now, and fewer pedestrians made it easier to watch for a tail but more difficult to blend into a crowd. The irony of countersurveillance.

The old man, who had a head full of fluffy white hair, disappeared only to reappear as she ducked into the Yau

Ma Tei Fruit Market, a long building with open air fruit stalls. A woman in a smart overcoat appeared, disappeared, and reappeared.

A net was slowly ensnaring her. Kira's ability to tell who was following her and who was an ordinary citizen began to seep away from her, and she imagined this was what it was like to slowly go mad.

The fruit market was crowded with people avoiding the rain. Wall-to-wall folding tables were overflowing with wampees, jackfruit, guava, durian, coconuts, and melons. She paid for a bunch of grapes and munched them as she walked, ever mindful of the pedestrians around her. When the old man with the fluffy white hair reappeared, she tossed the remaining grapes and made a beeline for the exit.

How to escape?

She needed to get somewhere remote, off the beaten path, away from the crowds. There, perhaps, she might nab one of the people tailing her and extract some intelligence, or shake the tail altogether.

From her explorations of the city, an idea jumped out at her, and she headed for a subway station as thunder rumbled in the distance.

Outpost was on the move. It no longer made sense to remain near the Nga Shing hotel as they tightened the noose on the target. To the annoyance of the taxicab driver, Outpost, who smelled of body odor and vomit, sat in the rear of the bright red Toyota as it sped south along Nathan Road, in the direction of the waterfront.

Reports of her location appeared in Outpost's phone via text messages.

Jordan Street station
King George park
Yau Ma Tei Fruit Market
Kowloon Station

This last update was his destination. Through a surgical mask, which he wore to keep his face hidden, he urged the taxi driver to go faster. To emphasize the urgency, Outpost shoved a one-hundred-yuan note through the plexiglass opening. The cab surged as the driver touched the accelerator.

At Kowloon station, she emerged into the middle of an ultra-manicured shopping district with luscious greenery and towering buildings, the kind of place where well-heeled visitors might wake up at the Ritz-Carlton, or try on Diesel jeans before gorging on Godiva chocolate and dining on steak and frites at an imitation French bistro. The pavement was slick with moisture, but the rain had slowed. She dodged a family of Koreans in matching pajama outfits and walked through an archway past a sign for the Ritz-Carlton Spa. The tallest building in Hong Kong jutted behind her.

Navigating this area on foot to arrive at her destination was tricky. Austin Road was a busy highway skirting the Waterfront Block area. To her left along a service road was the West Kowloon Waterfront Promenade, where walking trails, museums, restaurants, and more green space dominated the area. She hurried across a grass-covered walking bridge that went over Austin Road and arrived at a construction fence. Beyond were two partially constructed buildings covered with scaffolding and yellow sheeting flapping in the breeze. A crane towered overhead but remained still, its crew gone for the evening. After tightening the strap on her satchel, Kira jumped, caught the top of the construction barrier, and pulled herself up and over, landing among pallets of paint cans and piles of unused scaffolding. The hectic city disappeared behind her.

The construction area was to become the east zone of the Kowloon Waterfront Promenade and was a dozen city blocks long and half that distance in width. It ran from Nga Cheung Road on the western side all the way to Canton Road, with the Pique Center on the east side. When it was completed, the promenade would offer dozens of shops and museums along with an extensive walking and jogging trail system, but now it was a massive dirt lot chock-full of front-end loaders, construction trailers, and stacks of equipment. And it was devoid of pedestrians who might be tailing her.

Let them try to follow her here. Either they would reveal themselves, in which case the area offered many private spots for her to interrogate her pursuers, or Kira would sneak out the other end of the construction zone and lose the tail.

Careful to remain in the shadows lest she be discovered by a random security guard, Kira made her way east.

Outpost was in a position to witness the 14K raid on the East Kowloon construction site. The noose tightened as the wave of surveillance pushed their target into a location perfect for the attack. They couldn't have planned it any better. Outpost counted as a dozen men flowed out of two vans and streamed through a wide-open gate in the chain-link fence. No security guards were in sight. He guessed they had all been recalled.

Anticipation surged as Outpost eyed the twelve men. Each gang member was fierce and determined. Some wore face masks, and they all dressed in black and carried a club or a knife. One portly man carried a machete. *These poor suckers have no idea what they're up against.*

A text pinged softly on his phone.

Ten men entered from the west side.

Outpost's confidence wavered. That made it one woman against twenty-two men.

His heart raced and a pit formed in his stomach.

Did she need help?

And do I have the courage to help?

One misstep, and his life and the lives of his ailing parents were forfeited.

Let's see what happens.

Her plan was to nab one of the people following her and make them talk. A crude plan, but it might yield intel on who was attacking her. The Glock remained in her shoulder bag as she crept through a corridor made by ten-foot stacks of wood planking.

As darkness took over the city, a few halogen lights illuminated the construction zone, and the steady sprinkle of rain fell from low clouds. The half dozen lights weren't enough for the large area, and plenty of spots were filled with shadows. The rain gave Kira comfort. The moisture might cause her pursuers to falter or lose a step.

Her adrenaline spiked as four men, all dressed in black, passed by her spot in the shadows near a trailer that had been converted to a construction office. Each man carried a weapon, and they walked in a formation as if they were on patrol. Two carried clubs with spikes on the end and another carried a knife, while the fourth, the heaviest man, wielded a machete.

Who guards a construction site with a roving band of men, one of whom carried a machete? These were not garden-variety security guards.

A sensation crawled along her skin as she realized the trap she had fallen into.

These men are hunting me.

The notion made her smile.

They think *they're hunting me.*

The construction trailer where she hid in the shadows had a set of wheels at one end and a fifth wheel at the other, so it could be hauled away by a tractor when the job was done. On either side of the wheels were chocks, while two legs supported the trailer's fifth-wheel end. A set of wooden steps led to a door on the side. Underneath was stored all manner of construction gear, including stacks of scaffolding, rows of concrete barriers, and heavy machinery on a pallet. Kira shrugged off the shoulder bag and hid it deep among the scaffolding, but not before she removed the pistol. She checked the mag.

Nine rounds in the magazine. One in the chamber.

Four men in the hunting party.

With the pistol held in two hands, she crept along the shadows and followed the four men.

SEVENTEEN

Hong Kong

Kira darted through the shadows formed by stacks of concrete barriers and hid behind a row of overflowing dumpsters. She flanked the group of four thugs as they walked toward her position brandishing their weapons. The heavyset one carried the machete against his shoulder. The rain made the ground slick with mud, which didn't bother Kira.

With the Glock in her hand, she stepped from her hiding spot as the four thugs approached, and when they saw her, their eyes went wide. Two men dropped their clubs and went for pistols which were secured in their waistbands.

Nothing could be done about the noise from the Glock. With a two-handed grip, she walked at the group, firing at the men who fumbled for their guns. One man collapsed from two bullets to the chest, while the second thug took one in the thigh before he spun around from another bullet in the shoulder. She kept walking and aimed at the third man, who stood transfixed, ten feet from her, his knife raised, eyes wide.

Panic consumed him, and he took off running, which left the pudgy one with the machete, who shouted something akin to a battle cry and charged her, the big blade held above his head.

What is it with these guys and their machetes? Kira fired twice and dropped him. She spun with the gun in a two-handed grip and searched for the runner. He was gone.

The gunfire and the runner might attract more thugs or security guards. She shoved the Glock into her waistband and snatched the machete from the ground where it had fallen. Two of the men on the ground were dead, but the pudgy man groaned, and Kira squatted next to him and rested the large blade on his chest. The man's breathing was raspy, and blood bubbles formed at the corners of his mouth. The tip of a black tattoo escaped the man's shirt collar, and Kira ripped the front to reveal elaborate drawings of bloody knives with the term 14K in various locations on his neck and chest.

Somehow the 14K triad had followed her from the brothel.

How did that happen?

She pushed those thoughts aside for now. Time to stay alive and gather intel. Figure it out later.

She slapped the thug's cheek. "Hey, you awake?"

The man's eyelids fluttered before he expelled his last breath.

Still on her haunches, she pivoted and peered through the rainy gloom. Voices carried from behind a front-end loader. She snatched a pistol from the mud and crouched next to the oversized wheel of a mobile crane.

Five 14K thugs materialized out of the fog, and she recognized the man who had taken off running, whose eyes were wide with panic. The five men were sodden from the rain but alert. Two carried pistols, while the other three wielded clubs. The man in front smoked a cigarette and walked with a strut.

She didn't have time to examine the pistol she had retrieved from the ground, and she wasn't about to trust her life to an unreliable weapon, so she shoved it into her waistband.

With the machete in her left hand and the Glock in her right, she was on the group in a blur of silver steel. As before, she targeted the gun-wielders first. The long machete flashed and sliced a man's neck. She swung the blade again and knocked the pistol from the second man's hand. She whirled and parried the swing of a club and used the momentum to bring the blade around to slice a fourth man's abdomen.

The second thug, the gun knocked from his grasp, lunged in the mud to retrieve the weapon. Her Glock bucked as she fired twice, and the thug slumped. Two of the 14K gang members remained standing. The former cigarette-smoker held his club like a baseball bat, but his arms quivered and his nostrils flared. The other man who remained on his feet was the former runner. He turned on a heel and sprinted away.

Not this time.

Kira put two bullets into the runner's back, and he stumbled and fell face-first into the mud as the Glock slide locked out on the empty gun. She faced the remaining attacker from three feet away. A tattoo of the numbers *1* and *4* plus the letter *K* were on the side of his neck. All at once, his eyes narrowed and he swung the club at Kira's head.

The attacker was faster than she expected. She dropped the empty Glock and attempted to parry with both hands on the machete handle but only managed to deflect and slow the attack. The club, which had rusty nails set into the business end, glanced off her shoulder, and the nails drew blood.

She ignored the wound and brought her blade around in a two-handed thrust and sank it into the attacker's side. He screamed, dropped the club, and fell to his knees.

Shouts rang out from the darkness followed by slapping footsteps in the mud. She yanked the weapon to dislodge it from the thug's oblique and darted into the shadows made by towering stacks of two-by-fours. With her back pressed against the wood, she leaned the long blade against the lumber and checked the gun she snatched from the fallen 14K gang member, a Chinese-made QSZ-92. The barrel was nicked and gouged, and a star in a circle was embedded in the polymer handle. Somehow, she knew the star meant the pistol was chambered for the 9 mm Parabellum and not the smaller in size but higher velocity 5.8 mm. She eased the slide back to make sure one was in the chamber. With the gun in both hands, she peeked from her spot.

Another roving patrol of four men had found the dead and injured triad thugs. One of the newcomers, a thin man whose pants hung loose on his waist, stood with a mobile phone pressed to his ear, talking fast and gesturing wildly with a gun in his opposite hand, while two colleagues knelt by their fallen comrades. A fourth, a man with the number 14 and a large K tattooed on his forehead, stood with his feet spread and a pistol clenched in a fist while his panicked eyes darted to and fro.

Let's hope this thing fires. While using the cover of a stack of lumber, Kira held the pistol in two hands with fully extended arms and pulled the trigger twice. The one with the forehead tattoo staggered back from two bullet holes in his neck, his arms pinwheeling, and screamed. He fell into one of the men who knelt by the corpses.

Gun fires high.

The thought arrived unbidden in her mind as she compensated for the untrue pistol and fired again. The side of the head of one of the kneeling men burst from two bullets, and he crumpled.

The scrawny man with the phone put both hands in the air while the kneeling man jumped to his feet and reached for something at his waist. Kira didn't wait to find out what it was and put two bullets into his chest. As he toppled over, Kira walked ahead, her gun trained on the man whose arms were in the air. "Drop the gun."

"Don't shoot, don't shoot." The thin man appeared to be in his teens or younger, except for his eyes, which were hooded and guarded.

"Drop it."

The matte-black polymer pistol plunked into the mud.

"Drop the phone."

The silver flip phone tumbled to the dirt.

"Kneel on the ground."

The man complied.

"You guys are 14K, yes?" She held the pistol up.

The man was silent, so Kira waved the gun. "Yes?"

"Yes, yes."

"How many of you are there?"

"I don't—"

Kira kicked the man in the stomach and he fell back. While he struggled to his knees, Kira put the pistol next his temple. "I'm not going to ask again. How many?"

"Twenty, I think. Maybe twenty-four." The scrawny

man's chest heaved. "There were twelve in our group and there was another group coming in on the west side. We meant to trap you in the middle."

She had taken out twelve attackers, including this one, which left ten or twelve more—if the man was truthful. "How did you find me? How did you know I was here?"

"I don't know. I'm just following—"

She pressed the pistol against his cheek. "Don't make me kick you in the stomach again. You had the phone. You were reporting in. You're in charge of this little squad, aren't you?"

His head nodded vigorously.

"How did you know I was here?"

"It was a tip. We were tipped off. We had to scramble."

"A tip? A tip from who? Who tipped you off?"

She figured they followed her from 383 Lockhart Road. If they were tipped, that meant someone else had been following her. Her mind spun. "Who, damn it?"

"I don't... I don't know. I really don't. I got the call, grabbed my guys, and showed up here. We were shown a picture, your picture, and then we went in. That's it. I swear."

Working fast, Kira used one of the dead men's belts to secure the scrawny man's hands behind his back and gagged him using a dead thug's T-shirt. She left him there among the seven dead and wounded triad members while she found a deep shadow to hide in. While she crouched along the edge of a fence running along the southernmost edge of the construction zone, the rain increased in intensity.

It didn't take long for her to hunt down and either kill or incapacitate the remaining thugs. As a hard rain blew across the construction zone and turned the dirt into a muddy swamp, she used the QSZ-92 to take out five more of the 14K before she ran out of ammunition. A few of the triad thugs scattered and ran as she used the machete to wound another two. After she wiped the gun's handle of her fingerprints, she tossed it over the fence into Victoria Harbour before returning to where she had dropped the Glock. There was something about the Austrian-made handgun she appreciated. It shot true and it was indestructible. She found another QSZ-92 next to a dead thug, and she ejected the Chinese gun's magazine and stuck it into her pocket as sirens blared in the distance.

The noise grew louder quickly, and the authorities arrived faster than she anticipated. Before she was able to escape from the construction site, two white vans with the ubiquitous red stripe of the Hong Kong police roared into the muddy yard near her position at the west end near Canton Road. Dozens of police in olive-drab uniforms and riot gear flowed from the vans and established secure positions.

From her hiding spot in the shadows formed by a massive yellow earth mover, she watched as a man barked orders to a dozen heavily armed and uniformed officers with automatic rifles, body armor, sidearms, and night-vision goggles attached to their helmets. There was probably an identical force entering the construction zone on the east side.

Killing gang members was one thing but killing police was another, and Kira had no intention of engaging with law enforcement. There was no time to retrieve her shoulder bag with the cash, which she'd left in the center of the construction site, so she ducked under the heavy machinery, hugged a stack of planking, and kept to the shadows while she moved east.

The rain pounded into the mud and pavement as she approached the high fence comprising the construction zone's border on the east. The fence was ten feet high and was covered in white plastic sheeting made dirty from the mud and rain which prevented people from seeing through to the other side. It was meant to keep pedestrians from seeing into the site, but it also worked in reverse, and once she was over the fence, the sheeting hid her from the authorities inside the construction zone.

"Hey! Hey, you! Stop!"

Without a backward glance, she grasped the metal chain-link fence above her head and scampered up, swung a leg over, dropped onto the pavement on the other side, and absorbed the impact by rolling.

When she rose to one knee, she was staring into the barrel of a pistol.

EIGHTEEN

Hong Kong

The nickel-plated .45 hovered a foot from her face, and was held steady by a Chinese man in a leather jacket. Raindrops beaded on the jacket's surface and there were tiny splashes of water on his thick rimless glasses. A neatly trimmed mustache adorned the man's chin reminiscent of Fu Manchu, and his gold pinky ring glinted in the sparse light from a nearby streetlamp.

She froze. The empty Glock was in her pocket next to a QSZ-92 magazine. The two were not compatible, so she had prioritized escape from the authorities over transferring the 9 mm slugs to the Glock's mag. She was weaponless.

The man with the Fu Manchu, who she placed at maybe forty years old, put an index finger to his lips, waved the gun, and waggled his head in the direction of a black van twenty feet away. The van's side door was open and two more men were visible inside, each holding a pistol.

Fu spoke in a whisper. "Get in the van."

Outpost was a man of extensive field experience outside his home country's borders. A North Korean didn't enjoy this level of operational autonomy without having proven himself time and time again. He was present in Burma in 1983 when the bomb exploded, killing twenty-one and narrowly missing the South Korean President. He was in Vladivostok in 1996 when a South Korean official was bludgeoned to death in retaliation for the deaths of twenty-two North Korean sailors. And he was in the airport in 2017 when the half brother of North Korea's leader was killed by RGB operatives. While Outpost didn't pull the trigger on any operation, his surveillance skills were critical to each mission's success. Because of his prowess and contributions, Outpost's aging parents lived in luxury in Pyongyang and received the health care they needed in their dotage.

Despite Outpost's breadth of experience, he had never been part of anything like this. From his position behind a dumpster, he watched as his subject dropped from the fence top and was surprised by a man with a pistol. The man, wearing a leather jacket and a flowing mustache, guided her into a black van. The van sped from the parking lot as the door slid shut, and Outpost barely got a photo of the vehicle before it disappeared into the dense traffic on Canton Road. When he examined the photo on his phone, he noticed the van's license plate was obscured.

The other detail Outpost noted, because it was his job to do so, and because he was good at his job, was a marked difference about the target. When she entered the construction zone, she was toting a leather shoulder bag. As she dropped to the ground after scaling the fence from inside the construction area, the bag was not over her shoulder.

While Outpost prepared to make his report up the chain of command, he contemplated whether to mention that detail.

The interior of the van reeked of tobacco and smoke, and the man with the Fu Manchu sucked on a cigarette while one man drove and another held a pistol trained on her. Plastic cuffs secured her wrists. One of the men had performed a cursory pat down, and Fu slid her Glock into his belt, but they missed the pocketknife with the red handle.

Sloppy.

No one spoke, and no one opened any of the windows, and so Kira endured the noxious fumes.

So far she had been allowed to see their faces, which was not a good sign. Fu was obviously in charge, and the other men were the muscle. All three were fit, adept with their weapons, and operated with precision movements, a far contrast from the young thugs who had attacked her at the construction site. No tattoos were visible. These were not 14K.

Outside the window the city flashed by in a watery kaleidoscope of reds, yellows, and blues. The wipers beat a metronome on the windshield as they merged onto Canton Road and passed Kowloon Park when the road turned into Kowloon Park Drive. A left onto Salisbury Road took them past the Peninsula Hotel and the Signal Hill Garden. A massive tower rose overhead along the harbor front, and an abrupt left took the van down a ramp and into an underground garage beneath the tower.

The fact she was permitted to see their faces and know

their destination meant one of two things. Either she was about to be a dead woman, or these were friends. Helpless to know which, she was manhandled from the van and marched through a set of metal double doors leading into the underground belly of corridors below the tower. After a brief walk through a concrete hallway, where one of the men pushed her along behind Fu while the other muscle remained close behind with a drawn pistol, they trooped onto a freight elevator, where Fu hit a button and the conveyance descended with the clanging and rattle of metal on metal.

When they exited, the air was noticeably humid. Pipes and ducts were exposed overhead, and moisture seeped along cracks and crevices in the concrete. A series of corridors took them deeper into the belly of the tower until they arrived at blue metal double doors, where the warren of hallways was devoid of humans. Fu pushed the doors open and led her into a room where two leather sofas and two leather chairs were arranged around a silk rug in the middle of the room. The walls were bare concrete, and the only other furniture was an empty credenza along the far wall.

Fu pointed at one of the sofas. "Sit."

She sat. The lighting was fluorescent, and more ducts and pipes crisscrossed overhead. She supposed video cameras or other surveillance devices might be hidden among them, but doubtful. This was the kind of room where nothing happened. At least nothing anyone wanted recorded.

She didn't wait long. After she crossed her legs to find a comfortable position on the sofa, given her hands were secured behind her, the metal double doors banged open and a man flowed inside.

That was the only way to describe how he entered. It was almost as if he floated through the doors, but there was nothing ethereal about his attire. Small in stature, but with an enormous head, the man wore an immaculately tailored suit with an open collar and a cravat. He rushed in, arms wide, and stood ten feet away from her. His spectacles were rectangular and the lenses yellow. Fu took a position two feet behind the newcomer.

"Do you know who I am?" The man with the yellow glasses folded his arms together and touched his chin with a finger.

Kira shook her head.

"Ah, it's to be expected, I guess." He waved both hands at her. "Better this way, maybe." With a flourish as though he wore flowing robes, he sat in a leather chair across from her and crossed his legs. "My name is Bao." He pronounced it like *pow*. "The media calls me Big Head Bao, but they romanticize our little club." His cackle was high-pitched.

Kira made no response and bounced her leg.

"A woman of few words," Bao said with another laugh. "I like that."

Big Head Bao stood abruptly and perched one butt cheek along the arm of the other sofa. He fidgeted a lot and had trouble sitting still.

"I should thank you, young lady." Another high-pitched laugh.

"Why is that?"

He jumped to his feet. "Where are my manners." He made a snipping gesture with one hand before he snapped his fingers. One of the muscle approached Kira from the rear and used a knife to release her bonds.

She rubbed her wrists to get the blood flowing.

Bao spread his arms. "Now, where were we? Yes, you deserve my deepest appreciation. You've damaged my enemy. You single-handedly shut down one of the 14K's operations, and killed or maimed, what?" Bao looked at Fu. "Twenty?"

Fu waggled his hand back and forth.

Bao spun back to face Kira. "Twenty of my enemy's soldiers." His face broke out in a smile.

"You're a rival gang to the 14K," Kira said.

"Gang." His lips puckered as he paced. "Such a dramatized notion made popular by the news media and American Hollywood. We are a guild, an association, a society of like-minded men"—he gestured at Kira— "and women. People who band together for a worthy cause. We run businesses that employ people and put food on the tables of those in our communities. We help fund the police and the fire departments. We operate many charitable organizations that help those in need when our government cannot do so. Our name means good fortune, longevity, and abundance, which is what we work hard to bestow on our communities. Unlike some of our... ahem... competitors, we are not violent. Unless provoked, of course." Bao winked. "We provide pension schemes for thousands of older men and women in our communities. We make large investments in the film industry and provide jobs and entertainment to hundreds of thousands." Bao grinned, displaying a set of gleaming teeth.

"Let me guess. You're White Phoenix." The so-called triad group was one of Hong Kong's largest.

With a vigorous nod, Bao spread his arms, palms up, and sat again, this time on the far end of the same couch where Kira sat. When he crossed his legs, his white patent leather platform shoes gleamed in the light.

A little vain, are we?

Bao cleared his throat. "You, my dear, have a price on your head."

Kira raised her eyebrows.

"The reward is, well..." Bao glanced at Fu, who shrugged. "The reward is enormous by some standards yet in the big scheme"—Bao jumped to his feet—"We don't need the money, but the benefits to us of turning you over to the North Koreans go beyond the cash payment." Another glance at Fu.

"Go ahead and try."

Bao's smile disappeared as his enormous head whipped around to peer at her. "You are at a disadvantage, my dear." Bao swept an arm around at his two muscle and over to Fu, at which point his hand turned into the shape of a gun that he pointed at Kira. "You were taken rather easily, don't you think?"

Kira tilted her head to one side. "If you wanted me dead, I'd already be dead. If you were going to hand me over, you'd already have handed me over."

This appeared to perplex Big Head Bao, who put his hand to his pursed lips and paced.

"You may not know this" —Bao turned and put his fists on his waist—"But the 14K have a relationship with the North Koreans. This is how they found you. How they tracked you all over the city. The 14K also handles the smuggling operations in and out of North Korea on behalf of the North Korean government. Dear Leader over there likes his Western cars."

Bao waved his hand in a generally northeastern direction. "Against the sanctions, the 14K smuggle contraband into North Korea and bring out counterfeit US currency." Bao laughed in a high-pitched giggle. "That trade is very lucrative for the 14K."

Kira rose to her feet, and the rustle of clothing behind her told her the muscle had tensed. She paced in the direction of Big Head Bao, who slid away from her in the direction of the sideboard. Fu stood his ground. She approached Fu and stood close enough to touch him. Fu's eyes were on his boss, in what Kira guessed was a plea. A plea to release the hold Bao had placed on him. For some reason, Bao didn't want her hurt or damaged.

In a move so fast the muscle had no time to react, Kira slid the rusty pocketknife from her sleeve, ducked, came up behind Fu, and shoved the blade far enough into his jugular to draw blood. Her other hand snaked under his jacket and yanked the Glock from Fu's waistband and stuck it in her pocket. Then she pulled free his nickel-plated .45, which she pointed at one of the bodyguards.

As the two muscle stood frozen, Fu slowly raised his hands.

No one spoke.

Bao stood near the beverage cart with a tumbler in his hand full of brown liquid and ice. The glass was held in the air, and his pinky was up. His free hand dipped and swayed, a maestro conducting an orchestra. "Bravo, bravo! You've made your point, young lady. Now let him go and let us resume our civilized discussion."

Kira pocketed the knife and shoved the .45's barrel into Fu's neck. She pressed the gun tight against his skin as she yanked him along and slowly walked backward to the door. As she maneuvered herself and Fu through the outer office, through the hallway, up the elevator, and out through the garage, the tall Chinese was docile. When she reached open air, she pushed Fu face down on the concrete, dropped the magazine from the .45, ejected the round from the chamber, and tossed the pistol onto Fu's back before she disappeared into Hong Kong's nighttime crowds.

Commander Pak stood in his familiar spot on the tiny metal balcony overlooking the *Damanzaihao's* fishing operations while men in slickers and rubber boots worked among massive bins of shiny fish below. When the rain slowed and the lightning rolled east, the business of fishing resumed. The cigarette in Pak's hand was burned to the filter, so he flicked it in a shower of sparks and it floated through the air and into a bin of wiggling fish. None of the workers glanced up.

They wouldn't dare.

The smell of fish, the ever-present dank air, the cramped quarters, it was all getting to him. The oldest child of a working-class North Korean family, Pak was conscripted into the army but rose through the ranks on hard work, talent, and ruthless cunning before he was selected to join the RGB. Now a lieutenant commander in the General Reconnaissance Bureau, his position came with its own privileges, including enough money to live as he pleased and the autonomy to move in and out of North Korea as he wished.

He had also parlayed his success in the RGB into a second role as the external director of the operations smuggling Western luxury items into North Korea and exporting counterfeit American dollars. It was a function Dear Leader himself took enormous interest in, and usually the close proximity to the man himself had its perks. But Pak wasn't interested in the luxuries afforded him by living outside the DPRK.

If one visited his luxurious flat, they would find cartons full of noodle cups, endless bottles of water, a large television for Premier League soccer, and little else. If one gained access to his personal computer, one which the regime wasn't aware of, they might find information on a half dozen offshore bank accounts where Pak stashed the cash he skimmed off the smuggling operations. Eventually Pak planned to accumulate enough cash to allow him to disappear. Or defect.

Except now he was in peril of losing everything. Who was the mythological Greek character who flew too close to the sun? Icarus? Icarus's father warned him of his hubris, but Icarus used wings made of feathers and beeswax, and when he flew too close to the sun, the heat melted the wax and he plunged into the sea and drowned. Pak glanced at the roiling gray water off the starboard side. A failed mission would mean he would be recalled to Pyongyang and relegated to some back office in the north, away from the influence he now wielded. Away from his offshore bank accounts.

The satphone buzzed. Pak clenched his eyes shut briefly before putting the phone to his ear. Before his boss spoke, Pak said, "We need to shut this thing down. It's a disaster." All calls were recorded, and it was best to be on record first.

There was a brief pause by Colonel Ryo. "Do you understand the damage she did to us with our friends?"

Pak's stomach clenched. It was an involuntary reaction to hearing his boss's voice.

Stay focused.

"I activated the fail-safe," Pak said.

"It might be too late. The damage is done."

Pak's eyes roamed over the ship as his thoughts churned. "We served her to them on a silver platter. It was their choice to send amateurs. I warned them myself. That thing in the construction zone is on them. Their incompetence led us to where we are now, and now we have to clean it up."

"Let's hope the fail-safe ends this thing before it gets worse."

Pak's throat clicked as he swallowed on a dry tongue. "I'm confident he will, sir."

"You need to get back to Shenzhen. I've arranged a meeting between you and our 14K contact. He's going to want reparations. Before you meet, I will have a proposal to bring to him."

"Copy that, sir."

"And Commander Pak?"

"Yes sir?"

"They wanted to recall you. I insisted you were instrumental in getting our deal with our friends back on track. Don't make me a liar. Get this cleaned up, and mend the fences."

The call ended.

"The construction site is mass carnage," Neo said while sitting in the van, where he had caught a few winks.

His voice was in Wu's ear via a secure comms line. He was patched into the local police channels and still monitored the North Koreans' as well. "Twenty-two dead or injured. Officially they're calling it a street fight between two rival triads, but the police are perplexed."

Wu smiled. "Child's play for her. Where is she now?" Wu was perched on the sill of her tiny flophouse-style hotel room with the window cracked while she blew smoke through the opening and flicked ashes into a ceramic coffee mug.

"Her hotel."

"This is it," Wu said. "It's gone too far, even for them. They'll shut it down now. Has she turned the phone on?"

"Once, briefly. You should have given her a charger."

"She can buy a charger."

"Chargers cost money." Neo chuckled.

"Money is not a problem for her. Do you have the message ready to send?"

"Affirmative, ma'am. Are you sure this is a good idea?"

"No. But when are we ever sure in this business? Besides, with how this has escalated, we need to act before it's too late."

"Right. But is now the right time? She's already probably vulnerable after the visit to our fortune teller friend and the melee in the construction zone."

"I'm not concerned about her vulnerability." Wu softened her tone. "Remember, we're recruiting a well-trained but potentially hostile asset. Besides, she chose the red bag. She wants answers."

"Then why send it at all?"

"I want her to know we're here to help her."

"Build up the trust."

"Exactly." Wu absently flicked ash through the open window. Despite the early morning hour, taxis, cars, and lorries splashed through puddles in the street below. "Plus, this one is different. Until now her adversaries have been amateurs. Her next test will not be amateur."

"Should I send it now?"

Wu inhaled hard on the cigarette butt and exhaled while she stubbed it out on the inside of the coffee mug. "Send it."

Sleep didn't immediately come, and Kira tossed and turned on the scratchy sheets. A film of perspiration covered her skin, and her body ached from the cuts and abrasions still healing. Visions of the three tarot cards haunted her, and when she drifted off, she jolted awake as a flurry of swords flew at her from a stormy sky. Kira got out of bed and splashed water on her face before returning to the damp sheets. The tiny window air conditioner blew out tepid air, which did nothing to tame the humidity. She lifted the mobile phone and flipped it open. The gray-haired woman's warning rang in her mind.

Turn it on only when you need it so you're not tracked.

Her rational brain told her to leave it off, so she set the phone aside, rolled to her side, and folded one of the pillows so it fit under her head. Sleep didn't come, and her mind was awhirl with jumbled images and thoughts from the last forty-eight hours. When the monkey mind got the best of her, she grabbed the phone and turned it on.

After it booted up, an alert popped up on the tiny screen, a text message with a photo and some words. She clicked on the photo. A young man reclined in a chair next to a tiny table in an outdoor cafe. Taken from afar, maybe through a telephoto lens, the photographer had caught the man unaware. He was handsome and square-jawed, with a wry smile. One of his hands rested on an espresso cup while the other held a mobile phone and he scrolled with his thumb. He filled out a sport coat with muscular shoulders. Instinct told her the man was Korean.

She clicked to close the image and scrolled to the text message, which made her sit up in the bed.

This man is coming for you.

NINETEEN

Shanghai, China

The safe flat was located high in a luxury apartment tower situated along the Huangpu River not too far from the hipster bars and eating establishments on Hongmei Road. If an analyst successfully traced the flat's ownership through a bewildering web of shell corporations, they would discover the rent was paid by a Singapore bank known to launder funds on behalf of the North Korean government.

The apartment's interior was furnished in sleek modernist decor with lots of leather, chrome, and shag rugs on the dark oak floors. A bar cart with top shelf liquors stood in a corner, and the master bathroom's soaking tub was situated with a view out over the river. The pantry was empty, however, and there were no plants or personal touches to the place. Reserved for only the most distinguished of North Korean visitors to China's most populous city, the rooms were seldom used. A local service kept the apartment dust free, washed the sheets, and stocked it with toiletries.

The young Chinese escort, known only as Mei, knew none of this, of course. Through her agency, which enjoyed a protected status among the China Party elite, she was given a time and a location via text message. When the black Mercedes sedan dropped her under the portico, the bellman was away and she could not know the foyer security cameras were switched off.

Tall for a Chinese woman and proportioned like a Western movie starlet with curved hips, narrow waist, and significant bosom, Mei was in high demand by a tiny set of entitled clients and commanded large sums by her employer. Fat party bosses, foreign dignitaries, and polished business moguls all boasted of her company, and she enjoyed many repeat customers.

Mei had no complaints. Plucked from a farm in northern China near the border of Mongolia, she lived a life those from her village only dreamed about. Endless shopping with credit cards mysteriously paid, a wide array of party drugs available to suit her whims, and she was granted access to the most exclusive parties in town. A trainer kept her fit, and her meals were made by a chef. She was assured her family was being taken care of, and she often wondered how she became so fortunate.

The only item of interest in the apartment was a silver metal briefcase standing upright on the glass coffee table. Unable to help herself, she tested the clasps and found them locked. What did it contain? Stacks of cash? Maybe a bag of the pink pills for her enjoyment?

Mei found a bottle of rosé in the fridge and poured herself a glass, which she took to the master bedroom where a king-size bed lay ready. She balanced the wine glass on the edge of the tub and turned on the hot water. Her gown dropped to the floor, and she wiggled from her thong. Both garments went on a hook so they wouldn't wrinkle. After testing the water with a toe and adjusting the temperature, she drizzled fragrant oil into the water and put her silken hair up in a bun. As she settled into the hot water, she rested her arms along the tub's sides and gazed out to the expansive, multicolored skyscape of Shanghai.

It was in this position that she first saw her client. Quietly he stole into the suite and appeared in the master bath in a dark, well-tailored suit. The man was tall and fit with broad shoulders, and his tightly trimmed hair was shiny black. His face was sculpted for a magazine cover with a strong jawline, proportioned nose, and wavy hair. And young! Deliciously young, with smooth skin colored from the sun and eyes twinkling with a hidden knowing. Perhaps this knowledge would translate into expertise between the sheets.

He ignored her, and she remained silent while she watched him. Tight buttocks swayed under the wool trousers as he walked. When he shrugged out of the jacket, his back muscles rippled under a silk shirt hugging his frame. Waves of anticipation surged through her loins. What luck!

How would he want her to behave? Some men preferred she dominate and take charge by removing their clothing and straddling them on the bed. This man was different. He was in charge.

When he removed his trousers to reveal white silk boxer shorts, the man gazed at her partially submerged body. She lifted her leg from the water and rested her ankle on the tub's edge as her finger's trailed along her oily skin. How a gentle night of lovemaking would be a much-needed break.

When he shed his clothes, she bit her lower lip. His abdominals and obliques were tight, and his arms were heavily muscled. Thick quads—maybe he was a cyclist—were revealed as he bent to remove his boxer shorts. His entire body was hairless: shaved, waxed, whatever. She didn't care. What a difference from the disgusting Texan last weekend. When the Korean man straightened, her eyes traveled up his chiseled chest.

Yes, she noticed he was Korean and not Chinese. The differences were subtle, but after a half dozen years in this business, she recognized the signs. A longer, more feminine nose, smaller eyes, and lighter skin.

As he approached, she rose from the tub and oily water slid from her smooth skin. She offered her hand and he stepped in, and they settled into a sitting position so she leaned back into him. Oh, what a lucky night. She slid her hands along his silky shins.

No words were spoken, and when the wine was gone, they rose and stepped into the shower, where he let her wash and rinse his skin. If she noticed that he didn't touch her in the shower, she didn't care. She was too busy gazing into his open, friendly, and loving face while caressing his body. When they moved to the bed, her fantasies came true as he took control and the sex was tender.

Until it wasn't.

He flipped her roughly to her stomach and pushed her into the bed as his hand clamped onto the back of her neck and crushed her face into the pillow. She struggled to find breath as her chest heaved. Another hand pinned her arms back and wrenched one arm up as pain shot through her shoulder. At first she went with it, but the agony became unbearable and she screamed.

Which was muffled by the pillow.

Mei struggled as panic consumed her. His iron-like strength held her in place. Her lungs screamed for air, and when he flipped her over, she sucked in oxygen until he pressed a knife to her neck. She opened her mouth to scream, but no sound came.

With a finger to his lips, the Korean pushed the knife so it drew a thin line of blood on her skin. That was going to anger her employer. The one rule all clients adhered to was to refrain from damaging the merchandise. Her body went rigid.

The last thing she felt was tremendous pressure as he thrust into her. The last thing she heard was the groan escaping his lips. The knife plunged into her jugular and pierced the carotid artery.

Pain faded as darkness consumed her.

His overwhelming urges sated, the tall North Korean placed the spent condom in a Ziplock baggie, showered the blood from his skin, and dressed before he pulled on a pair of latex gloves. Using a bathroom towel, he wiped clean everything he had touched, drained and washed the tub and shower with bleach, and covered the woman's body with the duvet. As he worked, he was careful to avoid the large pool of blood and the blood spattered on the walls and floor. The wine glass was washed with soap. There might be DNA in the bed in the form of body hair, maybe a fingerprint on her body, but his handlers did the deep cleaning. They always caught everything.

On the counter was a bottle of expensive California cabernet, which he opened. With a glass of the red in hand, he sat on the edge of the leather couch, where he tipped the silver case onto its side and flipped the lock dials to the correct numbers. Inside were straps of Hong Kong dollars, a

Chinese passport with his photo and a fake identity, a medium-sized tablet computer, and a compact pistol. Two magazines and a short suppressor wrapped in an oily rag were alongside the gun. After he checked the pistol—a German-made SIG SAUER—he pushed home a magazine full of 9 mm slugs and screwed on the suppressor. The gun went into a specially made holster inside his suit jacket.

With the weapon attended to, he turned on the tablet and let it boot up while he sipped the cabernet. The tannins swirled on his tongue, which he savored. At the password prompt, he entered a memorized alpha numeric string of characters and was granted access to a dossier on the file system, a target package with images and a document.

First were dozens of pictures showing a young black-haired woman with Asian features. Beautiful, was his first thought. Troubled, was his second. Bobbed hair framed a grim face. None of the pictures showed her smiling. She wasn't Korean; maybe she was Chinese or Japanese. Pinched eyes, petite nose, olive skin. Probably a mixed breed, with a hint of the Mediterranean in there.

Most of the images were of the target wearing a North Korean army uniform. Some showed her holding a pistol at a gun range and some were taken at an obstacle course, while others depicted her in hand-to-hand combat, always with a male opponent. The pictures portrayed her as self-confident, efficient, highly competent, well trained, self-assured.

Interesting.

He turned his attention to the document, a short form with a bureaucratic heading at the top. The form was a standard-issue RGB assessment of a trainee's performance. Her name, according to this document, was *Ha-Yoon*. Might as well be Jane Smith in Korean. The document lacked any detail on her heritage, upbringing, or family. Instead it focused entirely on her training in weapons, hand-to-hand combat, and operational capabilities. According to her North Korean handlers, she was the best on record, the best they ever produced.

Anger erupted inside him, and he slammed the tablet onto the couch cushion and stood.

I'm the best they ever produced.

The emotion vanished as he paced and he replaced the anger with a thought, as he was trained to do.

This is a suitable test. I don't intend to fail.

He returned to the sofa and resumed reading. Missing from the file was how the operative escaped, or more likely, the assassin thought, how the RGB lost control of their asset. Of course, they would never admit they lost control. Instead they would formulate this elaborate scheme to clean up their mess and claim victory.

But still, what went wrong?

The target's last known location was Hong Kong. After the killer wiped down the silver case, the wine bottle, and the wine glass again, he departed for the train station, where he napped on the high-speed train to Hong Kong.

"I'm pulling the plug." Joe's voice was a low growl.

Wu rolled her eyes as she stared out over the millions of twinkling lights surrounding Victoria Harbour. The rain had stopped, but the lingering nighttime clouds cast a purple glow over the city and Kowloon Bay. The hotel lobby where she sat was on the 103rd floor of the International Commerce Centre. Ordinarily she would avoid such ostentatious digs, but she needed to get eyes on a new development, a new development not unanticipated, and one which was about to take the operation to a new level. A level she wasn't sure Kira was ready for.

"You said I had forty-eight hours. I sent the team back as you asked. But I have another twenty-four, and I intend to use those hours."

"I didn't take into account the massacre of two dozen Hong Kong citizens." Joe was in Tokyo, and they were speaking on a secure mobile line.

"Hardly citizens. They were members of the 14K triad, which, as you know, run smuggling operations for North Korea in addition to prostitution and drugs. These were bad guys, Joe. No one will miss them."

"Except now the Hong Kong police will investigate. This brings heat that you don't need and she doesn't need. That our agency doesn't need. If Hong Kong authorities discover we're running an operation in their city, it will damage relations before we even get started."

"This only helps our plan, Joe." Wu craved a cigarette and cursed the indoor non-smoking laws. "The more pressure on her, the better."

Joe was quiet for a spell. He was stoic and contemplative—a man of measured choices and words. When he made a decision, it was one born from weighing consequences and benefits. "I don't like it."

"I don't love it either, but we'll have squandered a massive opportunity. I know I keep repeating this, but we have spent a lot of time and resources on this. She will be an asset we can use. We need her on the team."

From the corner of her eye, a tall Korean man walked into the lobby and approached the reception desk. Mid-thirties with a shock of black hair and designer sunglasses. A glittering watch escaped his left cuff. Wearing a tailored silk suit and carrying a silver attaché case, the Korean man resembled a young but wealthy executive in Hong Kong on business. Wu knew otherwise.

More silence filled Joe's side of the line as Wu watched the tall Korean receive a packet of keys and walk to the elevator.

"Twenty-four hours, Joe. That was our deal. If we can't close her by then, I'll bring her back to Tokyo, and we'll let the chips fall."

The line went dead as the tall Korean stepped into the elevator and disappeared.

The last eight hours were torture for Outpost. The problem was a wide-ranging kaleidoscope of emotions he had never experienced before. This was new territory for him, and the feelings and sensations were so foreign to him, at first he assumed he was sick. Stomach flutters, a thudding heart, and anxiety.

First he chalked it up to fear, but eventually he admitted he had some kind of familial affection for the target. His trainers in the early days described it as Stockholm Syndrome, where a kidnap victim begins to identify with their captors. Except in this case, the operative develops emotions for their target, or a case officer develops feelings for the spy they're running. It's natural, and his employer's remedy was fear. If Outpost acted on his emotions, he and his family would suffer. As the tall Korean assassin stepped from the taxicab under the portico of the Ritz-Carlton hotel, he pushed all his thoughts into the dark recesses of his heart.

There was another challenge for Outpost to overcome,

which was also new. He had withheld details about his target's movements from Control, making no mention of the man with the mustache who abducted her. The red dot on his tracker only went a short distance before it stopped at the location of a hotel several blocks away. After a short time, the red dot again meandered through the city before it returned to the Nga Shing hotel, where Outpost witnessed her trudging up the stairs of the dingy hotel.

Why did he choose not to relay any of those details?

TWENTY

Hong Kong

Fatigue caught up with her. First the infiltration of 383 Lockhart Road, which was followed by the fateful surveillance detection route through the city, illuminating the group following her, the attacks on the construction site, and the subsequent meeting with Big Head Bao. Her legs felt heavy, and keeping her head upright took real effort.

After she departed Bao's, curiosity trickled into her mind. Why did the gangster want to talk with her? Her escape was instinct—she didn't like being held against her will. Any discussion with Bao would be under her terms, not his.

As she crouched in the shadows formed by a dumpster in an alleyway, she cataloged her options. Returning to the construction site now to retrieve her shoulder bag with the cash was out of the question. The area would be swarming with police. She had a little cash left in her pocket, maybe a hundred yuan—enough for a meal, not enough to change places to sleep.

With the adrenaline surges, the physical battles, and the pursuit, if she didn't get sleep soon, fatigue might affect her judgement. She needed her wits about her. Her priorities were food and rest. After which, maybe she would be willing to have another discussion with Bao. Clearly, the gang leader of the White Phoenix possessed information that might be helpful.

She was stuck with the Nga Shing Hourly Hotel, even if her instincts screamed at her to find a different place to sleep. One more night at the Nga Shing, and tomorrow she would retrieve the bag with the cash and find a new place to sleep.

Despite the fatigue, she took time to do a short SDR. This late at night, the streets were full of club-goers. She walked three blocks north, hopped into a cab, ducked into a subway station, exited the other side, and jumped in a second cab. The taxis took some of her remaining cash, but it was worth it. She was too exhausted to walk her SDR. The cab dropped her a block from the Temple Street Night Market, which is where she found a bowl of noodles and chicken kabobs. She slowly ate a second order of noodles while squatting with her back against a brick wall and deposited the empty bowls in the towering pile of dirty dishes next to the street vendor's steaming caldron of broth. When she walked past stall number 42, the decrepit shelter was empty.

The food revived her, and she decided to walk the twenty minutes north to her hotel. After taking a zigzagging route, where she passed the shuttered Yau Ma Tei Fruit Market, Kira was confident no one was tailing her. As she approached the stairs that would take her up a flight to the

Nga Shing's lobby, she ducked into the doorway of a shuttered ramen stand and squatted to observe the hotel's entryway. Kira remained in that position for thirty minutes and noted the people coming and going. This late at night, and this far from the nightlife of the Tsim Sha Tsui neighborhood of Hong Kong, there weren't many.

The only curiosity was the homeless person who lay in a sleeping bag on a cardboard box across the street from the Nga Shing's doorway. The man—she assumed it was a man, although his head was not visible—was there the entire time Kira stayed at the Nga Shing.

Like any good operative, Kira cased the Nga Shing hotel before ever setting foot in the lobby. Back stairs led from the alleyway behind the place. The narrow back stairs were meant for service, and the tile walls were covered in grease. They also accessed the manager's quarters.

After she left the doorway, Kira gave the homeless man a wide berth and took a circuitous route to the back alleyway, where she expected to see a second homeless person or some other form of disguised sentry. But the alley was empty.

She hurried to the Nga Shing's rear door, slipped in, and trudged up the back stairs, where it smelled like rotting vegetables and rancid cooking oil. In the hotel lobby, the skinny old man sat in the plexiglass booth with his head in the crook of his arm. Otherwise the place was empty. Thankfully, there was no sign of the mottled orange tabby.

Once in her room, she locked the door and wedged a chair under the door handle. She fieldstripped the Glock, wiped dirt and grit from the pieces using a bathroom towel, and reassemble it before loading the magazine with 9 mm rounds from the QSZ-92 magazine. She placed the gun on a towel on the toilet within arm's reach and stepped into the shower. With the curtain open, she stood under the hot water and sudsed herself clean. Along with the fatigue, an overwhelming sense of despair washed over her as she stood with her head under the scalding water.

After a brisk towel dry, she redressed and crawled onto the bed. With effort, she pushed the despair from her mind as she went back over the last twenty-four hours. Her raid on 383 Lockhart and the subsequent flight through the city in an attempt to shake a tail. The feelings of dread as the network of street watchers closed in. The attack in the construction zone. Did surveillance catch her at 383 Lockhart?

Who wants me dead?

Am I any closer to figuring that out?

If the 14K hadn't followed her to the construction site, as Big Head Bao said, whoever watched her must have tipped them off to her location.

Can I trust Bao?

Instinct said no, but that didn't mean what he said wasn't true.

Something niggled in her mind, and she remembered the soldier on the beach, his pack of cigarettes, and the paper with the address 383 Lockhart. The man obviously visited the brothel, and he was well known to the staff.

Was the North Korean soldier a guest of honor at the brothel at 383 Lockhart? Was he sent there after his arrival in Hong Kong, ostensibly from North Korea, for a preoperational meeting between the 14K and the North Koreans?

If Big Head Bao were to be believed, the 14K worked on behalf of the North Koreans to smuggle illicit contraband into the country.

Did the North Koreans tip off the 14K as to her whereabouts?

The logic was far-fetched, but it was possible.

Fatigue overwhelmed her as she rested the pistol on her chest and drifted off to sleep.

Rhythmic thumping of a headboard banging on the other side of the wall woke her, and she leaped up, the gun outstretched in a two-handed grip. Pale morning light streamed through the thin curtains, and nothing moved in her tiny room. She padded to the bathroom, where she rubbed her face with cold water, peed, and fought to tame her hair. Despite the sleep, her eyes were puffy and rimmed with red. Nothing to be done about it now. Coffee, food, and retrieval of the satchel. After that she would see about a meeting with Bao.

In the lobby, the skinny man dozed in the plexiglass booth. The tabby and the wizened man with the scraggly goatee were nowhere to be found. The lobby coffee was hot and strong, and she sipped from the cardboard cup as she departed the hotel and took off north along Sai Yee Street. To be safe, she spent two hours performing an SDR and saw nothing alarming.

Odd.

Yesterday, they were all over her.

Along her route, she noshed on fruit and more coffee until she stopped at a noodle cart near the vacant Temple Street Night Market. A steaming bowl was pushed at her after she handed over the necessary cash. The boy behind the cart wore a dirty white tank top and sported a gold earring with a ship on it. The ship was one of those old clipper ships, like the *Mayflower*. How Kira knew this, she had no idea. She found an open spot on the dirty curb and sat and ate.

Her thoughts turned to the gray-haired woman, who hadn't appeared in the last twenty-four hours. Kira's hand crept to the leather thong around her neck, which secured the tiny red velvet bag under her shirt. As she caressed the velour bag, she wondered where the gray-haired woman was, and why she wasn't helping her more directly.

Does she have the power to make this game stop?

Is she somehow aware of it, yet unable to end it?

Is she able to offer more direct help, but somehow doesn't wish to?

What's her endgame?

All questions, and no answers. The only thing the last twenty-four hours had produced was a tentative introduction to a triad gang leader who might turn her in for the reward.

I'm alone.

She jumped to her feet, pushing aside the sensation of vulnerability. She knew the antidote: Action beats intention. Taking action is always the answer.

More than anything, she needed cash. Cash for a new hotel room. Money to buy a new outfit and a more balanced meal than noodles and fruit. She dumped the empty bowl in the bin next to its soiled cousins and hastened along the road in the direction of the construction zone.

TWENTY-ONE

Hong Kong

The Korean killer with the square jaw and well-tailored suit cautioned himself to be vigilant. The dossier specified the target was extremely well trained, and his handlers constantly warned him not to be arrogant. Cocky was okay, confident was preferred, but arrogance got you killed—at least, according to his handlers.

The assassin didn't agree. Raised in privilege and born of a superior bloodline, the killer excelled at every sport and easily leaped to the top of his class in any martial art or weapons training. Told by his teachers and trainers that he was a natural, he was never bested in the gym or in the real world. And of course there was his uncle, who was descended from gods. His uncle was invincible, and so was he.

For a moment the Korean's thoughts drifted to the beautiful woman he had enjoyed in Shanghai. A warmth washed over his insides at the memory of the knife slipping into her neck, and his groin stirred. When he was done with this assignment, he would reward himself again.

He set aside the temptation and focused on the mission. Locating his target was relatively simple. Several methods were at his disposal, even for a target using only cash and not carrying a mobile phone. When he arrived in Hong Kong, he checked the operation's chat room that was buried in a secret website. It didn't surprise him to find the target still alive, the previous teams all failed. The other participants in the little exercise were amateurs, and the target was a pro. This is why he was activated. The reward was still available, and the target's last known location was Hong Kong. Information he already possessed.

His next action was to make contact with the fish factory ship floating just over the horizon in Causeway Bay. This was a resource not available to the rest of the game's participants, but the advantage didn't bother the assassin. It wasn't his fault he was born into the right family. He wasn't doing this for the reward; the cash offered for killing the target meant nothing. He did it for the scalp, as his uncle liked to say.

The tremor in the commander's voice came through the phone when the assassin's identity was revealed, and instantly the assassin had a team at his disposal. The commander confirmed that the target remained in Hong Kong, and an analyst on the commander's team supplied him with the log of the target's movements through the city plotted on a digital map.

Endless random circles of red, which the assassin assumed were the target's SDR routes, dotted the map. One location which the target frequented became evident: a low-rent hotel in the Mong Kok neighborhood where she probably slept. The analyst team on the factory ship also provided him with a file folder of Hong Kong police reports. He read through the incidents at 383 Lockhart and the construction site with close interest.

After another hour of reviewing the logs of the target's movements, a plan formed in the assassin's mind. One obvious weakness in the target's behavior was evident, and the assassin wondered why she frequented the same hotel. Patterns were a weakness and violated basic principles of tradecraft. Perhaps the woman craved familiarity while her mind was clouded by memory loss, or perhaps the tactic was part of a larger plan. Either way, the assassin would take her there.

At the Nga Shing Hourly Hotel.

From her vantage point on the covered walkway over Austin Road, Kira's view of the construction site below was clear. The meat wagons were gone and the bodies had been removed from the area, but the entire site crawled with law enforcement. A circle of officials in suits stood talking with three men in hardhats, while the group gestured and pointed at each other and appeared to be yelling. Kira guessed the construction team wanted to resume their work while the police wanted to seal off the area until their investigation was complete.

Both entrances to the construction site were crowded with a dozen or more security guards as crews of men unloaded truckloads of halogen lights. More security personnel poured from white vans, and police in baby-blue blouses and flak jackets cordoned off areas using yellow tape.

Retrieving the bag of cash might not be so simple.

While the activity unfolded below, she thought of other ways to replenish her funds. Robbery was always a possibility. Mug a rich person. Attack an armored truck. Rob a bank. All of those would take time to plan and could go awry and put her at more risk.

She remained in her position for another thirty minutes as the halogen lights were deployed and security patrols were organized. Eventually the hard hat wearers stalked off, and the law enforcement officials resumed their investigation.

The only hope of retrieving the cash was to do so under the cover of darkness. For that, she had to wait for nighttime. She pushed away from the fence and decided to perform an SDR before she returned to the Nga Shing.

The tall Korean's eyes adjusted to the murk of the Nga Shing's lobby as a cat with mottled fur lay in a narrow beam of sun near a rotating fan. Until the cat's paw twitched, the assassin thought the feline was dead. Grease from the McDonald's fryers downstairs hung in the air.

A haggard old man sat in a plexiglass-encased booth, and the assassin showed him a picture of the target. "This woman. She's here?"

The old man held his head up with a hand while his elbow rested on the table.

When he got no response from the hotel manager, the assassin slid a hundred Hong Kong dollars through the slot. "How about now?"

The proprietor shook his head.

"I know she's staying here. I need her room number."

Still nothing. The killer pursed his lips, crumpled

another hundred-dollar bill, and tossed it through the opening so the old man would have to pick it up off the floor.

The proprietor leaned back in his chair, crossed his arms, and smiled.

The plexiglass box where the old man sat had a door on one side. The door was fitted with a round metal handle, and when the assassin jiggled it, the knob turned. When the tall Korean stepped into the booth, the old proprietor's smile vanished.

"He entered the Nga Shing hotel. Target's not there." Outpost was on the satellite phone with Control. "I haven't placed eyes on her since she disappeared into the construction site yesterday evening."

A lie.

"How's he look?" Control's voice was clipped.

As Outpost watched from his cardboard box in the doorway across the street from the Nga Shing, the Korean assassin emerged onto the street. "He just came out of the hotel. Looks determined."

The tall man's head and shoulders towered over the other pedestrians, which made him easy to spot.

"He spent five minutes inside the hotel before he went into a Starbucks across the street. Guessing he's waiting for the target to appear."

"Call me with the first sign of her or any other news," Control said. "We need him to be successful."

It was a rare editorial from Control, and a pit formed in Outpost's stomach. "Copy that."

The assassin hurried down the stairs and squinted as he emerged into the sunlight and fresh air. He entered the Starbucks across the street, purchased an extra-large frozen mocha something or other, and found a spot at a narrow wooden bar running along the window that offered a clear view of the Nga Shing's entryway.

It wouldn't be enough to end her life and dispose of the body. This was a moment to be savored, a time to be enjoyed, a reward, a celebration, something provided by his uncle to thank him for his service, and he intended to relish her aroma and bathe in the woman's dying breath.

As he sipped the frozen drink, the sugar and caffeine surged through his veins. Whatever the drink was called, it wasn't available in Pyongyang, and it was delicious.

The straw gurgled on an empty cup as his target walked by.

TWENTY-TWO

Hong Kong

Her mind was preoccupied as she completed the SDR and headed for the Nga Shing. So far, despite the continued attacks, she had drawn a blank. After the bizarre meeting with the old fortune teller, her infiltration of 383 Lockhart, and the attack on the construction zone, she was no closer to figuring out who wanted her dead. She had a mysterious key in a red velour bag, a picture of a man who might attack her, and a satchel of cash she couldn't access. The one idea that stuck in her head was to make another meeting with Big Head Bao. The triad leader for some reason didn't want her dead. Maybe he had information he was willing to share.

The notion percolated as she approached the front of the Nga Shing. The homeless man who slept in the doorway opposite the hotel was still there, and the street was busy with pedestrians. Tourists, locals out on errands, and businessmen mingled in a familiar maelstrom of humanity. A half dozen ubiquitous red taxicabs lined the street.

She took the steps up two at a time. The voice nagged at her again to get out of the hotel, to find another place to stay. As soon as she retrieved the satchel with the cash, she'd find another place to sleep. In the hotel lobby, she gave the orange tabby a wide berth and eyed the aged proprietor, who's head rested against the wall in his protective booth, his face hidden by his arms. As she put a foot on the bottom step, a soft whistle came from behind.

She whirled and scanned the lobby. The room was empty save for the cat, whose eyes were narrowly open, and the old proprietor, who watched out of one eye while the other eye was pinched shut with a black and blue ring around it. Almost imperceptibly, the old man shook his head.

Alarm crept along her spine as she returned to the stairs leading to the street. No one was there, and she stopped to dig out a few bills, which she held up, but the old man waved them off. As she turned to descend the stairwell leading to the street, the old man tipped his head slightly in the direction of a closed metal door.

With a slight nod, Kira changed direction and opened the metal door, which led into a clean hallway in need of new paint. She walked past a room with a tiny kitchenette and a sagging couch with an oxygen tank next to it. There she took the back stairway that opened into an alleyway. She stopped and scanned both ways before she stepped out. No one was in the narrow lane between the two tall buildings.

After making a left, she hurried along the broken pavement of the alley, made two more left turns until she was back on the street where she ducked into the McDonalds, ordered a bag of fries, and found an open seat with a view out the window.

With her hat pulled tight, she ate the fries slowly and watched the street.

It's too easy.

As the young woman walked by, the tall Korean compared her to the image of his target he had memorized. Pitch-black hair, cut short. Tight lips, square jaw, a feline nose turned up slightly at the end. Small, petite, compact. Despite her size, the file specified unnatural strength and dexterity and stamina.

Light skin coloring, which made the handlers back home guess there was some American or European blood in there despite her Japanese appearance. Almond-shaped eyes with coal-black irises. Hollow cheeks, but that wasn't unique for anyone who was raised in the Democratic People's Republic of Korea, even for those like her with privileged status. Petite and trim, she wasn't his type. He liked them taller and fuller, but she would do. And afterward, he would satisfy his craving as a reward.

Despite the cap she wore pulled low and the scarf around her neck, it was the target. He sipped the last of his sugary drink as she turned off the street and bounded up the stairs to the Nga Shing.

The assassin waited a good thirty minutes. Before entering Starbucks for his drink, the killer had familiarized himself with the hotel's layout. Back stairs led to a tiny living quarters for the old proprietor. A side door off the back led to a hallway to the McDonald's and a tourist store filled with cheap jewelry and knickknacks.

With any luck, she might be in the shower or maybe asleep. His plan was simple: Enter the room and soften her with body blows until she was disabled. Administer a light sedative. After which he would take his time and enjoy the fruits of his labor until the inevitable loss of control. The hotel room would be a mess, but his North Korean cleaning crew, who stood by, would sanitize the room. By then he would be back at his uncle's private estate near Wonsan on the Pacific Ocean.

He smirked at his good fortune to be born into the right family.

After he tossed the empty plastic cup into the garbage, the assassin pushed through the door and jaywalked across the street to the tiny hotel.

TWENTY-THREE

Hong Kong

Since she had checked into the Nga Shing motel, the only humans Kira noticed were two old men. The same two old men. The stick-thin one sat in the lobby watching the muted television while smoking endless cigarettes during the daytime. At night he slept in the plexiglass booth. The heavier-set old man with the random white hairs growing from his chin looked to be the proprietor and lived in the back room and manned the plexiglass booth during the day.

Otherwise Kira had not seen another soul, either in the lobby or in the hallways. *Am I the only guest in the hotel?* When Kira saw the tall, handsome Korean man jaywalk across the street and make a beeline for the hotel's stairway, alarm bells went off in her head and her skin prickled with anticipation. It was same man in the picture she had received from the gray-haired woman.

This man is coming for you.

The man attempted to appear disheveled by wearing

dirty jeans, soiled Converse shoes, and a ripped T-shirt. But his hair was too styled, his eyes were too bright, and his teeth too white. A shock of dark hair fell over his eyebrow. A glittering watch was loose on his left wrist. Despite the gray-haired woman's warning, the man's appearance meant only one thing: answers. As with the men in the hut, there was no fear. Only purpose.

Kira tossed the oil-soaked french fry bag into the garbage and pushed through the door into the McDonald's kitchen. Sullen workers glared at her as she hastened through the tight quarters and through a rear door into the hallway. There she dashed up the stairs to the old hotel proprietor's apartment. The rusty pocketknife went into her waistband with the blade open. She held the Glock near her leg.

Kira peeked through the door into the lobby of the Nga Shing. The thin old man with a wisp of hair combed over his head sat staring at the television, hung in the corner, playing an old American Western on mute. A curl of smoke came from his lap, where the cigarette was hidden from her vantage point. The old proprietor sat in his plexiglass cage, leaned on an arm, and eyed the television. The orange cat lay on her side washing a paw and stopped to peer at Kira through amber eyes.

There were two ways to the hotel rooms: The stairs, which were accessed through a swinging metal door, or a narrow elevator whose buttons were caked in grime. She slid through the metal door and eased to the stairs. The old manager lifted his head and gazed at her through one rheumy eye. The other was closed, puffy, and black and blue. Watching for a tell, Kira raised an eyebrow. The man did nothing but put his chin back on his forearm.

Anger surged. There was no call to mistreat the hotel

proprietor. He had done nothing wrong. With her finger tight on the trigger and the pistol clutched near her leg, she eased up the stairs.

Threadbare carpet covered each riser. At each step, she tested her weight to ensure it wouldn't creak. With her back against the wall, she made her way to the first-floor landing. Each hallway was accessible through a metal door with a narrow window crisscrossed with wire mesh. The lighting was tungsten, the walls pale lemon, and the carpet gold. Rooms 100 through 110 were on this floor. Kira crept up to the next landing and along another flight of stairs to the third floor. No one was there.

Her room was halfway along the hallway on the left. At six feet by ten feet, it was small and reminded her of a jail cell, but it had a window overlooking the back alley and access to the fire escape. A single bed accompanied a table with a small television next to a door leading to a bathroom barely large enough to stand in. If the attacker waited for her in the main room, he would be exposed. He was probably standing in the bathroom and was hidden from view as the door opened. When she entered, he would attack from behind while she strolled into the room. That's how she would do it.

The lock required an ordinary metal key be inserted into a loose doorknob. With the gun in her left hand, she used her right to ease in the key, turn it, and push the door open. The dark room yawned at her, lit only by a neon-red blinking light pulsing through the window.

She went in low and swung the gun over to aim into the bathroom. The door closed behind her. It was her first error in judgement. The bathroom was empty.

A shadow sprang from the bed area. The heel of a hand crashed into her forearm, and the gun almost came loose.

She squeezed off a shot, but the bullet thunked into the wall over the bed. Through the murk came a fist, big as her head, and it plowed into her cheekbone with a crunch. The blow rocked her on her heels as the back of her head slammed into the wooden door. The attacker was on her with a flurry of punches, and she wasn't able to hold onto the gun and defend herself at the same time.

Partially stunned from the fist to her face, she parried the attacks with a blur of her arms and the Glock clattered to the linoleum. Big, tall, strong, and fast, the killer threatened to overwhelm her as her back butted against the door. A strike hit her torso and another crashed against her neck. If she didn't do something, the attacker would bury her.

She drew the knife, feinted, and swung for his midsection. Too fast, he deflected with a forearm, and in a blur of speed he chopped down on her wrist. The blade went flying to the floor and skittered under the bed.

She parried three blows, swung a foot, and connected with the attacker's shin with a crack. Low to the ground, she punched into the lowest and most vulnerable spot: his knee. One, two, three quick strikes and his leg buckled. He scuttled backward, favoring his back leg. With dazzling speed, she struck again, this time with a kick to the same knee.

Pick a weakness and exploit it.

Relentless, she struck the leg with a one-two punch that landed two crushing blows with hands calloused from a life of fighting. The man's size, an asset while on attack, was a liability on defense, and the leg was hard to protect. As she fought, she kept an eye out for the gun.

It was there. Next to the door. Behind her.

The attacker exploited the brief glance with a flurry of attacks of his own. Using his longer reach to his advantage, he came at her with punches and open-palm strikes, all against her neck and chest. The blows counted and pain flared. She parried a few, and others connected. A throbbing ache covered her chest.

He avoided her face and head. Why?

His strategy was to wear her down with body blows.

The attacker let up for a second, and his eyes went to the gun, as if taunting her. *Go ahead, grab it.*

Instead of falling for the trick, she lashed out at the leg again with a flurry of open-palm heel punches connecting with the knee. The man was forced to back away. As he did, she connected with a straight kick that collapsed his leg. As he went to the floor, she punched at his neck with another open-handed heel strike that the attacker parried.

The leg collapse was a feint by the taller man, and it almost did her in. The attacker hoped the force of her strikes would propel her into the center of the room and enable him to jump to the door and grab the gun. She recognized the feint and danced back, her hands held up to protect her face.

The attacker came at her again using his long arms to connect punch after punch into her chest and stomach. Ignoring the burning pain of the strikes, she once again parried and aimed a sweeping kick to his knee. That one connected and the knee wobbled, and he bounded up and changed his stance to present the opposite knee.

This time she fell for the bluff. As she attacked an opening, he flicked his foot up and caught her under the chin. Lights flashed across her eyes and the room swirled as she fell back. More punches crushed into her obliques, stomach, and chest. Strong, smart, well-trained, and fresh, this one was not like her other opponents. This one was a professional.

Her back crashed into the door as she absorbed the

attack, and she went into a feint of her own. She curled into a ball to protect her body as she sank closer to the floor.

It almost worked.

She darted her hand out to snatch the gun, and the attacker realized almost too late what she was doing. As Kira's hand gripped the polymer handle, she swung the Glock and fired. The aim was off, but the idea was to scare the attacker into slowing his onslaught. The gun popped, and the bullet plunked into the wall near the window.

Instead of hesitating, the attacker rushed at her with stunning speed and knocked the gun aside. Kira's hand hit the doorjamb, and the gun clattered to the floor and skidded into the doorway of the bathroom. She swung her left fist and caught him in the chin, which drew blood as his lip split.

The attacker fell back and his hand came away red when he touched his lip. Fire blazed in his eyes as he gazed at the pistol. It was on the floor, equidistant from them both.

They both dove for the gun.

TWENTY-FOUR

Hong Kong

On the ground, Kira had a decided disadvantage to the larger man. He was taller by more than a foot, and his wingspan was wider by at least two feet. He had fifty pounds of well-defined muscle over her slight frame. As she dove, Kira realized she had no chance to reach the gun, so instead she grabbed his arm.

The attacker's long arm stretched out for the gun, and his hand felt around on the cracked linoleum inches from the gun handle. The killer heaved while she hung on to his heavily muscled forearm.

He would get to the gun first. He was too strong.

So she went for his eyes.

The killer lunged, and his hand wrapped around the gun handle.

She let go of his arm and grasped at his face with both hands and jabbed two thumbs into his eye sockets.

The assassin screamed, and the gun clanked to the floor as his hands went to his face.

She clung on and dug deeper.

Strong hands clamped on her wrists and yanked her hands away from his face. The assassin's bloody face contorted with pain, fury, and something else.

Panic.

Interesting.

He held two vice grips wrapped around her thin wrists and he levered them as though he might break them. Her wrists throbbed, and she thought her arms might snap at any second. With her hands pinned, her legs fought for purchase on the slick linoleum.

Inventory of vulnerable spots: scrotum, neck, tops of the feet. None were available in her prone and compromised position.

Tears flowed from the killer's eyes, and he glared at her through the swelling. His mouth contorted into a hate-filled grimace as he bared his teeth and fought to break her arms.

She did the only thing she could think of, which was to ram her forehead into the bridge of his nose in a downward arc.

Cartilage gave way with a snap, and he gasped in surprise. But his hands still grasped her wrists in vice-like grips.

So she head-butted him again. Blood spattered on the yellow bathroom wall and on the front of her T-shirt. Drops of the viscous red liquid spattered on the floor.

He screamed, and his grip weakened.

She wrenched her arms free and lunged for the gun. As her body flew across the floor, which was now slick with blood, her hand wrapped around the weapon's handle and she flipped so she was on her back holding the gun out straight with a doublehanded grip.

A large, blurry object moved.

She fired.

A door slammed.

The attacker was gone.

Get up, damn it.

Her mind screamed out to chase the killer, to finish him off. Her body didn't comply, as pain consumed her. The gun was still aimed at the bathroom doorway, and no amount of will could force her body to get to her feet. Instead the Glock slowly wavered until it pointed to the ground. Blacks and reds swirled in front of her eyes as she fought to stay conscious.

Pain and exhaustion ravaged her muscles and bones, and an image of black and blue skin covering her midriff and chest swam at her. *Stay awake, damn you. If you pass out, you're a dead woman.*

Nothing happened, except her vision blurred and her hands held the pistol in a death-grip. Unable to move, she lay there with her back on the floor and her head propped against the bloody wall. She wavered in and out of consciousness.

Time disappeared.

Fuzzy shapes appeared. She made an attempt to raise the pistol, but it was too heavy. Amorphous blobs grasped her arms and legs and half carried, half dragged her from the room, along the hallway, and into the elevator.

Everything went black.

Shenzhen, China

An endless, windswept rain pattered against the thin sheet metal siding of the three-story warehouse. Commander Pak stood next to a row of windows with a view of the Shenzhen Safari Park hills to the east. If the windows faced west, he would see endless rows of containers and cranes comprising the enormous shipping operations of Dachan Bay Terminal. Located along the north border of Hong Kong on the east bank of the Pearl River, Shenzhen's population of eighteen million made it the third largest city in China. The Port of Shenzhen is one of the largest in the world, which also made it an ideal location for Commander Pak to run his smuggling enterprise.

The RGB analysts had been sent home to Pyongyang to await their next assignment. Outpost was reassigned to report status directly to Pyongyang. The *Damanzaihao* steamed north to Nampo, a seaport on North Korea's Taedong River, to disgorge its illegal catch of yellowfin tuna. The cramped room of surveillance gear was shuttered, and the room was locked until the next operation. The failsafe was activated, and the operation was over. At least Commander Pak's participation in it had ended.

The woman's fate was out of his hands, which put a pit in his stomach. Still, Pak was a survivor—one had to be in the North Korean RGB—and now his life depended on fixing the relationship with the 14K.

He sipped black coffee from a tin mug and peered out at the rain. The first meeting did not go well. The man in charge of the 14K was named Hump Nose Ho, and his reputation belied the comical nickname. The 14K triad was a loose-knit group of self-interested thugs until Ho, fresh out of prison, united the various clans through extreme violence and adept negotiation. Ho, his skin heavily marked with prison tattoos, had ranted and raved about the loss of his men and the destruction of a major source of his income in the prostitution operation and made a case for millions in reparations. Now Pak awaited word from Pyongyang on what amount he was authorized to provide.

The mobile phone in his pocket buzzed, and he removed it and answered.

"It's done," Colonel Ryo said.

Pak bowed his head as sadness washed over him. "We have confirmation?"

"Waiting on Outpost, but the fail-safe entered the hotel fifteen minutes ago and the target was seen entering. The fail-safe has never disappointed, so it's just a matter of time."

A strange sensation overcame Pak. *What if she prevails?* "Excellent. Do I have approval on my proposal to our friends?"

"I'm waiting to hear. Once your negotiations are complete, you're to return to Pyongyang for debrief."

Pak's head hung and his scar radiated with a faint burning sensation. *A debrief.* "Copy that, sir."

After the transmission ended, Pak walked to the coffee urn and refilled his cup. He had no intention of returning to North Korea. Ever. Who knows what fate awaited him in Pyongyang. Days, weeks, maybe months of interrogation followed by a post to Tongbōn-p'o, a frigid outpost on the northern border with Russia. If he was lucky. Or maybe he would be shipped off to a labor camp. Either way, his lavish lifestyle was probably over. Nothing to be done about that now.

He removed a picture from a hidden compartment in his wallet. The image was of a black-haired girl about the age of seven. Small for her age, the girl stood in a flower bed, and her mouth was open with laughter. His fingers crept up and stroked his scar as he gazed at the picture before he put it back in the secret spot in his wallet.

There was only one way to save himself, and he retrieved a mobile phone from a drawer in the desk. The prepaid phone was made in China. If Pyongyang caught wind of Pak's secret phone, he would be marked for immediate execution.

One final card to play.

He dialed a number from memory.

TWENTY-FIVE

Hong Kong

Outpost sat in the front seat of a red taxicab, which was procured for him by his new contact at the RGB, and now he idled with the lights off, double-parked with a view of the front of the Nga Shing hotel. After his target entered the hotel thirty minutes prior, there was no further sign of her. The Korean assassin entered the hotel ten minutes ago, at which point the rock settled in his gut.

She was in trouble. This killer is the real deal. This was different than before. It would be bad.

While he sat and watched, he tapped a finger on the steering wheel. Who would appear from the hotel door? The tall assassin or the raven-haired woman? A part of him hoped for the assassin. Despite the heart-wrenching loss, wasn't it better to get this over with? Return home, visit his parents, and wait for his next assignment?

When the tall Korean emerged from the Nga Shing, the rock in Outpost's gut fell into his intestines. The assassin limped badly, his shirt was torn, blood covered his clothes, and he held two hands up to his face. He staggered like he was drunk, and pedestrians gave him wide berth.

As the assassin stumbled away from the Nga Shing, Outpost wondered what to do next. Was she dead? If she was dead, he needed confirmation.

The red dot on the tablet remained hovered over the Nga Shing. Of course, that meant nothing. The device buried under her skin in the flesh of her triceps was programmed to give off a signal until the battery died, regardless of whether the host was alive or dead.

As Outpost sat back onto the seat of beads taxi drivers use to ease the long hours in traffic, sadness overwhelmed him. What if she was dead? The idea tore at him until he pushed it away.

Don't get emotional.

He tugged his bucket cap snug on his head, slipped from the cab, and crossed the street to the steps leading to the Nga Shing lobby. When he arrived at the landing, no one was visible. A black-and-white television played a muted American Western. A mottled orange tabby woke and hissed at him. A fan whirred slowly and creaked as it rotated on an arc. A haze of cigarette smoke hung against the ceiling.

A grunt and a curse in Chinese sounded from along a hallway. Outpost crept down the cracked linoleum until he arrived at a doorway that was open a crack. Through the opening, two old Chinese men lowered the body of a small woman onto a fabric couch. Outpost strained to see through the dim light, and he stepped closer.

One of the old men shifted, and Outpost got a better view of the body on the couch. Raven-black hair and blood everywhere.

It's her. Is she dead?

The woman cried out, although her eyes remained closed, as if she were in the middle of a bad dream.

Relief flooded him as he returned silently to the lobby and exited to the street.

She's alive.

Unlike when she was in the jungle, consciousness arrived abruptly. She jerked awake, leaped from where she lay, and landed in a crouch. A ray of sunlight filtered through a dirty window and illuminated an orange and fuzzy blob on the floor.

As the room swirled, she fell. A man-shaped amoeba caught her before she hit the ground and helped her onto the soft bed, where she dozed off into a dreamless state.

The next time awareness crept into her mind, she cracked her eyelids enough to see a dark room. The room was shabby and small but clean, and striped wallpaper covered the walls. Street sounds trickled in from a window next to where she lay. Sirens, horns, and the tin-like bleats of motor scooters. The astringent scent of cleaning fluid poorly concealed the smells of urine and feces. It took her a moment to place the odor. It was the smell of an overused, unclean cat box.

Everything hurt. Her torso, her forehead, and her legs ached. Even raising a hand from under the tattered wool blanket sent shooting pain radiating along her arm and into her spine.

That can't be good.

Darkness returned as she drifted off to sleep.

A salty, brothy smell woke her, and a pale light fought

its way through the dingy window. The cat box odor was as strong as ever.

Everything was blurry, and a fuzzy old man sat next to her bed. As she blinked away haze, he held out a cup. "Drink."

It was a struggle to prop herself up on one arm long enough to let the old proprietor hold the cup to her lips. The hot broth scalded her tongue, but when she was able to taste again, she gagged and almost spit it out.

"What the fuck *is* that?"

"You must drink it. Drink it all." The man's eyes were hooded with concern.

"Why? What the—"

"Drink."

She drank, and it was awful. Piping hot and flavored like chalk dust laced with urine. *Did this come from the cat box?* She barely choked it down.

When the cup was empty, she laid back onto the thin pillow and tried not to retch. Bile filled the corners of her mouth, but she closed her eyes and fought through it. She may have drifted off. When she opened her eyes, the old man was gone.

But the cat was there and lay curled against her feet on the ratty blanket in the sunlight. Kira was in the hotel proprietor's living quarters. Across the room was the threadbare plaid couch and next to that was a large canister of oxygen. The black-and-white television was off. A pot of something boiled on a hot plate.

Every part of her body hurt, but now the ache was duller. Maybe the broth contained a sedative or painkiller. A pleasant numbness washed over her, and she drifted back to sleep.

The next time her eyes opened, a warm twilight shone

through the window, and the cat was nestled into the crook of her arm. Two men were in the room. The old hotel proprietor stood at the stove while the rail-thin Chinese man wheeled a mop bucket and disappeared through a door. It was the man who had sat smoking and watching the mute television in the Nga Shing lobby.

Alarm surged within her and she sat up, which sent a wave of dizziness swirling through her head, but she fought it and stayed upright. "Am I... Where..."

The old proprietor rushed over and gently pressed her back.

"I need to go." Kira's head was heavy.

"Safe here." The strength in the old proprietor's hands reassured her, and she allowed him to guide her back into a lying position. The bruise around his eye was now purple and yellow. Several strands of hair flew around his fleshy head when he moved about the room, and moles and age spots covered his otherwise bald pate.

The man hastened to the stove and returned with another steaming cup of the barf brew.

"What if he comes back?" Kira flexed her leg muscles but felt only pain.

"No come back. Bodyguards."

"A bodyguard?"

The old man nodded his head vigorously. "Drink this."

She pushed the drink away and rose a few inches from the bed. *No bodyguard is going to stop that killer.*

With surprising strength, the old man eased her back with one hand while he held the broth up to her mouth.

"White Phoenix," he whispered. "You safe here."

White Phoenix. Big Head Bao's triad. How did he learn of the attack? Perhaps the hotel was on that gang's turf, and they didn't take kindly to the violence that had taken place under their roof? She let the old proprietor feed her the broth and she managed to swallow all of it, after which she fell asleep again.

The sleep and broth cycle happened twice more, and when she awoke, her muscle pain was remarkably better. Nighttime sounds filtered through the open window, and the orange tabby was curled on the bed against her arm. She tested her muscles by petting the cat's fur. The fur was soft, and the feline stretched, rose, kneaded the blanket, and settled with her paws against Kira's arm. Kira's ligaments creaked, but the pain was now a background haze.

"She likes you." The old man sat at a nearby table, where he used chopsticks to eat a bowl of food.

"Yeah, well until now I'm pretty sure she wanted me dead." Kira let her fingers linger on the soft fur. "What's in that broth?"

The old man shrugged. "Ancient family recipe."

A hard object was under the wool blanket next to her hip. She reached under and touched the handle of the Glock. The folding penknife with the red handle was next to it. The old man must have put them there.

"I'm sorry about the damage to the room. I have money. I'll pay."

The old man shrugged again. "What damage?"

When she sat up, her head swam but it cleared after a moment. As she swung her feet to the floor, a vision of the hut on the jungle island appeared. There she had been in much worse condition. Probably drugged, beat to hell, unaware of her surroundings. Here, the broth helped clear her head and dulled the ache in her bones.

Where can I get more of that magical potion?

The clothes she wore during the fight were clean and folded on a rickety wooden chair, so she shed the simple cotton pajamas and top someone had dressed her in, folded them neatly, and pulled on her old olive capri pants and T-shirt. The shirt had two new holes, and a muted-pink stain covered the front.

Time to upgrade the wardrobe.

For that she needed funds, and she remembered that her bag of cash was hidden at the construction site.

Hopefully still hidden.

Her head was clear, but her body creaked. *Once the magical brew wears off, will the pain come back?*

She did a few knee bends and stretches, and as she moved her body, a memory jolted her.

A red velour bag.

A key.

She felt her pockets, but the key wasn't there. She ran her hands through the sheets in the bed. No velour bag. No key.

Panic engulfed her.

She turned to the old man and spoke in Chinese. "Did you see a small cloth bag, or a key? A key was in the bag. It was in my pocket, here." Kira pointed at her right front pocket. She had taken it from around her neck and put it in her pocket for safe keeping.

The old man shook his head. "No bag. No key."

She approached him and he shied away, so she stopped. "Please. Are you sure? It's important."

Again, he shook his head and waved his hands. "No bag. No key."

"Maybe it's upstairs, still in the room?"

He handed her a room key with the plastic fob attached. After she shoved the gun into her waistband, she hastened out of the living quarters and bounded up the stairs. The door to her old room was closed, so she used the key and pushed it open. A vision of the battle washed over her, but she ignored it. The blood was gone and the bed remade, as if the fight had never occurred. Kira searched the entire room. Under the bed, among the sheets, in the bathroom, and in the cupboard serving as a closet. But no velour bag, and no key.

With a heaviness in her gut, she went back downstairs, where she asked the old proprietor's helper, the skinny man, who also shook his head.

Where did it go?

After one last search around the proprietor's tiny apartment, including in the bedding where she recovered, the laundry area, and the bathroom, she realized the key had vanished.

The old man sat on the couch, hands on his knees, an oxygen hose attached to his nose. He kept murmuring, "No bag, no key."

Kira hung her head and admitted defeat.

"I must go," she said. "I can't stay here. Your life is in danger if I stay. Even with your bodyguards."

The hotel proprietor heaved to his feet, removed the oxygen strap from his nose, and tossed the tube to the couch before shuffling to a cabinet hanging askew on the wall. He took something from the cabinet and handed Kira a cellophane baggie containing a sand-colored powder.

"One spoonful in hot water." He tapped the baggie with a crooked finger. "Go easy. Powerful stuff." The old man also pressed some bills into her hand.

Kira hesitated before she took the cash. She put her arms around the old man's neck and kissed his cheek. "I'll pay you back tenfold."

TWENTY-SIX

Hong Kong

The assassin made his way through the lobby of the Ritz-Carlton, his face partially hidden by a cap and sunglasses covering his swollen eyes. At this time of night, the night bellman was present, and the Korean gave the sleepy employee wide berth. The only other occupant in the expansive and modern lobby with the red and beige swirl carpet was an old lady, her gray hair thinning and matted, with sunglasses on her face, who appeared to be asleep, sprawled on a cream-colored leather chair. A martini, halfway consumed, sat next to her on the black lacquer table. When the assassin got to his room, he slammed the door and assessed the damage.

That bitch. That little bitch.

After he yanked off his jeans, he examined his right knee, which was puffed up two times its normal size. He hoped it wasn't permanently damaged.

But his face was the primary concern. His beautiful

face. The face that made women turn. The face that asked more questions than gave answers. He took off the sunglasses to reveal two eyes partially swollen shut. Black and blue bruising blossomed around both eyes. His nose, expertly crafted last year by his uncle's own plastic surgeon, was crooked and humped, and his nostrils were rimmed in blood.

That bitch will pay.

He slammed his fist against the wall and put a crater in the plaster as drywall flecks sprinkled to the carpet.

That bitch!

The worst part wasn't the black mark on his record or the failure tallied on the competition scorecard. It wasn't that she got away or that she was still out there. Or that now another team might notch the win. No, based on the woman's skills, there was little chance another team might take her down. None of that was the worst part.

The worst part was his face. When the woman connected with the second headbutt to his nose, it wasn't the pain that sent him running. It was the fear lacing through him. Fear that she had permanently altered his looks. Without that face, who was he? How could he walk through a crowd and know, just know, everyone stared in awe?

Now as he gazed in hatred at his bent nose, he would have to endure the indignity of his uncle's laughter and contempt as he begged for another round of plastic surgery.

No! Never. There must be another way.

The assassin washed his face and dabbed the wounds with antiseptic ointment before sending for a bin of ice. While he waited, he stripped off the rest of his clothes and put the contents of his pockets on the credenza. A money clip with a thick wad of cash and room key, as well as a small red velour bag with something hard and tubular inside. He opened the gold silk drawstrings, and a key dropped into his palm.

What the—

A knock sounded at the door, so he wrapped a towel around his waist and took the ice bucket from the steward, wrapped a bag of ice cubes around his knee, and lay on the bed, where he draped another bag of ice over his face.

The key was in his hand, and he rubbed the hard metal with his thumb while the ice numbed the pain. It was an antique, with bronze patina, squared bits, a round shaft, and a seahorse carved into the end.

While he lay prone, fighting to endure the icy numbness on his face and knee, his mind wheeled from memories of the fight to images of the woman to a single imprint of her face. Something was there he had never noticed before. In every other fight, the assassin entered the combat as the clear superior. Stronger, faster, meaner, and more highly skilled, superior in every way. It put fear into his opponents and guaranteed the assassin the upper hand. Every face he encountered dissolved into fear when the fight started, as it dawned on his opponent that they were destined to lose.

This time was different. The woman's face was blank, a resolute mask, a confident shell of nothing. No fear, only determined confidence. Thinking back, it made him anxious, a feeling he had never experienced.

He ran the tip of a finger along the jagged ridges of the key.

A kaleidoscope of emotions ran through him as he lay on the soft bed, the ice dampening the swelling. Curiosity: Who is this woman? Intrigue: How did she get this way? Fear: Maybe I'm not invincible? And one that surprised him more than the others. Arousal: *I want you.*

I'm coming for you, bitch.

Famished.

Her stomach rumbled as though she hadn't eaten for days, and when she found herself standing in front of the noodle cart with the kid in the white tank top and the gold earring with the clipper ship, she ordered two servings. With one steaming bowl balanced on her knees, she scarfed the noodles and dumplings from the other and drained the broth. After that bowl was empty, she started in on the second portion. By the time the second bowl was empty, she was close to feeling normal again.

Kira stacked her empty bowls next to the half dozen others and paid for a bottle of cold water, which she chugged as she strolled west along Temple Street.

Her muscles complained as she walked, but she ignored the soreness. Instead she focused on the key. It had been in her pocket, that much was certain. The only explanation was it must have fallen out during the melee. If the bag was not in the hotel room, which Kira confirmed for herself, there were only two possibilities. The old hotel proprietor or his helper found it and kept it, or the killer had somehow ended up with it after the fight.

The old hotel proprietor or his helper were a distinct possibility, except why would one of them lie about it? Both men were kind enough to help her, so why would one of them keep something clearly belonging to her? Neither man would have attached any significance to it. Even she didn't know what the key was for. She dismissed this scenario.

Her thoughts turned to the assassin. Did he see the key on the floor and snatch it? The killer was hurt badly and wanted to escape. It seemed unlikely, but when all other explanations have been exhausted, the most unlikely option must be true.

A coffee shop was on her left, and she ducked into it. After she paid cash for a strong black coffee, she sat with her back to the wall where she enjoyed a good view of the street. The coffee was hot enough to scorch her tongue, but she sipped it anyway and visualized the fight.

She had come in low, with the gun aimed into the bathroom, where she guessed he was hiding. Instead the killer was in the tiny bedroom, and he batted the gun away and attacked with an onslaught of body blows. Did the door remain open, or did it close?

The fight played out in her mind.

The door swung closed. She remembered her back against it with nowhere to go. She attacked a vulnerable spot, his knee, and there were feints, body blows, and more strikes to his knee.

Find a weakness and exploit it.

They both dove for the gun and she grabbed his arm. She headbutted him twice, jammed her thumbs in his eyes, he screamed, and the panic on his face...

Was the panic due to her assault on his face? What a weird thought, but not out of the realm of possibility. Was the attacker, a highly capable fighter, losing the battle? If her memory was right, the fight to that point was a draw. She damaged his knee, but she also took a lot of body blows. Over a longer fight, his advantage was his size and stamina. So why did he bolt, unless he was panicked from her assault on his face? She damaged his looks, and that struck the assassin's nerve. Inadvertently, she had found his weakness.

Her thoughts went back to the fight. As the attacker writhed on the ground from the savage eye wounds, Kira dove across the floor, sliding in the blood, and grabbed the gun. She flipped onto her back and aimed, but the attacker was gone.

Or was he?

She gulped the coffee and let the caffeine fire the neural networks in her brain. At the time, her mind was in combat tunnel vision with the adrenaline and cortisol narrowing her focus. Now, after the fight, a vision appeared while Kira lay flat on her back, her arms outstretched, the gun in two hands. It took her a moment to find the target. Her own vision was hazy and the gun wavered as she searched for the assassin. In her peripheral vision, a shape pulsed in and out of view. The shadow was on the ground, and a hand had shot out and grabbed something off the floor. Her arms were paralyzed, and the gun was frozen in place. Before she could summon the strength to bring the gun around, the shadow was gone. Her tunnel vision prevented her from seeing the movement.

Now with a clear memory, the events came back to her. The assassin grabbed something off the ground before he fled. That must have been the key.

Shit.

A flood of emotions surged. Frustration and panic, but those emotions were soon replaced by a warm sensation. The warmth from an idea. If the assassin realized the key was important to her, it meant he believed he had leverage over her. That was knowledge she might exploit to her own advantage.

She drained the coffee and exited the coffee shop.

The hunted was now the huntress.

TWENTY-SEVEN

Hong Kong

The first order of business was to retrieve the shoulder bag with the cash and figure out how to get a message to the tall Korean assassin.

After she meandered through the city and watched for a tail, she jumped into a red taxi, and a waft of fetid body odor assaulted her nose. The cabbie was dressed in filthy military fatigues complete with a bucket cap. She was relieved to step out of the cab at the corner of Canton Road and Austin Road West near the construction zone. The Glock was in her waistband, hidden from sight by the hoodie. She didn't want to have to use it.

This late at night the thoroughfare was busy, and she hastened past the Sky Corridor and Sightseeing Deck and found the elevated greenway spanning the road and offering easy access into the construction zone. She kept to the shadows, stopped at the fence, and looked out over the construction area two levels below. The police were no longer present, but several two-man security patrols walked through the area as the new halogen lights cast a bright glow over the lot.

While she tracked the security patrols, her mind wandered to the assassin. Her guess was he wouldn't take failure lightly and was eager to finish the job. She needed to find a way to get a message to him. A pattern of security patrols emerged as a kernel of an idea occurred to her. She knew someone who may know how to get the assassin a message.

When she was confident of the patrol's patterns, she made her way to the parking lot on the east side of the construction zone where she had been captured by Big Head Bao's team. There she timed her ascent over the fence to coincide with the pattern of the patrols. She dropped to the dirt and crouched.

While her timing was right, she didn't account for an errant guard who decided to relieve himself next to a forklift. Dressed in a dark uniform complete with weapons belt, the man zipped up his pants and turned in the same moment as Kira landed in a crouch. They were both equally surprised, but Kira recovered more quickly.

Before the guard was able to yank his weapon, she took three steps and used her momentum to jab her fingers into the man's windpipe. At the last instant she pulled back so the strike stunned him but didn't end his life. His hands went to his throat as he gasped for air. She swept his feet out from under him, pinned both his arms behind his back, and used her weight to hold him while she yanked the gun and tossed it ten feet away, where it landed partially concealed behind a pallet of paint cans.

Now she had a problem. The guards traveled in pairs, and this man's partner was close. A search of his weapon belt uncovered a set of plastic handcuffs, which she zipped onto his wrists. With her rusty pocketknife, she cut a length of his sleeve and tied it firmly around his head so his mouth and eyes were covered. She dragged him along the fence to an area where metal pipes were stacked like cordwood and left him hidden in the darkness.

"Li?"

The voice came from where Kira had disabled the guard. She crept around the stacks of pipes to flank the second guard, who stood with his hands out, palms up, slowly turning to look in all directions. When his back was to Kira, she stole behind him and crossed his throat with her arm while she snatched his pistol. Her left arm cut off his air, and she eased him to the ground as he blacked out. After she dragged him behind a stack of two-by-fours, she gave him the same treatment with the cuffs and a gag and tossed his pistol into the open end of a cement mixer.

She hurried through the shadows along stacks of wood, storage bins, concrete barriers, scaffolding, and shipping containers to where the office trailer sat bathed in yellow light. She figured she had only a few minutes before the two-man patrol was missed. As she hid in a shadow next to a front-end loader, a pair of security guards ambled into a pool of light about fifteen meters from her position. One swung his baton while the other man's fingers were hooked on his weapon belt. Their eyes roamed the construction site while they walked. She kept to the shadows and waited for them to pass.

When they disappeared, she ran from her hiding spot and crouch-walked until she reached the trailer. Under the trailer were six stacks of the scaffolding end units stored on pallets. Each end unit was in the shape of two rectangles next to each other on the long side, like an H in a box. The scaffolding was stacked on their sides so they formed two large holes. She counted three stacks from the end and thrust her arm over the thick piping and cast around in the hole. There was nothing there. No leather shoulder bag.

A pang of panic shot through her. *Maybe it's in the next hole over.*

After she scuttled two feet to her right, she reached into the scaffolding and felt around. Her fingers brushed leather. Relief flooded her as she yanked out the satchel. It was as heavy as she remembered it, but to be sure, she glanced inside. The rolls of Hong Kong dollars were still there. She slung it over her back and fastened the flap.

"Hey! Hey, you!" The voice called out in Chinese.

Two guards stood out in the open bathed in yellow light. One guard held a long black flashlight and pointed the beam at her, although he was too far away for the light to reach her hiding spot. The second guard was frozen with one hand on his gun, which remained holstered, and the other hand holding a mobile phone.

She whipped out the Glock and fired two shots. She purposefully aimed low and wide, but the loud reports created their intended effect. The two men ran. One darted to his left and took refuge behind a pile of concrete barriers, and the second man sprinted to his right.

As the men scattered, Kira took off at a run. She wove around the trailer and sprinted on a vector away from the two guards and shoved the Glock into her shoulder bag.

Shouts erupted behind her.

She increased her speed and threaded through stacks of shipping containers and pallets of paint and drywall mud until she reached the fence forming a barrier between the construction site and Victoria Harbour. Without looking to see if she was followed, Kira jumped to grab the top of the fence. The fence rattled, and she hung suspended for a split second.

A bullet whizzed overhead, and a second clanged off the fence two feet from her hand.

With a heave, she swung herself to the top of the fence and hesitated with her thigh on the top bar, balanced, with both hands grasping the bar. In front of her, a million blue and red lights twinkled off the black water.

A shot careened off the fence, and another bullet split the air near her ear.

She stood and balanced for a split second before shoving with her feet to propel herself out into the air, straightened her body, and put her arms out. The shoulder bag flopped against her back as she soared through the air, and she plunged into the water with barely a splash.

Gradually the blood pulsing in his ears receded, and Outpost positioned his taxicab with a view of the fence where his target exited the construction zone last time, the time when she was abducted by the man with the flowing mustache. It felt so long ago now, and Outpost had never ascertained where his target was during that short window of time. It was only one example of the degradation of his performance, which he only surmised was a direct result of his newfound feelings for his target.

Another indiscretion was the cab ride. Of course he was powerless to stop it. The target emerged from the hotel, spied his cab, and jumped in before he was able to drive off. Adrenaline and emotion surged as he was close enough to smell her, and he fought to concentrate on the traffic. He felt as though he was driving through a tunnel where everything else around him receded into the background.

As his racing heart subsided, Outpost watched while the red dot on the small tablet meandered through the construction site, stopped for three minutes, and floated south. When the red dot slid into Victoria Harbour, Outpost's eyebrows shot up.

A soft ding woke the assassin. It was the alarm on his phone, which sat on the bed an inch from his ear. Instantly a hot pain enveloped his head, and he pawed for the bottle of painkillers on the nightstand. After he dry-swallowed two of the white pills, he rested a moment to let the chemicals take effect. His fingers touched the wound on his nose. The bridge was swollen and painful to the touch. While the needle-like pain dulled, his hand wandered to the other side of the bed, found the warm form under the sheet, and let his fingers linger along the swell of her buttocks. Small and boyish, the woman wasn't his favorite flavor, but her nursing skills made up for her angular form. Sent by the North Korean military, the nurse lived and worked in Hong Kong and was reserved for moments like this when operatives might need medical help.

He ignored the pain in his knee as he set both feet on the ground. His head swam, and he rested for another moment before he snatched his phone and padded to the bathroom. He almost dropped his phone when he saw himself in the mirror. Both eyes were circled by black and yellow bruising. His nose, although bandaged, was crooked. His vision was blurry, although the nurse assured him it would clear. His right knee throbbed and was swollen to the size of a soccer ball.

Before he stepped into the shower, he tossed back a handful of the white pills.

After a quick rinse, he dressed in slacks and a casual shirt and left the room to find breakfast. Dark sunglasses partially hid the wounds around his eyes. A butterfly bandage covered the bridge of his nose. It was ugly, but he couldn't stay in the room forever. With a pronounced limp, he went in search of food.

The lounge with the expansive breakfast buffet was nearly empty except for an older couple who hovered over a guidebook near the window and a forty-something Chinese woman who was immersed in her paper. Behind the paper, her locks shimmered silver and Wayfarer sunglasses perched on her head.

He carried a plate of food from the buffet to a table by the window. In the daytime, the city below was a pattern of cement-colored buildings punctuated by green spaces and the blue harbor as a tinge of yellow smog ringed the air. The mass throng of the city bustled while he dined in silence 102 floors above the mosh pit of humanity. Aromas of caramelized coffee beans intermingled with fruity berries wafted through the breakfast space. It was bone quiet save for the occasional clink of a spoon on china. He swallowed four more of the white pills with his food.

While he sipped coffee, he made another examination of the velour bag and its contents. He had some vague recollection of seeing it on the floor and snatching it as he darted from the room. It was risky, given the woman was bringing a pistol around, but instinct told him it was important. Dried blood discolored the velour and soaked into the golden drawstring. He untied the silk strings and slid the key into his hand. It was long, maybe two inches, with jagged teeth on one end and a seahorse carved into the other end. The seahorse had blood dried in the tiny crevices within the carving.

He didn't recognize the key, but that wasn't a surprise. It must be important to her. Maybe important enough to make her come to him.

And when she did...

The assassin grinned as he sipped his coffee.

TWENTY-EIGHT

Hong Kong

Kira felt like a new woman.

Except for the gun pointed at her head by the man she called Fu.

A fresh set of clothing, although she bought the same cargo pants, light T-shirt, and hoodie, because they were comfortable, functional, and lightweight in the humid Hong Kong weather. Instead of the black cap, she went with a dark blue one. After a full meal complete with vegetables, tofu, and water—lots of water—her muscles still creaked. The cuts and scrapes were painful, but overall she felt ready.

After she crawled out of Victoria Harbour and returned to the Nga Shing Hourly Hotel, there were four burly and capable-looking Chinese men sitting around a card table. Cigarette smoke hung thick along the ceiling, and they were boisterous as they slapped mahjong tiles on the table, drank long-necked beers, and chided each other. Two wore pistols on their belts, and two guns were on the table among the game tiles and the ashtrays. The old proprietor sat in his booth, held his head up with an arm, and watched the four men with half-closed eyes. The bruising around his eye had turned yellow. The tabby walked over and rubbed her side against Kira's leg, and a glimmer of a smile appeared on the old proprietor's face. "See? You safe."

She had nodded and pushed one of the thick rolls of cash held with the rubber band through the hole in the plexiglass. The old proprietor glanced at the money and looked away, but he shoved a key with a plastic fob through the slot. A different room than before.

Before she fell asleep, Kira had gone over her plan in her head for the hundredth time. It was far from a perfect plan and had no guarantee of working. But she didn't know another way to find the assassin or get a message to him. Her sleep was dreamless and deep.

When she woke, she fieldstripped the Glock, cleaned the parts as best she could, and reassembled the gun. After she showered and dressed in her new clothes, she returned to the lobby to find a different set of men reclining on the couch while draping their legs over the chair arms, watching a kung fu movie on the black-and-white television. The card table was cleaned off and sat in the corner, and coffee replaced the beers. The plexiglass booth was empty, and the roll of cash was gone.

After she poured herself a black coffee from the urn, she approached the four men. "Take me to Big Head Bao."

They stared at her blankly, and she repeated her demand several times before one of them flipped open a mobile phone, dialed a number, and spoke into the mouthpiece.

That's how she found herself in the underground

garage of the Rosewood Hotel with a silver-plated .45 semi-automatic pressed to her temple while one of Fu's men patted her down. There was a tiny bandage on Fu's neck where she had cut him with the knife.

"Sorry about your neck." Kira raised her eyebrow at Fu.

Fu made no reply.

Earlier Kira had stowed the leather satchel with the cash, the rusty pocketknife, and the baggie of magic dust in a carry-on suitcase and stored it in the Hong Kong Station luggage storage. She handed the Glock over to Fu, and when his henchman finished the search and proclaimed her weapon-free, Fu led Kira along the concrete hallway to the freight elevator. This time the hallway was populated with a half dozen men toting AK-47s. The large metal elevator clanked and shuddered as they descended. After another series of bare gray concrete corridors, which were guarded by a team of four men, Fu pushed through a set of double doors and led her into a small antechamber. Two tall men stood on guard, each wearing a sidearm and a semiautomatic rifle slung over his shoulder. Serious firepower this deep in the compound.

A Chinese woman sat at a receptionist-style desk and clacked on a keyboard. Her hair was pulled back in a severe bun, and the woman's blouse was clasped tight at the neck. When she rose to usher Kira to the door, the hem of her gray wool skirt fell to her ankles. After she pushed through the double doors, Kira stepped into Big Head Bao's inner sanctum.

She knew this because the massive mural on the wall behind Bao's desk said so. It was graffiti art displaying a comically large rendition of Bao's head while splashes of color oozed across the entire wall. The words *Inner Sanctum* were painted in fluorescent reds and purples, and the letters were almost as tall as Kira. It took Kira a moment to rip her eyes away from the artwork.

"You like it!" The White Phoenix triad leader emerged from behind a massive glass desk. Today he wore a red silk jacket with a Mao collar and tails reaching to the backs of his knees, vibrant white trousers, and white patent leather shoes that shined in the spotlights. The shoes were platforms with two-inch heels, and he made no effort to hide the risers.

"It's...um... It looks exactly like you."

"Why thank you." Bao beamed. "I commissioned it. It's by SEEN. Do you know his work?"

"No, but if you pay me enough, I'll spray-paint you something."

Bao peered up at the artwork. "SEEN is the godfather of graffiti. From New York. I flew him here last year and he painted it while I watched. It was... breathtaking." He swooped over to Kira, took her arm, and ushered her to a crimson leather chair before he leaned back on the edge of his desk. "I'm so happy you're here to see it."

The rest of the office was sumptuous and comfortable despite the concrete walls. The ceiling was two stories high, made of concrete, and covered in sections with sound tiles. Enormous Persian silk rugs covered the floors, at some points two and three deep. A leather couch was against the wall, while an Eames chair was next to a credenza with a turntable and speakers. A record jacket of The Rolling Stones' *Tattoo You* leaned against a floor standing speaker. A bar cart stood in a corner, and three massive ninety-eight-inch televisions were mounted one on top of the other on the far wall, their screens black at the moment.

"Where are my manners?" Bao flowed over to the bar cart and made an elaborate show of dashing vodka into an ice shaker, rattling the shaker all about in a two-handed grip, and pouring them two martinis. He tossed in toothpick-speared olives and practically flew back to where she sat, all without spilling a drop.

"Now. Why are you here again, Ms...."

"Kira. You can call me Kira."

He bowed slightly. "Ah, Ms. Kira then. Last time you left in a bit of a rush, and I was disappointed not to have been able to continue our discussion."

"I need your help."

Big Head Bao sipped his martini and stroked his chin as if that were the sagest thing anyone ever said. "Tell me more."

"My request is predicated on a guess that you are in contact with the people who want me dead. Based on what you told me last time we spoke, you are aware of the bounty on my head. I think you know who wants me dead. If that's not a true statement, I'll be on my way." She placed her martini untouched on a table.

"Your assertion may or may not be true." Bao folded his hands over his stomach. "But let's assume for the time being it is true. One might surmise that you wish those people, whoever they may be, some kind of harm."

Kira shrugged. "I also believe you have a particular gripe with the same people who want me dead. Maybe you have a territory dispute or some turf war going on."

"Now why would you think that, Ms. Kira?" Big Head Bao leaned on his desk. Gone was the ADD-style pacing and swooping around. The triad leader was motionless.

"Because you didn't kill me for the reward. Because you didn't turn me over to them. There's no other reason you didn't collect the bounty than you want to fuck them over, whoever they are. You want to prolong their misery. Also, I noticed a much higher level of security than the last time I was here. Conflict is escalating."

More stroking of his chin. More nodding. Bao drained his martini and set the glass on the desk. "Maybe I meant to turn you over to them before you gouged out my man's neck there." Bao nodded to the back of the room where Fu stood, arms crossed, feet wide.

"Nope. You wouldn't have let me in here. Why risk it? Capture me, kill me, and hand me over. Easy, and you're on to your next conquest." Kira shook her head. "The way I see it is you were about to ask me to do something for you. Maybe hire me or somehow try to make me to do something for you."

Bao rose and hid a smile by strolling away from his desk. The red silk jacket flashed in the overhead spotlights. "Brawn, beauty, and brains. You have the entire package, my dear. So now you propose a trade."

Kira's eyebrows went up. "I do. I want you to pass along a message to those who are after me."

Bao stopped twirling. "You merely want to send them a message? You don't wish to know who they are? Where are they located?"

Kira shrugged. "I'll take whatever information you're willing to give. But most of all, I want to get them a message."

The triad leader paced with his fists balled and balanced on his waist before he spun around. "I'll do one better." His eyes went wide. "I'll let you send them a message yourself."

TWENTY-NINE

Hong Kong

Kira's eyebrows went up.

"But the task I require, my dear, will not be an easy one." Bao's eyes narrowed behind the rectangular yellow glasses. "By giving you access to these people, I put myself and my organization at great risk. The stakes go up tremendously."

Kira sat motionless.

"Also, they must not know how you gained access to them. They must not know it was the White Phoenix."

"I can abide by that constraint." Kira figured Bao was calculating how much he was able to trust her.

Big Head Bao's face became grave, and he paced with his hands clasped behind his back, but there was none of his signature levity. There was a business deal to be done that required all his concentration. Kira observed the transformation with great interest. Big Head Bao didn't become who he was by bouncing off the walls. This was a formidable man who rose to his position of power through cunning and ruthlessness.

"What do you need me to do that your formidable team isn't able or willing to do?" Kira glanced at Fu, who stared at her with dead eyes.

Bao pinched his lower lip, glanced around the room, appeared to settle on something, and leaned with his palms on the glass desk. "As you may know, the White Phoenix has a long and rich history and has been in existence for more than a hundred years. The media and law authorities call us a triad." Bao's face scrunched up. "That is mostly a Hollywood and Hong Kong cinema concoction designed to sell movies. They portray us as gangsters, heavily tattooed, riding around on fast motorbikes, killing everyone in our path."

"The heavily armed guards in the hallways are what then?"

"We are not a marauding band of murderers and thieves. In actuality, we are a guild. Our primary structure is to coordinate resources, combine efforts, and grow commercial organizations. We invest in many businesses from manufacturing to technology to service businesses and everything in between. We create jobs and support our communities where the government either can't or won't."

Bao paced with his arms clasped behind him. "The first so-called triad was started as a secret society with the sole mission to overthrow the Qing dynasty back in the early nineteenth century. The group was called by many names, the Tiandihui, the Hongmen. The Qing ruled in tyranny for three hundred years, and many people died under their regime. The Qing labeled these secret societies as criminal organizations in one of the first fake news or propaganda efforts designed to poison civilians against these groups to prevent their numbers from growing. In the beginning, the Tiandihui were patriots and they saved many lives."

"Naturally these secret societies needed funding. They were labeled criminal enterprises and they were forced into the drug trade, primarily opium, to fund themselves. One thing led to another, and many of the groups attracted bad people and evolved into more diverse illicit activities. They thrived in the chaos and aftermath of the Second World War. When the communists came to power on the mainland in 1949, the new government cracked down on crime, and many of the gangsters moved to Hong Kong." Bao put his arms in the air. "And here we are."

"Fascinating." Kira cocked her head. "You're not whitewashing triad history, are you?"

Bao let out a big sigh. "I'm not going to pretend that every so-called triad is a group of saints or not involved in illegal activities. The 14K clearly violate that assertion. But people want their vices. If they want to escape by using chemicals or human flesh, they're going to do it with or without us." He shrugged. "I'd argue that we do more good as citizens than bad."

Kira crossed her arms. "The operation I took out on Lockhart Road had underage women who were forced to work for slave wages and live in squalor."

Bao put his hands up in a defensive gesture. "The White Phoenix do not traffic underage women. We do not hold women and force them to work. You have my personal guarantee."

"If I find out otherwise, I'm going to end those operations, and I'll shut you down."

Bao waved his hands in a jazz hands gesture. "Trust me, trust me." He shook his head. "I shudder at the mere idea of it. We may not be saints, but..." More head shaking. "No, no, no."

Kira was unsure whether to believe him or not. Big Head Bao was her only route to find out who wanted her dead, and why. Her only path to retrieving the key—the key to unlocking answers to her past. Nothing else mattered. "What do you need me to do?"

After a deep breath, Bao resumed pacing with his arms clasped behind his back. "As I was saying, after World War Two, many of the secret societies fled to Hong Kong to avoid the crackdown by the new communist government. Around that time, a new triad was formed which took on the name 14K. While many of my predecessors simply wished to run their businesses in peace, the 14K sought to establish themselves by forcibly taking territories and opium trade routes, and using bloody violence to do so." Bao visibly quivered.

Do I believe this guy, or is he delusional?

"Today the 14K are very violent," Bao said. "They do not live according to the same code as the rest of us. For decades, we and others have worked to cripple their operations. Worked to tame them. Worked to negotiate with them and bring them to heel. Until recently, they were splintered and without cohesive leadership. They ran as independent subgroups who called themselves 14K but were really just a random band of violent thugs."

"Let me guess. Things are escalating?"

Big Head Bao nodded. "Twelve years ago, a man named Hump Nose Ho was arrested and jailed for loan-sharking and attempted murder. Ho was a mid-level enforcer for 14K then, was released six months ago, and ever since he's been on a mission to pull together the various 14K factions into one massive enterprise. There's an extraordinary level of violence against any 14K leader who opposes him, and he aggressively seeks to expand his territory."

"Are you asking me to take out Ho?"

Bao snorted. "You'd never get close to him. He travels with a large contingent of bodyguards, always rolls in an armored Mercedes, and lives in a fortified compound in Macau."

Oh, I'd get close to him. "So what then?"

The triad leader stroked his chin. "About ten years ago, the 14K made a deal that strengthened their position considerably. Looking back, we're all kicking ourselves for not making the deal before they did. It's a deal that fortified their position with the Chinese government and with one of the Chinese government's allies, North Korea."

Kira's eyebrows went up. "Go on."

"I thought that would get your attention." Bao stopped pacing, although his arms remained behind his back. "The 14K handle all the illicit smuggling operations in and out of North Korea on behalf of the North Koreans." Bao used his fingers in an air-quotes gesture when he said the word *illicit*.

"Why the air quotes?"

Bao snorted. "Because the 14K kick back a significant amount of their earnings from North Korean smuggling to the Chinese government. So while technically illicit, they're legitimatized.

"It works like this: Kim Jong Un likes his luxury items. Cars, caviar, expensive wine, but they're all prohibited from entering North Korea because of sanctions. So the North

Koreans employ the 14K to move the merchandise across the Chinese border in exchange for counterfeit US currency made in North Korea. The North Koreans are the largest counterfeiter of currency in the world. They ship the bills out by the truckload through their border with China to the 14K up north in Shenzhen, where the 14K launders it and distributes it around the world."

"How did you guys miss out on such a lucrative deal?" Kira tapped a finger on the leather of the chair she sat in.

"Ugh." Bao rolled his eyes. "My predecessor was asleep at the wheel."

"So you want to steal this trade from the 14K."

"Of course we do." Bao stroked his chin. "We want to make the 14K appear weak and unable to keep the business. When the North Koreans grow tired of their inept capabilities, we'll be there, ready to take over. For months, we've disrupted their shipments while also making business offerings to the North Koreans. Unfortunately, the 14K have wised up to our strategy."

"Hence the increase in guards."

Bao shrugged. It was an elaborate gesture with his hands, shoulders, and a tip of his large head to the side. "Their answer to everything is more violence."

"Where do I come in?"

"Hump Nose Ho has a daughter. She was educated at Harvard in the US. She did a stint with some investment bank in New York before returning to Shenzhen to join the family business. She's the brains behind the smuggling operation while her father handles the... er... muscle work, so to speak. She runs the logistics, shipping, and the transfer of goods. She also handles the money laundering of the North Korean counterfeit currency."

"A daughter, huh?"

"Ho is in his sixties. Anyway, we've been stealing a few small-scale shipments of the currency here and there. In most cases, we grab a truck and firebomb it with the currency inside. It's small potatoes, but it's getting the North Koreans' attention."

"Where do you get your intel? How do you know where the shipments will be?"

"I'm not going to tell you that."

Kira shrugged. "You probably have people on the inside at 14K. People at a low level who work for cash. By the time they get you the tip, you have to act fast, and each attack is crude."

Bao waved his hand and swished behind his desk, where he produced a tablet about the size of a paperback book. "We've compiled a short dossier on Ho's daughter. Her activities, her known associates, her security detail. Where she lives, where she works. She lives like a successful thirty-year-old who is rising rapidly in her career, albeit a wealthy one. She uses a chauffeured car to visit a private gym each morning at 6 a.m. From there, it's to the office where she eats and works until late. Almost no social life, no known boyfriends or girlfriends, and when she travels, she flies private from Hong Kong International."

"Why don't you just kill her? Her pattern is repeatable and predictable. Sure, she must have some bodyguards, but it looks like she lives and works out in the open. Do a car intervention on her way to the gym or find someone to rig a bomb on the underside of her car."

Bao thrust his hands in the air. "Unlike what you may think, we're not barbarians. Ms. Ho happens to live and work in Tsmi Sha Tsui, a region here in Hong Kong that I control. How would it look if one of our citizens blew up in a bombing or there was a shootout in our streets? Innocent civilians might get killed, and it would be a sign of weakness under my leadership. Even if she is a family member of the 14K. In the eyes of the world, she's a non-guild member and an ordinary, hardworking citizen." Bao shook his head. "No, we've considered such an operation and ruled it out. It was a smart choice by Ho to locate her here. Naturally, our strength is also our weakness."

"Then what?"

"One of the mistakes Ho made when locating her in my territory is I have people in the building where she lives. She owns a penthouse flat at the top of the Peninsula Hotel, and of course, the hotel's general manager and many of his staff are on my payroll. We have arranged to gain access to her apartment."

"For what purpose?"

Bao held up a small memory stick. "On this device is a computer program. A worm, I'm told it's called. Once installed on her computer, it will allow my people to gain access to her machine. We'll own her, so to speak. She's worth more to us alive than dead."

"You have a team of computer hackers on staff?"

Bao chuckled. "Ms. Kira, we are a multibillion-dollar operation with the resources of similar-sized corporations and institutions. Why are you surprised that we possess computer- hacking capabilities?"

Kira shrugged. "If you have access to her apartment, why do you need me?"

"Excellent question. Obviously she takes her laptop computer home with her at night. She also takes it with her to work."

"You need me to enter her apartment while she's at home and plant the worm?"

Big Head Bao leaned back on his desk, crossed his arms, and nodded.

"And, if I'm caught, you need plausible deniability. No connections to White Phoenix."

Big Head Bao smiled and winked.

THIRTY

Hong Kong

The Peninsula Hotel in Hong Kong is one of that city's oldest, most historic and luxurious properties. Opened in 1928 by the Kadoorie family, the Peninsula Hotel in the Tsim Sha Tsui neighborhood of Hong Kong is the flagship of a brand that has grown to twelve properties around Asia and North America. Known for its iconic fleet of Peninsula-green Rolls-Royce cars, the hotel is located on the spot where the governor of Hong Kong, a British colonial official, surrendered to the Japanese on Christmas Day 1941. Today the baroque-styled hotel is home to sumptuous shopping and dining, and is known as one of Hong Kong's most elite lodging establishments. Or so said the internet page she read about the fancy-pants hotel.

Kira slipped through doors at the Peninsula's rear loading dock amid dumpsters filled with the remains of that night's gastronomic culinary experiences. Several white-frocked waiters enjoyed a cigarette before knocking off their shift, and they ignored her as she followed the food and beverage manager through the spotless kitchen and through to a back hallway tight with spare chairs, folded tables, and tall food carts. She was given a room service staff uniform: black pants, white shirt, white jacket, black tie, name tag, and jaunty cap. She was thankful for the cap, as it added to her disguise. The other precautions were a black medical face mask and pair of black latex gloves, which were often worn by food service staff and raised no undue alarm. No fingerprints would remain behind, either in the woman's apartment or in the service area of the hotel. Her face would not appear on any camera footage.

Kira was supplied with a wheeled cart complete with a salad and a heaping plate of steak frites under a metal cover, along with a champagne bottle in an ice bucket. In addition, a single rose sat in a crystal vase in the corner of the tray. If the room service crew wondered who she was, no one said a word. The food and beverage manager, an American from Indiana named Grant, who was also on Bao's payroll, ran interference in the cramped room where the cart was prepared.

She wheeled the cart into the hallway and followed Grant to the service elevator, where he held the door for her as she boarded the lift and punched the P for penthouse. The door closed, and she was alone. Bao had assured her the security cameras in the service elevator and the penthouse lobby area were disabled temporarily. Kira didn't believe him, hence the mask. The tiny USB drive was in her pocket, and she was unarmed save for a fixed-blade combat knife strapped to her left forearm and hidden by the loose-fitting jacket.

"Whatever you do, don't kill her." Big Head Bao's final words rang in her ears.

Yeah, right. If she wakes up and sees me, I'm going to slit her throat.

This late at night, most of the service staff was cleaning up and heading home, which left a skeleton crew of house management and room service. She rode the lift thirty floors to the penthouse, where there were four owned apartments. Ms. Ho resided in number 3025, which faced south and east and presumably offered spectacular views of Victoria Harbour.

Bao's prior surveillance of Ms. Ho indicated an early to bed, early to rise schedule. They learned this by observing her through high-powered scopes from the Sheraton, which was situated to the east and across Nathan Road from Ms. Ho's apartment. For the past month, her lights blinked out at 10 p.m. sharp.

Let's hope she's a heavy sleeper.

Kira had studied the unit's floor plan. The main door accessed a tight entryway which led to a living area with an open kitchen to the left. A guest bedroom or office was to the right, while the master bedroom suite was on the far side of the living area. With any luck, the woman's laptop might be on a desk in the living room or perhaps in the second bedroom. Kira removed a plastic keycard from her jacket pocket and waved it over the lock. There was a faint *snick*, and she pushed on the door.

It caught on a security bar on the inside.

The security mechanism was designed as a traditional two-bar system fitting over a ball attached to the backside of the door. When the door opened, the ball slid along the two bars and caught at the end, which prevented the door from opening farther than an inch.

Kira was prepared. Using her foot, she held the door open as far as it would go, slipped a leather thong around the two bars of the security latch, and tied the leather string in a circle. With the thong held between two fingers, she let the door close to a half inch and slid her hand through the opening. With her hand inside the apartment, she was able to yank on the thong, which popped the ball through the opening in the two bars.

After leaving the food cart pushed against a wall in the external lobby, Kira slipped into the darkened apartment. The lights from the seven million people crushed together on the Kowloon peninsula cast a blue glow into Ms. Ho's apartment through floor-to-ceiling windows. The living area was sumptuously decorated in muted earth tones, and the kitchen, a marble and chrome affair, was spotless. Kira didn't find a computer in the living room or the kitchen.

She crept along the short hallway and stopped to listen at the door to the primary bedroom. No sound. No television. No snoring.

Bao's team, who were assembled across the street on the thirtieth floor of the Sheraton, reported Ms. Ho's lights winked out at ten o'clock, right on schedule. Kira returned to the main room. There were no personal items. No pictures of loved ones. No keepsakes from the occupant's time in college. Only a sculpture of the bust of an ancient Chinese figure Kira didn't recognize and a portrait of Chairman Mao that looked like it was painted by Picasso.

Homage, or satire?

She went through into the guest room, which was furnished like an office with a modern desk made of teak, a white leather couch, and extensive bookcases displaying a collection of economics and finance textbooks. The desk had a spectacular view of Victoria Harbour. It also held a laptop.

Jackpot.

Kira left the door to the office open and sat in the desk chair. The computer was silver with a fruit logo on the cover. She followed the instructions Bao had provided and lifted the lid, which woke the computer from its slumber, and she was greeted with a login screen and an icon of the face of an orange fox along with the woman's name. Kira ignored the login field and groped along the side of the machine for the USB port. She found plenty of ports: something for the monitor, something long and thin, and two tiny ones along with a magnetic mechanism to hold the battery charger which was attached. But no USB port.

Shit.

Her pulse quickened as she glanced around. The desk, like the rest of the apartment, was clean and orderly. She opened the drawers, and she hit pay dirt in the top one, where she found a half dozen dongles made of white plastic. One of them fit the USB drive and had a tiny plug on the other end that fit into one of the tiny holes on the left side.

When she plugged the whole shebang into the laptop, the screen changed to display a field of whirling numbers and characters. According to Bao, this meant the software on the USB stick was attempting to hack through the woman's password.

How long was this going to take?

It turned out to take two minutes, after which a pinkish-gray desktop appeared, cluttered with files and software icons, and she was granted access to the computer's file system.

Not so organized on your computer, huh?

Bao assured her the worm software would only take a few minutes to install, and sure enough, a tiny window appeared with a countdown timer, except the timer showed ten minutes. Her skin broke out into a light sweat, and she went into the living room to ensure the apartment's resident hadn't woken. The flat was silent.

Ten minutes was an eternity. To occupy her mind, Kira snapped off the latex gloves and used the laptop's trackpad to hunt around in the woman's machine. Like her martial arts and weapons skills, her familiarity with the computer was intuitive.

She found a trove of documents relating to Ms. Ho's business that were over her head. Manifests, invoices, journals, ledgers, and endless copies of email correspondence. All the documents were in Chinese, and there was nothing in Hangul, the common language between North and South Korea.

When the countdown timer read five minutes left, a drop of perspiration beaded at her temple.

She kept scrolling and stumbled upon a few personal files, documents with Ms. Ho's personal budget and copies of bank records showing healthy balances. Ms. Ho was a wealthy woman. Kira clicked on a document titled *Journal*, and it displayed a password box. Unsure of how to make the USB worm unlock this password, she closed the journal and kept scrolling.

Two minutes left on the timer.

She clicked into a folder named *Pics* with a couple hundred images, and Kira absently opened random pictures to pass the time. Dozens of images of Ms. Ho in America were found, some taken at what looked like a wealthy collage complete with ivy-covered brick buildings and grassy quads.

When Kira clicked a subfolder labeled *Pak*, the hair went up on the back of her neck. There were only twelve images in this folder, each one showing a handsome man with a shock of black hair and thick black eyebrows who might be either Chinese or Korean. Tall, thinly built, with hollowed cheeks but handsome, with a V-shaped jawline and rugged features like he spent a lot of time outside. A ragged scar ran from his chin across his cheek to his temple, and maybe it was the light or the photograph, but the scar glowed with a faint jade-like color. Recognition hit her hard, and weakness flooded her body as her knees went folded.

I know this man.

But from where? He was young enough to be her brother but perhaps old enough to be her father. The man's face was vivid in her mind and sent shivers all along her spine. Fear and hate blossomed in her, but there was also another emotion she didn't immediately place. Something warmer, maybe paternal. The warmer feeling made her shudder. Regardless, this man was important in her life—or had been at one time.

After she got her emotions under control, Kira examined each picture closely. As she clicked through the images, Kira got the sense this man was Ms. Ho's boyfriend. Maybe they lived apart and he sent her images of himself every now and again. Perhaps a similar folder was on his machine containing pictures of Ms. Ho. It wasn't until the tenth image that her suspicions were confirmed. This one showed the tall man with the scarred cheek standing in a park with his arm around Ms. Ho.

When she clicked on the eleventh picture in the list, an image of the man wearing a military uniform appeared, and she caught her breath. The recognition and sense of déjà vu hit her hard. The picture looked like it may have been a digital reproduction of a Polaroid, or maybe someone had used their phone to snap an image of the physical picture. It was slightly yellowed, and in this one the man was much younger. She exhaled slowly. The man's uniform was North

Korean army and similar to the one Kira wore in the picture she found on the boat.

When she clicked on the last image in the stack, she stopped breathing. Her heart raced, and her legs went rubbery. The countdown timer indicated the worm was done, but she ignored it. If the homeowner walked in, Kira would have been unable to react.

The image was also old and yellow with age, probably a digital reproduction of an older picture. The handsome man with the scarred face was in uniform, but he stood in what appeared to be an outdoor gun range. In the background were a half dozen uniformed North Korean soldiers standing with arms extended, and each held a pistol in a one-handed grip. The image caught the soldiers in a frozen posture, and five of the soldiers stood with their backs to the camera, their right hand extended, their heads facing downrange. These five soldiers were far away enough and obscured by their posture to render them unidentifiable, but it was the sixth soldier's face that caused Kira's heart to skip a beat.

The sixth soldier was shorter in stature than the men and stood facing the camera. The soldier's left hand was extended, but her head was facing the camera, just beyond the shoulder of the man with the scarred cheek.

The face was hers.

THIRTY-ONE

Hong Kong

The handover was an uneventful affair. Kira visited Big Head Bao's inner sanctum and stood around as a team of computer jockeys, as Bao called them, confirmed they were in control of Ms. Ho's laptop.

Bao's face lit up as they downloaded gigabytes of information, and he upheld his end of the bargain by handing Kira a slip of paper containing an internet URL, a username, and a password. "The operation to hunt you is orchestrated through a chat room. Instructions, information on your whereabouts, and reward offers are sent into an account's private inbox. Anyone can apply for an account to receive information about the bounty."

Teams of killers around the world hunting her in exchange for a cash payment. Kira shuddered. "How much is the reward?"

Bao shrugged. "Haven't looked in a while, but it goes up the longer you stay alive."

Kira's eyes narrowed as she waved the slip of paper. "Whose account is this?"

"Mine." He shrugged. "I hope you take this as a sign that I'm not pursuing you or the bounty."

Kira's eyes narrowed. "I guess we'll see about that, won't we?"

―――

After she exited Bao's building, she rode the train north to Fanling, a small town in the New Territories north of Hong Kong, on the light blue East rail line, where she ate breakfast and drank black coffee at a tiny table in a modern coffee shop run by a local family. No reason to go to Fanling, other than it was different, non-routine. This far north, among the Chinese general public, she felt more at ease, and the breakfast was a short respite from her problems.

Before she left Ms. Ho's apartment, she snapped pictures of the images in the Pak folder using her flip phone. While she ate and sipped her coffee, she scrolled through the images. The one of her was both curious and unsettling. Clearly Ms. Ho was in a relationship or had been in a relationship with the man with the scarred cheek and V-shaped jaw. But the man's face niggled at Kira's memory. His face was like a word she couldn't remember. His identity was there, somewhere in her mind, but she couldn't place him.

The anger surged again, and she flipped the phone shut before she tossed a few yuan notes on the table and exited the coffee shop. *Why can't I remember anything?*

It was the scar. Something about the roughly healed wound stuck in her mind. The cut must have been deep, and at least in the photos there weren't stitch marks along the scar. As hard as she concentrated, she was unable to place him.

With the opaque memory of the man's scarred face in the back her mind, she returned south to Hong Kong Island, retrieved a roll of cash from her stored luggage, and entered the Pacific Place mall. There she let herself have thirty minutes of guilty-pleasure shopping and exited with a small black backpack, designer jeans, a safari-style blouse, two new scarves, and a new ball cap. Her old boots were replaced with Converse high-tops, and wraparound sunglasses hid the bruises on her face. The last stop was at an electronics store, where she purchased a small laptop.

One tactic that was drilled into her head long ago was to avoid routine. Routine got you killed, and even though she was disappointed to wave goodbye to the old proprietor, she petted the orange tabby, who mewed in return, and wiped her room clean at the Nga Shing before checking out. In an alleyway, she hot-wired a Honda sportbike with a 650cc engine and a lot of miles. With some of the Lockhart cash, she bought a new black full-face helmet with a dark visor and motored up the windy roads into Hong Kong's Peak neighborhood, one of the most exclusive neighborhoods in the world.

Atop Victoria Peak, Peak Road is considered one of the most expensive real estate addresses in the world. Neighborhoods of 10,000-square-foot homes were interspersed with towering apartment buildings with spectacular views of Kowloon Bay, Victoria Harbour, and the South China Sea.

Before setting out, Kira consulted two sources of real estate offerings and learned homes routinely went for 75,000 to 100,000 Hong Kong dollars per square foot. Her list contained five options, and she took a perverse pleasure in shopping for a new home.

As she cruised along the windy road at a moderate speed, she reviewed her criteria. The home had to have been on the market for a while, which was not difficult to find given the asking prices. It must be a single-family home and not a unit in a high-rise. It also needed to be vacant but furnished. Seclusion was also important—it wouldn't do to have a nosy neighbor see her coming and going.

After two hours of driving and searching, she found the right house. A wrought iron gate gave way to a long drive ending at a lush hillside beside a white stucco house perched with stunning views of the city and bay below. The home was the highest on the mountain so no other house overlooked it. Verdant flowers and freshly trimmed shrubbery made her think a landscaping crew took care of the grounds. Priced at twenty million US dollars, it had been on the market for two years.

She parked the bike off the main road among some greenery, trudged along the black iron fence until she was hidden from view, and vaulted over. The house was four stories with massive patios and balconies overlooking Victoria Harbour. A separate garage with a carriage house above it sat to the north. Enough furniture remained inside to stage the house for an improved buying experience. To her good fortune, the electricity, cable television, and internet were all functional. The only issue was the home's alarm system.

Using the pocketknife, she jimmied open a window on the first floor and stepped inside. She checked the time on her mobile phone as she scampered down the wide, curved staircase to the kitchen, where she found the alarm box pulsing with an alert. Like most systems, this one allowed several minutes for the owner to punch in a code.

Next to a handful of Realtor business cards on the granite countertop sat a three-inch-thick binder, which she flipped open. The folder contained all the useful information about the house. Warranty information, age of the roof and appliances, instructions about how to use the HVAC system. And right on top, in plain sight, was a booklet for the alarm system. On the back of the first page was a handwritten code, which she punched into a keypad near the garage door. The system showed *disarmed* on the LED readout.

Next she reprogramed the alarm system with a new code, which she memorized. The alarm monitoring company and local law-enforcement would be automatically notified of the change, which was a routine occurrence and should not raise red flags. But if a Realtor or the owner arrived unannounced, the alarm would blare and wake her with enough time to make an escape.

The Wi-Fi password was also noted in the binder, and in a kitchen drawer she found a key, which belonged to a side door from the kitchen that exited into a flowering garden well hidden from the street.

Having secured herself a place to stay, she departed the home and rode the motorcycle to a grocery store, where she filled her backpack with provisions, including coffee, packets of ramen, fruits and vegetables, and a newspaper.

By the time she returned to the house, the sun was a red orb low in the yellow sky. After she dragged a chaise lounge to the edge of the master bedroom's patio, she sat down with a bowl of hot ramen, a view of the sunset over the harbor, and her new laptop.

With the machine open on her lap, she stopped after

opening a browser window. Without some kind of secure software, such as a VPN, her browsing would be open to sniffing, tracking, and snooping.

How do I know all this stuff, but I don't remember who I am?

Focus.

One thing at a time.

She downloaded a free VPN service and signed up for it using a free Gmail account. With the VPN active, she accessed the URL Big Head Bao had given her.

After the browser thought for a moment, a webpage appeared in Hangul, the Korean alphabet. Reading the text was easy for her. It was a fan website for the Korean pop music sensation BoA.

She clicked on a video and watched the singer, a young, dark-haired Korean woman named Kwon Bo-ah who apparently went by the moniker BoA, who danced, sang, and writhed on stage.

Am I wasting my time?

In the upper right-hand corner of the website was a login area with text fields for username and password. With her enthusiasm waning, she tried the email address and the line of alphanumeric characters from Bao's slip of paper. When she clicked *Go*, the website let her into a chat room where fans of the K-pop star conversed with each other about the singer's performances. Kira scanned the webpage, where she found chat rooms for all manner of topics, including the performer's recent foray in the American music scene, her outfits, and rumors about her plastic surgery. Kira moved the mouse to shut the window but stopped when she noticed an alert indicating private messages were on the site. She tapped the mouse to open the private mailbox.

The mailbox contained dozens of messages, almost all of them read. Each message subject line started with *Operation Gumiho*. Kira read every message in the user's inbox in chronological order until she reached the one unread message.

Update: Reward Increase.

The message went on to say the reward amount increased to $100,000 after a second failed attempt in Hong Kong. Sources indicate the target remains in the Hong Kong vicinity.

The message ended with the phrase *Good Luck*.

They're going to need it.

After the initial panic from uncovering the communication mechanism by which her enemies coordinated their efforts, Kira read through all the messages a dozen times. The username where all the messages originated was *thanatos*, which was as anonymous as all the receivers of the messages. If she had more sophisticated tools, she might hack into the message board and find out more information about thanatos. Unlike the hand-to-hand combat, weapons usage, and the counter-surveillance techniques, the computer-hacking skills and knowledge didn't appear easily.

Maybe that's not one of my inherent skills.

She closed the message and scrolled through the others. After each failed attempt—the attack on the island, the boat attack, the soldiers at the beach, the attempted kidnapping on Nathan Road, the attack in the construction zone, and the fight in the Nga Shing—a message from thanatos was sent less than twenty-four hours later with an updated reward. Each note was terse in its tone and brief, with little information about her location. Either there was another system for tracking her whereabouts, or it was up to each team to locate her on their own.

The first thanatos message, dated two weeks prior, laid out the rules. Each entrant was responsible for their own gear, financing, and tracking. If apprehended by local law enforcement, the team was disqualified and disavowed. Capturing the target alive had no value. Most importantly, the target was to be killed and proof of death must be via photo, submitted through this chatroom. Death was to be confirmed through local law enforcement. In other words, the body must not disappear. Payment was to be made through wire transfer.

Using the laptop's built-in camera, Kira took a picture of herself with her eyes rolled back and her tongue sticking out. She held the newspaper so the date was visible in the image. Careful not to reveal any background that could be used to locate her, she angled the laptop's built-in camera so only her face from the neck up was visible along with parts of the chaise lounge. She typed a message to thanatos:

Shek O beach at midnight in forty-eight hours.

She attached the picture and hit *send*.

THIRTY-TWO

Hong Kong

She picked Shek O Beach after hours of research. For Hong Kong, it was fairly remote. Busy in the summer with hordes of locals arriving by bus from the city, the beach was mostly deserted at night. There was little nightlife surrounding the area, and by the time darkness fell, most visitors would depart the little community for the city. Miles of rugged shoreline hugged the D'Aguilar Peninsula, which jutted into the South China Sea, where a dozen hidden bays and desolate coves provided cover. There was less of a chance a citizen might stumble into a battle, along with plenty of places to melt away into the wilderness should the authorities appear.

This was also a peninsula that held vague memories of playing there as a child, which warmed her heart as she reconnoitered the area on her motorcycle. The terrain came back to her while she hiked the trails, toting a backpack full of food and her pistol, her hat pulled tight and sunglasses wrapped around her head. The exercise felt good, and midweek the visitors mostly gathered at the beach, with almost no one on the trails winding up to the Satellite Earth Station, a fenced facility bristling with antenna and radars operated by Hong Kong Telecom. If anything was her home turf, this was it.

Finally, some memories.

As she hiked, a plan took shape. The objective was to capture the tall assassin and interrogate him, which would, she hoped, lead her to the source of the price on her head. How else to end the bounty than to end the life of the person who opened it up, who was responsible for the contest? The tall assassin, she figured, had some answers. And he had the key in the velour bag.

Would he show?

If he was anything like her, he would want retribution for his previous failure. Killers like him hated to fail, and his arrogance and cocky confidence would compel him to appear.

Other killers might also show. Those attackers would need to be dealt with before she could concentrate on the tall assassin. Which was why she needed a plan.

To execute her idea, she needed some gear. Throwing her leg over her motorcycle, she wedged on the helmet and rolled into traffic on Cape D'Aguilar Road, which would take her along Shek O Road and eventually into the city.

Colonel Wu relocated to the Ritz-Carlton, where she took a room under the name Mrs. Wang using a forged passport and an untraceable Department 82 credit card. It wasn't that she required the luxurious accommodation, but she wanted to be closer to the North Korean killer.

Is the operation nearing its zenith?

The mobile phone balanced on the railing buzzed with an incoming text message, and Wu caught the device before it fell. Her back was to an enormous pillar, and she sat on a buttery leather stool with her left arm on the railing. A martini, up, neat, and with three onions skewered on a toothpick, rested on the ledge next to the window, where she had an expansive view out over a daytime Victoria Harbour from the 102nd floor. Endless ships and ferries crisscrossed the harbor. The only thing the view inspired was a craving for a cigarette, which was forbidden in the lounge, so she enjoyed a rare alcoholic beverage.

Wu had seen a lot in her long career, a life that had taken her from the lap of luxury in Hong Kong to China, to America, across Europe, back to China, and now finally to Japan.

As the child of a mixed-cultural marriage, most of her life was spent trying to determine who she was, where she belonged. Caught between two cultures where enough animosity remained among the Chinese from Japan's various military excursions into China, Wu never felt entirely comfortable in either place. Required by her father to enlist in the Chinese Ministry of State Security, she worked hard to maintain clandestine relationships on the Japanese side. Had the Chinese been aware, she would have been tried and convicted as a double agent, but she didn't think of it that way. She was merely living the paradox she was born into. Ultimately, her time in the Chinese agency ended at the hands of a Russian operative who persuaded her to betray her Chinese team. She had been ready for the betrayal, and the plans to switch teams to Japan, her mother's country, were already in motion. It was a decision made easier by her father's brain-wasting illness. Her own age and wisdom had brought her priorities into stark relief.

Wu's fingers crept to the faint scarring along her scalp line as she viewed her profile reflected in the pane of glass. The plastic surgery was subtle, not enough to fake out China's facial recognition cameras, which relied on fundamental facial structures that plastic surgery didn't hide, but the nipping, tucking, and nose job gave any human enough pause to make them wonder. The reconstruction, performed in Switzerland, fooled her boss Joe, a man she had known since childhood.

Across from her sat a mother cradling a baby swaddled in a blanket, while the father sat close scrolling on his phone. The woman wore a burka, and her eyes never left the baby's face.

A family. Wu saw a lot in her life, but that's one thing she didn't know. Families, boyfriends, girlfriends, they were all entanglements. Complications to get you killed, end a career, or put a team in jeopardy. Sure, there were flings and entanglements—Joe's face as an eighteen-year-old floated through her mind—but each had ended, and when they did, she was relieved.

Now she was staring down fifty with nothing. There was money in the bank, of course, a few offshore accounts that made her a wealthy woman, but she cared about none of it. She owned no possessions other than a scant few items of clothing and a television that was a useful distraction during moments of downtime, a way to avoid the voices in her head. She eliminated any items of sentiment, dodged pictures, took no keepsakes, and was fast to forget any relationship that came and went. The apartment where she stayed in Tokyo was paid for by Department 82. She slept better in a surveillance van than she did in that apartment.

Why keep doing this? Is there a cottage somewhere in the Japanese Alps, away from everything, where I can go and leave all of this behind? What would I do there? Sit, meditate, and grow mad? Probably eat the barrel of a 12-gauge shotgun. Prop up the weapon and tie a string to the trigger so I can fire it while the barrel is in my mouth.

The buckshot would exit the barrel at 1,100 feet per second and blow the back of her head clean off.

Maybe.

Her body might sit there for a long time and decompose right there on the polished mahogany floor. The kami, the spirits inhabiting the natural world, would not be pleased.

She didn't fear death. Never had. It was an edge that allowed her to take calculated risks, and ironically, allowed her to survive this long. Life rewards the risk taker, after all. She read that somewhere, and her life was a testament to that axiom.

But why go on? What's the point?

Her phone buzzed again, which she ignored and instead contemplated leaving her seat to take a smoke out on the balcony. After which she might pitch herself over the railing and into the night.

The thought made her shudder. What a horrible way to go. All that time to regret the choice as you plummet through the air. *Whoops, changed my mind.* Nope, not the best way to go. Pull the trigger on the shotgun. A flash of pain but ever so brief. And final. You're done.

It's too early.

There's more to do, like finish the recruitment of the raven-haired assassin. It was a purpose of sorts. The asset might become a key weapon in Japan's arsenal. With rising tensions in Southeast Asia, North Korea's renewed nuclear weapons testing, and China threatening to invade Taiwan, Japan recently promised to increase military spending, and the prime minister created the ultra-secret Department 82 to give the country an edge in counterterrorism and intelligence.

And there was the matter of Kira's parents. Anxiety panged in her stomach as she shoved her thoughts away, but not before their faces slid by in her mind.

I'm sorry I let you down, my friends.

And there was Kira. After all her suffering, she deserved a chance. And Wu was determined to give her one.

Wu eyed the three-word message in the secure chat application she used with Neo.

She made contact.

The lounge was half full of well-heeled tourists and suave businessmen from Asia. A piano in the far corner twinkled with an Adele song as waitresses with high cheekbones and short skirts sashayed back and forth ferrying drinks. It wasn't Wu's type of place, but the other bars and restaurants in the hotel were worse: blinking lights and DJs, or dainty plates of food eaten by misguided tourists. No thanks.

With a gulp, she finished the vodka and ate the tiny onions before leaving her spot in the lounge and taking the elevator down the 102 levels to the street below. Someone told her, maybe it was the lady at check-in, that this was the highest hotel in the world.

The things people care about.

Once outside, she crossed over Austin Road and ducked through a gap in a chain-link fence to access the West Kowloon Terminus, a gigantic construction area devoid of people at this time of night. Despite the absence of people, the area was lit brightly by dozens of halogen lamps rigged to tall poles.

To her right was West Kowloon Cultural District, a green space with walking trails and amazing views. She was more comfortable among the grime-encrusted construction zone than in the coifed man-made park.

After lighting a cigarette and inhaling the comforting cloud of smoke, she worked the buttons on her phone to access the secure chat application.

Neo: She made contact with thanatos

Her cigarette forgotten, Wu walked along a row of three shipping containers stacked on top of each other and emerged next to a fence. The plastic sheeting had ripped away, offering her a view of Victoria Harbour.

Here the odor of dead fish mingled with an acrid smell of fuel. Trash and oil slicks floated on the water. This is what the Harbour really looked like, not that filtered view the tourists saw from a hundred stories up. Reality was comforting. With a flick of her fingers, she sent the cigarette arcing into the bay in a shower of sparks before she typed her response.

Wu: Tell me

Neo: Through the chat room, sent a private message directly to thanatos

Wu: Did you trace her IP?

Neo: I surmise she used a VPN as the message originated in Finland

Wu: Smart girl. What did the message say?

Neo: "Getting me dead will cost you a lot more than one

hundred thousand dollars. If you a want a real shot at me, come to the Shek O Beach at midnight."

Wu chuckled.

Wu: When?

Neo: Two days from now.

Wu: Shit. She doesn't know what she's getting herself into.

Neo: She's taking the initiative, just like we expected.

Wu: Does she think the North Korean is going to show up and fall to his knees?

Neo: You sound like a nervous parent

Wu ended the secure chat and lit another cigarette as she walked back to the hotel.

That's exactly what it feels like.

The assassin reclined in the soft velour sofa and enjoyed the action through the window. Through the one-way glass below, a trio of mostly nude dancers spun on silver poles and writhed on stage. A woman lay with her head on his lap, blindfolded, and either dozed or pretended to sleep, or maybe she was passed out from the white pills he offered her. She was still breathing, so she would be fine. He didn't blame her, the last hour was a lot.

The room and the woman cost him a wad of cash, but it was the only place private enough so no one saw his face. The proprietor, an old friend of his great-uncle's regime, arranged everything, including the blindfold.

At his elbow was a glass of red wine, and in his pocket was a bottle of the white pills. He swallowed two more tablets with a gulp of the cabernet as the phone buzzed in his pocket.

He answered. The voice on the other end was feminine and melodic, which was the signature of his remote handler. He had no idea if it was the same woman, or several women all taught to sound the same, or perhaps a male using a device to disguise his voice as a comely female. He wouldn't put it past his uncle to manipulate him in such a way.

"The target will be at Shek O Beach at midnight in two days' time."

"How do we know this?"

"The target sent a message to the thanatos inbox."

Curious.

"A trap." The assassin pushed the comatose woman's head away and walked to the glass. His flexed his knee, which felt much better after a series of cortisone shots and the multiple rounds of stiff anti-inflammatories.

"Obviously. The message went to the community, so there will be competition."

The community. The asinine contest dreamed up by someone high up in the Reconnaissance General Bureau. Someone who needed to get rid of a mistake. Someone pandering to the Supreme Leader.

"There is no competition. Give me the details."

He listened as his handler, whom he pictured as a young and shapely clear-skinned woman in her mid-twenties, provided more information about the target's proposed meeting at Shek O Beach at midnight two days hence. No doubt the Pyongyang military geniuses were astonished how the target, who they perceived to be a brainless tool of death, was smart enough to contact them through the chat room. The assassin had predicted the target would turn the tables and go on the offensive. If she didn't, he would be disappointed.

"There's something else. The target wrote something else."

The assassin's eyebrows shot up. "What else?"

"It's a question. She wrote, 'How is your face looking?'"

Anger surged and the tall Korean assassin punched the wall, leaving a fist-sized hole in the plaster as he roared, "You're a dead woman!"

THIRTY-THREE

Hong Kong

Outpost was in his element. Mud-soaked, dirt caked on his face, and smelling like soil, loam, and vegetation, the North Korean lay among a thicket of Buddhist pine and blue Japanese oak near the so-called Dragon's Back, an undulating trail winding across the peninsula's ridge top. From his location, views of the beach and the bay below were easily accessible through a high-powered scope attached to a tiny tripod. A satphone was in his pocket, powered off, and he had enough rations and water to remain in his position for seventy-two hours.

He was not surprised when the orders came to report directly to Pyongyang. It was routine and he cared little for what might happen to Control. His job was to lay low and perform his tasks with precision and speed. His reports to Pyongyang were monitored carefully, perhaps as far up the chain as Dear Leader. His elderly parents would continue to be taken care of, and Outpost got to do what he did best. The familial feelings for the young woman faded.

As the moon slid across the sky, he waited and watched the tablet as the red dot floated along Tai Tam Road and into the park.

———

It happened to be a moonlit night on Shek O Beach, with the small orbiting moon waxing gibbous, or three quarters bright. She didn't plan it that way, and she didn't care too much, except perhaps the lighter sky may impede any team's night-vision goggles, putting them all on more equal footing, since she didn't have that kind of equipment.

It took most of the previous day to gather the necessary gear and most of today to prepare for the outing. She monitored the chat room, but there were no additional messages. Sleep was difficult, and her mind bounced between fleeting images of a childhood in Hong Kong and the past week of hellish battles. She found herself more comfortable in the day-to-day operations game of countersurveillance and mission preparedness than she did in trying to remember her past.

The old Chinese hotel proprietor's magic powder was gone, and she was back to a morning routine of body-weight workouts, including endless push-ups, sit-ups, and squats. While her muscles and bones were still sore, and dozens of scabs and bruises were scattered across her torso and face, her mind was clear. She made a mental note to return to the Nga Shing hotel and acquire a lifetime supply of that powder once this was finished.

From her perch on the cliffside overlooking the beach, she watched for movement. Although it was unlikely any team appearing here for a chance at the bounty would show themselves, these kinds of things drew all sorts of thugs who called themselves killers but had few skills. From her spot, the tiny crescent of sand called Shek O, which means rocky bay, stood silent. Hulking black rock formations dominating the beach appeared tiny from up here, and more of the rock formations jutting from the placid black water made a series of tiny islands sheltering the bay. The beach was a twenty-minute hike along a steep trail from her vantage point.

For the occasion, she dressed in black cargo pants, light combat boots, and a black form-fitting top. The Glock was secure in her waistband. The only other weapons she brought were a collection of replica throwing knives. A visit to an army surplus store deep in Hong Kong's Sham Shui Po neighborhood yielded the combat boots and the throwing knives, which were marketed to collectors, most of whom had no idea how to use them. An hour of practice in the mansion's living room made her confident. She smiled at the idea of a real estate agent appearing for a showing only to see one wall of the living room pulverized by hundreds of tiny knife holes.

Also in her bag was some parachute cord, a few energy bars, and a bottle of water. All her senses were on high alert. Things would be so much easier if she had a sniper rifle and a night scope. But she would make do. That was the way.

As the midnight hour rolled in and out, nothing stirred. Hitching up her backpack, she slid through the underbrush and emerged onto a tight game trail. Seldom used by the tourists because of its steepness and the fact that it wasn't marked on any map, she encountered no one. After a hundred meters, she stepped off the track, into the overgrowth, and crept silently in the dark.

As she hiked, hazy flashbacks came in waves, ephemeral

visions of time spent exploring these cliffs and trails. In many of the mirages, she held the hand of a woman who towered over her. Try as she might, Kira wasn't able to pierce the murky haze of the visions to see the woman's face.

Damn it. Who is she?

Despite the frustration, the familiarity of the forest and footpaths comforted her. To her right through the foliage, the trail wound around an outcropping with an overlook of the beach. Careful not to disturb the trees in front of her, Kira stopped and peered through the branches. Two dark forms huddled on the rock shelf with a long, dark object between them. Ever so slowly, moving branch after branch out of her way and stepping lightly on the dirt ground, Kira edged closer. Gradually the two forms took the shape of humans, one huddled with his eye on a scope, the other prone with his face pressed to a rifle stock.

A blade flew silently through the air and impaled itself into the shooter's neck. A second blade sank into the spotter's windpipe. She darted after the knives, using a third blade to end the lives of the sniper team before she retrieved her blades, cleaned them off on the men's uniforms, and sank into the underbrush.

Wishes may only come from fairytales, but sometimes kismet provided. After waiting ten minutes to ensure no one noticed the activity, she eased from the thick foliage and performed a quick search of the dead men's bodies. The rifle itself was a QBU-88, a bullpup-style gas-operated semi-automatic rifle with an effective range of 500 meters. Like the terrain around her, Kira found herself familiar with the weapon. The brochure indicated a range of 1,000 meters, but that was a lie. She folded the tripod, slung it over her shoulder, and stuffed two additional ten-round box mags into her cargo pockets. The shooter had a mobile phone, which she left behind. The scope was a Chinese knockoff with night vision on a small tripod, which she stuffed into her pack before ducking back into the undergrowth.

How many more sniper dens were there around the cliffs overlooking the beach?

After checking two more spots on the cliffside where she might consider setting up a sniper rifle, she took out one more team. The remaining locations were empty.

At the last spot she checked—a sheltered, rocky ledge with a small cave where she found an empty pint bottle and a condom wrapper but no attackers, and thankfully no used condoms—she made her own overlook with the scope.

It was now about 12:30 a.m., and nothing moved on the beach. She scoured the sand, water, surrounding cliffs, and dark restaurants with the night-vision scope. No one. After stowing the scope in her pack, she set off through the underbrush on a little-used game trail that sloped down to the beach.

Did she take out all the sniper rifles? She suspected there was a team or two lurking to the side of the beach ready to pounce.

Time to set some bait, and the only bait she had was herself.

———

The choice of Shek O beach didn't surprise Wu, for she knew more about Kira's upbringing and past than she ever planned to admit—to Kira or anyone else. In times of crises, people like to return to where they know, locales where they are comfortable. Wu was pleased with Kira's choice, as Wu herself was familiar with the beach and surrounding area.

Hunkered along a black chunk of rocky island called Ng Fan Chau with her eye to a rifle scope, Wu touched the comm device stuck in her left ear.

"Report," she whispered. A quick check of her watch showed 12:30 a.m.

"Nothing, boss. It's quiet. Nothing happening."

The report came from a SFG operator, who Wu requisitioned from Tokyo along with a few other resources. She convinced Joe that this was the endgame, one way or another. Either the asset survived, in which case they would bring her in, or she died, in which case they would retrieve the body and bring her home.

The SFG operator was stationed at the edge of a small mansion's grounds off the east end of the beach and only a minute boat ride across the black water from Wu's position. The home was vacant, and the soldier was hidden in a camouflage blind also with a night-vision scope on a tripod. "Wait."

Wu's eye left her scope and peered at the moonlit beach.

Her SFG operator sounded again in her ear. "Movement on the west side of the beach."

Wu swung her rifle scope to the left. A jumble of rocks covered the west end of the sand, behind which was a shuttered BBQ restaurant with open seating on a wooden deck overlooking the beach. During the daytime, the bar was popular with locals who came out to watch the beachgoers from the city. It took her a moment to find the movement, and when she did, she sucked in her breath.

A dark shadow the size of a young woman appeared among the rocky formations at the west end of the beach. The form hovered and glided among the stones, invisible except to the sharpest eye or clearest night-vision scope.

A faint buzzing sounded on Wu's left out over the water. It was almost whisper quiet, and only her ears, honed from decades of attentive audible observation, were able to pick it out. Her eye left the scope and she scanned the water.

A black shape the size of a rubber Zodiac attack craft skimmed along the water with four heads bobbing to the rhythm of the surf.

———

As she clambered over the rocks and through the stone formations, Kira sensed a dozen eyes were on her.

Probably my imagination.

Her head on a swivel, she picked out several places where someone might be hiding. A row of large homes with short fences walling off their pools ran along the eastern shore across the bay from her position, and a rocky outcropping was in the middle of the bay within eyeshot of the beach. Someone or a team may be waiting in one of the darkened restaurants lining the beach.

Kira crouched and leaned her shoulder against the pitted rock worn away by millennia of water and wind. The air was heavy with salt, and there was no breeze. The still water shimmered black in the moonlight.

She scanned the beach. At 200 meters long, the small strip of brown sand was usually jammed by visitors. At this hour tonight, no one was around. Maybe her adversary didn't take the bait, maybe he was laid up with a broken knee, or maybe he didn't want to show his marred face in public.

Several things happened at once. At the far end of the

beach, a solitary figure appeared. At the same time, her ears detected a faint sound from over the water.

The lone form at the eastern end of the beach grew closer, a tall man with a leash attached to a medium sized dog. He strolled as the dog frolicked in the water. The buzzing from out over the water grew louder in an approaching crescendo. From her vantage point, the far western portion of the bay was hidden from view by the rocky formations, so she shifted her position to find a better view of the water.

A bullet whizzed, and another chunked off the rock near her face. She ducked and leaped to another spot behind a rock as more bullets flew and ricocheted off the rocks.

After she poked her head out to get a look at the beach, the man and his dog ambled in her direction, still a hundred meters away, apparently oblivious to the whizzing bullets.

Who walks their dog this late at night?

The pair were far enough away that she wasn't able to make out his features. But there was no limp in his gait, and Kira was sure the killer's leg was severely damaged.

She returned her gaze to the black ocean and spotted the source of the gunfire. A small boat raced at her with four black human shapes on board. She dropped prone onto a smooth rocky platform, partially hidden behind a waist-high chuck of rock, flipped open the rifle's bipod legs and flicked off the safety.

No time to dial in her target, but the range was closing fast.

THIRTY-FOUR

Hong Kong

Colonel Wu tracked the racing boat using the night-optics scope on her rifle as four men in dark outfits braced themselves against the gunwales. One held up a rifle. Foolish to fire from the speeding boat, but maybe they were testing their luck.

An urge told Wu to leave the rifle and dash to where her own Zodiac raft was tied up and speed to Kira's rescue. The maternal instinct caught her off guard. It was a primal impulse from the recesses of her brain, and instead, she cautioned herself to remain calm, have faith in her asset. This was not a problem for the young assassin. Wu's comms crackled, and the voice of her SFG soldier appeared in her ear.

"We got a civilian. Walking along the water's edge."

Wu swung her scope across the beach from left to right and found a man ambling along with his dog. Through the scope, she scrutinized the dog walker. Tall, thin, and wearing a light jacket, the man was older with scruffy facial hair. No weapons were visible, but he walked with no discernible limp, stoop, or other malady that might afflict the aged. The dog was a golden retriever who bounced carelessly along the beach, sometimes in and sometimes out of the gentle surf.

"We sure he's a civilian? Awful late to be out walking your dog."

"Negative, boss. Not sure. Didn't see where he came from."

Sharp cracks came from her left, which she realized were bullets plinking off the rocks interspersed with the sounds of suppressed muzzles reverberating over the water. Wu swung the rifle to her left and found the speeding boat. It was on a plane approaching the beach at speed. One man, hunched low in the back, manned the tiller while two others crouched with assault rifles, spraying the beach with gunfire. A fourth man lay prone on one rubber gunwale, prepared for landing.

To help Kira or not to help? And what about the civilian?

"Boss, any orders?"

"Stay put."

"What about this civilian?"

That's no civilian. There was no evidence to support her claim, only her intuition.

"I said stay put."

"Copy that, boss."

―――

The buzzing from out on the water grew louder among the whizzing bullets and turned into the sound of a muffled engine. From Kira's position crouched behind a rock formation, she picked the black boat out from against the black surf. Four human forms rode in the speeding Zodiac, two on knees braced against the tubular gunwales, firing on her position with assault rifles. They were aware she was there but didn't know her precise location. Instead they were laying down fire to cover a beach landing.

With her eye to the rifle scope, she acquired an enemy's head, which bounced around in the optics as the boat planed through the placid water. Take out the boat driver first, which might slow their progress and create turmoil on board. With no time to dial in the target, she shifted the scope a fraction to acquire the torso. Better to make a hit in the body and do some damage than miss a head shot all together. After she sucked in her breath, she willed her body to calm and her heart rate to slow.

How do I know how to do this?

When her pulse receded, she pulled the trigger.

Blam.

The unsuppressed rifle blast echoed around the bay. The boat's driver shuddered and lurched, and his hand fell away from the tiller.

The boat raced ahead. One of the gunmen abandoned his prone position and moved to the helm. A cascade of bullets plunked off the rocks around her position as the remaining shooter keyed on her muzzle flash. She ignored the gunfire and maintained her position.

A slight adjustment, and the scope found the shooter. She pulled her trigger as the boat hit a small wave.

Blam.

The bullet plunked into the rubber splash guard. Again she pulled the trigger, and this time the round hit the oncoming shooter. The bullet entered the man's shoulder and he spun, dropped the rifle, grabbed his arm, and fell into the boat.

Only seconds remained until the Zodiac hit the beach. Now closer, it offered a larger target. Another rifle shot from Kira ended the life of the driver. The fourth man, who was prone on the bow, rolled from the black raft into the water while the boat plowed through the remaining twenty meters of water and onto the sand.

Using her scope, Kira scanned the black water but didn't see the fourth attacker's head. Lifting her eye from the rifle, she peered at the placid water. A quick glance along the beach didn't reveal the civilian. He was probably chased away by the rifle blasts. The dog wandered the beach alone.

That's odd. Why would the man abandon his dog?

How long until the police showed?

There was a sound behind her, something scraping on rock. With her adrenaline-heightened senses, it was louder than a rifle crack.

The three men in the black Zodiac fell one by one from rifle shots among the rocks, and Wu stopped holding her breath.

That's my girl.

"The civilian is on the move, boss."

She lifted her eye from the scope as the tall dog walker sprinted across the beach. Rather than run away from the gun battle as she would expect a civilian to do, the man ran toward it with limp. The dog stood on all fours on the beach, tongue out, watching the running figure.

Wu returned her eye to the scope and followed the

sprinting man. From this distance, in the dark, hitting a running figure was a tough shot.

And we don't know his status. Attacker? Or dumb-ass beach walker trying to help?

She took her eye away from the scope, scanned the water for the fourth boatman, and found him on the waterline maybe a dozen meters to the east from where the boat had beached itself. She swung the rifle and picked up the man's head in her optics. The round, black shape disappeared into the inky blackness, so she returned her gaze to the beach, and the civilian disappeared among the rock formations.

Be ready, Kira.

Wu's vantage point was both a blessing and a curse. Help, or don't help.

The head of the fourth man reappeared on the water, closer to the cliffs and now to the left of Wu's position.

The sound of a scuffle came from among the rocks and rolled across the water: a clang of metal against stone, a grunt.

The head in the water moved rapidly to the shore.

Using her night-vision scope, Wu searched for Kira or the dog walker among the rocks.

Nothing.

The head in the water glided to the beach, hugging the rocky shore until shoulders and a back appeared. Wu acquired the form in her scope, took a moment to calm herself, breathed out, and fired.

Pfft.

The fourth boatman slumped into the water.

THIRTY-FIVE

Hong Kong

Kira flung herself to the left and held onto the rifle, careful to keep the jutting rocks between her and the shore. The knife blade flashed in an arc right where her stomach had been a split-second ago. The glint of moonlight off the knife's razor edge caught her eye, and she rolled again as the attacker swiped the knife a second time. The blade was familiar: a tanto-style black-coated KM2000. Popular among German soldiers, but this attacker wasn't German. His features and his movements were familiar, but something was off. His hair was gray, and his face was distorted.

It was a disguise. From afar, he appeared old and wizened. Up close his appearance was muddled, but it was the same killer from the Nga Shing.

As the assassin thrust the knife again, she swung the rifle and connected with his arm to deflect the blade. With a grunt, the man easily parried her second swing and knocked it from her hand, where it clattered to the rocks a dozen steps away. His balance off, the attacker stepped back, favoring his left leg. She yanked the Glock free from her waistband.

She performed a fast draw and fired with the pistol close to her waist. The draw was practiced and smooth and she got off two shots, but the attacker was gone. A split second later, a whirling foot caught her hand and knocked the pistol to the sand.

The tall killer followed the right-foot crescent kick with a left-foot roundhouse kick that connected with her arm and sent her spinning to the ground.

So much for his knee slowing him down. Maybe he had some of the special powder.

The pistol was several meters out of reach. She rolled and scampered to her feet and produced her own knife, one of the throwing blades from the army surplus store.

The attacker stood with his blade in an attack position, feet apart, opposite hand up. "I must say I'm enjoying our encounters." He spoke in Korean.

A closer look by the moonlight revealed a wound across the attacker's nose and deep bruising around his eyes that he poorly hid with makeup. In this knife fight, she was at a sizable disadvantage with her short arms and smaller knife.

"Your face looks like shit."

The taunt resulted in a snarl by her tall attacker. "It'll heal. You, however, will not heal when I'm done."

She flicked her knife in an underhanded, no-spin throw while drawing a second knife with her left hand. She rushed in with the second blade using a hammer attack. The thrown knife impaled itself in the attacker's deltoid. Despite the wound, he parried her hammer attack by stepping aside, gripping her shoulder, and using her momentum to fling her into a rock outcropping, where she hit the stone with a jolt. When she spun and shook off the collision, a whirl of motion came at her.

He was on her with a lightning-fast attack of the knife in a traditional thrust of the seven-inch blade. Her attempted parry with her off arm barely knocked aside the blade, and the tip plunged into her oblique and sliced deep into her side. The attacker followed the lunge with a left hook to her jaw. The punch was off-balance and lacked momentum, but his fist caught her face hard enough to send stars shooting through her vision.

Still close, he thrust the knife and sliced open her quadricep. The Korean whipped the knife around and the tip dug into her bicep, where it hung up on bone.

Dazed from the punch and woozy from the loss of blood, she took advantage of his proximity and thrust her knee into his groin.

With a grunt, the attacker fell back, hunched over, and his eyes hardened.

Her breath was ragged as she backed away from the rock. Dizziness swam over her, and she fought it and pushed it away.

I'm losing blood.

The attacker's eyes blazed with fury, and he came at her as she attempted another knife toss. The blade glanced off his chest. Before she could draw another knife, the attacker's knife sliced through the air and caught her across the abdominals in a deep, long cut.

Kira's hand went to her stomach, where she felt warm, viscous liquid. Her knees grew weak as bile rose in her throat.

The attacker's face broke out in a grin as he stood back and tossed his knife from one hand to the other.

Death by a thousand cuts.

The beach and the rock formations around her wavered and swirled as her vision clouded. *Wake up, damn it.* A flick of her wrist and another blade appeared in her hand, which was slick with blood. The attacker separated into three men, shimmering and morphing back into one before separating again. The muscles in her legs grew weak, and she fought the urge to sit.

The blurry form in front of her paced and faltered. He leaned over with his hands on his knees before standing and ripping the throwing knife from his shoulder.

A moment of clarity flooded her vision as the man straightened and stepped toward her with the knife out. The blade swayed and he fell to a knee. His chin sank to his chest before he struggled to rise.

Again the man in front of her wavered in and out of focus, splitting into three men and returning to a single attacker.

Time floated as an apparition appeared in front of her eyes. It was a woman all in white, with a white robe and snow-white hair to her waist.

Wu?

No, Wu was shorter and squatter and from the streets. The apparition was ethereal, monastic, tranquil. Larger than life, the woman in white towered over Kira with her arms outstretched like a cross. Her face was deeply wrinkled, but her eyes shone and sparkled with a knowing grin on her face. The woman in white floated a foot above the rocks, and a feeling of warmth washed over her.

Is this the end? Is this when I meet my maker?

The glowing apparition dissipated and in its place rose the attacker, dark and hooded with devilry. The seven-inch blade sliced at her in a final coup de grâce meant to end her once and for all, except now there were three of them, attached like triplets, hazy and shimmering.

Which is the real, flesh and blood man?

The middle one.

A surge of adrenaline coursed through her as she realized the woman in white was not the end but instead was the beginning. It was someone she knew, somehow, somewhere. Someone who would help her. Help her heal. Help her remember.

I'm not ready to be done.

Kira ducked and sidestepped to her left and moved inside so she was under the knife attack. As his knife drove down in an arc, she shoved her own blade into the man's sternum. With all her weight behind it, the blade sank to the hilt. The razor-sharp knife pierced his breastbone and the tip plunged into his left aorta.

The attacker's blade swung and impaled her shoulder.

That's going to leave a scar.

It was her only thought as the attacker's heavy body fell on top of her and his blood ran freely from the embedded knife handle onto her back, shoulder, and neck.

Shit, shit, shit.

Through her scope, the two fighters staggered back from each other. Both were wounded. Kira took a step and stumbled on the rocks. The Korean put his hands on his knees before he caught another wind and raised the large knife for a final assault. He came in high and thrust the blade down in an arc at Kira's neck.

Kira ducked low and to the side, brought her own knife up, and almost dodged her attacker's knife before it sliced into her shoulder. Wu lost sight of Kira as the two fell to the ground in a tangle of arms and legs. The mass of two humans hit the rocks and remained still.

Damn it.

A siren wailed in the distance.

Come on, Kira. Get up.

Across the bay, among the black rocks that glistened in the moonlight, nothing moved.

Screw it.

Maternal instinct took over, and Wu let it. Dread grew in her belly. It wasn't so much that she succumbed to the maternal instinct, but instead she chose to use it, to harness it. There was a time to let Kira fly free and a time to bring her in.

If I'm not too late.

Wu hitched the rifle to her back, shouldered the rest of her kit, and scrambled down the slick rocks to the water's edge where a black Zodiac was hidden among a formation of black boulders. She shoved the craft into the surf, leaped aboard, and cranked the engine.

Am I too late?

As she made a wide, sweeping turn and pointed the vessel to the scene of the fight, something stirred among the black rock formations. Wu wedged the tiller into the crook of her leg, yanked a tiny night-vision scope from her vest pocket, and trained the lens on the two bodies.

The big Korean attacker lay face down over Kira's smaller frame.

He moved.

The sirens were loud, and so was the surf whooshing in Kira's ears.

Or are they birds darting and weaving around her head?

Songbirds, that's it. Calling from far away. A pretty sound, the happy call of one feathered friend to another, or maybe to her.

Come, Kira. It's okay now. Everything is okay.

Aches and sharp pains permeated her body. Her stomach, in the same place the thug from the jungle cut her. Her shoulder throbbed. And so much pain in her side that maybe it was cut open with blood gushing from the exposed flesh.

I should stanch the blood.

Despite the logical thought, she remained motionless.

Did she pass out?

Don't know.

Dead weight was pressed on her sternum while thick, viscous liquid mixed with the ocean water made everything slippery. With a weak heave, she pushed at the weight, but it was unyielding. As heavy fatigue washed over her, an unwavering desire to go to sleep permeated her mind. That's all there was.

Lay here and fall into a peaceful slumber with the ocean sounds in my ears.

The birds called to her. The songbirds evoked visions of sunny skies with white fluffy clouds and butterflies. Lots of butterflies in a field. A field of soft clover. An apparition shimmered in the sunlight.

The woman in white.

She stood hovering above the waving grasses with her arms outstretched, white robes fluttering in the breeze. A black and yellow butterfly landed on the woman's shoulder.

A rising and falling wailing jolted her, and the vision

vanished. Sirens. Sirens mean safety. Rescue.

Sleep now. The sun-washed clover is so comfortable.

The field of clover shimmered into view again, except the woman in white was farther away, a tiny figure floating in and out of view.

Among the wail of the emergency vehicles was the faraway purr of an engine.

I know that sound.

An outboard motor. The purr crescendoed in volume, its gentle buzz clear across the placid water. The songbirds, the clover field, blue skies, and the woman in white with the butterfly on her shoulder faded away as an image formed in her mind. An image she knew too well. Something she trained on constantly, repeating drills in a murky ocean.

Roll off into the surf and disappear beneath the waves. Catch the side-rope and hurl myself into the speeding boat.

So many drills. That noise was the engine attached to the rear of a Zodiac.

As the sirens grew louder, something jolted awake in the primitive part of her brain, the part of the brain that regulates fight or flight.

The buzzing of the approaching boat.

These sirens are not safety.

Danger.

Wake up.

Adrenaline surged. With a grunt, she pushed against the heavy body that lay atop her and managed to roll it to the side. The effort took everything she had, and she lay back in the warm water as nausea swam through her. As bile and liquid came up, she turned her head to spew it on the rocks. She fought the queasiness as she pushed herself to her hands and knees but slipped, and her chest hit the slick stone.

Something metallic glinted on the rock to her right.

A thought registered. *Something of importance.* A key?

With a heave, she got onto her knees, and she reached out to the tiny metallic object. It was one of her throwing knives. Not a key.

The key. Find the key.

After she snatched the knife, she scrabbled up the slippery rocks on her hands and knees to the killer's body and rifled through her attacker's pockets. It was a panicked effort, and her fingers slipped on the buttons and the Velcro held against her feeble attempts.

Slow is smooth, smooth is fast.

She slowed and methodically went through the attacker's pockets.

The loud sirens blared in her ear. Red and blue lights appeared and flashed repeatedly among the wet rocks.

How far is the road from the beach?

An image of the Shek O strand of sandy beach appeared in her mind.

I have less than a minute.

In one pocket was a wad of cash. The other pockets were empty.

No key.

In a flash of desperation, she ripped open the Korean's shirt. Gold glinted in the blue and red flashing lights. The antique key with the seahorse was on a leather thong around his neck. When she grasped the key and yanked, the thin strand of leather gave way, and her momentum, fatigue, and lack of balance sent her tumbling down the rocks and into the surf, where she fell with a splash. Her head hit a rock, and stars sprang through her vision.

Once again, the overwhelming desire to sleep overcame her as she lay back into the tepid water. Into the darkness.

THIRTY-SIX

Hong Kong

Rushing air pushed Wu's hair against her forehead. With the tiller trapped in the crook of her leg, Wu lifted the scope to her eye as Kira's form tumbled down the rocks and splashed into the surf.

Get up, damn it.

Wu cranked the throttle to make the craft go faster, but the engine was already wide open. The hull planed on smooth black water as salt water sprayed Wu's tactical clothing.

Emergency personnel swarmed the sand from both ends of the beach. Red and blue lights flashed over the scene from a dozen police vehicles. Men, with their weapons out, walked toward the rock formations. They were cautious but moved with intention and training. So far they hadn't appeared to have noticed Wu and her racing raft, which was black against the black water.

Kira still lay face up in a deep well of water at the ocean's edge formed by a cluster of rocks.

Wu's only viable weapon was a compact Glock 19 pistol in a holster at her side. It was a 9 mm with the standard fifteen in the magazine and one in the chamber. The barrel was retrofitted with a threaded barrel, and a short suppressor was attached. The weapon was ineffective at the current distance, especially with the boat bobbing on the surf as she sailed along at top speed.

If it came to it, would she kill a member of the Hong Kong police department to protect Kira? The question weighed heavily as the boat sped across the water and she gauged the timing of when the men might discover the fallen fighters and her own trajectory across the water. She kept the engine's throttle wide open.

Let's hope it doesn't come to that.

At first she bobbed in the water, but the water washed away the blood and cleansed her skin. It was warm, reminding her of bathwater, and it fueled her desire for sleep.

Her head went under, and she took in a lungful of salt water and jolted up, sputtering. When the water cleared from her throat, all energy left her body and there was nothing left. Not even the woman in white appeared.

Time to sleep.

She let herself lay back in the warm bath, and this time, when she went under, she stayed there. Water filled her lungs again, but she didn't notice. Darkness engulfed her.

Goodnight.

Wu aimed the craft straight at the rock formation. As the skiff bounced over tiny waves near the shore, the tall black rocks loomed in the murky darkness. From afar, the rocks appeared small and insignificant, but now they were the size of houses and effectively obscured her approach from the police and rescue personnel swarming the beach. As she let off the throttle to slow the boat's approach, she pulled the Glock free.

Blue and red lights danced, twirled, and glinted off the glistening stones. Shouts from the law enforcement team echoed across the water.

When the boat's bow bumped against the rocks, Wu leaped out and trapped the gunwale rope under a rock to snug the boat so it wouldn't float away. As she turned, there was movement in the corner of her eye. She raised the gun as a man in tactical gear appeared from among the towering rocks.

He froze. His right hand clutched a pistol, but he used both hands to steady himself against the slippery rocks and the barrel was pointed down. He wore a tactical vest and a ball cap with night-vision googles pushed up on the cap's brim. His eyes went wide as he stared at Wu's pistol.

With the pistol steady in a two-handed grip, Wu pointed the barrel at his chest. Probably a member of Hong Kong's special duties unit, a tactical unit of police who focus on counterterrorism and other serious crimes.

The soldier was five meters from her position. She put her finger to her lips. "Drop the weapon."

The man glanced at the rocks behind him.

"Drop it or I'll drop you."

The pistol clattered to the rock and splashed into a pool of water.

"Lay down."

As the soldier went to his stomach, Wu clambered over the rocks, yanked a set of plastic cuffs from his belt, and secured his wrists.

"Keep quiet, or I'll put a bullet in your head. Understand?"

The soldier did his best to nod while he lay on his stomach.

Wu turned and raced to where Kira had fallen, her head submerged in a pool of water. Wu yanked her up by the shoulders of her tactical vest.

Please be alive, please be alive.

Kira felt nothing when she was jerked out of the water by the shoulders of her tactical vest. Her lungs, full of seawater, didn't react. She didn't notice when her head hit something hard but yielding and she didn't feel the second pull, nor did she realize her back bounced off something wet. She didn't notice the momentum as the boat increased the speed, nor did she feel the chilly air against her wet clothes. The bumps against the surf went unnoticed, and she didn't hear the cracks of rifle shots.

All she saw was darkness, and the only sounds were the calls of faraway songbirds.

Bliss.

The tiny body was light, and Wu was able to haul her from the puddle of water and fling her over the Zodiac's gunwale into the boat.

"What's the situation?" It was her SFG operator in her ear, situated in a blind on the east end of the beach.

"She's lost a ton of blood." Wu panted and held a finger to Kira's neck. "Pulse weak, not breathing."

"Wounds?"

"Too many to tell. Blood everywhere." Wu positioned Kira on her back and started CPR. "Probably water in her lungs."

Wu pushed on Kira's chest, slowly, rhythmically, and counted to herself. "Come on. Breathe, damn it."

Kira coughed, and Wu held her head sideways so she wouldn't choke. Kira sputtered and spat out seawater.

"She's breathing again."

"And the assassin?"

Wu reached over and put a finger against the killer's neck. "Dead." Sirens blared as Wu tossed Kira's rifle into the Zodiac. She permitted herself another full minute to scour the area, found a throwing knife on the rocks, and tossed it into the boat. A Glock pistol lay in a puddle of water, and she tossed that into the boat before she yanked the blade from the North Korean's chest. A cursory glance revealed no brass casings. Using her mobile phone, she snapped a picture of the dead Korean's face.

Voices emerged from over the sand beyond the rocks.

Time to go.

"Exfill, exfill." Wu issued the command for her SFG operator to vacate his position, and pushed at the front of the rubber craft, splashed into the water along with the boat, jumped in, and scrambled to the rear to fire up the muffled engine. Kira lay on her back in a puddle of water, her shirt soaked in blood.

After she tossed the backpack into the water sloshing in the floor of the craft, Wu cranked the tiller hard to the right and opened the throttle. She yanked out her pistol and glanced over her shoulder at the shoreline. As the rocks receded, a half dozen men appeared in the vicinity where Kira fell. One man stooped to help the trussed police officer while another pointed out over the water and shouted.

As the boat got up on a plane, Wu trapped the tiller against her leg so the craft drove straight and squeezed off a half dozen pistol shots that pinged off the rocks over the men's heads. The police scattered and ducked for cover. A minute later, she cleared the rock formations guarding the bay and was out in the open ocean.

She dug out a satphone, and with one hand on the tiller she keyed in a number with her thumb. When it connected, she yelled to be heard over the engine and the wind. "Coming in hot. One wounded. Need medic standing by."

A kilometer out in the South China Sea bobbed the *Nishino Maru No. 68*, a 115-ton crab fisher flagged in Japan. In addition to the ship's crew of ten ocean-hardened Japanese, a half dozen Department 82 support staff were crowded in the ship's galley. Since they were blatantly violating Chinese territorial waters in a zone known for conflicts between China, Japan, and Taiwan, the crew was sweating it, eager to return to Japan's waters.

The reply was faint among the wind and engine noise. "Copy that."

The rubber gunwale of her craft bumped against the *Nishino Maru*'s hull, and Wu caught a rope ladder as it was tossed from above. A SFG soldier scampered down the ladder, flung Kira's inert body over his shoulder, and climbed up. When she was safely aboard, the *Nishino Maru No. 68* got underway, dragging the Zodiac alongside as it plowed north and east on a course that would take them to the American military base in Okinawa.

Mess gear was cleared from the galley table, and the bloody woman was laid out. On Wu's orders, two Department 82 analysts were stationed as guards to prevent the fishing boat crew from catching a glimpse of their new visitor. As a Department 82 medic tended to the woman's injuries, Wu stood over Kira and used one of the razor-sharp throwing knives to open a cut on her bare shoulder. She traced the knife's tip along a preexisting scar and made a deeper two-inch incision. After snapping on a pair of latex gloves, Wu dug her finger into the opening, fished around, and emerged with an electronic device about the size of a large vitamin. The device's existence was one of the pieces of actionable intelligence passed along by Colonel Choe, the North Korean defector. She used the butt of her pistol to pulverize the device and left the wound for the medic to close as she exited the galley to the decks above.

The dark sea rose and fell as Wu stood at the railing in a blustery wind and gave Joe an update with the satphone at her ear. "I'm sending you a picture of her attacker. I'm almost positive it's Kim Nam Il."

"No kidding. Isn't that—"

"Yup. It's his nephew. Another reason to get her out of there. Better she's not officially tied to his death."

Silence filled the gap between them for a moment before Joe replied in a measured voice. "You're right. I assume you're taking her to see Tomoe?"

"That's affirmative."

Outpost did everything possible to prevent emotion from creeping into his voice as he reported the facts to the unknown recipient on the other end of the satphone. The assassin was dead. Law enforcement swarmed the beach. The target was plucked from the rocks by an unknown operative in a black boat. The target's status was unknown. Possibly deceased. Possibly not.

He was told to remain in Hong Kong and await further orders.

When the blinking red dot on the GPS tracker winked out, a tear rolled down Outpost's face. Not because it meant she died. The GPS tracking device in her shoulder would stay powered on as long as battery remained. It meant the loss of a connection with her, and for that Outpost wept.

THIRTY-SEVEN

Near Kamikochi, Nagano Prefecture, Japan

Through the Land Rover's window rose a jagged granite cliff that disappeared into the mist. Scraggly juniper sprouted from various cracks and fissures, and along a ledge or two rose thick pines, their trunks curved up in an effort to find sunlight. From her position in the back seat, Wu rolled the window down and inhaled deeply, letting the heavy air laced with pinyon soak into her lungs. With a hand cradling a lit cigarette hanging out the window, she peered up in an attempt to make out the top of the cliff as the SFG soldier piloted the vehicle up the muddy road.

Fog encased the cliff face. Mist dampened everything, and the occasional raindrop splattered on the windshield, promising heavier precipitation later.

As a longtime resident and frequent visitor to these mountains, Wu knew the terrain well. Long ago she memorized the topography and spent countless hours trekking through the narrow trails and along the steep embankments.

The cliff top was accessible via a winding hike through cedar trees estimated to be thousands of years old. At the summit, one can walk out onto a rocky ledge, usually made wet by the constant fog and rain or snow in the wintertime, and on a rare clear day gaze over an expanse of snow-capped peaks and lush valleys.

Or jump off.

If one planned one's own trajectory correctly, the body would smash into gritty rock in an inaccessible valley and lay there for days, weeks, or maybe months, until an Asian black bear or maybe a raccoon dog picked away at the carcass's soft areas. The eyeballs, cheeks, fingers, and toes would go first. The bear might dig into the belly, open the intestines and stomach, and expose the innards to other wildlife like the red fox or the sable-like creature called the Japanese marten. Eventually the body would decompose, maggots would take over, and her cells would sink into the loamy dirt. Ten years later, her bones would be all that was left, her soul returned to the earth. She might return to conscious life as a Japanese snow monkey, the macaque, and spend her days in search of hot springs and succulent ferns.

Sounds nice, except for the trip down. Too much time to think about it, to have second thoughts, regrets.

She flicked her spent cigarette into the fog and glanced into the back, where a makeshift stretcher was fashioned. A small body lay on the stretcher under thick blankets to ward off the mountain chill. A SFG medic rode next to her, monitoring the patient's vitals. On the boat ride across the East China Sea, Kira's blood was replenished and her wounds were treated and dressed, and they fed her an IV of saline and vitamins every few hours. Still, she remained unconscious.

Periodically, headlights from the chase Land Rover

flashed through the rear window where three more SFG operatives rode. Wu lit another cigarette and ignored the medic's glares.

When a clearing opened in their headlights and a massive wrought iron gate towered overhead, the vehicles ground to a halt. The gate was black metal decorated with intricate carvings of lions and dragons. It towered overhead at least three stories and was conjoined to fifteen-foot-tall fencing on either side. The black metal fence was adorned with more of the animals, which were meant to help ward off evil spirits. Sharp spikes lined the top of the fence, and vegetation choked the fencing as it disappeared into a thick forest of conifers and cedar.

As the gate opened silently, Wu toggled a radio and spoke to the rear vehicle's driver. "Remain here. Leave the engine running. I won't be long."

Her SFG driver exited her vehicle, along with the reluctant medic, leaving Wu to drive through the gate, which closed tight behind her. She shifted into four-wheel drive low and picked her way up a rocky and muddy two-track.

The drive wound through an impenetrable forest overgrown with vegetation. Branches clawed at the sides of the Land Rover and scratched the paint as they climbed. All of this was special for the injured woman in the rear. Ordinarily, no vehicles were permitted on the monastery's property, and Wu hated to drive.

The grounds of the monastery were situated on this mountaintop for almost as long as the thick cedar trees grew. No one knew for sure, but records of the monastery's operation dated back to the Nara Period when Empress Genshō, the forty-fourth monarch of Japan, commissioned the Buddhist sanctuary and bankrolled a monk named Saicho to build and establish the religious compound. The empress herself was rumored to escape to the vast grounds for her own contemplative retreats. Since that time the Buddhists controlled the grounds except for a brief period during World War II when Emperor Hirohito commandeered the facility for a war-time escape. In the modern era, the grounds served as a functional monastery and a training facility for Department 82.

When a cupped-tile roof appeared atop a low-slung building built of cypress wood, Wu pulled from the track and came to a halt in front of three robed figures. In the center was a tall woman with flowing white hair, alabaster skin covered with an impossible number of wrinkles, and her hands clasped in front of her under the flowing sleeves of a white robe. Two shorter and younger women, both with silky black hair and wearing robes the color of sand, bowed slightly as Wu exited the Land Rover. The two aides withdrew the stretcher from the vehicle's rear and disappeared through the wide-open doorway of the building, leaving Wu alone with the woman in white.

Wu approached the tall woman and bowed deeply. "We are in your debt, sensei Tomoe, and I apologize for the use of the vehicle."

The white-robed woman's return bow was shallow, but her face was open with a dreamy smile. "You honor us, Colonel Wu. The transport cannot be helped under the circumstances. Come, join me, please."

The monastery's sensei skirted the long building and led Wu along a flagstone path through a grove of manicured pinyons where fine, bright-green moss covered the intertwined roots. Earth, loam, and grass fragrances filled the air as a light rain began. Mists swirled, at times obscuring the trees and buildings, other times parting to reveal splendid details of pinyon or carved balustrades.

They passed several buildings, all in the same low-lying architecture similar to the first structure, which Wu knew to be various temples and places of worship for the monks. More than a few of the buildings were constructed with open sides. A pond filled with red and orange koi fish was ringed by reeds that swayed in a breeze. Once past the group of temples, they hiked through a cluster of bamboo and thatch huts surrounding a field. The field was used for martial arts training. No one was present now. They walked through another stand of conifer to arrive at a structure open along all sides, made of dark mahogany and roofed with tile in the Japanese tradition.

After she kicked off her sandals, Tomoe led a barefoot Wu through the building to the rear, where two cushions sat next to a broad rock garden open to the rain. The two women sat cross-legged on the cushions, which made Wu wince as she bent her legs in the proper manner. An aide in a beige robe appeared and poured them each green tea from a large kettle. As the rain pattered on the garden's polished stone, the two women sipped under the protection of the eves.

"It wasn't so long ago that you appeared on my doorstep in a similar condition." Tomoe cupped her mug in two hands.

"Wasn't it? It feels like an eon has passed."

And you look exactly the same as you did back then. How does that happen?

"Time is an illusion, Colonel Wu. Time is what we make it."

Wu sipped her tea.

"Was it difficult to return here after so long?" Tomoe breathed in the steam from her cup.

"This isn't about me." Wu cast about for a place to smoke until she remembered where she was.

"Isn't it?" Tomoe's eyes crinkled at the edges as she smiled.

Ugh. Is everything a damn riddle?

A long moment passed in silence, interrupted by the aide returning to deliver a fresh pot of hot water and pour more tea. As the young woman departed, she practically glided along the black wood floor without moving her feet under the thin, sand-colored robe.

When the aide vanished from sight, Tomoe smiled again. "The timetable moved up, I see."

"It accelerated faster than we wanted. I know what it's like to wake up here alone and fearful. Eventually she'll realize this is home. I'd prefer to be here when she awakes, but alas, I have business to attend to in Tokyo."

"Anything to avoid staying." Tomoe sipped as one eyebrow went up.

"I'm here, aren't I?"

"Are you, though?"

When does it stop?

The nicotine craving washed over her, and Wu patted her pockets for the smokes before she realized they were in the Land Rover where she left them. On purpose.

"I can't make you stay." Tomoe cupped her tea mug. "But take a rest. Stay here with us. Train your mind. Rest your body. When you are done, you'll be better prepared for whatever awaits you in Tokyo."

"Joe needs me."

"Another illusion created by your own mind."

Wu bowed from her seat before she stood and shook out a leg to allow the blood to flow. "Sometimes duty supersedes the ego. Don't let her die, sensei. She's in an extremely fragile position."

Nodding into her tea, Tomoe frowned and remained seated. Turning her head, the sensei's eyes roamed the vast rock garden. "She will be taken care of here."

There is nowhere safer. Although invisible to the naked eye, the acolytes trained here in the ancient ways of the samurai, and its remote location made the monastery one of the safest places in Japan, maybe the world.

Wu took two steps and turned. "She still has severe memory loss. She has no recollection of her past. Let's keep it that way, at least until she can discover it for herself."

Tomoe's gaze lingered on the massive rock at the garden's center. "It would be better if you are here when she wakes."

Wu turned her back and strode along the slick black wood to the entrance, where she slipped her shoes on and walked out into the rain.

THIRTY-EIGHT

Four weeks later, near Kamikochi, Nagano Prefecture, Japan

Bombing Rocks Tokyo; Fifty-six Dead

Tokyo, Japan – A brutal act of terror rocked downtown Tokyo this morning that left fifty-six people dead, including school children and teachers. The incident, which took place in Shinjuku Gyoen National Garden during the peak of sakura viewing, has sent shockwaves through a city and nation unaccustomed to violence.

The bombing took place at 10 a.m. local time as busloads of school children entered the park to view the flowering cherry blossoms, a national treasure and symbol of peace between Japan and its closest ally, the United States. The explosion that originated in a landscaping van resulted in extensive damage to the surrounding area. Another seventy-six people have been taken to nearby hospitals, many with life threatening injuries.

The Japanese prime minister quickly condemned the attack.

———

Wu closed the browser on her phone and shoved the device into her pocket as the SUV parked in front of the monastery's wrought-iron gate. Investigation of the bombing fell to Department 82, and Joe was under pressure to produce results—fast. It took every ounce of energy Wu could muster to convince Joe to let her make the trip out here to the monastery. She trudged up the muddy drive and met Tomoe in front of a small torii gate painted bright red.

Tomoe bowed and led Wu along a worn dirt path that wound through dwarf juniper and rode the edge of a yawning chasm that opened into a valley. A stream raged at the bottom of the long cliff as it meandered on its path along the Chikuma-Shinano watershed. Today the air was clear, and the snow-capped peaks of the Japanese Alps were in high definition against a polarized blue sky.

The crisp air was full of loamy scents that soothed Wu's troubled mind. "I assume you heard about the bombing in Tokyo."

"I have." Tomoe walked ahead of Wu and practically hovered over the muddy and root-crossed trail while Wu trudged along behind, mindful to keep her footing. Despite having no internet, television, or radio in the compound, Tomoe was well informed. She maintained a team of spies in the external world who reported back information about world events.

The sensei halted and turned to Wu. "It's a shame, all this senseless bloodshed. I'm shocked that this kind of violence has found its way to Japan's shores."

"Conflict in the world is escalating," Wu said. "Japan is strengthening its military as North Korea fires test missiles over our sovereign lands. This is why the prime minister formed Department 82. This is why we need Kira."

Tomoe made a clucking sound in her mouth. "And yourself, I suppose."

Wu bit back a retort. Tomoe's preference was for Wu to remain in the monastery and ceaselessly train and meditate, do chores, and prepare to take over after Tomoe's eventual passing. But somehow, Tomoe remained ageless. Wu bowed slightly. "A ship was built for the high seas, not to remain in port."

When Tomoe made no response, Wu changed the subject. "How is she?"

The sensei stepped off the trail at a tiny clearing offering an expansive view of the surrounding mountain range and the valley below. Wu stopped next to Tomoe and breathed deep.

Tomoe crossed her arms so each hand went into the opposite sleeve. "Better than I expected she would be by now. Against my wishes, she's embarked on a rigorous fitness regimen, although she doesn't eat enough."

"That's a good sign." Wu removed her sunglasses and chewed on one of the earpieces. "The fitness, that is."

Tomoe made a harrumphing sound. "There is something you should know."

"Tell me."

"She hasn't spoken a word since arriving."

"Nothing in four weeks? That's troubling."

"Agreed, which is why I summoned you. I'm hoping a friendly face will spur her to open up."

The sensei turned and pushed aside overgrowth, while

Wu followed along a hidden path she knew by heart. During her own lengthy and tumultuous stay in the compound as a young woman, Wu trekked these trails thousands of times. As the path wound through thickets of conifers, they were offered glimpses of the surrounding mountains. After another ten minutes of walking, the trail opened into a small clearing where a wooden deck jutted out over an open cliffside. The observation platform was bare of furniture and offered no railings, and the wood was weathered to a mottled brown. At the far edge of the deck sat a solitary figure in the lotus position facing the open expanse of the valley below.

Tomoe stopped at the clearing's edge. "Please, Colonel Wu. Keep it brief."

After she bowed slightly, Wu trudged along the trail. She kicked a few rocks in an effort to make her presence known. Sneaking up on a troubled assassin was a bad idea. Before stepping onto the platform, Wu glanced over her shoulder. Tomoe was gone.

Wu edged around the side of the wooden deck until she was at Kira's two o'clock, at which point she sank into a painful cross-legged position. "I really must start a yoga practice." One knee jutted out over the expanse. Far below was the thin gush of a waterfall among the wet rocks and moss-colored sage. The whoosh was audible this far above. The green hues of the foliage popped in the warm, overcast light.

Long way down.

Kira's brown robes were threadbare and dingy but clean, probably the same vintage as the robes Wu wore during her stay decades prior. In the tradition of newly indoctrinated acolytes, Kira's hair had been shaved off, and now a dark stubble covered her head. Her hands were clasped under her robes. Black eyes sparkled as she stared out over the expanse, but her cheeks were gaunt.

"They tell me your wounds have healed nicely." Wu placed one hand on each of her kneecaps. "Do you have everything you need?"

The assassin stared out over the abyss.

From Wu's position, she studied Kira's profile. High cheekbones. Pert nose. Full but humorless lips. Wu shook her head. *Of course you don't have everything you need. You're missing your memories. But sometimes, that's a good thing.*

A butterfly with yellow and black wings and red spots flittered over their heads and landed on Kira's knee before taking off again and disappearing into the woods. Kira's eyes followed the insect until it disappeared.

"Tomoe says you're not eating enough."

The trainee's face remained placid.

"Listen, Kira. I know you're in pain. And I don't mean the physical kind. Losing one's memory is a terrible thing, but you're in a safe place. Tomoe and the rest of the acolytes will take good care of you. You can stay as long as you'd like. I'm unsure if Tomoe mentioned this, but I stayed here for four years when I was about your age."

The only indication the young assassin heard her was a slight frown when Wu said her name.

Wu pulled a photograph from her jacket pocket and set it on the wooden deck next to Kira, who looked at it with a sideways glance.

The image was of a tall, trim, and handsome Korean man in a military uniform with his breast covered with two rows of medals. The man's black eyebrows were furrowed in a frown and his V-shaped jawline belied little mirth. His rugged face was marred by a ragged scar running from his temple, across his cheek, and ending at his chin. "Do you recognize this man?"

The assassin's reaction was immediate and visceral. Kira's nostrils flared and her pupils dilated. Her breath came out in puffs until her gaze flicked away from the photo out over the valley, at which point her breathing resumed its placid state.

Wu slipped the photo back in her pocket. "I guess that's a yes, which confirms my suspicions about your time in North Korea. We believe that man is responsible for your incarceration in North Korea."

Kira cocked her head. "Incarceration?"

Wu nodded and stifled a smile. "I'm going to tell you what I know about your past, Kira." *Or at least some of it.* "Are you ready?"

Kira shifted so she faced Wu, but she remained in the lotus position. Like Wu, one knee jutted out over the empty chasm, and her hands rested on her knees. "Yes."

With a deep breath, Wu watched the black and yellow butterfly as it reappeared and fluttered along the edge of the chasm before it disappeared behind her back. Kira's eyes hadn't left Wu's face.

"You were abducted by North Korean agents when you were five years old."

Kira's little finger twitched.

"The North Koreans have a history of doing this sort of thing." Wu shifted slightly to take some pressure off her knees. "The idea is to bring skills to North Korea they don't have internally, like Japanese speakers to teach classes. They once kidnapped a South Korean movie star couple to help their own movie-making efforts."

"Kidnapped from where?"

"Here. Japan. A small town on the shore of the Sea of

Japan called Murakami about four hundred kilometers from here."

The young woman's eyes left Wu's face and peered out into the valley. "I'm Japanese?"

"You are."

The assassin's face softened as she took a deep breath, held it, and let it out. She bowed her head for a long moment and when she raised it, moist eyes found Wu. "I'm not North Korean?"

Wu shook her head.

Relief flooded her. "How long was I in North Korea?"

"From the age of five until you were placed on that island in the South China Sea."

Kira's eyes narrowed. "That's a long time."

Wu nodded. "Twenty years."

"I'm twenty-five?"

"Yes. Your birthday is in April."

"How do you know that man kidnapped me?"

"The man's name is Pak Yong-ju. He's a senior official in North Korea's RGB intelligence group. Rank of lieutenant commander, we believe. Most everything we know about Pak comes from a senior Reconnaissance General Bureau official who defected last year. Our working theory is after you were kidnapped, the North Koreans discovered you had a set of skills they wanted to exploit, or perhaps they trained you from an early age."

"To do what?"

Wu shrugged. "Clandestine operations. Counterintelligence, spying, black ops. Assassination."

"I've seen pictures of that man." Kira told Wu about the images on Ms. Ho's computer. First, the one showing her in the background, and the second image of Pak standing with the woman and the boy.

Wu's eyebrows came together as she listened. "That implies Pak had, or is having, a relationship with Ho, the daughter of the head of the 14K."

Kira nodded.

The silence was interrupted only by leaves rustling in the breeze as Wu considered the implications.

"You didn't have this intel?" A smile appeared on Kira's face before it quickly disappeared.

Wu bit the inside of her cheek. "We didn't."

"How did I come to be on that island in the South China Sea?"

"We don't know all the details, but we can speculate based on information provided by the defector. The groundwork and plans for the operation were formed during his tenure. The RGB realized they weren't able to control you. We're told you made a couple escape attempts, and you were disruptive and disrespectful to authority. Our guess is there was one final straw, and someone above the defector's level decided to make a game out of your... ahem... demise.

Rather than stick you into a labor camp, he decided to formulate a test. It was a test for the people you trained with. Again, we're speculating with some assistance from the defector, but they stuck you out on that island and informed their teams how to find you. The idea was to test their people and at the same time eliminate a problem."

"And how do you know me? My birthday, my age?"

As Wu sighed and bit back her nicotine craving, a Japanese leaf warbler flew overhead. The tiny wings sounded like gunshots in the stillness.

Kira's face fell. "You're not going to tell me, are you?"

The lesson Wu was taught percolated through her memory. Seduction is like foreplay. Don't go all in. Dole it out over time. Give and take. Give enough to keep them hooked. Take less than you give. Think of Maslow's hierarchy. Before she can graduate to love and belonging, the subject needs food, shelter, and safety. Build on those foundations. Establish the trust bits and pieces at a time. Once the base was strong enough, gradually add more until self-actualization.

"It's going to take time is all."

"Why?"

"Because this is bigger than you, and it's bigger than me. We want to help you. But—"

"You want something from me in return."

Wu tilted her head to the side. "Not so much that. Just like you have to trust us, we have to know if we can trust you."

The assassin bowed her head.

"Tomoe will take good care of you here." Wu glanced around the small clearing to ensure they were alone. "You're safe here. You can stay as long as you want. You can make a home here. You're among friends."

A tear appeared on Kira's cheek as she slipped the key from inside her robes where it hung on a leather thong around her neck. "Why did you give me this key?"

Wu smiled. They found the key in the young assassin's possession when they brought her aboard the Japanese fishing trawler *Nishino Maru No. 68*.

"I'm happy to see you managed to retain the key. That key will unlock a small box. In the box are several of your possessions. Things from your childhood. Things that may trigger memories."

Kira's eyes fell. "What happened to my memory?"

Wu shook her head. "We don't know. I'm sorry. I wish I knew."

Another tear rolled down Kira's cheek.

"There's one more thing," Wu said. She removed the picture of Commander Pak and set it on the wooden deck in front of Kira. "This man, this Commander Pak, has possession of your box."

"The box that fits my key?" Kira's eyes focused and her lids narrowed.

Wu nodded.

"Where is he?"

Wu shrugged. "Hong Kong or Shenzhen. It's all we know." Next to the picture, Wu set a bundle of yuan notes strapped with paper, a Chinese passport, and a mobile phone. Unlike the flip phone Wu provided her before, this one was heavy and resembled a small tablet. "That passport is clean. There is a legend behind it that will hold up to scrutiny. The phone is secure and cannot be tracked or hacked."

Wu rose to her feet, which made her knees crack. "I would join you, but I'm needed in Tokyo. Best not let Tomoe see that stuff."

When Wu stepped away from the platform to return to the front gate, the butterfly returned and settled on Kira's knee.

At 5 a.m. the next morning, an acolyte in a sand-colored robe appeared at the doorstep of the thatch-roofed hut at the edge of the cluster of tiny buildings that housed the trainees. Kneeling, as was the custom, she placed a tray on the ground with a pot of hot green tea and a bowl of rice, fish, and seaweed mixture. After a light tap of her fingers on the wooden door, the acolyte hurried away and back to the kitchen.

As the young woman scampered along the trail, she wondered endlessly about the newcomer. The student who lived in the tiny hut was different than the rest of the trainees, and the acolyte was filled with curiosity. For the first week the woman stayed in her bed, covered with wool blankets, and received only Tomoe as a visitor. During the second week the woman ventured out and began long training regimes that included running along the mountainous trails and hours of tai chi, karate movements, and other solo martial arts exercises. Despite or maybe because of the newcomer's injuries, her fitness levels were impressive. The woman spoke to no one, simply ate what was offered and made no requests. She abided by the simple yet unyielding rules of the monastery and made no complaints. Her only sign of emotion was to make deep bows with her hands pressed together in gratitude.

Once, when the black-haired newcomer stooped to retrieve the bowl from the acolyte's tray, a key hanging on a lanyard around the young woman's neck slipped out of her robes and the acolyte glimpsed a seahorse carved into the bronze handle. The woman's brow furrowed and there was a flash of anger before she shoved the key into the folds of her robe and her face returned to serenity.

When the young acolyte's kitchen duties were done, she returned to collect the tray, stunned to find the food untouched. This never happened. Curiosity piqued again, she listened at the door and heard nothing. Was the newcomer out on an early run on the wilderness trails? She took the tray and retreated a few steps, but returned as alarm blossomed in her mind. What if the woman was hurt or incapacitated?

After a rap on the door with her knuckle yielded no response, the acolyte pushed gently on the door. It swung open to a dark interior. She stepped inside.

The hut was empty, the bed was made, and what few belongings the woman had were gone.

With the tray of food left forgotten, the acolyte ran to find the sensei, a deep sadness within her heart.

THIRTY-NINE

Hong Kong

The month-long stay at the monastery taught her one thing about herself: She didn't like being caged. Sure, there were no locks on the door to her hut, and once, during a long hike through the property, she followed the tall wrought-iron fence to the solitary gate and determined it was also unlocked. The internment was an unwritten rule. Answers to life's mysteries were to be found within the gates and walls of the monastery, not without. Only by committing oneself to a years-long meditation may true enlightenment be discovered. Of course, that also guaranteed Tomoe years of free labor.

Kira chuckled to herself as she dodged a lorry, crossed Chatham Road, and hastened into the Garden of Stars. Behind her were a cluster of tall offices and apartments, but she was surrounded by greenery. Bronze statues were interspersed with clay tiles with handprints, each on a waist-high pole. In the garden, the cacophony of the city died away, and she found a spot on a bench across from one of the handprint tiles with the name Jackie Chan.

After she sat, she brought out the mobile phone Wu provided. The phone had heft, a thick glass screen, and beveled silver edges. There were no brand markings. After she powered it on, she found a browser and a secure chat application with a single entry.

Gray Sable: Did you make it across?

Kira powered off the phone and stowed it in her pack. It wasn't that she didn't trust the gray-haired woman who chain-smoked like she wanted to kill herself. She didn't know if she could. The distinction was important. What did Colonel Wu want? She acted like she wanted Kira to trust her, but she was also distant, remote, and withheld information. For what purpose? She had something to hide, something she didn't want Kira to know. What was her endgame? To what end was Colonel Wu deploying all the deception?

Why did Wu provide Kira with the information that Pak kidnapped her before she provided cash, a passport, and a phone? It was as if the woman primed Kira and set her loose. Was it a test, or was there a larger game afoot where Colonel Wu and this intelligence department wanted Pak dead?

Her thoughts turned back to the monastery, and despite her lack of trust in either Wu or Tomoe, the place was what she needed at the time: a balance of the feral and the civilized, a safe respite away from the constant pressure of being hunted, time to recover from her wounds. The physical wounds, that is.

Except the silence was maddening. There was nowhere to get away from the voices in her head. The ones that asked who she was, what her life was like, and how Wu was involved in it. The voices never quit, despite how hard she willed them to stop. The only way to make the voices halt was to train her body and her mind. Even the training became rote, so Wu's visit to the monastery was opportune. The place had served its purpose.

Now it was time to go. Act. Get moving. Chase a purpose. But purpose follows action. It was the only way to make the voices stop.

And Wu had provided her with a purpose. The box that fit the key. Find it, and find out something about herself. It didn't matter what it was. Her memory of herself was such a blank that anything might help. It also didn't matter that Wu may have an ulterior motive. Kira would only make one decision: Find the box, which meant finding Pak. The man who disrupted twenty years of her life, robbed her of her childhood, ripped her away from her parents, incarcerated her, and trained her to be a killer. Anger boiled over, but she pushed it away.

The best fighter is never angry. The Taoist mantra arose from somewhere in the recesses of her mind.

The park reminded her of the monastery: quiet and serene with nothing to interrupt her churning thoughts, so she hopped to her feet and made a circuitous route through the green space and around the block, all the while watching for a tail or surveillance. She noticed nothing, so she backtracked and crossed the footbridge over Salisbury Road to the Avenue of Stars, turned southwest, and ducked down the ramp into the parking garage beneath the Rosewood Hotel. If anyone knew Commander Pak's whereabouts in Macau, it would be Big Head Bao.

Unlike last time, Kira called ahead. After she was frisked, she walked into the cavernous office of the White Phoenix triad leader, where Bao strutted around in a fashion runway's version of military garb. Gone were the flamboyant platform shoes and silk shifts and yellow glasses. In their place were skintight cargo pants, a formfitting olive drab shirt with plackets, and army boots with some fashion logo Kira didn't recognize. There was also a sidearm in a sagging belt holster, like a Western gunslinger. The whole ensemble screamed runway revolutionary, some designer's take on military guerrilla wear.

"What?" Bao stood in the middle of his office with his arms extended.

Kira stifled her grin. "Nothing. I just... I liked the white platform shoes."

"I'm at war, sister. I can't get blood on those white platforms. Besides, my wife assembles the outfits." He waved at the desk. "I can't be trusted to get it right. What? What now?"

Kira failed to hide a giggle behind her hand. "You have a wife?"

"Of course! I'd be lost without her. What did you think, anyway?"

Kira shook her head. "Oh, nothing. Nothing at all." She caught the eye of a guard, whose face was blank. She had passed through two formidable barriers of guards on her way in, and four men stood around the permiter of the office wearing automatic rifles. The men in the room were not your garden-variety bodyguards. They were tall, muscular, attentive, and well armed.

"Why are you here, sugar?" Bao dragged a finger across the glass surface of his desk. "And where have you been? I thought you were dead."

"I'm not dead."

"Are you here to help with my fight against the 14K? A fight, I add, which has escalated since you single-handedly took out an entire platoon of their men. You kicked the hive. They're out for blood."

Kira crossed over five silk rugs on her way to the glass desk, where she placed the photo of Commander Pak. "Do you know this man?"

Bao picked up the photo. Gone was the sashaying and prancing and galloping. The triad leader's lips were set in a permanent frown, and his gestures were deliberate and slow. Battle-ready Bao was different than peace-time Bao. His frown deepened while he scrutinized the photo.

After he returned it to the desk, he walked over to a couch, sat, and crossed a leg. "I know this man." His brow creased, and that combined with the frown made his face dark. "The most important question is why do you have a picture of him?"

"How do you know him?"

"You answer a question with a question."

"I'm going to kill him."

Bao's eyebrows shot up, and there was a flicker of something on his face, but it happened so fast that Kira wasn't able to discern its meaning.

"I would caution a mere mortal against such folly," Bao said. "You, my dear, are no mere mortal, it seems. Still, it's a risky gambit. May I ask why?"

"My reasons are my own. Let's say it's personal."

"Is there any other reason?" Bao rose and walked to the bar cart, which was empty of any liquor bottles. Tall glass water bottles replaced the booze, and Bao poured himself a glass, chugged it, and filled it again before handing a full glass to Kira.

"No alcohol during war?" she asked as she sipped.

Bao nodded. "I need all my faculties."

"How do you know him?" Kira asked, and watched Bao's face carefully. The triad leader was reserved when it came to discussing Pak, and Kira wanted to learn why.

The triad leader paced. "He's North Korean. He partners with 14K. He's North Korea's outside representative for their smuggling operation. Cars and caviar go into North Korea, counterfeit hundreds go out. 14K handles the whole business, and Pak oversees the 14K. Essentially he's Dear Leader's watchdog. 14K brings the cars and whatnot into Shenzhen and arranges the transfer over the border in partnership with Pak's men, then they arrange for distribution of the fake currency on this side. It all goes in and out of the Port of Shenzhen, just north of here."

Kira nodded. "What happens to the 14K's operations if Pak is out of the picture?"

Bao eyes searched the far wall for a few silent moments before he shrugged. "North Korea sends another man."

"What happens if Pak is out of the picture, and the head 14K guy is also gone?"

"Ho?" Bao's eyebrows rose again. "Well, I suppose that business may be up for grabs. Maybe the North Koreans lose faith in the 14K."

"Especially after Pak and the 14K failed to take me out. Pak's stock with the North Koreans will be at an all-time low."

Bao tapped a finger against his chin. "Maybe the North Koreans look for another partner."

"And you eliminate a major source of income for the 14K, which negatively affects their ability to wage war against you."

"I'm picking up what you're laying down." Bao's fingers

stroked his chin. "It would help if the North Koreans didn't know we helped. What do you have in mind?"

"Can you provide a crew of White Phoenix who are unknown locally? Import a crew from somewhere else?"

Bao nodded slowly. "Manila."

"Can you find a location not known to be affiliated with White Phoenix? A place where we can hide some semitrucks?"

Bao nodded some more. "You'll take out Ho?"

Kira nodded.

"And all you want in return for all of this is Pak?"

"Yes, and I need him alive."

FORTY

Port of Shenzhen

The shadow dropped to the ground inside the fence and crouched to watch for movement. Her entry into the warehouse compound was silent and required only a pair of wire snippers, which made quick work of the barbed wire strung along the top of the fence. The signs warning of an electrified fence were either a ruse or the 14K never paid the power bill.

The sky was cloudy, and the low ceiling blocked out a slivered moon. The air was heavy with moisture, and odors of diesel fuel, brine, and mildew permeated the air.

She planned her entry location so her ascent of the fence and her subsequent drop into the interior of the compound was in relative gloom from the wall of an adjacent warehouse. Any cameras on the target warehouse might have difficulty penetrating the shadows. The downside of this location was that access to the warehouse itself required a sprint across twenty meters of open asphalt.

Her outfit was all black and included a black watch cap along with a black face covering. Her athletic shoes were silent. With reverence, she retired the rusty pocketknife in favor of two fixed-blade combat knives, one secured to each of her forearms. She withdrew a compact pistol with a long suppressor screwed into the threaded barrel. The Glock G44 .22 caliber was chosen for its small size and quiet action, and when combined with the long suppressor, it made for as silent a pistol as you can get.

A boot crunched to her right. Two men materialized out of the darkness twenty-five meters away. They hugged the fence, each man carrying an automatic rifle over his shoulder and a lit cigarette in his fingers. One man laughed and punched the other man in the shoulder. In another minute, they would stumble over her.

If she moved, she risked exposing herself. Instead, she steadied the .22 and waited. The tradeoff for such a small and quiet weapon was stopping power. The .22 is best for up-close work, where lethality can be assured. Twenty-five meters, now twenty, in the darkness, was not a guaranteed kill, even for her. So she waited, frozen in place.

When the men were at ten meters, she fired twice and dropped one of them. She shifted and fired twice more. The .22 spit two bullets that found the second man's neck, and he crumpled.

She stayed in the shadows and surveyed the interior of the warehouse complex, which consisted of the large main building with a half dozen loading bays and a roll-top door large enough to drive a small airplane through. A front entrance with a guard shack and a side entrance with a larger guard building were next to a large sliding gate in the chain-link fence.

The darkness was still. She followed the fence line until

the large shack at the side gate loomed in front of her. A pale blue light shone through the window, and the silhouette of a man appeared and disappeared. She put her back against the wooden siding and peeked through a lower corner of the window. Two men sat smoking and watching a small television. Two automatic rifles leaned against the wall within their reach. She crept around the building's corner to the door and pushed on the handle. Unlocked.

She turned the knob with her right hand and held the gun in her left. A push, and the door was open. Crouched, she fired twice and hit one guard in the chest with two slugs before she pivoted and shot the second man as he scrambled for his weapon. She dropped the mag, stuck it in her pocket, and slapped in another ten-round magazine before she darted across the open space and stopped with her back to the aluminum wall of the main building. A metal ladder was to her left that provided access to the roof.

No movement. No shouts of alarm. She scampered up the metal ladder and vaulted onto the roof. There she crouched and checked her watch. Right on time.

Two air ducts the size of tractor trailers were in the center of the football field-sized roof. The trap door providing access to the roof was locked from the inside. It took six long minutes hunched over a battery-powered angle grinder before she was able to cut through the trap door's hinges and slip inside, where she dropped onto a metal catwalk that ran from one end of the building to another.

The interior of the massive building was dark, lit only by the soft glow of security lights placed around the perimeter. One end of the building was filled with blue metal shelving rising as high as the ceiling and holding pallet after pallet of shrink-wrapped cargo. The other end was empty and clean but stored a half dozen forklifts and two delivery trucks, all of which sat dark.

A yellow light emanated from a tiny building at the far end of the warehouse near the massive roll-top door. Moving with enough care to ensure the catwalk didn't creak underfoot, she vaulted from the metal latticework, dropped to a pallet on a shelf, and used a support pole to slide to the ground. She used the shelving and the vehicles to hide her movements until her back was to the building with the yellow light. The noise of a kung fu movie filtered through the door, and a quick glance through a window revealed two men. One had his feet on top of a desk, while the other leaned his elbows on his knees and peered at the television.

Gun in hand, Kira planted a foot above the doorknob and the hollow wooden door splintered and banged open. She fired four bullets on the two security guards before she melted back into the shadows inside the warehouse.

After checking her watch, she was right on time. She circled the interior of the warehouse and found no more guards, and she returned to the guard shack and disabled the second-rate security camera system.

When her watch hit the appointed time, she used the remote switch in the tiny security office to open the massive roll-top door.

The tiny building at the perimeter of the warehouse compound was an ordinary guard shack with a floor heater, which the solitary security guard never used, a rickety chair, a television for soccer matches, and a tiny refrigerator that had never been cleaned. A sliding glass window was used to check the credentials of visitors, which was a seldom occurrence. Most access to the warehouse was through the truck entrance at the rear, where two and sometimes four security guards were stationed with automatic weapons and a more involved computer and telephone system. Here at the front of the facility, the lone guard's job was to refuse admittance to the periodic reporter or lost civilian and keep the gate shut. A dusty sawed-off shotgun with its stock wrapped in black electrical tape leaned against the wall behind the chair. The security guard wasn't sure if it was loaded.

The facility's primary security was the simple nature of the warehouse's affiliation with the 14K triad. The local police were all on the payroll, and the 14K controlled most of the Port of Shenzhen.

Which is why the lone guard was surprised when the SUV with the darkened windows stopped at his gate. The driver's window was opposite his sliding glass window, but nothing was visible inside the vehicle.

As the guard was about to slide his window aside, a rumble came from the warehouse behind him, and he turned. The massive roll-top door was on its way up. From his vantage point, four tractor-trailer rigs were idling outside the side gate. The side gate fence was in the process of rattling open.

What the hell?

There was no scheduled shipment for that night. A thought flashed that he should recheck the book to make sure he hadn't missed a delivery or the scheduled arrival of a VIP. Were the four tractor trailers empty and here to make a pickup, or were they full and dropping off? That's why he failed to notice when the SUV driver's window eased down and a nickel-plated handgun appeared.

Two bursts from a .45 caliber pistol punched through

the guard shack's sliding window and ended the young man's life.

The operation was a simple but risky one and took them five days to plan, which included importing a team of White Phoenix foot soldiers from Manila, reconnaissance of the 14K warehouse, and securing a new warehouse outside of the White Phoenix territory. They also relied on intelligence provided by a 14K gang member who was on Bao's payroll. Once the counterfeit bills were in their possession, Bao would pose as an intermediary and negotiate with his contacts within the North Korean regime to secure the currency's safe return. The deal was simple: Bao wanted control over the smuggling operations on the Chinese side and wanted Pak in his custody. The North Koreans should have no issues handing over the man who failed to protect their interests. Once the deal was consummated, Bao would hand Pak over to Kira.

While she waited for Big Head Bao's team to take positions around the exterior of the compound, Kira returned to the main warehouse and used her knife to slice open a cellophane-wrapped bundle on one of the pallets within reach. The package was the size of a large bag of rice, but she needed to cut through six layers of thick plastic. The bundle was wrapped so tightly that after she hewed through the layers of thick plastic, it burst apart and straps of one-hundred-dollar bills fell to the concrete. After some quick math, and if each strap of hundreds was ten thousand dollars, she figured each bale was a million dollars, give or take. Her rough count of the pallets came to at least a hundred million dollars in the warehouse.

Five minutes later, the warehouse and grounds were surrounded by well-armed White Phoenix guards from the Manila clan. Another crew of Filipino White Phoenix fired up the propane-driven forklifts to fill the four semitrucks with pallet after pallet of the counterfeit hundred-dollar bills.

The man known as Hump Nose Ho scowled and rhythmically clenched and unclenched his fists as the black Mercedes sedan sped through vacant city streets. The car was heavy with bulletproof glass, reinforced body panels, and run-flat tires. Two of his most loyal bodyguards were in the front. One drove while the other sat in the front passenger seat cradling a machine pistol. An SUV with four equally adept bodyguards followed. They were under attack, and Ho's mind was clouded by fury. The man in the passenger seat turned and held a mobile phone.

"Your daughter."

Ho snatched the phone and received the update. His hands clenched into fists as his daughter, his head of operations, relayed the number of dead men and the loss of a hundred million dollars of North Korean counterfeit currency. Someone had made a huge mistake, and Ho thought he knew who it was.

As he handed the phone back to his bodyguard, the sound of metal on metal erupted from behind the Mercedes. He twisted around just as the SUV carrying his henchmen flipped onto its side after it was broadsided by a lorry. It didn't occur to him that his motorcade was under attack until a black van cut off the Mercedes and forced it onto a sidewalk. The van's side door opened and a man with an automatic rifle sprayed gunfire into the front windshield, which cracked but held. When Ho saw the shooter's Fu Manchu-style mustache, his suspicions were confirmed and rage consumed him. The White Phoenix dared to attack him in a brazen street gun battle?

"Reverse, reverse, damn it!" Ho ducked and raised a semiautomatic pistol.

The driver thunked the transmission into reverse and hit the gas, but glass tinkled and metal screeched against metal as the big car's rear end rammed into the front of a flatbed Mack truck and jolted to a stop. A third vehicle, this one a large SUV, pulled alongside the Mercedes, and the black sedan was pinned in by vehicles on three sides and a brick wall on a fourth.

The automatic rifle fire stopped, but there was pounding overhead. It took Ho a moment to realize that the pounding was footsteps. Someone was on top of the car. He pointed his pistol up and fired, but the bullets banged on the reinforced steel and failed to puncture. That was when liquid started running down the windows, and Ho smelled gasoline.

Kira jumped from the roof of the Mercedes, hurled the gas can aside, and tossed a lit Zippo lighter onto the hood. Flames engulfed the car and crackled and hissed. The rear door popped open and a man jumped out with his hands in the air. His hair was mussed, and sweat rolled down his face. The man's nose was crooked, and his blue shirt under the gray suit jacket was soaked. "I give—"

Kira pulled the trigger twice on her Glock, and Hump Nose Ho crumpled.

FORTY-ONE

Hong Kong

The unmarked semitrucks pulled into a small warehouse near the Kwai Chung Container Terminal in Hong Kong's container port after an elaborate and circuitous route through Shenzhen and south into Kowloon, where they split up and were each accompanied by three vans loaded with Filipino White Phoenix muscle. The trucks were powered down, locked, and surrounded by a company-sized team of the White Phoenix foot soldiers from Manila. It was better to keep the bundles of counterfeit currency hidden away, so they didn't bother to unload the trucks.

Now it was a waiting game. Bao's team handled the communications with the North Koreans, which was brokered through the Chinese government. It was Bao's job to negotiate for the return of the currency, which involved transfer of control of the smuggling ring from the 14K to White Phoenix and the one thing Kira cared about: the handover of Commander Pak.

Bao and his team were holed up in his underground compound while Kira wandered Hong Kong's streets. She visited the Nga Shing Hourly Hotel and hugged the old proprietor and stroked the tabby's fur, who purred away while she lay in a beam of sunlight. Kira bought a new wardrobe of capri pants, a T-shirt, and a gray hoodie. Afterward, she walked through the Temple Street Night Market and found booth 42, but it was empty. The old mystic was nowhere to be found.

It was odd to feel relatively safe. Officially, the price on her head remained, but she monitored the chat room, and since she killed the Korean assassin, no new messages were posted. The tracking device was gone from her shoulder. Perhaps the bounty hunt switched to a new chatroom, but Kira doubted it. She had been underground for a month while at the monastery, so any assassin groups likely lost interest. And now Commander Pak had bigger problems on his hands—namely, how to find the North Korean Supreme Leader's missing $100 million in counterfeit currency. Losing that kind of load, and staying alive while reclaiming it, was enough to distract anyone.

Kira found herself at the noodle cart, where the young man in the soiled white tank top and dangly clipper ship earring served her a bowl of the steaming soup, which she ate while seated on the edge of a curb.

"You the one looking for Commander Pak?"

The question was uttered behind her and to the left. The broth and noodles slopped as she whirled, which was difficult from her seated position. A meter away, the young soup vendor stood behind the cart, his white tank top wet and soiled, and ladled soup into a customer's bowl. The customer, who hadn't been standing there before, wore cargo pants frayed at the cuffs and patched with material haphazardly sewn with thick thread. A military-style jacket hung on his slight frame while a bucket hat hung around his neck by a strap. His clothing was soiled, and dirt was smudged on his face. The man's profile was to Kira, and there was no one else within earshot. His face was vaguely familiar to her, but she couldn't place it.

Kira stood and dumped her dish alongside a dozen of its empty cousins. "I am." The soup vendor eyed her but concentrated on ladling a serving of the noodles into the man's bowl.

When the homeless-looking man turned, his cheeks were sunken and hollow, his eyes were hooded, and his lips were dry and cracked. He held the bowl in two hands as if it were an injured bird, and bowed slightly. The man's gaze darted over her shoulder and shifted back and forth over the sparse crowd. "It is not how it seems."

The soup vendor took the bin of dirty soup bowls to the curb behind his cart and busied himself, rinsing each and stacking them in the clean pile.

Kira glanced around, and no one was within earshot. No one appeared to be watching them. "Who are you?"

The old man carried his noodle bowl to a rickety table. He moved with jerky motions, his legs shook, and he collapsed into the plastic chair before he bent over to spoon some broth into his mouth. It was as if he hadn't eaten in a week. "Commander Pak, yes? You look?"

"Yes, yes. Please." Kira eyed a tourist who wandered into view but passed by the street food vendor. She sat in a chair opposite the man and hunched over the table. "Tell me who you are."

After he slurped a mouthful of noodles, he shook his head. "Doesn't matter. They will never give him up."

"What do you mean? Who won't?" A part of Kira

wanted to put her hand on the man's arm, to make a connection. There was recognition there somewhere. She had seen him before, but she still couldn't place him. The man looked Korean; maybe he was from the north. There were signs of malnourishment, and his clothing reeked of body odor and something else, maybe rancid meat.

The man glanced at his watch. It was a large modern timepiece that was out of place on his skinny wrist. "Commander Pak, he the son of Kim Jong Un's aunt. He's the Supreme Leader's cousin."

The homeless man slurped a spoonful of broth before he eyed Kira. "They will not hand him over."

An image of a tarot card flashed—the one with the man with ten swords stuck in his back—and her skin broke out in goosebumps.

Was the old mystic right?

Kira put her hand on the man's arm. "Thank you."

He yanked his arm away and leaped up from the table. "Be careful."

In seconds, he disappeared into the throng of shoppers and marketgoers, leaving the steaming bowl of noodles on the table.

The handover of Lieutenant Commander Pak was to take place at the same warehouse in Hong Kong's container port where Bao's team hid the four semitrucks of counterfeit currency. With Hump Nose Ho's death, Bao's negotiation position strengthened, and North Korea agreed to switch smuggling operations from the decimated 14K to the White Phoenix. Bao contacted Kira and told her to meet them at the warehouse, at which point Bao would hand over Pak and their arrangement would be finalized.

The warehouse building was old but in good repair, with walls made of brick and a concrete floor stained from decades of use. The smell of decaying fish was everywhere, and dank, briny moisture hung in the air and clung to Kira's skin. Yellow lights from the ceiling three stories high were turned on, but the yard outside the main building was dark.

The North Korean contingent arrived in a single white unmarked panel van. The vehicle stopped at the perimeter security checkpoint manned by Bao's Manila team and rolled across the container-filled yard and into the main building, where they were greeted by three of Bao's men carrying Chinese rip-offs of the Soviet-designed AK-47. Fu was nowhere to be seen. The two-story door remained open and allowed moisture from a misty rain to seep into the interior of the warehouse.

A pinch-faced North Korean official wearing a suit stepped out of the white van's front passenger seat while the side door slid open to reveal two bodyguards and a tall Korean with a shock of black hair. Kira's heart raced at the sight of Commander Pak. The man in the suit was short and wore a permanent scowl as he strode to the middle of the circle with his fists on his hips, while the two guards and Pak stood in front of the white van.

Kira observed the North Korean contingent's arrival from where she stood in the shadows of one of the semi-trucks, her hands in her pockets. Big Head Bao assured her that he had already negotiated Pak's handover with the North Koreans. He relayed that the North Koreans had grown tired of Pak's failures and were more than willing to dispose of him.

A tiny red van sat behind Kira and next to one of the semitrucks. Pak was to be put on the floor in the rear of the red van, bound, gagged, and hooded. Kira would drive away and allow Bao and the North Koreans to finish consummating their deal. All of that was arranged beforehand. Now Pak stood in the middle of the floor, his hands free. The homeless man's warning at the soup cart rang in her ear.

Her first in-person view of the man who had kidnapped her and incarcerated her before training her to be a killer, and then coordinating an operation to hunt her down, was surprisingly anticlimactic. He was taller than his North Korean countrymen and most of Bao's soldiers, and he stood passively with his hands clenched behind his back. He wore dark gray trousers and a light gray button-down shirt that clung to his skin in the humidity. There was nothing about his expression that conveyed fear or trepidation. His face was placid, his mouth was a tight slash of narrow lips, and his eyes were blank. White speckled through his black hair, and deep crow's feet were at the corners of his eyes. His eyebrows were dark, and his jawline was V-shaped. The jagged scar on his cheek seemed to glow in a faint jade-like color.

As much as Kira wanted to remember, only fleeting visions of this man percolated up from her memory. Some of the images were from the pictures on Ms. Ho's computer and the ones provided by Colonel Wu. Because her memory was blank, it was difficult for Kira to summon any emotion, but this man had answers she desperately craved.

Big Head Bao, flanked by two of his own security guards, appeared from the back of the warehouse and approached the group. He was dressed in a charcoal business suit, except the pant legs stopped at his calves, the jacket sleeves were rolled halfway up his arms, and his white silk blouse was open to the navel. He paraded to the center of the group, stood with one knee pointed to the side, and snapped his fingers.

All thirteen sets of eyes turned.

Fu and a second White Phoenix soldier appeared from behind a semitruck and trained their guns on her. The second soldier was massive in girth and height, and his jolly face wore a leering grin as he pointed a rifle at her.

Kong.

FORTY-TWO

Hong Kong

Kira froze, her hands still in her pockets.

"Come on out here, little one." It was Bao, calling out in his singsong voice.

This was not the plan. As Kira and Bao agreed, it was at this point that Pak was to be bound, hooded, and placed in the red van, and Kira would drive away to a prearranged safe house. Now it looked like Bao had made other arrangements with the North Koreans.

Just as the homeless man at the soup cart predicted. Exactly as the tarot card with the ten swords in the man's back had foretold.

Fu, who pointed the same silver-plated semiautomatic pistol at her as he did back at the construction site, waved the gun to indicate she should join the party in the center of the warehouse. Kong held a Type 56 assault rifle, which is a knockoff of the Soviet-designed AK-47. The rifle was puny in his hands, and his grin spread into a wide smile. "We meet again."

"Oh, Kira!" Bao strode in a circle. "Come on out here and join the little party, why don't you. You remember Commander Pak. He is eagerly awaiting your reunion."

Commander Pak put his hands in his pockets. While there was a serene expression on his face, the pinch-faced North Korean official stood to the side with his arms crossed and eyebrows furrowed. Including Fu and Kong, there were ten men with their weapons either pointed at her or at the ready.

Damn you, Bao. We had a deal. It didn't have to be this way.

Kira touched a tiny remote in her pocket, and a faint *snick* came from under the van.

Forewarned is forearmed.

A vision of the homeless man at the noodle cart flashed in her mind as Kira ducked and rolled. Kong's rifle spit bullets, and copper-plated steel jackets chinked off the concrete.

She rolled again as a scatter of bullets hit the floor where she had been a split-second prior and hurled herself so she was under the little red van. There, hidden in a specially constructed box attached to the chassis, were two Glock 21s chambered in .45 caliber. The remote in her pocket had popped the door open to the hidden compartment. She snatched the guns and rolled again to end up under the semitruck that stood next to the red van.

Two meaty legs were visible under the tractor trailer, and she pulled the trigger on each gun. The 21s kicked, and a bullet stabbed into each of the visible legs. Kong screamed, and the Type 56 rifle clattered to the concrete.

Without waiting to see Kong's gargantuan body hit the floor, Kira rolled again to get to the far side of the semitruck and rose to one knee. From between the two truck trailers, she had a partial view of the group in the middle of the warehouse. They still stood in a circle, despite the gunfire. The North Korean official frowned, and both sets of bodyguards raised their weapons, but they all looked around with wide and darting eyes.

Bao was not visible from her vantage point, but Commander Pak's eyes narrowed, and he stood in a ready position but looked unsure which direction to go. The group appeared paralyzed by fear and indecision.

Her primary job was to stay alive. Her second job was to walk away from here with Pak in captivity. He was no good to her dead. From her position on one knee, she fired both pistols. A slug tore into Pak's quad and a second hit the chest of a North Korean bodyguard. Pak grunted and collapsed, and the gray-suited official bolted out of her field of view.

She was mostly hidden between two of the tractor trailers, and the bodyguards were wide-eyed and jittery while looking for a target.

Kira stood and walked between the trailers, at the group, as each pistol barked. The 21s held thirteen rounds stacked in the magazines plus one in the chamber.

Each bullet counts.

A second North Korean soldier fell from a bullet to the chest. One of Bao's men collapsed from a slug to the gut.

She picked the .45s for maximum stopping power relative to the weapon size. The guns were larger in her small hands than she preferred, but she also didn't have a lot of choice. Ironically, Commander Pak had trained her in hundreds of pistols, and ultimately each was merely a tool. And these 21s were doing the job.

The twin pistols roared again, and two more of Bao's men fell. Now she had a better view of the open space in the warehouse where the group of men had been standing. The North Korean official disappeared, as did Big Head Bao. Pak writhed on the floor, both hands holding his leg. Five bodyguards lay dead. Kong, who was out of commission, although alive, was out of sight behind a tractor trailer. Fu was nowhere to be seen.

A bullet sang past her ear and a second plunked into the fender next to where she stood, and she ducked behind one of the trailer's tires. The gunfire sounded like a .45 semiautomatic from Fu's nickel-plated. She hit the ground and rolled again to get to the other side of the truck and sprinted behind a row of shelving. While she ran, the twin Glocks popped, and two more guards fell. Slugs zinged past her head as she dove behind the shelving and hit the deck, her chest heaving.

No time to hesitate. After she leaped to her feet, she slid between two sets of pallets that held some kind of machinery which sat under the first row of shelving. From her hiding spot, she peeked out. Pak still lay on the ground groaning. The bodyguards from both Bao's team and the North Korean contingent were dead. There was no sign of Bao, the North Korean in the suit, or Fu.

As an engine roared to life, the white van's taillights illuminated. Through the passenger window, Kira glimpsed the mustachioed Fu behind the wheel. The van lurched ahead and screeched to a stop long enough for the North Korean official and Bao to jump from hiding and sprint for the van's open side door. She popped from her hiding spot and strode at the van, the .45s yammering.

All her lead went into the van's rear in an attempt to hit Fu and prevent the van from escaping. Holes popped into the sheet metal and spidered the rear window as her pistol hammers clicked and the slides locked out.

The van door slid shut, and the tires screeched.

Kira tossed the Glocks and traded them for a Type 56 from a fallen bodyguard and pulled the trigger.

Slugs poured into the van's bumper and thunked into the rear metal panel, but the van's engine growled as it spun through the open warehouse door and turned out of her field of view.

No time to linger. More of Bao's men were outside in the yard around the warehouse and on the perimeter. She hurried to the center of the room, where Pak lay with a small pool of blood under his leg. His face was bathed in sweat, his chest heaved, and his breath puffed in short bursts. Pak was going into shock.

Don't die on me, damn it.

She squatted and examined the wound. It was a through-and-through that pierced Pak's vastus laterals, the long muscle that runs from the hip to the knee on the outside of the leg. After she ripped a sleeve away from a dead guard's shirt, she tied it snug around the wound and used another piece of material and the banana magazine from an abandoned Type 56 to fashion a tourniquet.

"Hold the magazine."

Pak was glassy-eyed. When Kira slapped him on the cheek, his eyes focused.

"Stay with me, Pak. Hold this. Not too tight. Just enough to slow the blood flow. You don't want it so tight that it cuts off the blood. Good, that's it."

With the Type 56 slung over her back, Kira grabbed Pak by the shoulders and dragged him across the concrete to the little red van. She heaved to get his torso up and onto the vehicle's floor. After two shoves, she was able to slide the van door shut.

Before she jumped into the driver's seat, she stooped over Kong. The sumo wrestler-sized gangster lay on his back, both calves dripping blood, his face bright red and bathed in perspiration. "You were Bao's man inside the 14K?"

Kong nodded.

"You gave Bao the intel where to find Pak and provided the information we needed to get into the 14K's warehouse to steal the counterfeit cash?"

Kong's big head nodded again.

"I guess I'm lucky I didn't kill you back at 383 Lockhart. Maybe I never would have found Pak."

The big man held his hands in front of his face. "Please don't kill me."

Kira shrugged. "Do me a favor?"

Kong nodded.

"Give Bao a message for me." Kira jumped into the little red van's driver's seat and tossed the rifle onto the passenger seat. Before she slammed the door, she looked at Kong. "Tell Bao that I know where he lives."

Kong's head collapsed against the ground and his body went slack. "Thank you."

"Don't thank me. You're more useful as a messenger than as a dead man. Maybe next time that won't be true."

After slamming the van door, Kira fired up the engine and hit the gas.

As the van sped through the warehouse, she glanced over her shoulder. "Keep your head down, Pak. It's going to get bumpy." The North Korean lay on his back, one hand on the tourniquet, the other braced on the side panel.

When the little red van emerged from the open warehouse door at speed, gunfire erupted from the yard. Kira hunched down, pinned the accelerator to the floor, and spun the wheel. From her reconnaissance of the warehouse, the weakest part of the fence was not the front gate, which was reinforced and covered by three of Bao's armed security guards, but an area of the fence near the side of the building and close to the street. She gripped the steering wheel as bullets plinked through the thin aluminum panels and buzzed past her head.

As the van's nose smashed into the fence, the chain link squealed on sheet metal and hung the van up for a moment before it broke free. With another wrench of the wheel, they sped along an empty boulevard and away from the container facility.

FORTY-THREE

Hong Kong

"I'm already dead. You might as well kill me now."

Commander Pak was taller than she remembered, especially for a North Korean, who are on average three inches shorter than their southern counterparts.

Maybe he's six feet tall, which put her almost at eye level with him as he sat in a beige upholstered chair, his hands secured behind him by two zip ties around his wrists.

Each of Pak's ankles were secured to a wooden leg of the chair, also by zip ties. His left pant leg was cut away, and Kira had dressed the wound. Pak's face was pallid and his eyes rimmed with red. The scar shone faintly in translucent jade.

"Sorry, Pak. You can't get off that easy."

It was twelve hours since the flight from Bao's container warehouse. In that time, Kira performed a lengthy and meandering route through Hong Kong to make sure no one tailed her before she drove the little red van along the winding road to the top of Victoria Peak and through the gate of the squatter house she used before. The little red van was now in the home's massive garage, and she and Pak were in the living room. Broad floor-to-ceiling windows offered expansive views over the bay and Victoria Harbour.

Since Kira snatched Pak and brought him to the safe house, a hazy version of Commander Pak's face reoccurred in her memories. Seeing him in person was the trigger she needed, except the images were obscured by swirling fog and there were only bits and pieces of haphazard film clips. Nothing coherent she was able to string together.

Pak's face was flat and stoic, the kind of face that doled out punishment without batting an eye. Maybe it was slightly fleshier and the jowls hung more flaccid than years prior when he strutted around the training facility with his arms behind his back, but the face was the same. Same narrow eyes, the same jagged scar running from his temple to his chin glowing in a faint jade color when the light caught it right. A face she would see in her nightmares for the rest of her life.

"Nothing you can do will hurt me." Pak's eyes shifted to the right. "It's only a matter of time before they get me. That was my last chance to bring you in. Now I'm as dead as you are."

"I'm very much alive right now, but it's just a matter of time for all of us." Kira crossed her hands over her chest and stuck out a hip. Somehow, having this man here in front of her, subdued and captive, was less than satisfying. The man who ordered beatings and held her hostage for her entire childhood. The man who turned her into a lethal killer. The man who took away her memories.

She rested her foot on the coffee table. "How did you convince Bao to double-cross me? Our deal was Bao was supposed to deliver you to me in exchange for my help taking over the 14K's North Korean smuggling operation. If Bao wanted the bounty on my head, why didn't he turn me over instead of going through the whole charade?"

Pak's eyebrows rose. "Simple. You were part of his deal with Pyongyang to take over the smuggling operation."

"Perhaps." Kira smirked. "I think Bao's deal with Pyongyang was to turn us both over. He was going to betray both of us."

Pak gazed out the window and shook his head.

Kira paced the room. "Doesn't matter now. The question is what to do with you. You failed to kill me. Your operation with the 14K disintegrated with the loss of the hundred million in counterfeit money. If I let you go free, you're right. Pyongyang will catch you and ship you off to one of those labor camps up north. Some failures can't go unpunished, can they? Even with your family connections."

Pak blinked at her.

"I see three ways out of this for you."

Pak closed his eyes.

"One is I kill you."

Pak flinched.

"I didn't think you'd like that one." Kira winked. "Another way out of this is I drop you at the North Korean consulate."

Kira rose from the couch and walked to the window. A deck stretched away from the two-story wall of windows and looked north over Victoria Harbour. On the far side of the sparkling blue bay was the daytime skyline of Kowloon. Far below her window, two tugboats positioned a massive cruise ship next to a pier.

Pak stared at her. "The third?"

Kira stared out the window. "I drop you at the South

Korean Consulate. The funny thing is, both consulates are close to each other. I looked it up."

Pak frowned.

"Only one of those options keeps you alive," Kira said.

Pak's eyes narrowed and his brow furrowed. "They're going to keep hunting you, you know. They have long memories. You won't be able to hide anywhere. Despite what you think, they can get to anyone anywhere."

"I don't think so." Kira put her hands in her pockets as a ferryboat lumbered through the water and disappeared from view. "How do you think I got out of Bao's warehouse alive?"

She turned to Pak, whose eyebrows were scrunched together. "Do you think I had those pistols ready on the off chance I would be betrayed?"

Pak said nothing but he looked away from Kira, and his eyes searched the ceiling.

Kira faced him. "I was tipped off."

There was a brief flicker in Pak's eyes, and the corner of his mouth twitched before his face resumed its blank expression. "Who?"

Kira shrugged. "I don't know. I had never seen him before."

"Someone from Bao's team?"

Kira shook her head. "It came from your side."

Pak's face drained of blood.

"My only read on it is someone on the North Korean side thinks you're done."

"That's not true. Why would they give me to you? They wouldn't risk a defection."

Kira crossed her arms over her chest. "Defection? They think I'll kill you. I was trained as a killer, right? Killers kill."

Pak hung his head.

"They're cutting their losses, Pak. Your bosses have decided it's you who has become the liability. You're done, Pak. You're expendable, and you know it. They know I'm unreachable now that their assassin was killed. But you... They probably think that I'll kill you as retribution."

Pak squirmed in his chair. "I have information. Valuable information. The South Koreans are going to want to speak to me. I can be helpful."

"Whether the South Koreans ever meet you is up in the air, Pak. Right now, I haven't decided what to do with you." Kira walked to the other room, grabbed a bottle of water, and poured some of it into his mouth.

Pak's head bowed, and he was quiet. Kira let him stew as she went into the adjoining room and twisted a mangosteen along the middle to remove the rind. When she bit into the tangy, sweet fruit, nectar ran down her fingers and a fragrant aroma filled her nostrils. The lychee and peach flavor was bold and reminded her of her freedom. She smiled. *I can have this whenever I want.*

When she returned, Pak stared at her with wide eyes. Kira took something out of her pocket. It was a brown leather wallet, worn with a patina from years of use. She opened it and fiddled with a flap until a secret compartment opened, from which she fished a picture. The picture was of a small, raven-haired girl of perhaps seven. Even at that age, her high cheekbones were prominent. The girl wore a school uniform comprised of a blue dress with blue suspenders over a white blouse and a red kerchief. The girl was laughing as she stood in a bed of blooming flowers. She showed it to Pak. "This is me, isn't it?"

He slumped as soon as he saw the image and when he looked up, his eyes blazed. Perspiration streamed down his face, and his shirt was soaked. His salt and pepper hair, ordinarily trimmed and neat, was in disarray.

"I think you do have something to live for." Kira slipped the picture into her pocket. "Something other than your bank accounts. Something other than your family relationship with Supreme Leader."

Outside the window, green trees rustled in a breeze under a blue sky. Far off, down the slope, the azure waters of the bay glistened in the sunshine.

Kira perched herself on the back of a couch. "I was the daughter you never had, isn't that right, Pak?"

Pak gazed at the floor.

She had found the wallet among the items in Pak's pockets after she secured him to the chair, and she discovered the secret compartment after a thorough search. When she found the photo, everything clicked into place. "They say that only when you've lost everything can you truly become your true self. Or something like that. Do you feel that way now, Pak? You're laid bare, no more secrets. I know your truth."

Pak nodded as a tear rolled down his scarred cheek.

"Good." Kira licked mangosteen juice from her fingers. "Let's see how cooperative you can be. The more cooperative you are, the more likely you'll see the inside of the South Korean Consulate here in Hong Kong, and the more likely you'll ever see me again. Do we have an understanding?"

Pak nodded.

"Good. Now tell me everything about how I was kidnapped. I want to know when, where, and how. Leave nothing out."

THE JAPANESE ASSASSIN

Murakami, Japan, circa 1998

The wooden-hulled boat ground against the sand as four dark-clad men splashed into the water and pulled the vessel far enough onto the beach where it was safe from the tides. One of the young men, unnaturally tall for a North Korean, ran with a rope a dozen meters up the beach and tied it off to a tree. The other three men grabbed packs and hurried after him. One tossed the tall man his pack, and the four set off through the underbrush.

The beach was remote, which suited the men's purposes, but it made for a long march through a forest. The team took pains to disguise the landing boat's origin. The tiny outboard didn't have any numbers and all markings had been removed from the boat's hull. The men's clothing and gear were all sanitized, and they carried no identification. They also brought no weapons, as this was a simple intelligence-gathering exercise and Lieutenant Pak, their team leader, wanted to minimize impact. If they were caught, they would spend the rest of their lives in a Japanese jail, which would be bad, but he didn't want to make a mistake and injure anyone, which would be worse.

The mission was simple. Land on Japanese soil, infiltrate a manufacturing facility, take pictures of everything in the factory, including the floor layout, the machinery, and anything else that would help replicate the factory at home, and get out. As with most so-called simple missions, there would be nothing easy about this one.

The four men sipped water from canteens and munched on salty rations as they marched. The distance, estimated from prior intelligence excursions, was about six kilometers from their landing zone, about an hour of walking. They landed the boat at 1:00 a.m. local time, which gave them an hour to walk, an hour to photograph, an hour to return to their landing craft, and an hour to get back to the North Korean fishing boat waiting for them just beyond Japan's territorial waters in the Sea of Japan. Unfortunately, their intel was poor, and Pak had miscalculated.

Not yet on his way to a senior position in the RGB, Pak had something to prove. He wanted desperately to impress his senior officers and gain a position of privilege to make his life easier. His relationship with the Kim family got him in the RGB, but he wanted to prove himself. His rush to pull off a successful mission, along with poor advance intelligence, had caused him to miscalculate.

He especially miscalculated the distance from the beach to the target factory, and that, combined with a beach landing, was farther south than anticipated, which lengthened the hike to two hours instead of one. When they finally reached the factory, they had trouble getting inside and smashed a window to gain entrance. Once in the factory, one of their cameras malfunctioned. Still, the team managed to take hundreds of pictures. By the time they humped back to their boat, the sun was a pink glow in the eastern sky.

There was also a young girl standing on the brown sand, peering at their boat.

FORTY-FOUR

Hong Kong, Present Day

"So you grabbed the little girl and took her with you?" Kira sat on the back of a couch with her feet on the couch cushions. "I mean me. You grabbed me and took me with you?"

Pak did his best to shrug with his hands secured behind his back. "Our mission was to leave no trace. The broken window in the factory could be explained by a burglary, and we took all the food, which could also be explained away. But a witness who saw four men leave on a boat? Even a little girl?" He shook his head. "It would have created an international incident."

"And submarined your career."

"There was plenty of precedent," Pak said. "North Korea kidnapped hundreds of people from Japan and South Korea. We took so many people, there's a program for it inside North Korea. You were placed with a family. A family of privilege, I might add. Taught the Korean language. You went to Pyongyang's best school."

"How old was I when you kidnapped me?"

Pak shrugged. "Don't know. You were small. We guessed five years old, give or take a year or two. You hadn't started to lose your teeth yet, which I think happens around six or seven."

"Where did I come from? How did I end up on that beach that early in the morning?"

Pak shook his head. "I don't know. We always wondered, but we didn't have time. The sun was coming up. We were in danger of being spotted, either on the beach or in the water. It was a long motor out to our rendezvous ship. I didn't think. We tossed you in the boat and left."

As frustration washed over her, she jumped from her perch and walked into the kitchen, where she paced out of Pak's sight. All he had revealed was that she was originally from an area called Murakami on Japan's west coast, on the shore of the Sea of Japan, which corresponded to what Wu told her. Were her mother and her father still alive, wondering what happened to their baby girl? Living with the anguish of not knowing for more than twenty years? She curled her hands into fists and punched the barstool near the countertop. She gave it a few pummels for good measure, and when her emotions subsided, she took some deep breaths and walked back out to the living room. Pak sat still.

"How did I go from privileged schoolgirl to intelligence officer trainee?"

Pyongyang, North Korea, circa 2009

. . .

Pak arrived in a black SUV at the luxury condominium complex in central Pyongyang wearing a full uniform, with his plackets showing the four small silver stars and single red bar of the rank of captain. Three men accompanied him: two junior officers and a livery driver. They wore sidearms and didn't bother to knock or announce themselves. The complex was on the Taedong river and offered a view of Mansudae Hill Grand Monument where two massive bronze statues stood, one of Kim Il Sung and one of Kim Jong Il.

When they barged into the apartment, one of the most upscale residences in Pyongyang reserved for the most loyal of Kim Jong Il's supporters, they found the home's couple standing in the living room with their arms crossed, staring at the teenage girl who sat alone in a chair in the center of the room.

On one of the couches sat a younger boy with a large bandage on the side of his neck and one of his arms in a sling. He glared at the girl who sat in the chair.

The girl was small and wore her coal-black hair in a bob cut off the shoulders. Her beige school blouse was buttoned to the neck, and there was a small bag at her feet.

Without a word to the homeowners, Pak grabbed the girl by her arm and half carried, half dragged her from the living room and out the front door. It was a mistake he made once, and he almost paid for it with his life. It was a mistake he wouldn't make again.

As Pak opened the rear door of the SUV and bent to lift the girl into the seat, she swung her arm and sliced a gaping cut into Pak's cheek using a homemade knife. Pak cried out and let go of the girl's arm while he pressed a hand to his face. The girl stood there, rooted in place, her eyes wide, while one of Pak's junior officers clamped his hand on her tiny wrist, relieved her of the weapon, and bound her wrists.

Later Pak marveled at the weapon. It was a small paring knife, sharpened by rubbing the blade on concrete, and the handle was cut in half and wrapped with electrical tape. *A prison shiv.* Two inches lower and it could have severed his carotid artery and killed him.

"I should have killed you right then." Pak hung his head.

"Why didn't you?"

"I thought I would harness your anger into something useful. For years, you acted out, getting into fights. You almost killed that little boy because he bullied you. You almost killed me. I thought I could train the anger out of you."

"What happened?"

"It worked for a while. We put you into our most elite and rigorous training program. One we use for young students and soldiers who show a high degree of potential. Only about ten percent make it through. You aced it. Other than one incident, it looked like it was working. You settled in and focused all your energy on the training. You broke all the records in pistol shooting and trained in a variety of martial arts. I think it gave you purpose."

"What was the incident?"

Pyongyang, North Korea, circa 2013

. . .

There were no separate barracks for girls, and she was the only girl trainee in the encampment. The building where the trainees bunked was a large, squat concrete block affair with a corrugated metal roof and windows that were permanently open to the air. In the summer, the interior was insufferably hot, and the nights were cold. Twenty men slept on cots on one end of the room and she, the lone female, was provided a cot and a trunk on the other end. No privacy screens were erected, and she was forced to wear a man's uniform. The latrine was also unisex, and Commander Pak, who ran the training program, attempted to enforce shifts so she would have some privacy. The men, however, ignored the rules and took it upon themselves to barge in whenever they saw fit.

She endured the leers, the stares, and the blatant overtures of the men by concentrating on outworking them. She was faster, stronger, a better shot, and a more accomplished Kumdo practitioner, the Korean martial art also known as *the way of the sword*. She easily defeated her male counterparts at taekwondo and various self-defense practices.

So it was with some panic that she found herself pinned down late one night by two men with unyielding grips while one of the officers, a lieutenant under Pak's command, stood at the foot of her cot and unzipped his uniform pants.

The two men holding her arms were strong but not overly large. One had his sweaty palm clamped over her mouth and held her left wrist, while the other had a two-handed grip on her right. The famine and North Korea's food shortages affected even the soldiers, because there wasn't enough protein to build big, strong muscles. The lieutenant who stood at the foot of her bed with his pants around his ankles had a round, fleshy face covered by perspiration. There was a protrusion in his boxer shorts, and the man fondled himself while he leered at Kira.

This is not happening.

Their need to keep her silent was their undoing. The man holding her left arm with one hand, while his other was clamped over her mouth, was the weak link. She flung her feet back so her body was in a C-shaped position and scissored her legs around the attacker's neck on her left side. She squeezed, cutting off the man's air pipe, and would have broken his neck if she hadn't let go.

The second man was smart enough to hold on to her right arm, but the attacker on her left let go.

Big mistake.

While her legs encircled the man's neck, she brought her left hand around and jabbed her fingers into the man on her right's jugular. Her awkward position prevented a hard strike, but it was enough to make him loosen his grip on her arm.

She wrenched her hand free and released her legs from around the left man's neck and bounded to her feet atop the cot. A twirling kick to the neck of the man on her right sent him to his knees, and she jabbed her fingers into left man's eye socket.

Instead of pulling out some kind of weapon, the lieutenant chose that moment to yank his pants up.

Kira reached under the bar on the left side of her cot, where she stashed a knife she had shaped from a piece of metal rebar by scraping it repeatedly on the concrete floor. As the fleshy-faced lieutenant struggled to fasten his belt, she swung the rebar knife in a wide arc and impaled the tip into the man's shoulder. She jerked the knife free as the lieutenant's scream woke the barracks.

He staggered while holding his hand over the wound in

a futile attempt to stanch the blood flow. Blood spurted from the wound and covered the wall in an arc as he lurched and fell to his behind with his back against a wall.

Kira swung the homemade blade as one of the men rose to his feet. The soldier raised a hand in defense, and the rusty knife sliced through his wrist and along the length of his arm. He screamed and staggered away.

The lights flicked on, and a man stood in a wide stance with a pistol in a two-handed grip. He wore the three silver stars and two red bars of a colonel on his epaulets, and his black eyes blazed. "Stop!"

Everyone froze.

The colonel walked over, pointed the pistol at the lieutenant's head, and pulled the trigger. The lieutenant slumped.

The shooter was Colonel Choe Su-gil.

Elation rose in her as Pak told the story. Not because someone attempted to rape her, and not because she killed her attacker, but memories of the event percolated through her mind. Visions of the two men on the ground writhing in pain. The lieutenant slumped against the wall, Colonel Choe holding the gun on the two men on the ground.

I remember.

Something about Colonel Choe flashed in her mind, but it was hazy. He played a part in her life, but as hard as she focused, she wasn't able to remember.

But she recalled the aftermath of the attack. The lieutenant's body was dragged away, and the two men who had held her arms were never seen again.

Kira was forced to clean the blood. She didn't place eyes on Colonel Choe again until much later.

Life went on in the training facility. From that moment on, no one bothered her. A privacy screen was put up. She was permitted time alone in the latrine. The training regimes continued.

Kira shook her head. "You didn't kill me then or take me away to a labor camp. Why not?"

Pak gazed at a faraway spot on the wall and grinned. "You had a benefactor."

Kira searched her mind. "Colonel Choe?"

Pak nodded.

FORTY-FIVE

Hong Kong

"Obviously, it was a mistake not to." Pak grimaced. "Looking back, all the signs and evidence were there. When you're living in it, it's easy to dismiss the signals and not see what it was all leading up to." Pak's eyes fixed on a faraway spot. "Like the frog sitting in the boiling water. But you were our best trainee. We tried to control you with various drug cocktails, some worked better than others, but they showed promise. And the fact you killed with what appeared to be no remorse or hesitation. We wondered if that was controllable. If we harnessed that, to turn you into—"

"A weapon." Kira was again perched on the back of the couch. While her memories were returning, there were still a lot of gaps. She didn't want Pak to stop talking. She craved more information about herself. Kira rose and poured more water into Pak's upturned mouth.

Pak swallowed, and some of the water dripped onto his front. "Yes."

"When did it all come apart? When did you realize I had to be..."

"Dealt with?"

Kira nodded.

"It was a long time." Pak shook his head. "You were either playing us or biding your time, or maybe it took you some time to figure out what you wanted, or maybe you took advantage of a situation that presented itself. When your training was done, we put you in your own house on Haeju, the naval base where we operated. You were well cared for. Your meals were provided, and you were given ample opportunity to train and stay fit, which you did religiously. At first you were sent on routine operations around the interior of North Korea. Nothing outside, and in fact we thought long and hard about whether to send you outside the border."

"So what happened?"

Pak's face clouded. "The order came from above. You were sent into China on a mission."

"What kind of mission?"

Shenyang, China, circa 2022

The RGB's intelligence, provided by the Chinese, revealed the target was staying in a shantytown in a slum area of Shenyang, a city of nine million about 250 kilometers west from the border of North Korea. The mission was to infiltrate the slum, find the man, slit his throat, and exit. The tiny team of her and two North Korean operatives from the RGB was supported by the local Chinese police force, who permitted them to operate on Chinese soil.

The operation went by the book: Transit over the border and across country to Shenyang, the safe house in the upscale neighborhood not too far from the slum, pinpoint the target's specific location, which was accomplished in partnership with the local police, until Kira snuck into the shantytown at 4:00 a.m. and found the target.

It was a dark and smoggy night—at least that's what the senior RGB officer said. Both handlers were experienced operatives with dozens of successful missions over the border in China, Russia, Taiwan, and the Philippines, and both men remained back at the safe house. One monitored comms with her—she was in touch via a mobile phone—while the second man liaised with a team from the Chinese police who was surveilling the shantytown and would report back if the target left the area. Kira was dressed in tattered clothing, grime-covered sandals, and a hat pulled low enough to hood her eyes. She was armed only with a matte black tactical knife, which was strapped to her right arm and hidden by her sleeve, which was loose for easy access.

She had no problem spotting the police surveillance team positioned on the outskirts of the shantytown. She maneuvered around them and into the slum without them noticing her. It was the stench that she remembered the most. A combination of rotting food, sewage, and stagnant water consuming the cramped passageways that ran between the lean-tos and huts the slum's occupants had erected on their own behalf. Electrical cords crisscrossed the moonlit sky overhead, and even at this late hour, an occasional lightbulb was visible through cracks in the metal and plastic makeshift walls.

The hut where the target stayed was little more than corrugated metal sheeting propped up to make two rooms. After remaining motionless outside for fifteen minutes to watch for movement, Kira entered into a kitchen and eating area, where a folding table held an electric hot plate plugged into a tangle of wires. Four folding chairs were positioned around another table, and trash was strewn among milk crates full of perishables and canned goods.

Her shoes were quiet on the dirt ground, and she waited and listened for any footsteps or rustling that indicated someone was awake. Nothing, so she padded through an opening in the metal that led to the second room. Here three mattresses were on the ground, only one of which was occupied. A lumpy object under a blanket snored gently, and Kira crept closer and drew the knife.

She knelt with her arm poised, the blade three inches from his throat, ready to swipe the edge across the man's jugular.

His eyes fluttered open and went wide.

At the same time, she recognized him.

It was Colonel Choe.

She froze. It was the man who had killed her attacker. The only one who had shown her any kindness. The one bright light in her captivity.

Her finger went to her lips and she withdrew the knife. Her voice was a whisper. "You need to get out of here. There is a team of Chinese police two blocks way." She gave Colonel Choe the location of the surveillance team.

She slipped out of the shanty, skirted around the local Chinese police surveillance team, ignored the calls for situation updates from the handlers, and snuck through a second-floor window of the safe house, slit the younger handler's throat, and shot the older man through the temple with the younger handler's gun.

After which she started walking northwest. Mongolia was up there somewhere. And freedom.

As the memories returned, Kira's head was ajumble. Colonel Choe prevented her from being killed or carted off to a labor camp in North Korea after she almost killed the three men who tried to rape her. The memory of seeing his face in the Chinese slum crystalized in stark relief. In that moment she had made an impulsive decision to let Choe live. Wu's words also came back to her from that morning sitting on the platform high up in the Japanese Alps.

We don't know all the details, but we can speculate based on information provided by the defector.

The defector.

Kira reeled. "Colonel Choe made it out, didn't he? He was one of the most senior defectors in the history of the Kim regime in North Korea."

Pak grimaced. "That's right. Choe ran the RGB for a decade. We never found him again after you let him go, and six months later he showed up in Thailand, got immunity there, and eventually made his way to South Korea."

"But I didn't make it, did I?"

Pak shook his head.

Some memories cascaded back in another jumble. "I made it as far as Beijing before you caught up with me," Kira said. "I made a mistake. I didn't realize how extensive your network was inside China."

Pak nodded. "That's right. We put a team together and

hunted you down in partnership with the Chinese. You should have seen the look on your face when we showed up. You were surprised."

Kira knitted her brow. "Why didn't you take me back to North Korea and put me in a labor camp right then and there? Or execute me? I disobeyed a direct order and killed two of your men. I let one of the most senior defectors ever to escape from North Korea go free."

Pak snorted. "Clearly, we should have. Instead, we put you in detention until we could figure out what to do with you."

"How long was I... er... detained?"

"It was about six months. You were interrogated, tortured. Drugs were administered, more potent and experimental cocktails we hoped would subdue you. Benzodiazepine mixed with xylazines and some opioids. We think your memory loss was a result of the high dosages and prolonged use of the drugs."

Kira's mind clouded over with anger. "What gave you the right—"

Pak's head hung. "You compromised a mission, and a high-ranking defector escaped. You killed your team and tried to escape."

"Why didn't you kill me on the spot?"

The question hung in silence, and Pak avoided her eyes.

"Let me guess," Kira said. "You didn't want to admit you were wrong all these years. That would be a huge black mark on your record."

Pak waggled his head, and his eyes found her and lingered. There was moisture there.

So that's it. Kira's eyebrows went up as she remembered the photo she found in Pak's wallet. "You couldn't bring yourself to kill me."

Pak looked away as a tear appeared on the side of his nose.

Kira's mind spun as the revelation sank in. "So you concocted this entire scheme in the hopes someone else would do it. You wanted someone else to clean up your mess, except you miscalculated."

Pak shifted in the chair and closed his eyes.

"Or did you?" Kira stood and walked over, grabbed Pak's chin and forced him to look at her. "You didn't think anyone would be able to get me, did you? I was too good. You figured none of the thugs you sent after me would succeed. You did all this to save my life? This entire plan was designed to help me escape?"

Pak did his best to shrug while his arms were secured behind him. "I didn't know, but I hoped."

"This was your endgame the entire time, but you didn't count on my partnership with Bao. You thought eventually, maybe after the tall assassin, that your bosses would give up. When all the killers inevitably failed, you were going to defect. That was your plan all along. If for whatever reason the plan succeeded, you would be able to return to North Korea a hero."

When Pak remained silent, Kira pulled the key from underneath her shirt. It was on a thin leather thong and tied around her neck with a knot. She held it out, and Pak's eyes went wide. "Where did you get that?"

"A friend. Where's the lock it belongs to?"

When Pak told her where the box was hidden, she groaned.

The street was nondescript and wedged between Connaught Road Central, an elevated highway, and Queensway in the Central neighborhood of Hong Kong Island. The towering building was called Far East Finance Centre, and there was a Bank of Indonesia on the first floor, indicated by an orange sign. A narrow ally ran next to the towering building, where the little red van pulled up and parked under a gold archway. It was midday, and the alley was packed with delivery lorries and men on scooters delivering lunches. A small plaque, also in gold, read *Consulate General of the Republic of Korea* in both English and Korean.

The van screeched to a halt, the side door banged open, and a black-clad figure jumped onto the street. She, if indeed it was a she, wore a black cap, black face mask, and black hoodie, which attracted no attention from the bustling pedestrians. Masks were a common sight on the streets of Hong Kong. The black-clad figure helped a tall man step to the curb from inside the little red van. If anyone looked closely, they might notice the man's hands were secured behind him and there was a bandage on his leg. The man also wore a wool cap and a fabric face mask.

The pair hurried through the door of the South Korean Consulate.

Two minutes later, the slight figure in the black hoodie emerged alone from the consulate, jumped into the van, and slammed the door shut. The van puttered away from the curb and disappeared in Hong Kong traffic.

FORTY-SIX

Near the Paracel Islands, South China Sea

The prow of the eighty-foot Princess yacht named the *Sakura Yūgure* bounced on a wave and kicked spray into the air, which sent a fine mist of seawater over the teak decking. The ocean's surface was alive with whitecaps, and gusts of warm air blew Kira's hair about her face. Dark cumulous swirled overhead in what the pilots called a low ceiling. So far, the rain had held off.

A member of Japan's Special Operators Group, dressed in civilian clothing, piloted the pleasure yacht from the flybridge while a second man from the same group navigated. Both were armed with concealed sidearms. Given that they were in disputed waters, they wanted to keep a low profile. Wu explained the Paracel Islands were claimed by both Vietnam and China, but China had de facto control and was busy establishing naval outposts on various islands in the chain.

Colonel Wu sat next to Kira, and they spent most of the

journey in silence. The churning wind on the foredeck prevented Wu from smoking, although every once in a while she visited the aft deck and lit a cigarette.

It was a two-day ride to get to this point in the Paracel Islands. The two SFG operators kept to themselves and took turns sleeping and piloting the large yacht through the night. Wu bustled around the luxury kitchen and prepared a simple meal of rice, beans, vegetables, and bottles of beer, which the team ate with gusto. When everything was cleared, Kira asked some questions.

"Whose boat is this?"

Wu toyed with her beer bottle's label. "A friend of the prime minister's."

"A friend of the prime minister of Japan lent you his yacht?" Kira sipped from the bottle of beer. The hoppy effervescence was tasty, especially cold. This bottle had a gold star on the label and was from the northern Japanese island of Hokkaido.

"This is how important you are to us, Kira."

"Is this when you tell me who *us* is?"

The rear of the boat sported a large, teak diving platform along with a plush seating area and large table. A full moon cast a wide beam of light over Wu's shoulder as she sat with her back to the wake and lit a cigarette.

Wu let smoke escape her nose and mouth. "Very recently, Japan's prime minister assembled a small, highly secretive team and chartered them with the task of creating a new intelligence agency. For decades, since the end of World War II, Japan's intelligence capabilities were a mess. Partly as a result of how Japan emerged out of World War II, partly because of bureaucratic ineptitude, and partly due to culture, we were never able to establish an effective intelligence gathering function. There are several departments whose job it is to gather and assemble intelligence, but they are mostly an administrative function of paper pushing and bureaucratic posturing. Little effective intelligence is produced.

"Anyway, the prime minister realized something was changing, particularly in the Southeast Asia region. China is growing and clearly aspires to become a world power. They continually threaten Taiwan. North Korea firmly established its nuclear capability and taunts the Americans. They regularly launch test missiles over Japan's mainland into the North Pacific. He realized if Japan hoped to stay a world power, our ability to gather and process intelligence would have to improve—and fast."

Kira leaned her elbows on her knees. "Are you on that team? The team the prime minister assembled to design this new department?"

"I wasn't at first. They modeled the new group after the Central Intelligence Agency. The plan was to recruit and operate assets in China, who would bring intelligence back to Japan. Pure intelligence, no operational capability. But we had an event on the Japanese mainland which influenced the PM's direction for the special department. That changed the model from one of pure intelligence to something more similar to Israel's Mossad, which is combined counterintelligence, operations, and foreign intelligence.

"That's when I was pulled in. I run the operational capability." Wu sucked in on the cigarette, flicked ash into the wind, and blew the smoke over her shoulder. "The problem, as you can imagine, is we can't simply produce operators out of thin air. The Americans develop their special forces soldier programs over decades, and yes, we have similar teams, but they're all military."

Wu pointed her beer bottle in the direction of the fly

bridge. "That's why these guys are here. They're on a special task force assigned to Department 82."

"Department 82?" Kira's eyes narrowed.

Wu nodded. "That's the working name of our little agency. It's top secret. Only the PM and a few top government officials he trusts even know of the department's existence. The PM has supported your . . . er . . . recruitment from the beginning."

Some of the pieces dropped into place for Kira. "This whole thing for you has been a recruiting operation?"

"In a manner of speaking." Wu rose and flicked her cigarette butt into the black ocean. "Interested?"

From the bow of the *Sakura Yūgure*, Kira watched the island grow larger on the horizon with trepidation and fascination. This is where it all started. Her freedom, anyway. The fact that Pak was really trying to save her hadn't fully sank in. The realization was enough for her to preserve his life by dropping him off at the South Korean Consulate. But did she forgive him? Forgive him for stealing twenty years of her life? For turning her into a killer? That was a question for another day. Or maybe never. Some things are best left in the past, where they might fade into nothingness. Wu joined her at the bow and together they stood in silence while the boat glided through placid waters.

It was midmorning when the yacht weighed anchor a hundred meters out from the rickety wooden dock jutting into the ocean. The squall had passed overnight, and a high-pressure system chased it and brought clear blue skies and bright sun.

The heat formed a sweaty sheen on her skin as she and

Wu puttered toward the dock in the rubber dinghy. They were lightly armed and dressed for the jungle in cargo pants, hiking boots, and lightweight but long-sleeved shirts. Kira carried a sidearm, and a tactical shotgun was slung over her shoulder, and Wu wore a pistol in a holster at the small of her back. The two SFG soldiers remained on the yacht.

The tiny beach area was familiar, and a pang of sadness weighed on Kira from the death of the old fisherman. Was he an innocent victim in the entire operation? She may never know.

An oppressive heat consumed them as they hiked inland, away from the sea breezes and along the narrow dirt trail choked with vines. Kira used the machete to hack through the brush and clear the way. They sipped water from canteens and nibbled on energy bars. When a crushed plastic bottle with an *Aqua Life* label appeared on the ground, Kira speared it with the tip of her machete and stuffed it in her pack.

The wide-open clearing appeared much the same as it did six weeks prior, not that Kira remembered much. "I was focused on getting off the island."

"I'll bet," Wu said.

The fire pit was cold, and the hut was larger than she remembered. It rose a good ten feet off the jungle floor, and the wooden ladder was still in place. After pausing a minute to listen, she scampered up the ladder, and Wu followed a moment later.

The interior of the hut was unchanged, except for two details. The body of Trucker Hat was gone and there was no sign of Cowboy Shirt, but the blood had been cleaned, although poorly. Otherwise, the two plastic bins were in place, the small metal mirror hung on a nail by the washbasin, and the cot was in the corner. The oil lamp still hung from a chain, and the ragged wool blanket lay on the floor where she had left it.

Kira turned to find Wu standing by the railing. "How did you know?"

Wu cocked her head. "Know what?"

"How did you know about this... this operation? How did you know I was out here? That the North Koreans made a game of hunting me down?"

"To know that, Kira, is for me to divulge a part of my background that is a closely guarded Japanese intelligence secret. If you decide for whatever reason not to join us, I can't have that information out there. It's too dangerous."

Kira nodded and peered over the railing. Below was a freshly dug pile of dirt about six feet long and four feet wide. Double the size of a normal grave.

So much for leaving Cowboy Shirt alive.

She went to the ladder, where she climbed to the ground. Wu followed.

Commander Pak's instructions were precise, and Kira memorized them. From the south-east corner post, she paced twenty steps north, which took her into the thick underbrush where she was forced to slash a trail using the machete. A bird called out and a monkey chattered at her in protest. When she stopped, she was standing on another pile of earth. Unlike the unmarked grave under the hut, this dirt was covered with vines, leaves, and branches. She removed a folding shovel from her pack, dropped to her knees, and went to work. Wu paced and smoked. After ten minutes of steady digging, a large pile of dirt was at her side. It took another five minutes of work with the shovel before the metal tip clanked on something hard.

FORTY-SEVEN

Paracel Islands, South China Sea

"What the hell is with this box?"

The two Japanese SFG soldiers piloted the craft northeast from the flybridge while Wu sat with Kira in the boat's expansive and opulent galley. The clouds had passed without moisture and gave way to flat waters, warm sun, and indigo skies.

Kira held the key, the one with the seahorse carved into the brass head, in her left hand. In front of her, on the galley table, was a box. It wasn't an ordinary box made of wood with a keyhole like one would expect. The box was made of some beige plastic material and metal, smooth to the touch but heavy. At only a foot square and six inches tall with a recessed handle, the box could have been a briefcase. There was no visible lock, and with the box resembling something out of a spaceship from the future, the antique key obviously didn't match. The key might have been something recovered from a sunken pirate ship.

Wu sat on one of the galley benches and hid a smirk by drinking from a coffee mug. She prepared the brew using a French press and Indonesian coffee she found in a cupboard.

"You know something about this?" Kira ran her fingers over the seams of the box where it opened on a set of hidden hinges. The seams were lined with thick steel. She dug her fingernails between the seams, but they were too tight. In a cabinet in a back room was a hammer and a screwdriver. She pressed the business end of the screwdriver into a seam and pounded at the screwdriver with the hammer in an attempt to pry open the box. The attempts made no mark in the steel but cracked the handle end of the screwdriver.

"How am I supposed to get this open?"

Wu poured more coffee from the French press. "Hold the key near the handle."

"Are you serious?"

Wu nodded. "There is a chip hidden in the head of the key."

Kira glared at Wu. "You didn't want to tell me that earlier?"

"I was enjoying watching you try to figure it out."

When she held the key next to the recessed handle, there was an audible *snick*, and a narrow opening appeared at the steel seam.

"The box is fireproof, waterproof, and impervious to drills, saws, firearms, and explosives." Wu tapped a fresh cigarette from a wrinkled pack. "I suppose if you wrap it in dynamite or C-4, you might pop it open, but I doubt it."

Kira dug her fingernails in the crack between the seams and lifted the lid. All the time and effort to get to this point washed over her, and her knees grew weak. She collapsed into the captain's chair that sat behind the helm. "How did you come to have this key?" Kira waved the bronze object in Wu's direction. "I assume you gave it to the fortune teller?"

"Actually, I had the safe and the key specially made, and I gave the key to her for safekeeping."

"How did Pak come to have the box?"

"Colonel Pak stole it. It was during an operation we ran to try to find you. I used it as bait."

Kira waited for Wu to elaborate. "How did you—"

Wu shook her head. "I can't—"

"—tell me. It's need-to-know." Kira glared at her.

Wu shrugged and stared back.

"All I need to do is agree to work for you and you'll tell me everything?"

Wu grinned. "Everything I know, which isn't much."

Kira turned to the box. The interior was a shallow cavity about the size of a cigar box lined with off-white felt. Three items were inside: two official looking documents and one picture. "This is it? Some papers?"

"That's all there was."

Kira peered at Wu for a moment as she processed that statement. *All there was? What does that mean?*

Apparently Wu wasn't in the mood to elaborate, so Kira examined the picture first. It was aged and yellowed, showing a small child standing on her own two feet, one hand grasped by a Japanese woman on one side while a Japanese man held the other hand on the other side. The woman had black hair swept over her shoulders and wore a simple blouse and work pants and smiled at the child. The man was frowning and staring into the camera. They stood in a field with a forested tree line in the distance. A Japanese farmhouse, called a *nōka*, designed in the traditional *minka* style, was behind the trio.

Wu put her cigarette out by dropping it into the dregs of

her coffee cup and perched herself on the edge of a bench near where Kira stood. Wu took the picture from her hand and pointed at the woman. "That's your mother. Her name was Shoko."

Emotion washed over Kira as she collapsed into the leather cushion. "Was?"

Wu nodded. "She's dead now. And this was your father, Yuki."

"They're both dead?"

Wu nodded and gazed at the picture. "And this is you." She pointed at the child and handed her the photo back. "You're the spitting image of your mother. She was a beautiful and formidable woman."

Kira gazed at the picture. Her mother was stunning, with high cheekbones and long black hair. A movie reel appeared in her head, a tall woman who held Kira's hand as they walked along an undulating forest path. "You knew my parents."

After standing from the bench, Wu paced to the rear of the galley, which was open to the air, and gazed out over the ocean. The yacht rose and fell gently in the breeze. "I did."

"How?"

"You deserve to know everything, Kira, but do you *want* to know everything?"

Kira stood. "Of course. You must tell me."

Wu dug the cigarette packet from her pocket and lit one with a match. "We worked together."

Kira paced and sat in the captain's chair. "What kind of... How do you mean 'worked'?"

"Your parents worked for the Japanese government as... Well, they were spies. They lived in Hong Kong for a decade and conducted operations around Hong Kong and on mainland China. They operated as a couple. Your father's cover was as a Japanese diplomat and your mother's was as a stay-at-home wife and homemaker. But in reality, your mother spearheaded the operations to send intelligence back to Tokyo. When she got pregnant with you, they were repatriated."

The familiarity of Hong Kong washed over her. The noise and filth of the city. The lush greenery of Shek O park and the turquois vistas of Tai Tam Bay. The warmth of her mother's hand as they walked. Moisture arose in Kira's eyes and she wiped away a tear. "They moved to Murakami?"

Wu nodded.

"How did they die?"

Wu inhaled the cigarette, held the smoke in for a few beats, and exhaled into the ocean air. "They were assassinated."

Kira jumped to her feet. "How? Why? Who?"

"We don't know." Smoke curled from Wu's nose as she talked. With the cigarette between her fingers, she turned to the galley table, reached into the box, withdrew one of the documents, and handed it to Kira. "Your registration papers. Similar to a birth certificate in other countries. This other one is your passport."

Kira took the documents and examined them. The passport was a standard-issue travel document with a maroon cover and gold lettering along with a sixteen-petal flower. She opened it to find a picture of her as a baby. She flipped through the visa pages, but there was only one stamp: Japan. The port of entry was Narita, and the date was 1994.

"Your parents got it for you when you were born after they realized they didn't want to continue their work and raise you at the same time. They knew they were going to return to Japan."

Kira lifted the birth registration. It showed her date of

birth as April 8, 1994. Place of birth as Hong Kong. The address was smudged and unreadable. Nationality was listed as Japanese.

She looked at the name on the birth registration document. The first name was listed as Kira. Her surname was written as Nomura. "Nomura?" When she looked up, her eyebrows were knitted together.

Wu nodded, took a drag, and returned to the window to blow out the smoke. "That's right."

Kira sank into the cushions as the realization hit her. The passport was validation. Confirmation, in an odd way, that she was a real person with a real life.

FORTY-EIGHT

Near Kamikochi, Nagano Prefecture, Japan

At 5:00 a.m., the young acolyte in the snow-white robes who was assigned the food delivery chore walked gingerly along the stony path balancing a tray filled with bowls of rice, fish, and seaweed along with pots of hot tea meant for two of the senior Rinpoche, or monastic teachers. Something caught her eye through the trees, and she stopped abruptly enough to cause one of the food bowls to tip. Chunks of cold fish and rice flecked with green seaweed spilled onto the tray.

But the acolyte barely noticed. Instead, her attention was on the tiny hut near the path, partially hidden by the Himalayan pines. It was the same hut she eyed each morning over the past month, hoping, willing its former occupant to return. Each morning, until now, the gray wood door stood shut tight, and detritus gathered on the tiny porch, despite the acolyte's best attempts to keep it swept in her free time. But now the door was ajar, and a curl of smoke wafted from the squat chimney.

Hope filled the acolyte's chest, and she was consumed with a ray of sunshine despite the clouds that threatened rain. She took the trail spur that led to the hut, walking with smooth steps as she had been trained, and put the tray on a wooden bench at the edge of the porch. She set the bowl of food that remained upright on the wooden bench and set a pot of tea next to it.

When she straightened and turned, she almost dropped the tray. A young woman stood in the hut's open doorway. Her raven-black hair had grown back and was cut at a bob at her shoulders, and the woman's dark eyes sparkled as she smiled at the young acolyte. The black-haired woman's hands came together in Anjali mudra, the universal position of prayer hands, and she bowed deeply.

The acolyte recovered her senses and bowed as deeply as she could while holding the food tray before she hurried back up the trail, her heart bursting with love.

The procession of Land Rovers contained one more vehicle than the last time Wu made the journey. The extra SUV was made necessary by the Very Important Person who rode in the rear seat of the middle vehicle on the driver side. That VIP was tall for a Japanese man and had a wave of silver-white hair combed almost in a pompadour, but it was held in place by a dab of product. His steel-gray eyes glittered, and white teeth flashed when he smiled. The smiles were seldom, but when they came, there were hints of the genuine warmth the man once embodied before a recent personal tragedy.

Colonel Wu studied Joe Nomura out of the corner of her eye as the four-by-four picked its way up the rocky trail. Wu had known Joe personally and professionally for decades and watched his career progression from afar. He was a man with high convictions, high principles, and high capabilities—a rare combination in government service. Now, in the wake of the recent Tokyo bombing and the resulting personal tragedy, she worried about his ability to lead under such a massive weight. So far, there were no cracks in his stalwart and opaque foundation.

The VIP wore his trademark blue suit, a blue that was so dark it was almost black. A blue tie was snug on his collar atop a swan-white shirt. Aside from the suit, the VIP resembled an aging surfer who made women swoon. Perpetually tan, Joe Nomura might have been a politician in another life. In this life, he ran the newly constructed and highly secretive Department 82, Japan's nascent counterintelligence and counterespionage department. Department 82 proposed to buck a national culture inhibiting intelligence gathering, and instead it had evolved into an agency with the sophistication of the CIA but operated like the Mossad. Joe called it a *Tiger Team* whose mission it was to protect Japan's shores and civilians from enemies both foreign and domestic.

And now Japan was under attack. There had been little progress toward uncovering the terrorists behind the bombing that had killed fifty-six of Japan's citizens. Joe was finally ready to meet the fruits of Wu's operation and help bring Kira in from the cold. They needed the help.

Wu popped a piece of nicotine gum into her mouth. *Is he ready for this? More importantly, is she? And am I?*

A steady rain beat a rhythm on the windshield and the wipers thumped back and forth. The driver, one of the SFG team assigned to Joe's protection detail, swerved to avoid a boulder in the middle of the road that had dislodged from the cliffs above. For a moment, Wu envisioned another boulder, shiny from the rain and twice the size of their vehicle, bounce down the cliffside and smash their Land Rover flat.

If I will it, may it happen?

Unlike before, the idea had lost its luster. Was her sense of purpose renewed? The idea of purpose had a gentle warmth to it. And wasn't purpose the so-called meaning of life? The thing that kept a person young, even as inevitable glacial aging chipped away at one's youth. A new team, a new boss, and a heavy responsibility to serve a country and people she loved. A people whose blood ran in her veins. That was important, but more acutely, Wu had a new charge. A young woman to look after, someone to help nurture and grow.

Is that my new purpose?

Assuming Kira said yes.

At the wrought iron gates, the procession slowed long enough for the portal to swing open, and they were through. After driving the steep kilometer-long two-track, the Land Rovers crunched to a halt in a clearing. Joe shrugged on an overcoat, balanced a fedora on his head, and snapped open an umbrella as he stepped into the rain. Wu, who wore a black slicker and Wellington boots, joined him as they were greeted by Tomoe.

The sensei stood in the rain, wearing her signature white robes, and it appeared as if the rain didn't touch her. Her white hair flowed across her shoulders, and two acolytes stood with her, both under umbrellas. Tomoe cast a glare at the vehicles intruding on her sacred space but said nothing as she bowed and led Joe and Wu a dozen yards into a squat building constructed of mahogany. The roof was gabled in a traditional style called *kirizuma*, and there were no walls. A fire burned in a center pit, and the trio sat on cushions near enough for the flames to warm them. Outside, the steady rain pattered on leaves.

"She returned to the monastery under her own accord?" Wu used both hands to accept a steaming clay mug of tea from an acolyte.

"She did." Tomoe folded her hands under her sleeves.

The acolyte poured tea for Joe and Tomoe, bowed, and backed away.

"Has she spoken?" Wu sipped, and the hot green tea scalded her tongue.

Tomoe shook her head. "Nothing. One evening she wasn't here. The next morning, one of our acolytes discovered she was back in the cabin we assigned to her before."

"This was yesterday?" Wu asked.

Tomoe nodded.

"The final test." Wu glanced at Joe, who sat comfortably cross-legged on the cushion and sipped his tea. "Where is she now?"

Tomoe drank from the clay mug clenched in her two hands. "She picked up where she left off. She's out training."

"In this?" Joe angled his head in the general direction of the rain.

Tomoe merely bowed her head once.

"I'd like to meet her," Joe said.

When the tea was gone, Tomoe led Joe and Wu down a long and winding path choked with undergrowth. The sound of clicking, the banging of wood, and the grunts of effort emerged through the trees. By the time they entered a small clearing, Joe's overcoat was soaked and Wu's slicker was covered in water. Despite the precipitation, the clearing was filled with a half dozen acolytes in sodden brown robes and bare feet. Each carried a long staff called a bō, held at the ready, and they surrounded a seventh trainee, who wore a soiled brown gi.

A shout went up from a tall woman who stood at the periphery, and the six acolytes attacked the seventh woman in unison. The woman in the brown gi spun into a blur of motion, her bō flying at an invisible speed. She fended off the initial attack as the staves clicked and chunked against each other and mud and water flew through the air.

In one moment the six acolytes attacked, and the next moment the woman in the brown gi was gone. One by one, her bō smacked into the torsos and backs of each acolyte, putting them out of the fight. The whole battle took less than sixty seconds, during which the woman in the brown gi went untouched. At the end, she stood among her fallen attackers, her chest heaving, bō held at the ready. When no one resumed the attack, she put one end of the bō in the dirt and bowed deeply to the tall woman at the periphery.

Joe chuckled. "They're going to be sore tomorrow."

"This man's name is Joe Nomura." Wu accepted the porcelain cup of tea from the acolyte and held it in two hands.

Nomura. The name rattled around in Kira's head. *Coincidence?*

Kira had followed Tomoe, Wu, and the tall Japanese man in the waterlogged overcoat along the path and joined them around the fire, where she sat cross-legged on the wooden floor. She wore the soaked and soiled brown gi.

When a white-robed acolyte offered tea, Kira refused the drink with a slight bow.

After the two outsiders shook the rain off their coats and hung them close to the fire, they sat near her on cushions. The man's city shoes were covered in mud, but his faint smirk belied a comfort with discomfort. He was tan, his white teeth flashed when he smiled, which was rare, and his stare was hard. This man had seen things and been places. Hardships, perhaps. There was sadness in his eyes, maybe from a personal tragedy lingering beneath the surface. Despite any personal adversity, whatever this man did in life, he did it with conviction, and Kira respected that. She directed her eyes to the floor.

"He's my boss." Wu blew on her tea.

Kira bowed once in Joe's direction.

Wu shifted on the cushion. "Like we discussed a few weeks ago, we'd like you to come work for us. We know what you endured at the hands of the North Koreans, but you're home now. We're here to help you. Protect you. Provide you a place to call home. A place that is safe. You're welcome to stay here, at the monastery, as long as you'd like, or we can provide you with an apartment or a house anywhere of your choosing. You'll be paid, of course, handsomely. In fact, we've already opened a bank account in your name, and you're on the payroll."

Kira heard the monologue but her attention was focused on Joe, who regarded her with thoughtful observation. He watched her, no doubt for some kind of reaction, but instead his face belied a deep pain.

Kira held his eye. *What is your pain, Joe? Why do you need me? Why do you want me? Will I be used, like the North Koreans used me? Isn't every employment an agreement to be used in some way? Used in exchange for compen-*

sation? Isn't that the main difference? The North Koreans trapped me and used me. The Japanese, my home, needs me. They need my skills. Is this a trap?

The money meant nothing to her, but the monastery, with its peace and serenity, training and learning, and teaching opportunities, meant everything, despite its confining nature. It was an effective refuge to distract the constant monkey in her mind. A sanctuary to recover and train her mind and body and find solace.

Joe set his mug on the polished mahogany floor. "Kira, I won't denigrate your experiences in North Korea by offering hollow platitudes of duty to country or our blatant need for your services. You know all that." He steepled his fingers. "Instead, we can offer you a home, a family, and best of all, our support and resources to help you with the answers you seek. The answers we all seek. What happened to your parents? What happened to you?" He smiled in that melancholy way that was a combination of a tentative grin and sad eyes. "Will you join us, Kira?"

There was something in Joe's voice, his smile. A heavy burden, a purpose larger than himself. There was pain, yet a deep ambition. Angst and sorrow, yet something familial, paternal, and sage. There was a mirror there, for her, something she shared with both Joe and Wu.

Let me help you, Joe.

Kira touched Joe's arm, stood, and bowed once, deeply, her forehead almost touching the polished mahogany floor before she walked into the rain.

EPILOGUE

Murakami, Japan

Soft brown sand squished under her boots as a whippy wind blew her short hair around her face. Kira wore a puffy jacket against the spring cold, which helped stave off the windchill. Whitecaps crested on the slate-colored ocean, and in the distance, the gray water merged into the gray sky, so it was hard to see the horizon line. Far away was the silhouette of a cargo freighter, but otherwise, the Sea of Japan was empty.

She crouched and ran her hand through the bronze sand, letting it trickle through her fingers. The dreams of escaping to a brown sandy beach felt like decades ago, and she never imagined she would find herself standing on one. The beach in her dreams was hot, sultry, and salty. This one was cold and windswept. Still, it felt right, as if she had accomplished a difficult mission. As the granules ran through her fingers, the sense of satisfaction drifted away, replaced with an emptiness that demanded something new.

"About one thousand kilometers that way is North Korea." Wu stood next to her wrapped in a wool peacoat, and her finger extended northwest. She wore the Wayfarer sunglasses despite the overcast skies.

"This is the beach?" Kira tossed the handful of sand, stood, and turned away from the ocean, her back to North Korea, and surveyed the desolate shore and line of trees and vegetation. "This is where they landed the boat? This is where I was standing?"

"Approximately." Wu led her to the tree line and the wind died as they entered the underbrush. A hundred meters from the beach, a dirt road ran parallel to a rail line. The Land Rover the two women had driven in was parked a dozen paces north.

"The North Koreans followed this road to traverse south until they reached the Miomote River." Wu used the light from her phone to illuminate a map she brought, which the two had reviewed before their trip. "The Miomote is fairly shallow and slow-running. They forded the river to access the factory on the other side."

Kira wasn't listening. It didn't matter what the North Koreans had done, or where they went. "Where was my house?"

"We'll take the truck." Wu climbed into the driver's seat and started the diesel engine.

After a moment, Kira climbed into the passenger seat.

Wu drove north along a dirt road choked with trees and vegetation until they encountered a metal gate guarding a two-track that disappeared into the forest. Wu brought the vehicle to a halt, got out, and used a key to unlock a padlock before she pushed the gate open wide. The Land Rover's tires crunched on the rocks as they drove through the gate.

"This is it. This was your parents' place."

Kira rolled open the window and stuck her face out as Wu drove through thick forest. The smells of loam and dirt and pine and something floral filled the air.

This was my home. The natural ecosystem refreshed her, even if there was a pit in her stomach. "It's a long way for a five-year-old to walk from here to that beach."

"We don't know how or why you were on that beach." Wu gripped the wheel in two hands. The air suspension smoothed out the ruts and washboard. Eventually the forest gave way to a broad, overgrown field where a large farmhouse, or nōka, sat on a rise overlooking the open space around it. Brown and white, the house was built in the minka tradition, which originated in the Edo period, some 400 years ago. This nōka had a steep gabled roof made of tile reminiscent of two hands held in prayer. A wood porch ran around all sides of the home. It was the same farmhouse in the picture of her parents. The same picture she stowed away in a pocket. The only picture she had of them.

They parked in a gravel section near the back of the home, and Wu used another key to open a waist-high gate, which led into an overgrown and untended rock garden. Yet another key opened the home's rear door, and they went through into a kitchen that smelled of mold. As Wu opened several windows, dust swirled in the rays of light.

Thus far, Kira had no memories of this place. The beach, the road, the gate, and the drive leading to the farmhouse jogged nothing until she walked into the kitchen and visions flooded her mind. They weren't crisp memories in sharp focus, but were hazy, like a silhouette through a gossamer fabric.

A woman at work at the kitchen sink, lanky with long, black hair held back in a lacquer barrette. A man who came in from the rear door wearing work boots and a heavy jacket. He shrugged off the coat and sat at the table, where a meal was served.

"I remember." Kira dragged a finger along the surface of the rough-hewn tabletop as her father ate. A tear formed at the corner of her eye, which she wiped away.

Wu pushed her sunglasses up onto her head as they walked through the home. The furniture was covered in dust cloths, but the home was clean and as the musty smell evaporated through the open windows, it was replaced by a pleasant and fresh earthen smell.

"We have the place cleaned once every couple of months," Wu said. The living room had exposed, dark wooden rafters, and the internal walls were made of shoji, the sliding latticework wooden framed partitions covered with translucent white paper.

"There are no family pictures." Kira trailed her fingers along an off-white sheet draped over a sofa-shaped piece of furniture. There were no personal effects of any kind.

Wu leaned against a door jamb. "Your parents weren't fond of that sort of thing, and after they died, the government came through and sanitized the place. Anything personal was handed over to Joe, but there wasn't much." She pulled a yellow photo from her pocket and set it on the table near where Kira stood.

The image showed three adults in a city. The background was filled with dozens of neon signs in kanji mixed with the hiragana and katakana of the Japanese language. The buildings were designed in the architecture of the Heian period, which made Kira think the photo was taken in Kyoto, one of the only Japanese cities whose architecture survived the bombing of World War II. Two of the people were her mother and father. The third was Joe Nomura. Kira recognized the likeness between Joe and her father.

"They're brothers, right? Joe Nomura is my uncle?"
Wu nodded.

Kira left the image on the table and walked to a window. In the back of her mind, she had known it, but the revelation hit her in the chest. *I have family.* "Where were their bodies found?"

On the long drive from the monastery to Murakami, Wu told Kira as much as they knew about the murder of her parents that had taken place on the property. Now she led Kira out the back door, where a small outbuilding sat twenty meters away. A fence ran from the porch, past the outbuilding, and stopped at the far tree line.

She pointed to the ground halfway to the outbuilding. "Your mother was found there, shot in the back. Two rounds. Nine millimeter. Her body's position indicated she was running."

Wu stepped off the porch and led Kira to the tiny building. "She may have been making a run for this shed."

When Wu slid open the outbuilding's sliding barn-style door, dank air enveloped Kira. The building was filled with farming tools and implements and a worktable but was clean and tidy.

Wu squatted near the workbench and pointed at the ground. "Your father put up a fight. He was found here, his body riddled with bullets. There was an assault rifle near his body with a dozen spent cartridges on the ground."

Wu rose and pointed at the far end of the farmhouse's porch. "Blood was found on the ground over there. We think your father had the assault rifle hidden in here, and he either winged one of the intruders or killed him. There was no body left behind."

"Who were they?"

Wu shrugged and frowned. "We don't know for sure.

Given your parents' line of work, there are two main theories. But no one knows. I have the case files, which have what little evidence was uncovered. I've been through the forensic evidence a hundred times, as has Joe. So far, all we have are theories. Now that you're officially on the team, we can get you access to the file. I'm sorry, Kira. I wish we knew more."

Kira paced a tight circle in the little building. Something about this room was comforting; it was the closest she had felt to her parents thus far. She pictured her father at the workbench, maybe repairing a fence latch or sharpening a blade.

Kira put her hand on Wu's arm. "What are the theories?"

"One is the Chinese somehow discovered where they lived and sent a team." Wu closed the shed door, and the two walked back to the house. "Perhaps to send the Japanese government a message that no one was unreachable. Punishment for the many years your parents spent in Hong Kong spying on China and North Korea."

"And the second?"

Wu was silent a long time. The wind picked up, and purple-gray clouds gathered in the west.

Kira felt like Wu was considering how much to tell her. "It's okay. You can tell me. After all this, I want to hear everything. The good and the bad."

Wu let out a breath. "Your parents were assassinated the same night as Commander Pak's incursion onto Japanese soil. The same night you were taken. Maybe Pak's trip was, unbeknownst to him and his team, a diversionary tactic designed to lure attention away from your parents' house. That would explain why Pak's mission was so poorly planned. Maybe he was fed bad intelligence by his own superiors so he might be caught. The implication of that theory is that your parents may have been killed by the North Koreans. We don't have any facts to confirm it, but my instinct tells me it's true."

Wu shrugged as they walked back to the Land Rover. "It's possible your parents secreted you out of the house while they were under attack. Perhaps they told you to run. Maybe that's how you ended up on that beach. It's a theory, anyway."

Kira exited the shed and stood in the chilly wind as her fingers caressed her chin. "Why would the North Koreans have targeted my parents?"

Wu shook her head. "We don't know."

"It's too much of a coincidence that it happened on the same night I was abducted."

"Joe and I agree." Wu put her hand out with the set of keys dangling. "This farm has been preserved in your name. You own it. Joe and I have been taking care of it for you, but it's yours now."

After a moment, Kira shook her head. "There is nothing here for me. Can you sell it? Donate the money somewhere?"

Wu paused with the keys dangling from her hand before she pocketed them again. "Of course."

"Thank you." Kira walked to the Land Rover. "Let's go. I don't need to be here any longer."

The two climbed into the Land Rover with Wu in the driver's seat. As the vehicle picked its way along the tree-lined drive, trees slid by Kira's window. "One thing I don't understand. If you knew where I was, why didn't you come get me? Why did you leave me on that island in the South China Sea? Why didn't you pull me out of Hong Kong?"

A deep sigh escaped from Wu's lips as she guided the vehicle though the gate. After locking it behind them, she turned south on the dirt road. Eventually the road merged south onto the E7 in the direction of the monastery.

"The short answer is that we needed answers. We wanted to expose Pak. We wanted intelligence."

"I was a pawn. You used me."

Wu looked over at her, and Kira stared back.

"If we brought you in, we may have lost the opportunity to gain intel from Pak. We also didn't know who you were. Who you really were. You spent, what, eighteen years with the North Koreans? Maybe you had gone native."

"So it was a test." The terrain out the window changed from forest to farmland as the Land Rover accelerated.

Wu drove with an arm out the window. "We gave you a choice. Through your discovery of yourself, your skill sets, your own identity, we wanted you to discover your own path. If we had brought you in and stuck you in the monastery, where would you be psychologically? Did we put you to work with a therapist, or put you to work as a waitress in a coffee shop? No. You needed to discover your own self. The self-discovery process is a personal one. Only you can undertake that journey."

"Sort of like when you toss a baby into the pool's deep end and let them sink or swim." Kira thought back to when she woke in the jungle. The fight with the two men. The death of the old fisherman. The attack of the men on the yacht. "You gave me the key on purpose. To give me hope. To give me something to anchor to."

Wu nodded as she drove. "You could have run and hidden, or you could be living in London right now. Maybe you wanted to join the White Phoenix triad. We needed you to find your way back on your own, make the choice on your own. It's always better when it's your decision."

"It still is my decision." Kira peered at Wu.

When Wu narrowed her eyes, Kira smiled.

A BRIEF REQUEST

I would appreciate it if you would leave a review. An honest review means a lot. The constructive reviews help me write better stories, and the positive reviews help others find the books, which ultimately means I can write more stories.

It only takes a few minutes, and it helps more than you know.

Thank you in advance.

-Jack

JOIN MY MAILING LIST

If you'd like to get updates on new releases as well as notifications of deals and discounts, please join my email list.

I write a monthly dispatch with updates and reviews of what I'm currently reading and streaming. I never send spam. You can unsubscribe at any time.

Join my mailing list at www.jackarbor.com.

AUTHOR'S NOTE

I started this story in April, 2020, during the pandemic lockdown as a deeply personal passion project and to take a break from the world of Max Austin. I was knee deep in The Abyss, book five of that series, and it was a lot of brain power to make all the threads come together to end the series, and this story was a palate cleanser of sorts. There was a mysterious and anonymous raven-haired assassin in The Hunt, and I thought it would be fun to write her origin story as a novella. I figured I'd bang it out in a month and put it out there to see if anyone liked it.

Three-plus years later, Kira's origin story has developed into a full-fledged, 96,000 word novel. During that time, I launched The Russian Assassin book five, The Abyss, in 2020, and book six, Endgame, in 2022, effectively completing that series. I also outlined book two of The Japanese Assassin, and if anyone likes book one, I'll write the second one. Book two tells Joe Nomura's story as he leads Department 82 to solve the mystery of the terrorist bombings that rock Tokyo and appear as news items in this story. Of course, Kira helps him.

In 1957, my mother's family hosted an exchange student from Japan for his senior year of high school, a non-insignificant event so soon after World War II. Some years after that, I had the good fortune of being born on a now-defunct US Air Force base named Tachikawa just outside

Tokyo. Our families have remained close, and I consider his extended family to be my own.

In 2015, I convinced Jill to stop in Tokyo on the way to our honeymoon in Thailand. The stopover quickly became the highlight of our trip as we visited our family friends in Fujisawa, navigated the byzantine streets of Shinjuku, and went in search of world class sushi.

I remain beguiled by Japan and its people, who have always been warm and welcoming to Jill and me. I'm captivated by the country's beauty, mystified by the polarities of her culture, and entranced by her culinary offerings. I'm constantly in search of the perfect onsen, and I'm always planning a trip to visit, even when I'm there.

I hope you enjoy the story, and let me know if you'd like to read another Japanese Assassin tale. I'll probably write another one anyway.

Jack Arbor
Carbondale, Colorado
November 25, 2023

ABOUT THE AUTHOR

Jack Arbor is the author of eight thrillers.

Jack works as a technology executive during the day and writes at night and on weekends with much love and support from his lovely wife, Jill.

Jill and Jack live outside Aspen, Colorado, where they enjoy trail running and hiking through the natural beauty of the Roaring Fork Valley. Jack also likes to taste new sake and listen to jazz, usually at the same time. They both miss the coffee on the East Coast.

You can get free books as well as prerelease specials and sign up for Jack's mailing list at www.jackarbor.com.

Connect with Jack online:
- (e) jack@jackarbor.com
- (i) instagram.com/jackarbor/
- (f) facebook.com/JackArborAuthor
- (w) www.jackarbor.com
- (n) newsletter signup

ALSO BY JACK ARBOR

The Russian Assassin, The Russian Assassin Series, Book One

You can't go home again...

Max, a former KGB assassin, is content with the life he's created for himself in Paris. When he's called home to Minsk for a family emergency, Max finds himself suddenly running for his life, desperate to uncover secrets about his father's past to save his family.

Max's sister Arina and nephew Alex become pawns in a game that started a generation ago. As Max races from the alleyways of Minsk to the posh neighborhoods of Zurich, and ultimately to the gritty streets of Prague, he must confront his past and come to terms with his future to preserve his family name.

The Russian Assassin is a tight, fast-paced adventure, staring Jack Arbor's stoic hero, the ex-KGB assassin-for-hire, Max Austin. Book one of the series forces Max to choose between himself and his family, a choice that will have consequences for generations to come.

The Pursuit, The Russian Assassin Series, Book Two

The best way to destroy an enemy is to make him a friend...

Former KGB assassin Max Austin is on the run, fighting

to keep his family alive while pursuing his parents' killers. As he battles foes both visible and hidden, he uncovers a conspiracy with roots in the darkest cellars of Soviet history.

Determined to survive, Max hatches a plan to even the odds by partnering with his mortal enemy. Even as his adversary becomes his confidant, Max is left wondering who he can trust, if anyone...

If you like dynamic, high-voltage, page-turning thrills, you'll love the second installment of The Russian Assassin series starring Jack Arbor's desperate hero, ex-KGB assassin-for-hire, Max Austin.

The Attack, The Russian Assassin Series, Book Three

It's better to be the hunter than the hunted.

A horrific bombing rocks the quaint streets of London's West Brompton neighborhood and Max Austin finds himself the target of an international manhunt the likes of which the world hasn't seen since the hunt for Osama bin Laden. The former KGB assassin must put his fight against the Consortium on hold while he seeks redemption.

As Max chases the bomber from the gritty streets of London through the lush Spanish countryside and into the treacherous mountains of Chechnya, he's plunged into a game of cat and mouse with a wily MI6 agent determined to catch Max at all costs.

Can Max find the terrorist and clear his name before it's too late?

The Attack is the third installment in The Russian Assassin adventure thriller series that pits Max Austin against his arch-enemy, the shadowy consortium of international criminals that will stop at nothing to kill Max and his family. If you like heart-pounding, page-turning thrills, grab this adventure starring Jack Arbor's grim hero, the ex-KGB assassin-for-hire, Max Austin.

The Hunt, The Russian Assassin Series, Book Four

Friends are the family we chose for ourselves.

A man on a mission to save his family. A friend missing and presumed dead.

Max Austin is no stranger to mortal danger and hard decisions. But when the former KGB assassin is confronted by the choice to rescue a friend or save his family, he'll have to dig deep to keep those he cares about alive.

Haunted by a mysterious shadow that dogs him at every turn, he journeys through the treacherous Turkish desert, the harsh confines of Washington, DC, and the dirty alleyways of Cyprus searching for clues from his past. Along the way, he finds himself a step behind his adversaries who are intent on eliminating Kate Shaw before she can reveal her secrets. This time, failure in Max's quest will mean death for his friends and family alike.

Will he find Kate Shaw, or will this be Max's last mission?

The Hunt is the gripping fourth installment in Jack Arbor's Amazon bestselling series, The Russian Assassin, staring his stoic hero Max Austin. With a barreling pace, lovable characters, and unputdownable action, you'll see why Arbor's books sell like hotcakes and why readers clamor for more.

The Abyss, The Russian Assassin Series, Book Five

Every betrayal begins with trust.

A man fighting to save his heritage. A race to find a secret cache of documents. A deadly family secret revealed.

It's Christmas eve. Max and Kate are convalescing in the snowy woods of Colorado when violence strikes. On the run again, the ragtag family must trade their deepest secrets for safety.

Tormented by mysteries from his past, Max learns the truth about his father's treachery. A vast cache of documents that expose the inner workings of the Russian government are hidden from sight. The CIA, MI6, China's Ministry of State Security, and other clandestine groups are hunting for the secret archive along with Max's mortal enemies.

In a race against time, Max visits the grandiose ski resort of Chamonix and escapes a fateful train ride through the South of France before trekking across the treacherous borders of southern Russia. Deep in the heart of Siberia, Max must confront his past to decrypt his father's mysteries before his enemies beat him to the prize.

Will Max uncover the Vienna Archive and reverse his family's fortunes before it's too late?

The Abyss is the fifth installment in Jack Arbor's Amazon bestselling series, The Russian Assassin, staring his stoic hero, Max Austin. With a breakneck pace, endearing characters, and endless action, you'll see why Jack's books fly off the shelves and why readers holler for more.

Endgame, The Russian Assassin Series, Book Six

Who dares look the Devil in the face and tell him he's the Devil?

A vast trove of secret documents. A worldwide conspiracy that dates back generations. Enemies who will stop at nothing.

Max Austin has secured the Vienna Archive, an extensive hoard of secret documents that exposes the underbelly of the Russian empire. He's desperately seeking answers. Answers to help him end his family's nightmare. The answers elude him, and the archive puts a gigantic target on his back.

Pursued by the world's most elite intelligence agencies, Max puts into motion a brazen plan to end the kommissar's threat to his sister and nephew once and for all. From the icy backwoods of Finland to the corrupt streets of Moscow and finally to the civil war battlefields of Virginia, Max fights to stay alive long enough for his plan to unfold. With his back against the wall, he makes a deal with the devil in a desperate attempt to end the game forever. It's a deal he may come to regret.

Will the archive unlock the Asimov family secrets and give Max the ammunition he needs to ensure his family's safety before his father's past catches up to him?

Endgame is the gripping final installment in Jack Arbor's Amazon-bestselling series The Russian Assassin staring his audacious hero, Max Austin. With a full-tilt pace, captivating characters, and relentless action, you'll see why Arbor's books fly off the shelves and why readers holler for the next Max Austin story.

Buy Endgame today to finish the wild ride one reviewer wrote, "If you like Mitch Rap or Scott Harvath, this series is for you."

Cat & Mouse, A Russian Assassin Novella, A Max Austin Thriller

"Coincidence is the word we use when we can't see the puppet master." ~Andrei Asimov

An assassin's life is a balance between precision and chaos. But what happens when a mission goes wrong and a ghost from his past appears as an enigmatic stranger?

Former KGB assassin Max Austin is deep in contemplation over a botched job, nursing his sixth vodka, when a strikingly beautiful woman walks into the bar. She's the spitting image of a former lover, and in Max's perilous world, there are no coincidences and everyone is a threat. As the seduction unfolds, he becomes determined to find out why she was sent to entrap him.

After an unforgettable night of passion, Max discovers clues that his new lover may not be the woman she professes to be. As he tracks the mysterious seductress through the shadowy streets of Paris, he races to reveal the truth behind an intricate web of lies. Is his own mind deceiving him, causing him to see things as he fears them to be? Caught between the ghosts of his past and the perilous reality of the present, Max must discern truth from deceit before he becomes the victim of his own perceptions.

Will Max fall prey to his own paranoia before he can unearth a lethal plot against him?

Cat & Mouse, second edition, is Jack Arbor's gripping prequel novella to his Amazon-bestselling series, The Russian Assassin. Set against the vibrant backdrops of

Rome and Paris, the rollicking thriller offers insights into the complexities of Max's background. It's a fast-paced romp that takes the reader on a wild ride through intrigue and danger before culminating in a shocking finale.

Grab your copy today and immerse yourself in a story where every turn is unexpected, and every emotion is as real as the danger.

THE JAPANESE ASSASSIN
(A KIRA NOMURA THRILLER, BOOK ONE)

This book is a work of fiction. The characters, incidents, and dialogue are drawn from the author's imagination and are not to be construed as real. Any resemblance to actual events or persons, living or dead, is fictionalized or coincidental.

Paperback ISBN: 978-1-947696-15-0

Copyright 2023 by Jack Arbor and Ajax Media Group, LLC. All rights reserved.

No part of this book may be used, reproduced, or transmitted in any form or by any means, electronic or mechanical, including photocopying, recording, internet transmission, or by any information storage or retrieval system, without the express written permission of the publisher, except where permitted by law or in the case of brief quotations in critical articles and reviews.

Requests to publish work from this book should be sent to: jack@jackarbor.com

Edition 1.0

Published by Write More Studio

Cover art by: www.damonza.com
Bio photo credit: www.johnlilleyphotography.com

Made in the USA
Las Vegas, NV
29 October 2024